NATURE OF THE BEAST

As Evanna tried to think of something to say, anything that would help her keep her heartbreak hidden, she reached up to rub at a slightly sore spot on her neck. Shock raced through her as she gently ran her fingers over what was definitely a bite mark. Scattered memories of their fierce lovemaking passed through her mind and she suddenly recalled that brief sense of a sharp pain on her neck before desire had fully engulfed her body and mind. The way Berawald paled a little, looking both worried and afraid, eased her shock and smothered her rising anger. He had bitten her but she felt sure it was in the throes of passion, something she found somewhat flattering. The only weakness she had felt at the time had come from that wild lovemaking, so she knew he had not truly fed on her.

"Ye bit me," she said, trying to look cross as she stared at him.

"Ye bit me, too." He pointed to the mark on his shoulder, feeling quite pleased with it until she grew pale. "'Tis naught, Evanna. 'Tis but a wee love bite."

"Are ye sure, Berawald?" While part of her was thrilled that she might be enough like Berawald to have some future with him, another part was appalled that she could well be far more *different* that she had believed . . .

HANNAH HOWELL

ADRIENNE BASSO

EVE SILVER

NATURE OF THE BEAST

ZEBRA BOOKS
KENSINGTON PUBLISHING CORP.
http://www.kensingtonbooks.com

ZEBRA BOOKS are published by

Kensington Publishing Corp.
119 West 40th Street
New York, NY 10018

All Kensington titles, imprints, and distributed lines are available
at special quantity discounts for bulk purchases for sales pro-
motion, premiums, fund-raising, educational, or institutional use.

Special book excerpts or customized printings can also be created to fit specific needs. For details, write or phone the office of the
Kensington Special Sales Manager: Attn. Special Sales Depart-
ment. Kensington Publishing Corp., 119 West 40th Street, New
York, NY 10018. Phone: 1-800-221-2647.

Zebra and the Z logo Reg. U.S. Pat. & TM Off.

ISBN-13: 978-1-4201-0435-6
ISBN-10: 1-4201-0435-7

First Kensington Books Trade Paperback Printing: September
2008
First Zebra Books Mass-Market Paperback Printing: September
2009

10 9 8 7 6 5 4 3 2 1

Printed in the United States of America

CONTENTS

DARK HERO

by Hannah Howell

1

BRIDE OF THE BEAST

by Adrienne Basso

99

KISS OF THE VAMPIRE

by Eve Silver

203

Dark Hero

Hannah Howell

One

Scotland, summer 1512

Berawald MacNachton ignored the little spirit cautiously approaching him and continued to watch the sun set. He was safely tucked just inside the mouth of his cave enjoying all the colors of the waning day and had no inclination to deal with spirits now. He took a deep breath to inhale the sweet scent of the summer air heady with the aroma of the flowers growing close to the opening of his new home.

He frowned and took another sniff. The pleasant aroma of flowers was tainted by a far less pleasing scent. He sniffed again. It smelled like a dirty little boy.

Looking toward the small spirit he had been calmly ignoring, Berawald studied it more closely. It had inched to within a few feet of him and he began to suspect that this was no spirit. Pale and dripping with mud as it was, he had thought it was the spirit of some poor, drowned child. Most areas near water, as his home was, had a few ghosts of the drowned wandering around. Instead, it appeared that he was being cautiously approached by a cold, wet little boy who had *almost* drowned.

Now that the child was nearly close enough to touch, it was easy to see that he was too solid to be a spirit. And spirits rarely smelled like wet little boys. Berawald sighed. He was not really in the mood to play the child's savior, but his conscience gave him no choice in the matter.

"Child, what is it that ye want?" he asked the boy. "Are ye lost?"

"Nay, I dinnae think so," the boy replied in a trembling voice. "Evie kens where we are, I am thinking."

"Evie? Who is Evie?" Berawald looked around but saw no one else.

"My sister."

"And she has allowed ye to wander off alone?"

"Nay, she is ill, I think. She carried me 'cross the water, then fell down and wouldnae get up and I waited and waited but she still didnae get up and so I covered her up with some leaves and branches and all and came looking for some help because I am too little to carry her about."

Berawald was not surprised when the little boy took a deep breath. He had not taken a single one during that avalanche of words and was probably desperately in need of air. As he sorted through all that the boy had just said, he began to frown. There was a good chance the child's sister was dead, yet Berawald saw no spirit lurking around the boy. In his experience, the spirit of a woman who died trying to protect a child tended to cling to that child even after death, at least until she was certain the child was safe and cared for.

He sighed again and cast a last look at the sky. The sun was nearly gone now. It appeared he was about to rescue a damsel in distress. He had only been in his new home for a month and already trouble had found its way to his door. Silently scolding himself for such uncharitable thoughts, Berawald stood up and waved the boy closer to him.

"And what is your name, lad?" he asked the boy.

"David Massey," the child replied as he took a deep breath and stepped closer to Berawald.

"Come with me, then, David, and we will see if we can quickly get ye dry. After that we shall go and find this sister of yours." Berawald smiled faintly as the boy quickly stepped up to his side. Few people hurried closer to a MacNachton.

It was fully dark by the time Berawald got David a little cleaner, dry, and dressed warmly in one of his old shirts. Ready to go hunt down the boy's kinswoman, he reached for a lantern only to see the boy already striding out of the cave, unafraid and clearly unhindered by the shadows. Grabbing his bag of healing supplies, Berawald hurried after the boy.

"Can ye find your sister in the dark?" he asked David, following the boy but still carrying the lantern just in case it was needed.

"Och, aye. The dark doesnae trouble me." David cast a quick, nervous look at Berawald. "Nay much. Nay when someone is with me. Evie isnae far away. We best hurry."

"I could carry ye and we could move faster."

"Nay, I can walk verra fast."

The boy was nearly running by the time he finished speaking. Berawald knew he had no right to claim any great knowledge of, or experience with, children, but he felt certain the child's confident stride and lack of fear in the dark were very odd. Even most adult Outsiders tended to scurry home once the sun set. If they had to venture out at night they always took a light with them, as well as a few sturdy friends if they could. He also sensed a lie, could see it in the hasty, almost timid glances the child kept casting his way. As far as he knew none of his kinsmen had a small, blue-eyed, red-haired child, and certainly not one who would be allowed to run about without a very heavy guard. MacNachtons cherished each of the few children they were blessed with. But before he could ask a few probing questions, David stopped.

"Weel, where is your sister?" Berawald asked after looking around and seeing no one.

"Right there." David pointed to the ground.

Berawald looked down. Just a few inches from the tip of his boot was a pile of branches and leaves. He crouched down and immediately tensed. Mingled in with the smell of dead and dying leaves was another scent, one that knotted his belly with a sharp hunger. Sweet, rich, and temptingly fresh. The woman beneath the brush was bleeding.

Firmly reminding himself that a child awaited his aid, Berawald wrestled his craving into submission. It was possible he had ignored his need for too long. As soon as he healed or buried the woman beneath the leaves, he would have to tend to that matter. MacNachtons might have ceased to be the dreaded Nightriders of old, but some things never changed.

Kneeling by the pile of brush, he began to remove it. David moved quickly to help him. Berawald had no idea what to do with the boy if the woman they worked to uncover was dead, but he decided he would face that problem when, and if, it was necessary. When the last of the forest debris was removed, Berawald abruptly lost all interest in the little boy. All of his concentration became intently fixed upon the woman sprawled on the ground.

Once his shock eased a little, he tried to convince himself that his fascination was with all that red hair that swirled around her slender body, but he knew it was more. Much, much more. Berawald could not even see her face clearly, but that did not dim any of the strong pull he felt toward her. He suddenly realized he was praying, heartily and continuously, that she was not dead or dying, and forcefully shook himself free of the fascination that held him so tightly in its grip.

"Is she dead?" David asked in a tremulous whisper, his small hand held a few inches away from his sister as if he both ached and feared to touch her.

Berawald listened closely and silently breathed a sigh of relief when he heard the faint but distinct sound of a heartbeat. He told himself that bone-deep relief he felt was because he did not wish to have to tell the child that his sister was dead. A soft, inner voice mocked him as a liar, but he ignored it. Now was not the time to figure out all the strange feelings and thoughts besieging him.

"Nay, she isnae dead," he answered, "but she is wounded and bleeding. How did this happen?"

"Some men came after us. They hurt her but we got away."

"Before we go any further, lad, ye should tell me why they hurt her. I cannae risk sheltering someone guilty of some crime. I may wish to help, but there are others close by whose safety could be put at risk. I must think of them." Even as he spoke the hard words, Berawald found himself trying to think of some place he could take her that would ensure her safety as well as his clan's.

"Evie has ne'er broken a law!"

"Yet ye were chased away from your home, aye?"

The boy's small shoulders slumped and he began to idly stroke his sister's hair. "Aye. They killed my fither. He made me and Evie run when the men came stomping up to the door. Some men killed Maman when I was just a bairn. Fither escaped with me and Evie that time. He didnae escape this time."

"I am sorry for your loss, laddie, but ye still havenae told me why this happened."

"They say we are witches or demons." David's expression and tone of voice were belligerent, but Berawald saw the fear in his eyes. "We arenae. We are just a wee bit different, ye ken? There be nay evil in just being a wee bit different."

"Nay, there isnae. Mayhap later ye will tell me why, aside from all that red hair ye and your sister have, anyone would cry ye and her demons or witches. First, we must get your sister warm, dry, and mended. I promise I will do all I can to heal her."

The moment Berawald turned the young woman over onto her back, he began to regret that promise. Despite the paleness of her skin, despite all the scratches and bruises marring it, she was beautiful. Breathtakingly, heart-stoppingly beautiful. In fact, her loss of color only enhanced the fine

bones of her face, adding a heart-wrenching ethereal look to
her beauty. It was not easy for him to tear his gaze from that
face and look for the wound that scented the air with her blood.
When he found that wound low on her side, he reached for
his knife and saw David grow very pale.

"I must cut away some of the bodice of her gown, lad, so
that I may bandage her wound," he said in as low and sooth-
ing a tone as he could manage. "'Tis best if I try to ease the
bleeding ere I carry her to my home. Where are your belongings?" he asked as he started to bandage what appeared to be
a sword cut at her waist.

"On t'other side of the burn," David replied. "Evie was
going to go back to get them after she set me down here but
then she fell down. I couldnae wake her up."

Glancing at the swiftly flowing, rain-swollen burn, Berawald had to marvel at the strength of the woman. It would
not have been easy for even a full-grown man to cross those
rough waters carrying a child. The small, slender body he
tended to certainly did not look capable of such a feat of
strength.

"After I have your sister settled I will go and collect your
belongings," Berawald said.

"The water is verra cold, ye ken."

"Aye, I suspicion it is, but I am neither a wee lass nor
wounded. I will survive."

"Will Evie?" David whispered.

"I believe so if we hurry to get her warm and dry. Carry
the lantern and my bag. I will carry your Evie."

Berawald picked up Evie and, after assuring himself that
David could manage the sack and the lantern by himself,
headed back toward his home. Carrying the woman proved
to be a torment for him. Even though she was bandaged he
could still smell her blood. It was mixed with the equally
heady scent of her skin. A man should not be presented with
so much temptation at once, he thought wryly. He had to be
insane to take her right into his home, but there was no other

choice. Just because she plucked at all of his weaknesses, some he had not even known he possessed, he could not leave her outside to die. Nor could he turn his back on the little boy who had asked him for help.

It was not until he stepped into his cave that he considered how odd his living quarters would seem to someone outside his clan. He glanced back at the boy. David was looking around with no more than a calm curiosity. Berawald noticed that the boy had still not lit the lantern. Shaking off a strong urge to demand exactly what David meant when he said he and his sister were different, Berawald continued on, going deep into the hillside he now called home.

"Ye live in a cave?" David asked when Berawald finally entered a large chamber and halted.

Still seeing nothing but curiosity on the boy's face, Berawald nodded. "'Tis a strong home, which gets neither too cold nor too hot. Light some candles if ye can, lad."

As David hurried to obey, Berawald laid Evie down on a table set before the fireplace. He hurriedly lit a fire in the area he had hollowed just below a natural tunnel in the rock that served as an excellent chimney. Filling a bucket with water from his storeroom, he poured most of it into a large pot hung over the fire. He then gathered a blanket from his own bed and set it down on a bench near the table. Even as David moved to stand next to him, Berawald began to strip the wet clothing off the young woman, silently praying she would remain unconscious until he was finished tending to her wounds. He also prayed that he had the strength to hide all the fierce, confusing emotion she stirred inside him.

"Evie willnae like ye taking off her clothes," said David as he took Evie's wet boots and set them near the fire to dry.

"Weel, I cannae tend to her wounds as needed unless I do so," replied Berawald.

"I ken it, but she still willnae like it."

"Then we willnae tell her."

"I be thinking she will ken it when she wakes up naked."

Berawald briefly grinned. "True enough. We will just leave her alone for a wee while until she accepts the need of it."

It was difficult not to laugh when David responded with a solemn nod, indicating that he thought the plan was a very good one. Berawald's good humor faded quickly, however, when he finished stripping Evie of her clothes and removing the rough bandage he had put on her earlier. The wound at her side was long, ragged, and ugly. It would leave an equally ugly scar no matter how well he tended to it or how neatly he sewed it up. The sight of her bruised and battered body was almost enough to still a sudden rush of desire as well.

Covering her to just below her tiny waist with the blanket and laying a strip of cloth over her full, rose-tipped breasts aided Berawald a little in fixing his concentration on her wounds. A few of the larger bruises she wore would require watching to see if they worsened, indicating some unseen injury, but at the moment, all he could tend to was the slash on her side. Occasionally ordering a pale, silent David to hand him something, Berawald carefully cleaned the wound, even washing away all the blood and dirt in a wide area around it. He stitched it closed using the smallest, neatest stitches he could. She would still have a scar, there was no way he could change that outcome, but he was determined to make it as small a one as possible. As he worked, he returned to silently and continuously praying that she would not wake up until he was done.

The moment Berawald finished bandaging Evie with a clean strip of linen he dressed her in one of his shirts. With David's help he made her a bed near the fire. Next he scrubbed off the table, poured himself a tankard of wine, and served David one filled with cider. Setting the drinks on the table, he gathered what food he had on hand and set it on the table as well. There were not many foods he ate aside from meat, but he could see that David had no complaints about being served bread, cheese, and fruit.

"Will Evie get better now?" asked David as he sat down at the table.

Seating himself across from the boy, Berawald nodded. "Oh, aye, I believe she will. As soon as I am certain she is resting easily, I will go and gather your belongings." Seeing the look of worry the boy tried valiantly to hide, he added, "Ye will be safe here, lad. The way into these caves and tunnels isnae easily found. We only got in here easily because I ken the way so weel."

David nodded and returned all his attention to his food. It was evident that the boy had gone a long time since his last meal, and his last meal had undoubtedly been a meager one. He was obviously finding it a struggle to recall his table manners.

Turning his attention back to Evie, Berawald felt that surge of desire yet again and inwardly shook his head. There were many good reasons why he should have ignored young David's plea for help. He had the sinking feeling that Evie might well be the biggest one of all.

Two

Evie woke to pain and had to clench her teeth against a moan. Her mind hazy, she struggled to understand why she felt such a compulsion to keep silent. Her memories of the past three days slipped back into her mind in little, scattered fragments, slowly stirring a fear inside her that briefly made her forget her pain. Then she realized that David was not at her side and that fear rapidly became panic until she heard his laughter. He was close at hand and he sounded content, safe. The need to see that for herself made her ache to look for him, but she continued to hold herself still. She forced herself to relax as much as her pain would allow and began to try and judge just how badly she had been injured.

The worst of her pain was low on her right side. She suddenly remembered barely escaping being cut in two by Duncan Beaton's sword. She had feared that the slow, continuous loss of blood from that wound would kill her. However, it appeared that someone had tended to the wound well enough to keep her alive. As far as she could tell she had no broken bones, but there were a lot of bruises that would keep her in pain for a while longer.

One thing firmly grabbed her attention despite her concern over her injuries. She was not wearing her clothes. Moving as little as possible, Evie stared down at her body and had her worst suspicions confirmed. She was wearing a man's shirt and nothing else. Evie sincerely hoped some plump, graying shepherd's wife had cared for her, giving her the old shepherd's only clean shirt. That calming hope was just taking root when a low male chuckle kicked it in the teeth. That was not the laugh of some old, gnarled shepherd.

There was no longer any time left to ignore her surroundings. David sounded content and safe, but now that she knew a man was with her brother, Evie had to make certain of her brother's safety herself. For weeks now, no man had been safe—for her or for David. After cautiously testing that she could move all her body parts, even though too many of them protested the movement, she began to turn her head toward the sound of David and the man talking softly.

It took all of Evie's willpower to smother a gasp when her gaze finally settled on David and his companion—his tall, dark, and incredibly handsome companion. They were seated across from each other at a table set only a few feet away from her, a chessboard set between them. The strange urge to warn the man that playing chess with David was a waste of time swept over her. Then she noticed that David seemed to be studying his pieces with a knowledge he had never revealed before.

Pushing aside a pinch of jealousy that made no sense, she decided to ask for two things she desperately needed—a drink and a privy bucket. Evie was startled when all that emerged from her open mouth was a hoarse croak. It proved enough to catch the attention of David and his companion, however. Before she could more carefully study the man, David cried out in delight and rushed toward her. One soft-spoken but concise command from the man was all that kept David from hurling himself upon her bruised and aching body. David stumbled to a halt, knelt by her rough bed, and very cautiously leaned forward until he could give her the gentlest of embraces.

"I feared ye were going to die and then I would be all alone," David said, his voice uneven.

Evie felt the damp of tears where her brother nestled his face against her neck. She winced as she moved her hand up to stroke his bright curls, but ignored the pain. David needed comfort. He had just lost his father. Evie swallowed her own grief over that loss, wondering when and if she would ever have the chance to face it, release it, and then put it aside. Silently scolding herself for being selfish, she forced her mind back to her grieving, frightened brother and, much more importantly, the man who now stood next to David and watched her with the darkest eyes she had ever seen.

"Hush, David, I will heal," she said, and then looked up at the man. " 'Tis ye I owe my life to, is it?"

"I think ye would have survived anyway," he said. "The bleeding was easing and it was a shallow cut."

David sat up, keeping his hand on Evie's arm as he shook his head. "He did a lot, Evie. He got me all dry and warm and then we went back to the burn where I had left ye and he stopped the bleeding, then carried ye back here and stitched ye all up and e'en cleaned ye up a wee bit and he has been taking care of ye for three days."

All thought of reminding David yet again that he should not string so many words together without at least taking a breath fled Evie's mind as his last words finally sank into her mind. "Three days?" She looked at the man still watching her so closely. "Did I have a fever?" Even as she cursed herself for the sin of vanity, it took all of her willpower not to reach for her hair to make certain she still had it.

"A wee one but mostly ye just slept." Berawald clasped his hands behind his back to stop himself from giving in to the strong urge to touch that hair she was so obviously worried about. "I am Berawald MacNachton." He noticed no sign of alarm over the name and so continued. "And e'en if ye had been taken severely ill, I wouldnae have cut off your hair. Ne'er understood the need for it and ne'er saw that it did much good."

"He didnae put leeches on ye, either, Evie," David assured her, casting a brief look of awe at Berawald. "Didnae bleed ye at all. He said ye had already bled enough."

"Something I wholeheartedly agree with and nay just because I am the one in need of healing this time," Evie murmured, and then tried to hold out her hand to the man. "I am Evanna Massey."

"I already told him that."

"I am sure ye have, David, but 'tis still a courtesy that should be followed."

Berawald took her faintly shaking hand in his and kissed her knuckles. "Pleased to meet ye, Evanna Massey."

"I thank ye for helping me and my brother."

"'Twas my pleasure." He noticed her surreptitiously glancing around his cave. "Is there anything ye need?"

"Do ye need a pot, Evie?" asked David.

Evie did not need the fleeting grin that passed over Berawald MacNachton's too handsome face to tell her she was blushing over David's question. She could feel the heat of it on her face. David was too young to understand how badly a woman needed to preserve some scrap of modesty before a grown man, especially when that man was such a handsome stranger. She doubted it was a lesson she would be able to teach him for quite a while, either. Before she could make any response, however, Berawald picked her up off the bed, blanket and all.

"If ye would just show me where to go," she began.

"Ye would stagger there yourself?" Berawald asked. "Ye have been abed for three days, even lost a lot of blood ere I stitched ye closed. Ye might make it to where ye need to go, but ye would use up your entire strength to do so. I might then have to come and get ye because ye are too weak to rise up from where ye are squatting."

That was blunt, Evie thought, feeling her face heat up with yet another blush. It was also true, but she wished he had spoken with a little more concern for her modesty. She also wished she had the strength to get down and walk, for being held in his strong arms, her cheek resting against his broad, hard chest, was making her feel decidedly twitchy.

He set her down and Evie realized they had reached their destination. She looked around in amazement. The room resembled a garderobe, one that might be found in a very fine castle. A wooden boxlike bench with two holes in the top was against one of the stone walls. Stone slabs covered most of the floor and a thick sheepskin was laid out on the floor directly in front of the bench. Evie turned to say something to Berawald only to find him gone, and that made her frown. Surely she had not been so caught up in her thoughts that she had missed hearing him leave.

Shrugging her shoulders and softly cursing the pain the movement caused, she moved toward the bench. She was already weak, her knees trembling with each step, but she felt sure she could manage to do what she needed to do without his help. As she settled herself on the bench she began to pray that she would not need to call for help to get off it. Noticing a bucket of lime next to where she sat as well as a bucket of water to clean herself with, Evie decided her savior was a very meticulous man. It was even more reason to avoid needing his help. A meticulous man would not be one who would allow her to keep her secrets.

After she was done, had washed up, and then thrown some lime into the hole, Evie leaned against the cool stone wall of the small room to catch her breath. It annoyed her beyond words that doing so little could make her feel so weak. She finally looked at the room she was in more carefully and frowned. It resembled a cave, yet that made no sense. People did not usually make their homes in caves.

"Do ye need help?"

That deep voice echoing down the small passage leading

to her pulled Evie out of her confusing thoughts. "Nay, I can come to you." Keeping one hand on the wall and clutching the blanket around her shoulders, she started to walk down the passage, praying with every step she took that she was not mouthing an empty boast.

Berawald picked her up as soon as she inched her way out into the main room. He ignored her muttered protests as he carried her back to bed. She was pale and covered in a light sheen of sweat, her slender body trembling with the effort of walking only a few feet. He knew she did not need to be told that she would never have made it back to her bed on her own. Tempting though it was to say it, it would be a little like rubbing salt into her wounds.

Once she was settled back in her bed, he helped her drink some cider that he had mixed a few herbs into. He ignored her grimaces and silently pressed her to drink it all down. Just carrying her that short distance had stirred him so much, and so fiercely, that he was very eager to put some distance between them.

"Herbs to strengthen my blood?" she asked after she finished the cider and settled her aching body more comfortably on the bed.

"Aye." Berawald moved to stir the pot of broth he was brewing for her. "Are ye a healer, then?"

"I have done some healing work." She sighed as she saw what he was doing. "'Tis broth, aye?"

He had to bite back a laugh over the heavy tone of disgust in her voice, and that surprised him, for he rarely laughed. "'Tis indeed broth for you. David and I shall dine on something much heartier later."

"Cruel mon. I shall try to be asleep by then, I think."

"Sleep *is* the best medicine."

Her voice was soft, a little husky, and Berawald felt as though it caressed him each time she spoke. He had long ago accepted that he was not a passionate man, not like so many others in his clan. He was no virgin, doubted any man who had lived as long as he had could be, but he had never felt any true craving for a woman. He felt one for this woman and it worried him. His kinsmen would undoubtedly urge him to seduce her, to satisfy the need knotting his insides, but his every instinct told him that would only make the craving worse. He needed to get her healed and strong as quickly as possible and send her far, far away.

That thought had barely finished passing through his mind when he cursed himself for a heartless bastard. She and David were in danger. He had not pressed the boy too hard for information about that danger, but he was certain that some dire threat was dogging the heels of the pair. It was the only explanation for why they were in his woods; in the midst of MacNachton lands—lands most other people avoided—and for why she had been so badly wounded. As soon as she had the strength for a long interrogation, he intended to get some answers. Only then could he make any real decision about her and her brother. And he would not let those big green eyes of hers make him falter in getting the information he needed. For now, however, he would simply work hard to help her regain her strength.

Evie looked around the large chamber. The man's home definitely looked like a cave. That made no sense to her, for he was clean, well spoken, and handsome enough to make a woman's heart skip. He was the sort of man one expected to find living in a fine manor house or even a castle.

Before she could stop herself, she asked, "Are we in a cave?" She knew it was probably rude to ask such a question and felt herself blush, but she did not apologize.

Berawald looked at her and smiled faintly. "Aye, we are."

Since she had already crossed the line into rudeness, she decided she would keep right on walking. "Ye live in a cave?"

He heard only curiosity and a touch of surprise in her voice. "Aye. 'Tis spacious. As I told young David, 'tis also never too warm or too cold."

"It can be damp."

"I dinnae think there are verra many abodes in this land that arenae a wee bit damp."

She smiled faintly. "True, but I have ne'er heard of any but hermits or outlaws who lived in such places."

"None live in ones as comfortable as this. Hermits prefer ones that are nay more than niches in a hillside. This place wouldnae allow them to enjoy the suffering they often crave. And, I am nay an outlaw. Nay, I found this place several years ago and decided to make it my home. My clan owns the land and the keep was getting rather crowded. So I worked to make this cave more comfortable and moved into it this past spring. 'Tis safe here," he added quietly. "The entrance is nay easy to find, I can hear if anyone approaches, and since the path into this place is long and narrow, 'tis easy to defend."

"Is it easy to flee from if ye are attacked?" she asked, unable to bury her fear of being trapped by her enemies.

"Aye, and the ways out are even harder to find than the way we came in."

Evie tried to hide her relief, but the sharp look in his dark eyes told her that he had noticed it. He asked her no questions, however, and that pleased her. She was not sure yet if she could trust him with the answers. If only her life was at stake, Evie had the lowering feeling she would need only one long, soulful look from his beautiful dark eyes to tell him all he wished to know. The fact that David's life was also at risk was all that gave her the strength to keep silent.

"Good. 'Tis always best to have a way out."

"Time for your broth."

"How delightful," she muttered.

"'Tis good broth, Evie," said David as he knelt by her bedside.

She smiled at her brother and then dutifully consumed the broth Berawald fed her. It was good and, in truth, it was probably a great deal heartier than many another meal she had had in her life. By the time she was done she felt pleasantly full, warm, and very tired.

"Are ye going to sleep again, Evie?" asked David.

"Aye, I believe I am," she replied even as she closed her eyes and had to smile when David proceeded to tell her a bedtime story.

Beneath the shelter of her lashes, however, she watched Berawald MacNachton, her savior, her mysterious healer, and a man who lived in a cave. He was—without question—an astonishingly handsome man. Tall, leanly muscular, and graceful as only a skilled warrior could be. His features were cut in clear precise lines, barely escaping a look of frightening harshness. A well-shaped, slightly full mouth helped soften those sharply cut lines as well. His nose was straight, neither too long nor too wide, his chin was strong, his ears well shaped. Even his eyebrows were perfect, nicely arched and not too thick. Worse, he had long thick lashes she envied and admired so much that she might need to go to confession. He had long black hair that hung down to the middle of his broad back and was tied back with a strip of leather.

Much too fine a man for her, she thought sadly as she let the need for sleep start to conquer her. She would regain her strength and leave as soon as possible. Not only could she bring danger to his door, but she could all too easily bring it to her own heart. A man like Berawald MacNachton was one who could sorely tempt a woman, and she had no time to deal with temptation. She and David were being hunted and they had to keep moving. Her last thought was to wonder why the thought of leaving should cause her heart to twist painfully in her chest.

Three

Seated by her bed, Berawald waited patiently for Evanna Massey to finish waking up. It had been a week since he had found her and her brother. It was past time for him to get some answers to all the questions he had. During his hunt last night he had come across signs that indicated men were tracking along the border to the MacNachton lands. He strongly suspected they were the men David and Evanna were running from. It was time to tell his clan about his guests and that they could well be bringing a threat their way, one that was approaching all too swiftly. When he did speak to his kinsmen he wanted to be able to tell them why the threat was drawing so close, why it sought out two apparent innocents, or even that his guests were not so innocent and that he had sent them on their way.

At the mere thought of casting Evanna and her brother out of his home, Berawald felt a pinching pain in the area of his heart. Despite his best efforts, both Masseys had wormed their way into his affections. Evanna had such a tight grip on his heart and his lust he was not sure he could push her out of his home even if she was guilty of some heinous crime.

And each time he considered the possibility that she was guilty of something, it was only a fleeting consideration. He feared his opinion was being influenced far too strongly by soft green eyes, sweet smiles, and a beautiful voice.

No matter what he decided to do with the Masseys in the end, he still needed answers. It was all right for him to make an error in judgment when only his own life was at risk, but he would not share that risk with his whole clan. There were men hunting his kinsmen, men who wished to put every MacNachton in a grave. Berawald had seen what those men were capable of and he could not allow sentiment or lust to cloud his thoughts.

There was also something a little strange about David and Evanna Massey. In the week they had lived with him he had seen few spirits. Since the day when he had begun to change from a boy to a man he had had little peace from the visitations of the dead, yet he had known it from the moment the pair had entered his life. He could still see the occasional ghost, but the constant noise of them, the constant rattle of voices in his head, had gone away. It was as if the Masseys had brought some shield with them, one that thickened the wall between the dead and the living. He had never experienced such a thing before, or even heard of it, but he wanted to know the secret of it. Such a skill could help him to finally live as normal a life as any MacNachton was capable of.

Unlike many other Outsiders he had known, the Masseys did not seem to crave the sun. Evanna did not bemoan her inability to go outside, and David never did more than watch the sunsets, and occasionally the sunrises, with him. That a boy of five would be so content inside for day after day did not seem right, not when he was one of those who could go out and enjoy the summer sun the few times it deigned to show itself. Berawald knew fear could be keeping the boy close and hidden, but he could not shake the suspicion that it was more than that.

There were other things that he had noticed that troubled him. The Masseys did not even blink an eye when he ate his meat barely seared; David had even requested some for himself and Evanna. Berawald doubted that was because they had had so little meat in their lives that they had no idea how it should usually be served. He felt sure both Masseys caught sight of the occasional spirit that still wandered through the cave, yet they said nothing. And Evanna was healing at a very rapid rate for an Outsider. With their red hair and bright eyes, he could not believe they were Mac-Nachtons, and yet he began to wonder if there was some of his clan's blood in their veins. The problem would be in trying to verify his suspicions without exposing the secrets of his clan.

Berawald was yanked from his thoughts by a soft noise from Evanna, and he turned his head to find himself staring into her sleepy green eyes. The slow smile she gave him made him ache to pull her into his arms and join her on that bed. He crossed his arms over his chest to keep himself from giving in to that urge. She was a weakness with him, and until he knew the truth, he could not allow himself to give in to it.

Evie's smile faded away. For the first time since she had met the man, Berawald's beautiful face had a predatory cast. She felt a tickle of fear but smothered it. He was not her enemy; enemies did not save their prey and heal the wounds of the ones they were hunting. Something was troubling the man, however, she decided as she struggled to sit up.

"Is David all right?" she asked as a sudden fear for her brother swept over her.

"David is fine," Berawald replied, feeling a little guilty for frightening her and fighting to not allow that guilt to make him back off from demanding some answers. "I have been waiting for ye to wake up. 'Tis time to remove your stitches. In truth, I think they could have come out soon after ye woke up several days ago. Ye heal verra quickly." He noticed the way she briefly glanced to the side, fleeing his gaze, and suspected she was about to lie to him. He wondered why that should hurt him as it did.

"I have always been a fast healer and 'twas but a shallow cut," she finally replied. "Ye said as much yourself."

"Aye, I did. 'Twas a sword cut."

She sighed. "Aye. I was a wee bit slow to move aside, I fear."

"Evanna, why would someone try to kill you?"

She could tell by the look on his face that he would not cease to question her until he had an answer to that question. Evanna knew he deserved at least some of the truth. He had aided them and now sheltered them. She was afraid to say too much, however. The truth was why she and David were running for their lives, why both their mother and their father were now dead. She did not think Berawald would ever try to kill them simply because they were different, but she knew he might turn away from them. Just the thought of his dark eyes looking at her with disgust, with even a hint of fear, turned her heart into a cold stone in her chest.

It astonished her that, after so short a time, she could feel such a strong, deep need for him to look upon her with favor. Evanna thought it a little cruel of fate to deliver her into the hands of the first man to stir her interest now, when she had no time to play flirtatious games or see if the feelings he stirred within her were reciprocated. She wanted Berawald MacNachton, liked everything she had seen and learned about him so far, but she could not allow herself the luxury of learning any more. Her brother's safety was all she could think about or act on, at least until their enemies no longer hunted them.

"We are different from them," she answered softly. "'Tis all that is needed sometimes, aye?"

"Aye, but just how are ye different? E'en the most ignorant need some reason to fear or hate ye enough to want to kill ye, to want to kill David who is naught but a bairn."

"As ye have seen, I heal quickly, quickly enough to rouse suspicion." Pleased that her bed now rested against the wall near the fire, Evanna sat up and leaned against the cool stone.

"David is the same?" Hearing a slight rasp in her voice, Berawald rose to pour her a tankard of cider.

"He is. Thank ye," she murmured, accepting the drink and taking a deep swallow before continuing. "'Tis so plain that such a gift must be a blessing, nay a curse, yet it troubled people. We tried to hide it, but 'tis nay always possible to hide such a gift. Once when my father was gone away, my mother was badly injured in a fall. The village healing woman cared for her."

"And your mother recovered from her injuries with a suspicious speed."

"Aye. The whispers began then and soon superstition began to stir in the hearts of the villagers. In the end the verra gift that helped my mother survive such a hard life as we had, killed her. They came in the night intending to kill all of us and caught my mother outside fetching water. Our father got me and David to safety, but I think he left his heart with my mother's body. We moved away to another village and enjoyed a few years of peace, but it soon began all over again. This time superstition killed my father. He stood firm when the attack came, giving me the chance to get David away from there."

"But ye are still nay safe, are ye? Moving away willnae stop it this time, aye?"

"Nay, we arenae safe. I am nay sure we will e'er be safe, but I must try. For David. As ye said, he is naught but a bairn."

"'Tis hard to think that a healthy body and a quickness of healing could set a mob at your heels."

He was not exactly calling her a liar, but Evanna barely subdued a flinch of shame nevertheless. She truly hated lying to this man, to see in his fine eyes the knowledge that she was lying to him. Even assuring herself that she was not really lying, was just omitting a few facts, did not ease the guilt she felt. She also knew she would have to give him more, enough to satisfy his curiosity and his doubts, but not enough to rouse fear or superstition. It would not be easy, especially when she was so loath to lie to him.

"Weel, there is all this red hair," she said.

Unable to stop himself, Berawald reached out to stroke the thick, deep red braid that was draped over her slender shoulders. "True, but I havenae heard of many who were killed simply because of the color of their hair. Red hair isnae so verra rare in this land as to cause immediate alarm."

"True. Weel, ye do ken that redheads have fair skin." The way he moved his long fingers from her hair to lightly brush them down her cheek made her insides clench with the need to touch him back, with what she suspected was a fierce, white-hot lust. "This fair skin is, weel, easily damaged by the sun. 'Tis nay just slowly darkened as so many others' skin is; it burns. David and I try to stay out of the midday sun, as my mother did. For reasons I cannae e'en guess at, some people felt all those things, all those wee differences, marked us as demons."

Berawald said nothing for a moment, just nodded and tried to look sympathetic as he clasped his hands together in his lap and savored the lingering feel of her skin against his fingertips. He knew superstition well, and the fear it bred could indeed be stirred by such small things, but he also suspected there was a lot more to it all. His clan was being hunted, the hunters gaining strength and becoming more organized every year. It was very possible that one of those hunters had discovered the Masseys, seen their differences, and realized how closely those differences matched those of the MacNachton clan. That would be enough to set those dogs on the heels of the Masseys. In finding the Masseys they would be very close to finding the MacNachtons.

It was certainly enough to make him think that, somewhere in her lineage, Evanna would find a MacNachton. He needed to talk to his kinsmen. Several of them were diligently searching for all who might have a connection to or knowledge of their clan. A few instances in the past had revealed that some MacNachtons had bred children with Outsiders and, either uncaring or not knowing, left those children unclaimed. Being that their clan was very small, few children being born, the laird was calling on every MacNachton to search out all who might have some blood tie to their clan. The existence of the hunters had made it even more important to gather all their kinsmen into the fold. Berawald could not shake the feeling that the Masseys were some of those unknown and distant kinsmen. It would be tricky to gain the information needed to ascertain that without telling Evanna more than he wanted her to know right now.

"Weel, ye and David will be safe here," he said, deciding it was time to seek some advice on how to proceed now that she had healed. "I believe I will remove your stitches now."

Evanna grimaced. "I hate the feeling of that."

Carefully arranging the hem of the shirt she wore and the top of her blanket so that only the bandaged wound showed, Berawald gently removed that bandage. "I ken. I have always thought it just felt odd, that there really wasnae any word to describe it." Not that he had had stitches more than once, for his own ability to heal quickly meant there was little need for them.

"Aye, odd is a verra good word for how it feels." When he just frowned down at her uncovered wound, Evanna began to feel a little uneasy. "Is it all right? It hasnae putrefied or the like, has it?"

"Nay, 'tis completely healed and verra clean."

"Weel, then best to get the stitches out." She was pleased that he had not made any comment on how unusual that was and closed her eyes tightly. "I am ready."

Berawald had to smile, for she looked like a small child about to be forced to swallow a particularly revolting potion. Each time he tugged a stitch free, she grimaced. He would have felt bad about that except that he knew he was not really hurting her. It was amusing, however, that the woman who had remained strong through so much thus far would now whine and complain over something so simple and relatively painless.

"There, 'tis done," he said, and smiled when she opened one eye to peek down at the reddened scar that marred her fair skin. "The redness will fade soon."

At the same moment that Berawald finished tugging her shirt back into place, Evanna reached down to pull the blanket up higher. That movement brought her face close to his, her mouth within inches of his sinfully tempting lips. She met his gaze and saw a flare of interest in their dark depths. Her whole body responded with a keen interest of its own. Her lips tingled as if he had already touched them, the heat in his gaze enough to warm them.

Berawald was not sure which one of them moved first, but suddenly his mouth was on hers. He trembled faintly as the warmth of her full, soft lips soaked into his body, raising a heat he had never felt before. When her small, soft hand touched the back of his neck, he felt that light caress fly straight to his groin. That heedless part of him rose in full salute and demanded that he take more of what she seemed so willing to give. The gentle, closemouthed kiss they were sharing was no longer enough; he needed to taste her.

Nipping gently at her lower lip, he took quick advantage of her soft gasp that caused her mouth to open slightly. The taste of her, the sweet heat of her mouth, killed all rational thought and control. He pulled her into his arms and kissed her with all the hunger he could no longer hide, from her or from himself.

Evanna was briefly shocked when Berawald thrust his tongue into her mouth. No man had ever done that to her before. The way he stroked the inside of her mouth with his tongue and the feel of his strong body pressed close to her as he pulled her into his arms quickly dimmed that shock. Desire throbbed inside her with each stroke of his tongue. She reveled in the taste of him, in the way he made her feel. She wanted to wrap her whole body around his and never let him go.

It was not until the warmth of his hand curled around her breast that she was able to regain any of her senses except for need and desire. Her surprise over such an intimate touch, the slight tensing of her body, passed quickly beneath the heat of that caress, but he had noticed her brief withdrawal. A heartbeat later she found herself freed from his embrace and she nearly cried out in protest.

He stared at her in horror for a moment and then muttered an apology. Before Evanna could say a word, he fled the room and disappeared down a deeply shadowed passage. For a moment all Evanna could do was stare after him in stunned amazement before uncertainty began to taint the wonderful feelings he had left her with. She huddled beneath the blanket as a chill quickly replaced the heat his kiss had filled her with.

Despite her efforts to just forget his odd behavior, her mind began to sort through all the possible reasons for his sudden abandonment and none of them made her feel very good. Had she been such a terrible kisser? she wondered. Had her total lack of skill turned him away? Perhaps he had suddenly recalled what few truths she had just told him and realized he could not abide them.

Evanna shook her head, trying to force such thoughts from

her mind. She did not know Berawald well enough to guess at his reasons for his actions. Perhaps when he returned she could find out what had sent him running off into the night. She could only pray that when he returned, she would either hear an explanation that soothed her doubts and hurts or see by the look in his eyes that he had not fled her arms because he had suddenly realized he was kissing a demon.

Four

Berawald cursed himself with every step he took toward Cambrun, his kinsmen's home. He had given in to temptation, something his body still ached for, and nearly devoured an innocent maid. And there was little doubt in his mind that she was innocent. Her kiss had been one of a woman who had rarely, if ever, been kissed. That should have gentled him. Instead, for some inexplicable reason, it had stirred his lust to new heights. What was even more alarming was that, with every beat of his pounding heart, the word *mine* had echoed in his head.

She was not *his*. He was not sure she could ever be his or would ever want to be. That knowledge did nothing to silence the primal cry of possession in his heart, however. Berawald had to face the fact that he wanted to claim Evanna Massey in every way a man could claim a woman. It made no sense, for, although she was beautiful enough to stir any man's passion, he did not really know her. The feelings tearing through his body ought to be inspired by far more than a beauty of face and form. Surely a man needed to really know a woman, know her mind, and her heart, before he became so needy and possessive.

Shaking away his confusion, he entered through the gates of Cambrun, grunting a response to the calls of welcome he received from the guards, many of them his cousins. The sight of spirits clustering near him and the murmur of their voices in his head did nothing to improve his mood. He had quickly become accustomed to the quiet he enjoyed around the Masseys. What he needed to concentrate on was getting some advice and maybe even some answers to all the questions he still had. He also had to tell someone about the men he had seen creeping around the edges of MacNachton land. Since the laird and his lady were off visiting one of his sons, Berawald headed down into the bowels of the keep to find his cousin Jankyn.

When he entered Jankyn's chambers, Jankyn's wife took one look at his face and swiftly excused herself from the room. Berawald realized that he must look as bad as he felt, but she gave him no time to offer an apology for his foul mood. When he turned back to Jankyn that man handed him a large tankard of wine. One sniff was enough to tell Berawald that it was some of the specially enhanced wine and he gulped it down, savoring the strength it gave him.

"Sit," Jankyn ordered, pointing to a chair by a table set close to the fire. "What has the usually distracted but cheerful Berawald looking as if he wants to kill someone?" Jankyn poured himself some wine, refilled Berawald's tankard, and sat down facing him.

"I apologize for scaring Efrica," Berawald said.

"I doubt ye frightened her. She but sensed that ye needed to speak with me about something of importance and that ye would probably prefer to do that alone. So, speak."

"I have guests." Between sips of wine, Berawald told Jankyn about David and Evanna.

Jankyn frowned in thought for several minutes after Berawald had finished his tale. "She heals quickly?"

"Aye, verra quickly. It was a shallow cut on her side only

in that it didnae go deep enough to damage her innards, but it was long and bled freely. Isnae a week too soon for an Outsider to recover from such a serious wound?"

"'Tis completely healed?"

"Aye, naught but a faintly reddened scar is left. The bruises and scratches she was covered with faded within two, three days."

"That *is* unusual. And for that someone cried her a demon or a witch?"

"She claims the charge was born of that and having such red, red hair as well as having pale skin so delicate that it cannae bear being touched by the midday sun. Her brother is the same. Neither of them was troubled when I ate some barely seared meat and David e'en took some of it for himself and Evanna. I wondered if they might have some MacNachton blood."

"It seems verra possible to me. I shall see what I can find in all of the available papers. It also makes it more alarming that she is being hunted."

"Ye think that these men might be more than simple, superstitious villagers, aye?" Berawald had begun to suspect that they were, but he wanted someone to agree with him.

"Again—verra possible. The ones who mean to eradicate us ken a lot about us, far more than I like. Each thing ye have told me about the Masseys would certainly be enough to stir up their dangerous suspicions."

"E'en though they are both redheaded, one with green eyes and one with blue?"

"I am nay sure these men would realize the rarity of that. Or, and this is even more alarming, they ken weel that our kinsmen have spread their seed far and wide."

"'Tis what I fear," Berawald murmured. "There is one other thing—I think they ken about the spirits."

"They see them, too?"

Berawald nodded. "They havenae said anything but I am

absolutely certain that they do. E'en more curious, 'tis as if
they shield me from the spirits simply by being close to
hand. In the week they have been with me, I have been little
troubled by the spirits that seem to crowd this land, and the
voices in my head have been almost completely silenced.
'Tis as if, by their verra presence in my home, they have
strengthened the walls between the living and the dead. The
moment I reached Cambrun, the spirits and the voices in my
head were all back as if they had never left me."

"That is verra interesting, verra interesting indeed, and it
must be verra pleasant for you." Jankyn smiled faintly. "And
this Evanna—she is beautiful with her red hair, green eyes,
and delicate skin?" He laughed softly when Berawald blushed.

"Aye, she is beautiful, and, aye, I ache for her. But she hasnae
told me the truth, nay all of it."

"The truth comes hard for one who has learned the need
to remain silent simply to stay alive. Who kens that better than
we do, aye? She must also strive to keep her young brother
safe. If she tells ye all, is she risking him as weel? That is
what preys upon her mind and will continue to do so until
she feels completely safe, or as safe as any of us can feel in
this dangerous world. She might weel trust ye with her own
life, but hesitates because her every action affects David as
weel."

Sighing, Berawald dragged a hand through his hair. "I
understand that. I do. But right now what I truly need to decide is what to do with them. I saw signs that men had been
tracking along our borders, but cannae be sure if they are the
same ones hunting her and David or enemies of our own."

"I will tell our laird when he returns and will see that the
borders will be watched much more closely immediately, although we watch them verra closely now. Whether these
men are the hunters who plague our clan or simply foolish,
superstitious men hunting the Masseys, they are, in the end,
a danger to us all. My instincts tell me that her hunters are of

the same group of men as ours are. Ignorant, superstitious villagers wouldnae trail the Masseys for so long or so far. They would be weel content with the fact that the pair had left the village."

"That is what I thought. So, will ye let me ken if ye find any connection between the Masseys and the MacNachtons?" Berawald asked as he finished his wine and then stood up to leave.

Jankyn stood up, moved to Berawald's side, and lightly slapped him on the back. "I will. The search would go much faster, though, if ye could gather a wee bit more information for me. Her mother's name, where they have lived, grandparents' names, and such as that. Since ye said that she told ye the gift of healing quickly had come from her mother that would imply that the mother was the carrier of the Mac-Nachton blood and thus the name Massey may do me little good."

"Ah, of course. I hadnae considered that."

"Talk to the boy if ye can. It sounds as if he has full trust in ye and will speak more freely. He is too young to fret o'er everything he says or be weighted down with fear that any secret he may let slip could hurt his sister. And, Berawald?" Jankyn asked as Berawald opened the door to leave.

Pausing in the doorway, Berawald looked back at Jankyn. "What?"

"If ye want the lass so badly, then take her."

"She may nay want me," Berawald said, voicing aloud the fear that had lodged itself so firmly in his heart. "Nay when she learns the truth about me."

"It seems to me that her truths are verra similar. Ye havenae been so heated o'er a lass since, weel, for as long as I have kenned ye. That means something. Dinnae ignore it."

As he made his way home, Berawald considered Jankyn's advice—all of it. If he could get no more information out of Evanna, then he would overcome his reluctance to take advantage of a child's naïveté and get some out of David. He had taken them into his home and there was danger following them. He had a right to know all about them and what he might soon face in order to keep them safe.

Jankyn's advice to just take what he wanted, to just take Evanna, was a little harder to decide on. It was tempting and it filled his mind with some very heated ideas of just how he could do that, where he could do it, and how often he would. He was not sure he ought to give in to that temptation, however. He was the man who had saved her and her brother, had healed her, and was now protecting her. Somehow it did not seem right to take advantage of that. Even worse was the thought that, while he was caught up in an emotional turmoil and heart-pounding lust, she might just be feeling grateful. To reach for what he wanted only to discover that it did not really exist could leave him with a wound that might never heal.

For a moment he stood at the mouth of his cave and considered that. That he would even feel such a fear confirmed his opinion that it was already a lot more than lust that made him want Evanna. She had been with him for a week but had only been awake for about four days of that time. They had talked, even played chess a few times, but he knew very little about her or her life before he had found her at the side of the burn. What he felt made no sense at all, but he could not deny that he felt it, deeply and fiercely.

As he prepared himself to go inside and face her again, Berawald realized many of the spirits he had been seeing had faded away as had all the noise in his head as he had drawn close to his home. Here was proof that the Masseys had more than the gift of healing quickly from their wounds. For just a moment he savored the renewed silence. Berawald suspected that any spirits who had a true grievance, a real need to be heard, would still be able to reach him or he could reach out to them if he chose to, but this quiet was a gift he was loath to give up. Perhaps it was a sign that Evanna Massey was destined to be his, that she completed him, he thought as he entered his home.

"Where is Berawald?" David asked.

It took Evanna a moment to push aside her increasing despondency and smile at David. "I am nay sure, but he will nay doubt return soon. I could play chess with ye if ye want."

"It can wait."

Smothering the pinch of hurt and jealousy she suddenly felt, Evanna got out of bed. She was not accomplishing anything by lying there feeling sorry for herself. After donning the plaid Berawald had given her to act as her skirts, she began to walk around what she thought of as his great hall. Now that her stitches were out she could begin to wear her own clothes, although, sad to say, they were not as comfortable or as fine as the ones he had given her. Her strength had nearly returned in full and she tried to take some pleasure in that. The fact that it meant she and David could soon leave Berawald made that difficult, however. She knew she should leave, should no longer burden the man now that she was better, but she really did not want to go.

And why should that be? she asked herself as she marched around the room, a humming David skipping along behind her. She really did not know the man, and despite her complete inexperience with men, she knew a strong lusting in a man often meant no more than that—a strong lusting. The heat in his gaze could be coming from just one part of his body, his mind and heart not being involved in it at all. Unlike her own, she thought with a grimace.

"Did ye just hurt yourself?" David asked as he trotted along beside her. "Ye just made a face."

Slowing her pace a little to match his, Evanna shook her head. "Nay. I was just thinking."

"Oh. I like it here, dinnae ye?"

Evanna suddenly realized that her brother had settled in for a long stay with Berawald and nearly cursed. "'Tis a cave, David."

"Aye. A really nice cave. I e'en have my own sleeping chamber. I like Berawald and he is teaching me chess."

She stopped, crouched down before her brother and grasped him by the shoulders. "David, m'love, this isnae our home. As soon as I am strong enough for traveling, we must leave here." And take our troubles with us, she added silently.

"Why? Berawald has a lot of room."

"But that doesnae mean he wishes to fill that room with a woman and child, ones who arenae e'en his kinsmen."

"I dinnae want to live on the streets and eat rats!" he wailed.

"What are ye talking about? I ne'er said we would do that."

"We cannae go home e'en if we have one still. That means we dinnae have a home, and people without a home live on the streets of smelly, dirty towns and eat from midden heaps and eat rats and get all dirty and have fleas and I want to stay warm and dry and eat good food. We can stay. Berawald will keep us safe."

Evanna used the billowy sleeve of the shirt she wore to dab at the tears streaking David's angelic face. "We cannae ask that of him. The mon saved us, healed my wounds, and has sheltered us for a week. It wouldnae be fair, or right, to abuse that kindness by lingering here and putting his life at risk. I certainly dinnae want to see him get hurt. Do ye?"

Berawald lurked in the deep shadows of the entry passage and shamelessly eavesdropped. He had to beat down the urge to rush over to the weeping David and assure the child that he would not be left to starve in the streets. The craving he felt to hold fast to Evanna and her brother was growing stronger by the hour. What Evanna told the boy about not wanting to see him hurt eased some of his concerns. She might not have told him the truth about herself, but she was not intending to ensnare him in any way. Maybe Jankyn was right; he should just take what he wanted. The secrets and the troubles that stood between him and Evanna could be sorted out later, perhaps even in bed.

"He would fight for us," David protested, hiccoughing a little as he struggled to control his tears. "He is a good, brave mon."

"And ye think we should thank that good, brave mon for his help by leading killers to his door?" Evanna asked softly.

"Nay," David mumbled, "but we dinnae have anywhere to go. We dinnae have Da to find us a new home, either."

When her brother began to cry again, Evanna sat down on the floor and pulled him onto her lap. She struggled to control her own urge to weep. Her father had been a good and loving man, even though he had lost a lot of his thirst for life when their mother had been killed. He had never harmed a soul or committed even the smallest of crimes, yet those men had cut him down on his own threshold, calling him a demon. Her father's last act in life had been to give it up to save her and David. The fact that she could not even give him a burial worthy of such a sacrifice would always grieve her.

"Is something wrong?"

Evanna looked up at Berawald and slowly shook her head. "Nay, 'tis but a moment of grieving for our father."

Before she had even finished speaking, David had torn himself from her grasp and thrown himself against Berawald, wrapping his thin arms around the man's waist. Evanna stood up, ignoring the fierce need to do the same, and turned her thoughts to David. Her brother was becoming dangerously attached to Berawald and that would make it all the harder to leave. She hated to bring the little boy even more grief, but they could not stay here much longer. Not only had they not been asked to stay, but it was wrong to bring a man, one who had shown them nothing but kindness, into their troubles.

"I miss my fither," David said, his face pressed against Berawald's taut stomach. "I miss him a lot."

Berawald eased the boy's tight grip and then crouched down so that he could look him in the eye. "Of course ye do. Ye didnae e'en have time to say fareweel, did ye?"

David shook his head. "And now I have to go live in the streets and pick through midden heaps and eat rats."

"David," Evanna began, not wanting the boy to try and wheedle any promises out of Berawald.

"Nay, ye willnae have to do that," Berawald said, cutting off the scolding he could see Evanna wanting to give the boy.

"But we havenae got a home now," David said.

"Ye will have a home."

"Berawald, ye must nay promise such things," Evanna protested even as her heart leapt with the hope that the home he offered would be with him.

"I must and I can," he said in a voice that broached no argument. "Nay matter what else happens, I will ensure that ye have a home, David. A safe home. One with a big cat to eat any rats that venture too close to your door," he added with a smile, and was pleased to see the tearful smile that curved David's mouth. "Now, shall we play a game of chess ere we eat and ye have to seek your bed?"

Evanna watched Berawald and David move to the table where the chessboard was set up. The look in Berawald's dark eyes when he had made his promise had stolen her breath away. He meant every word of it. The way he had glanced at her, including her in that promise, had made her heart leap about in her chest like a wild thing.

Careful, lass, a voice in her head warned her. He had not said it would be his home he offered them. Holding on to that warning to control a giddy hope she could not fully tamp down, Evanna moved toward the fire. Cooking always calmed her and she definitely needed calming now. The very last thing she wished to do was reveal her growing feelings for him when he had yet to give her any real hint that he might, someday, return them.

Five

"Where is David?"

Berawald looked up from the ledgers he had been blindly staring at for far too long and blinked away the blurriness in his eyes. Evanna stood by his chair, her small hands clenched so tightly in front of her that her knuckles shone bone white. She had been quiet, a little nervous, and somewhat evasive in the two days since he had kissed her, but he had been unable to think of what to do or say to break this new awkwardness between them. Now, however, she just looked worried, very worried.

"He went to the burn to try to catch us some fish for dinner," Berawald replied, and watched as her worry rapidly turned to alarm.

"It isnae safe for him to be out alone."

"Be at ease, Evanna. I check for signs of strangers and threats each and every night, and no one has drawn near." He decided it would be a very bad time to tell her that there was a good possibility her enemies were lurking at the borders of his land. They were still too far away to pose any immediate threat, but he suspected she was not in the mood to accept any assurances about that.

Evanna tried to calm her fears but was not very successful. It had been quiet around the cave and Berawald did diligently go out and check for signs of her enemies every night, but that knowledge did nothing to make her fears about David ease. Everything inside her was demanding that she find David immediately and drag him back to the safety of Berawald's unusual home. She did not have the sight but she had learned long ago to trust in her instincts. Those instincts had kept her and David alive as they had fled from their enemies. She could not ignore them now. Nor could she ignore the ghostly apparition of a young woman standing near the passage out of the cave who kept jabbing her finger in the direction of the burn, although she would not mention that to Berawald. He did not seem to notice all the spirits that wafted through his home.

"I ken it," she said. "I ken that all ye say is the truth. Howbeit, I feel a true need to find David and see for myself that he isnae in any danger." When she saw how closely he was studying her, she gave him a trembling smile. She hoped he had not seen her glance toward where the ghost floated, still jabbing her finger and now stomping one wispy foot in impatience. "Nay, I dinnae have the sight, if that is what ye are thinking. I dinnae ken what ye would call it, but something inside me demands that I find David. Now." *And the ghost at your doorway looks as if she wishes she had body enough to come and kick me into motion*, she added silently.

Berawald chanced a brief glance in the direction Evanna kept peeking and tensed. A spirit stood there, and if her finger pointing and foot stomping were any indication, Evanna's instincts were being strengthened by that spirit. He attempted to open his mind to the spirit and nearly jumped to his feet when a loud *Go now! Get the laddie!* pounded in his head. Even though he was sure Evanna and David could see the spirits, they still had not told him so and now was not the time to discuss the matter.

"Then we shall go and find David," he said, keeping his

voice calm although he was beginning to feel his own fear for the boy.

It was only a moment later when they had their cloaks on and were walking swiftly toward the burn. Evanna suddenly wondered why Berawald never questioned David's need to go fishing now, after the sun had gone down, or wonder why the boy was not troubled by walking around by himself in the dark. Few children could be so calm outside after sunset, and certainly not when alone. She kept her need to go racing to the burn screaming her brother's name tightly leashed by chewing over that puzzle as they walked. When Berawald suddenly grabbed her arm and yanked her to a halt, alarm shattered her thoughts and she barely stopped herself from crying out.

"David," she whispered.

"Quiet," Berawald said, his mouth close to her ear. "Someone is with him."

It took every scrap of willpower she had not to break free of his hold and race to her brother. Common sense told her she would only get herself killed if she did that, but David was like her own child, the last of her family. The very thought of anything happening to him made panic seize her in a tight grip, and common sense did nothing to ease its chokehold.

"He is in danger," she whispered as Berawald gently but firmly shoved her toward some thick bushes growing at the base of a huge tree. "He needs help."

"And he will get it. But if ye go racing to his rescue without kenning the who, the how many, or the how weel armed, ye will just get yourself killed. And David as weel. Sit here and be quiet."

She sat. "Ye may need help." A cry came from the direction of the burn and she started to get up only to be shoved back down.

"Nay, I will need no help, lass." Berawald gave her a brief, fierce kiss and then strode away.

Evanna was still touching her mouth and struggling to

clear her head of both desire and surprise when she realized Berawald was gone. He had disappeared into the shadows as if he owned them. Hard as she tried, she could see no hint of his movements or hear any sound of his passing through the wood. And she had very keen sight and hearing. Suddenly, she knew that Berawald might well have been speaking the simple truth when he said he would need no help. He moved as swiftly and silently as the spirits that surrounded him so often. Berawald obviously had a few secrets of his own.

Despite his skill and his orders, she began to creep toward the burn. She knew she could offer him little aid in the battle he would soon face, but she could grab David and run if the opportunity presented itself. Getting David out of the way of any fighting that occurred would give Berawald a chance to act more freely. It was just an excuse to see what was happening to her brother and Berawald and she knew it. But it was a good one. She fully intended to use it mercilessly if, when the fight was over, Berawald felt any inclination to scold her for her disobedience.

Berawald felt a snarl scrape through his throat as he watched the scene on the banks of the burn. Three men stood over a crying David. It was obvious that one of the men had struck the boy, and he would pay dearly for that. The rage that consumed Berawald surprised him a little, for it went a lot deeper than simply anger over seeing a large man abuse someone so much smaller and weaker than he was. The dark beast that lurked within every MacNachton demanded the freedom to seek revenge, but Berawald fought to keep it under control. When one of the men grabbed David by the front of his shirt, lifted him off the ground, and shook him hard, that control disappeared. The beast roared and snapped all the tethers Berawald had placed on it. Growling loud enough to cause all three men to look his way, Berawald leapt toward the man holding David.

A sound echoed through the wood that made Evanna look around for some huge, enraged beast charging through the trees. She suddenly realized it had come from the burn. She ceased to creep along and started to run. The sight of Berawald snapping a man's neck like a twig and hurling him through the air as if he weighed nothing brought her to an abrupt halt. When another man raced toward Berawald she started to cry out a warning, but Berawald moved out of the way of the man's thrusting sword so quickly he was behind the man in the blink of an eye. He dispatched the swordsman by hurling him against a tree so hard Evanna doubted there was a single bone in the man's body that was left unbroken. When he yanked the third man up by the front of his filthy shirt she could not help but gasp softly. Berawald held the big, muscle-heavy man by only one hand and shook him. She realized then that the growl she had heard had come from Berawald.

When David suddenly ran up to her and clutched at her waist, she shook herself free of her shock and checked him for any serious injuries. Once she was assured that he had little more than a nasty bruise or two, her gaze was immediately drawn back to Berawald. She could not see his face, but the man he held was staring at it in wide-eyed terror. Evanna was finding it difficult to believe what she was seeing. The strength and speed Berawald revealed were not just extraordinary; she was sure they were an impossibility for a normal man.

"I kenned it," the man babbled as he dangled from Berawald's grasp. "I kenned Duncan was right about them."

"What was the fool right about?"

Evanna frowned, for Berawald's smooth, deep voice had changed into a deep, rough growl.

"That the Masseys were demons. The bitch has run back to her own kind. Duncan means to send ye all to hell!"

"Ye will see hell ere I ever do." Berawald snarled out the

words and then bent his head to sink his teeth into the man's throat.

A weak scream of pain and terror escaped the man dangling from Berawald's hand, followed by a gurgling noise that sent chills down Evanna's spine. She pressed David's face against her belly so that he could not see anything and tried to look away, but she could not turn her gaze from the sight. The thought that Berawald had just sunk his teeth into that man's throat plunged into her mind. She told herself that was impossible, that men did not do that sort of thing, but the sound she heard in the otherwise still forest told her differently. When Berawald lifted his head, snapped the man's neck, and then tossed him aside, she saw the ragged wound in the dead man's throat, a wound that bled very little.

For just a moment Berawald stood, his fists clenched at his side, and stared up at the moon. He savored the feel of the blood singing in his veins, enjoying the renewed strength and power it brought him. A soft noise yanked him free of that personal satisfaction and the beast in him rapidly drew back. With the clearing of his mind, he realized he had forgotten that David had been close by, that the boy could easily have seen everything. He took a deep breath to further calm himself only to have his nose filled with an all too familiar scent. Evanna was there and she, too, must have seen everything. He slowly dropped to his knees. Suddenly his victory did not taste as sweet as it once had, for in winning the battle, he feared he had just lost the only prize he wanted.

"Is David unharmed?" he asked without looking at her.

"A wee bit bruised but nay more than that." Evanna had tried to speak calmly, as if watching one man rip out another man's throat with his teeth were something she saw every day, but she could hear the faint quiver of fear in her voice.

"Take him back to the cave."

"But, weel, are ye hurt?"

"Nay, I am weel. Just, just go."

"My fish," David protested.

"I will bring them," Berawald said. "Please. Just go."

He heard them leave and bent over until his forehead nearly touched the ground. The woman he desired, the one he wanted so badly he could barely sleep, had just seen him tossing men around as if they were no more than thistledown, breaking bones, and snapping necks. Worse, she had seen him feed. That was the trouble with letting the beast rule, with releasing the creatures that had been the dreaded Nightriders of old. Those men had never caged their beasts but had ridden out at night hunting down anyone they could so that they could feed the dark hunger that could so easily rule a MacNachton.

She will never want me now, Berawald thought as he slowly climbed to his feet and numbly went about the chore of ridding MacNachton land of the bodies. He had heard the fear in her voice. If she was even still at the cave when he returned, he knew what he would find. She would look at him with fear and revulsion. Evanna would finally believe that there truly were demons in the world.

Evanna sat David down on a stool near the fire and began to clean and treat the bruises and scrapes he had suffered at the hands of their enemies. She wanted to deny all she had seen by the burn, but she could not. Neither could she forget it. The problem she faced now was what to do about it. She still felt some fear over what Berawald had done, over what it could mean about the man she had come to care for, but she simply could not make herself believe that he would ever be a danger to her or to David. The beast in the forest was Berawald, but so was the kind, gentle man who had taken her and David into his home and cared for them.

"Berawald is different," said David. "Just like us only bigger." He frowned. "Nay, I mean more."

Or worse, Evanna thought, but quickly bit back the words.

"There do seem to be many similarities," she said gently, noticing that there was no fear in David's eyes when he spoke of Berawald.

"Do ye think I will be able to toss men about like that when I am grown?"

"I have no idea."

She supposed she should not be surprised that a small boy would find such a skill admirable. David had not seen Berawald bite that man, nor seen the man tossed to the ground, his throat torn yet bleeding very little. Even telling herself it could not possibly have happened, she could not shake the feeling that Berawald had feasted upon that man's blood. While she felt no sorrow for the deaths of those men, was even glad that Berawald had ended their lives, the manner in which he had killed the last man really troubled her. What troubled her even more was that she had not grabbed David and run, screaming, as far and as fast as she could.

"Is he all right?"

Since she had not heard him approach, Evanna was a little startled to look up and find Berawald standing just behind David. In his hand three cleaned and gutted fish dangled from a length of thick twine. A pained look briefly crossed his handsome face and she knew she had not hidden her fear very well. Most of that fear was born of being startled, but she could not deny that some of it was of him.

Yet where was that man who had growled like a beast, snapped necks, tossed men around, and ripped out throats? Before her stood a tall, handsome man holding fish ready for cooking, a look of uncertainty in his eyes, and no sign of the vicious battle he had just been in. When he gently caressed David's hair she felt no urge to yank her brother out of his reach. It made no sense and she was not sure it ever would.

"I am fine, Berawald," David said. "Thank ye for saving me and for cleaning my fish 'cause I really dinnae like doing that myself, ye ken. And do ye think ye can teach me how to throw men about like ye did?"

Evanna took the fish from Berawald's hand and moved toward the fire. She would cook them a meal. Cooking would help her think, would help her put some order into her tangled thoughts and feelings so that she might finally make some sense of them. She refused to be one of those who condemned someone who was different, as she and her brother had been condemned. And, she realized, as she recalled all too clearly what the last man had said, there might be some connection between her enemies and the ones the MacNachtons had.

If not for David's chatter their meal would have been a silent one. Berawald tried to take comfort in the fact that Evanna made no move to keep him away from her brother. The very fact that she was still in his home, that she allowed him to be so close to David, seemed to imply that, although she might be afraid of what he had done, she did not believe he would harm her or David. He would not make the mistake of thinking that meant she would accept him or let him touch her as he ached to, however.

They were going to have to have a talk, he decided as he ate the fish she served. He knew the food would not give him the sustenance he needed or craved, but he liked the taste. She would undoubtedly have questions, and after all she had seen him do to those men, he supposed it would be best to answer them truthfully. Perhaps the truth would ease the lingering fear he could almost scent in the air, but he did not hold out much hope for that.

Leaving Evanna to clean up after the meal, Berawald took on the task of putting David to bed. By the way the boy acted he had to assume that David had not seen him feed on that man. All the child wanted to talk about was how he could learn to toss men through the air. Berawald was relieved to see that he had not frightened the boy. He just wished he could take the fear out of Evanna's beautiful eyes, for it cut him to the bone to see it.

He shook aside that concern and told David a tale about a battle the MacNachtons had fought many years ago, careful to leave out all the more gruesome parts. The boy had come through the experience at the burn unscathed. Berawald did not want to be the one to give him nightmares now.

When David finally went to sleep, Berawald sat beside the bed for a little while longer. He knew he was avoiding the confrontation with Evanna, but there was more to it than that. The moment he had seen that David was in danger, he had realized that his affection for the child had sunk its roots deep into his heart. He felt as if the boy was his own flesh and blood even though he knew that was impossible. He had never bedded down with any woman outside Cambrun and had not bedded many of them, either. David was the son of his heart and Berawald feared that he would soon lose him.

With a sigh that felt as if it was pulled up from his very soul, Berawald lightly kissed the boy's bruised cheek and decided it was time for him to meet his fate. He had no doubt at all that Evanna would be stunned to learn that she held it in her small, pretty hands, but she did. It did not make him feel one bit better to know that, no matter what she thought or felt about him now, he would always have her gratitude for saving her and David's lives. That was not going to do much to fill all the empty nights ahead. He stepped into the main room, saw her staring into the fire, and braced himself for the blow to his heart he knew was coming.

Six

"Evanna? We have to talk."

That deep smooth voice pulled Evanna out of her deep thoughts and she nearly cursed aloud when it also felt as if he had just stroked her skin and warmed her insides. After all she had seen, she did not understand how just the sound of his voice could move her so. For all the thinking she had just done, she had come up with no solutions or answers. The biggest question she had kept asking herself was why she was still in his home, had even let him tuck her little brother into bed. That made no sense at all and that in itself frightened her.

She nodded in agreement and sat in a chair near the fire. She was too cold to move any distance from its heat. Whether that chill came from a fear of Berawald or a fear of her own inability to leave his side she did not know. When she finally looked at him she inwardly sighed. Even knowing what he had done, she still found him beautiful. Worse, she still felt everything that was womanly inside her reach out for him. Evanna began to wonder if getting wounded had somehow scrambled her wits.

Berawald stared at her and wondered how to begin. There

was still a hint of fear in her eyes, but mostly he saw confusion and uncertainty in her expression. He wondered if she had been trying to convince herself that she had *not* seen what he had done. It was tempting to try to help her along that twisted path of denying all she had seen, but he knew that would not work in the end. Not only was she too sharp of wit to delude herself for too long, but also they faced a battle against a murderous enemy. Her enemies were near at hand and he would undoubtedly unleash the darkness in him again in his attempt to keep her and David safe.

"Ye saw what I did, *all* that I did," he said.

"Aye, all of it," she replied softly. "I made certain David didnae see it, but I couldnae seem to stop myself from watching it all, right up until ye bit that mon's neck. Ye truly did that, didnae ye?"

"Aye, I did." He winced when he saw the fear in her eyes flare up, but she wrestled it back down, proving that she was willing to listen to him. "For ye to understand I have to begin at the beginning." He placed a stool in front of her and sat down, clasping his hands on his knees. "MacNachtons have lived here, on these lands, for hundreds of years. In truth, they hide here. Ye see, my clan has a few of what ye like to call differences."

"Oh, aye, I should think so. Most men dinnae end a fight by ripping out their enemy's throat with their own teeth."

Berawald wondered if he could take her sharp words as a sign that she was not as afraid or repulsed by him as he had feared. "Let me finish telling ye who the MacNachtons are, please. We arenae exactly certain where we began or why we are different. We still search for the answers to that. After so many years 'tis difficult to tell truth from legend. 'Tis the way for many clans, I think. In the past, the verra distant past, we were known as Night Riders. I fear our people had little care or respect for those who were nay of our ilk. We hunted in the night, hunted anyone who was fool enough to be out after the sun had set. Some e'en in their own homes. If even some of the tales are true, we made the Norsemen look like innocent bairns. Those ancestors probably deserved to be called demons.

"The change in our ways began with one wise laird and continued with each of his sons until now, until all we wish to do is to be left in peace. The mon who is our laird now wishes us to try to breed out the differences, to have as many of us as possible wed Outsiders—those not of MacNachton blood."

Evanna thought about that for a moment and nodded. "It grows more difficult to hide what ye are."

"Exactly. And to keep our secrets."

"Do ye have a lot of them?"

She studied him as he carefully weighed his answer. Her fear was almost gone, although she was not sure it should be. Yet all she could see when she looked at Berawald was the man who had helped her and David, the man who had healed her wounds, a kind man who made her blood run hot. Every instinct she had told her that he would never hurt her or David, but for the first time in her life, she wondered if she should heed those instincts. She feared emotion might be twisting them into what she wanted. In her heart there was a strong reluctance to turn from him simply because he was different, no matter how shocking those differences were. After all, she and David had suffered dearly because they, too, were different, and she refused to act as her enemies did.

"I am nay sure I would say there are a lot," he said finally. "'Tis just that they are of the kind that makes it verra difficult to mix in easily with others, the kind that seem to breed only fear in others. We are, in most part, of the shadows. The sun can kill us. 'Tis as if it drains us of all life. The truer a MacNachton ye are, the more deadly it is. We are stronger and faster than Outsiders. We can see clearly in those shadows we must live in." He hesitated to speak of the last two differences, the biggest of all, for they could easily shatter her current state of calm and her acceptance of him.

"Ye drank that mon's blood, Berawald," she said when he fell silent. She was still surprised that the mere thought of that did not send her rushing for a bucket to empty her belly into. "I saw ye bite him and I saw his wound when ye let him fall. Such a wound should have been flowing with blood, soaking the ground all round the mon, but there was barely a trickle."

"Aye, I fed on him. We are, by nature, predators. My ancestors gloried in the taking of blood, in the kill. That is what the old laird changed. We may nay longer treat the Outsiders as naught but cattle, havenae done so for a verra long time, but we are still predators."

"But if ye have changed, why drink of that mon?"

"Because we still need blood and dinnae ask me why, for I dinnae ken the why. It just is. If we dinnae get some, we die, slowly and painfully."

"Yet I have seen ye eat proper food. Ye just dined on fish with us."

"I can do that. Many of us can. It just doesnae give us the nourishment we need to live or keep strong. But there are those of us who simply like the taste of some foods. When we are badly wounded, have lost too much blood, or have suffered beneath the heat of the sun for too long, the blood of another is all that will save us. A mate or a kinsmon usually gives us what is needed. Most of the time we exist upon animal blood and verra raw meat."

"Unless ye are fighting an enemy."

He sighed and dragged a hand through his hair. "Aye, just so. But only if he has left us no choice but to kill him. Those men left me no choice. 'Twas them or ye and David."

"I ken that. I think 'tis the only reason I brought David back here. I kenned ye wouldnae hurt us."

"Never." He grasped her hands in his, pleased when she did not immediately try to pull free of his hold. "I would ne'er hurt either of ye. Tell me ye believe that if naught else."

Evanna stared into his dark eyes and knew he was telling

her the truth. The air of desperation that clung to him only enhanced her conviction. It was a little unsettling to think there was an entire clan of people like Berawald, but she suspected she would soon cease to be troubled by that. And when all was said and done, was it not a good idea to keep such a warrior close to hand? He fought for her and her brother. Who was she to question *how* he did so?

"I believe you," she said quietly, and could see the relief that flooded him. "E'en after seeing what ye had done, e'en while fear still gnawed at my heart, a large part of me kenned that David and I were nay in danger from you."

"There is one last thing of great importance," he said after clearing his throat of the lump of emotion that filled him at her words.

"Ye arenae going to tell me that ye can change into some beastie, are ye?"

"Nay, why should ye think that I could do that?"

"I heard ye. I heard ye snarl, growl, and roar like some huge beast. I e'en looked around for one until I realized the sounds came from you."

"Ah, that." Berawald knew he should release her hands, ought to cease caressing the backs of them with his thumbs, but since she made no move to pull them back, he held fast. "I dinnae change although there is a, weel, a feral look that comes o'er my face when the darkness rules." He took a deep breath to steady himself. "And my teeth grow a wee bit longer and sharper."

Unable to stop herself, Evanna began to lean closer to him. She did not understand how the light stroking of his thumbs over the backs of her hands could make her feel so warm and needy, but she was sure that she liked it. Just the way he spoke, the way he watched her as if searching for some sign that she would push him aside and was dreading it, made the last of the fear in her heart burn itself out. The space left behind was quickly filled with the heat he could so effortlessly stir within her and the ache that never seemed to leave her.

"I would think they must or ye wouldnae be able to do what ye did," she said, struggling not to lose herself in his dark eyes and not being very successful.

"Does it trouble ye that I have a need for blood?"

She could feel him tense for her answer and chose her words carefully. "It does, but nay so much as I thought it would. As ye have said, your people nay longer hunt down people, e'en innocent ones. I cannae e'en feel the slightest pinch of sorrow or regret for the deaths of those men. I was just shocked by what ye did. I kept wondering why I brought David back here, back to the lair of a mon who could do what ye did."

"And what answer did ye get?" he asked softly as he slowly lifted his hands to clasp her face and pulled her closer to him.

"I decided it was because I trust ye. As I have said, I simply couldnae make myself believe that ye would ever hurt us."

The relief he felt, the utter joy her acceptance brought him, snapped what few restraints he had kept on his desire for her. He kissed her, reveling in the taste of her. When she wrapped her slim arms around his neck, his kiss grew fierce with his need, with the overpowering urge to claim her as his own. He stood up with her in his arms. The only clear thought in his head was that he needed to get her naked and beneath him. His entire body throbbed in agreement with that plan and he headed for his bedchamber.

Evanna felt herself dangling from Berawald's arms and wrapped her legs around him to better balance herself. He groaned softly and staggered just a little before he swiftly steadied his pace again. She knew where he was taking her and what he wanted, but she felt no reluctance or fear. Now she knew the other reason she had not fled from him—it was because she knew this was right where she belonged—in his arms.

Her descent to his bed was so swift and abrupt it left her dizzy. She stared up at him as he removed his shirt and nearly growled in appreciation of the sight of a bare-chested Berawald. He had a broad chest, his skin dark and smooth and stretched over taut, strong muscles. Her hands itched to touch him.

"Evanna?" he asked, pausing at the side of the bed, his breathing heavy and fast.

She knew what he was asking with that one word. The fleeting thought that this was wrong, that she was about to give him what she should only give her lawful husband, went through her mind and was quickly banished. She wanted this, needed it, and for once she would take what she wanted and worry about the consequences later. In truth, with such deadly enemies at her heels, there might not even be a later. Evanna answered his question by simply opening her arms to welcome him.

Berawald groaned and nearly fell into her arms. He fought to regain some hint of control as he pulled and yanked their clothes off as fast as he could, and threw them aside. Every touch of her small hands, each taste of her skin, made even the slimmest strand of control difficult to cling to. The way her full breasts filled his hands made him tremble. The soft warmth of her skin beneath his hands and his mouth had him hardening to the point where he feared he would burst before he ever got inside her. Every soft sound of delight she made was pure, sweet music to his ears.

Evanna felt wild with need. When he drew the hard, aching tip of her breast deep into his mouth, she arched up, desperately trying to touch as much of his body with hers as she could. She doubted she would ever get enough of his kisses or the feel of his warm skin beneath her hands. Even the feel of his hard, hot manhood brushing against her did not dim her passion. It felt big and some small, still cautious part of her mind shied away from that, but mostly she wanted to touch him, to learn each and every part of his body. When he slid his hand between her legs to stroke her where the ache of desire was at its worst, she barely flinched.

"Berawald," she cried out when the intimate caress made her feel as if she would shatter into small pieces right in his arms.

"Och, lass, I ken ye are untried and it pleases me, but right at this moment I dearly wish ye werenae." He pressed his forehead against hers and fought for just a little more control, just enough so that he did not slam into her like some barbarian. "I fear this may hurt ye a wee bit."

Her eyes widened until they stung her a little when she felt something large start to enter her body. Evanna could feel herself begin to tense as if rejecting the invasion. Instinct told her that was the wrong thing to do.

"Kiss me," she ordered him. "Kiss me blind and then, weel, then just get the hurting part of this over with."

"I dinnae want to hurt ye."

"I dinnae want to be hurt, but I do want what comes after that. So kiss me."

He kissed her, struggling to keep the kiss soft and seductive, to lull her virginal fears and restore her passion. As he kissed her, he rocked slowly into her until he felt her maidenhead. Praying that it was a very thin shield and easily broken, he drew back and thrust into her, pushing right through that shield until he was buried deep inside her heat. He caught her startled cry of pain with his mouth. Despite his need to keep on thrusting, to savor her tight heat, he held himself still until he felt the tension caused by the pain begin to ease out of her body. As soon as she was once again soft and welcoming in his arms, he lifted his head to look at her.

"The pain has eased?" he asked, praying that it had, for he was not sure he could remain still for one more minute.

"Oh, aye. It was a quick one, nay more, and it faded just as quickly."

Evanna was bemused by how odd it felt to be joined with him, odd but very good as well. The memory of the quick glimpse she had once caught of a pair of lovers told her that they were not finished, however, as did her body. She was certain the taut stillness Berawald still maintained was not the way this should be done. The lovers she had glimpsed had been moving. Idly wondering how she could get Berawald to move, Evanna ran her fingers down his back and nipped his shoulder.

A soft growl escaped Berawald and he began to move—hard and fast. Evanna gasped as passion raced through her like a rain-swollen river. She clung tightly to Berawald, quickly learning to meet his every thrust, their bodies moving in perfect harmony. Her world narrowed to this one act, to the feel of him in her arms, in her body. She shattered, fire racing through her body from the place where they were joined. Even as she tried to pull him deeper into her arms and her body, she felt a sudden sharp pain in her neck. In some small sane part of her mind she decided that must be part of the loving and so she bit him on the shoulder again. Berawald roared as his body bucked and his seed flowed into her. Evanna finally sank completely beneath the blinding pleasure sweeping over her.

Berawald collapsed in Evanna's arms, retaining barely enough of his wits to ease his body a little to the side as he fell so that his weight did not crush her beneath him. When he finally had the strength to open his eyes, he found himself staring at a bite mark on her slender neck. He grimaced as he realized he had marked her and feared it was the mating mark. Now there was yet another thing they needed to talk about, he thought, and sighed. Later, he told himself. For just a little while he was going to savor the peace after the storm of loving He was going to thoroughly enjoy that sweet moment when it felt as if all was right in the world.

Seven

"How do ye feel about older men?" Berawald asked.

Berawald ignored her quizzical frown as he climbed back into bed and pulled her into his arms. She settled against his chest a bit limply and he grinned with masculine pride. After cleaning them both up from her loss of innocence, he had let her rest for a little while and had then made love to her again. Not only had he made her cry out his name several times, but he had *not* bitten her. Glancing at the mark on his shoulder, he wondered if he was worrying unnecessarily about telling her about that bite. She had some pretty sharp teeth herself.

"Ye cannae be that much older than I am." Evanna rubbed her cheek against his warm skin, loving the feel of him and the bone-deep pleasure that still tingled through her body. "I am three and twenty. What are ye? Five, mayhap six years older?"

Deciding blunt was best, Berawald did a little adding of numbers in his head and replied, "I am older than ye by four score years."

It took Evanna a few moments to understand what he had just told her. She raised herself up just enough to look at him and scold him for making such a poor jest, but then frowned. He looked perfectly serious. In fact, he was watching her warily as if he was awaiting her reaction to yet another shocking MacNachton difference.

"Nay," she mumbled, "ye cannae be that old. Ye look thirty or less."

"I ken it and I probably will for a long time yet. MacNachtons live a verra long time. The purer their blood, the longer they live. In truth, we arenae all that sure just how long we can live, for all too often, the elders reach a point where they are simply sick of life and end it."

"They kill themselves?" The thought of anyone committing such a grave sin briefly broke through the shock that held her in such a tight grip. If one could believe all the priests said, such people put their very souls at risk.

"A few. Most just hurl themselves about recklessly until they are killed. They lose all sense of survival because, we assume, they no longer wish to survive. It mostly happens when they lose their mate. As far as I ken, I am a Pureblood MacNachton." Noticing that she was staring at him in wide-eyed shock again, he decided to just keep talking until she shook herself free of it. "My cousin Jankyn isnae so sure, for he has no record of any Pureblood having a gift like I do."

Aware that he was about to tell her that he saw ghosts and he did not think it was a good time for that, he hurried on, "MacNachtons are verra alike, as twins can be. I dinnae ken if that was so in the beginning, but 'tis certainly the way of it now. Too often wed and bred within our own clans. Leastwise that is what our laird says. He believes that is why we can nay longer breed. My cousin was the last child born to a MacNachton, and by your thinking, he is verra old but he is a wee bit younger than I am."

Evanna rolled off him to sprawl on her back at his side and stare up at the ceiling. All of her little dreams were crumbling about her feet. There could be no future for her with this man. She could accept all the other differences between them, but not that he would stay young and strong as she grew old and weak. Not that he had asked her to stay with him, she thought as he turned on his side and looked down at her. She quickly buried her pain and disappointment, not wanting him to think it was because of the sort of man he was or, worse, make him start asking her what troubled her.

As she tried to think of something to say, anything that would help her keep her heartbreak hidden, she reached up to rub at a slightly sore spot on her neck. Shock raced through her as she gently ran her fingers over what was definitely a bite mark. Scattered memories of their fierce lovemaking passed through her mind and she suddenly recalled that brief sense of a sharp pain on her neck before desire had fully engulfed her body and mind. The way Berawald paled a little, looking both worried and afraid, eased her shock and smothered her rising anger. He had bitten her but she felt sure it was in the throes of passion, something she found somewhat flattering. The only weakness she had felt at the time had come from that wild lovemaking, so she knew he had not truly fed on her.

"Ye bit me," she said, trying to look cross as she stared at him.

"Ye bit me, too." He pointed to the mark on his shoulder, feeling quite pleased with it until she grew pale. " 'Tis naught, Evanna. 'Tis but a wee love bite."

"Are ye sure, Berawald?" While part of her was thrilled that she might be enough like Berawald to have some future with him, another part was appalled that she could well be far more *different* than she had believed. "David and I are different, too, ye ken. The sun doesnae burn us. Weel, it might do, but we wouldnae be aware of it or care, for by then we would be unconscious and dying. It weakens us. One reason I collapsed after carrying David across the burn was that we had been forced to flee our hiding place while the sun was still verra high in the sky. I used my own cloak to cover David and protect him. For us it is exactly as ye say, the sun drains all the life out of us. I wasnae in it so long that it could have killed me, but I was also wounded and so verra tired that any added weakness was dangerous."

He brushed a kiss over her mouth. "I already suspected that. Aye, ye might even have some MacNachton blood in ye. My cousin thinks so as weel, for ye also heal verra quickly, far too quickly for any Outsider. As I told ye, I could have removed the stitches from your wound before I did so, but I simply couldnae believe what my eyes told me. And both ye and David dinnae think anything odd about eating meat that has been barely passed over a flame. Ye see verra weel in the dark, too. David has none of the usual child's fears of the dark, acts as if it is right and proper to play or fish in the dark." He winked at her. "And ye bite whilst caught up in the heady grip of passion." He laughed when she blushed. "Now, tell me, how old was your mother and what was her maiden name?"

"Bell and I dinnae ken how old she was. Two score, may-hap two score and ten."

Berawald gently grasped her by the chin. "Think of her now, Evanna. Think of her with the clear eyes of a woman and nay the eyes of her child. Ye have seen other women of that age. How did your mother compare?"

It took Eyanna only a moment to find the answer to that question. She felt excited, for it meant there really could be a chance of some future for her and Berawald. An equal sense of unease plagued her, however, for she had suffered for her differences all her life, had lost both of her parents because of them, and did not truly wish to be burdened with even more.

"She didnae look much older than I do," she finally replied, hiding the unease she felt about accepting such a truth, for she did not wish to burden him with it. "But, Berawald, she had red hair. Much darker than my father's but still red. Mac-Nachtons dinnae have red hair, do they?"

"Nay, but she wasnae a Pureblood. I do think her family

got a dose of Pureblood MacNachton nay so verra far back in her line, however. Some of us do travel still. We have refuges scattered all over this land so that we might travel in safety if we choose to. We ne'er considered the possibility that any of our blood survived outside of Cambrun, especially since we have apparently lost the ability to breed, but we have recently had proof that there are some of our kin out there. A search has begun for them not only because our clan is in need of new blood, but also because they are most certainly in danger. As ye weel ken, the differences they will have make them a target for superstitious people or the ones who hunt down MacNachtons. I dinnae e'en want to think of how many have been killed or have had to spend their whole lives in hiding."

Evanna wrapped her arms around him. "It was the duty of the one who sired them to see to their safety, to tell your clan that there was a child somewhere." She kissed the hollow of his throat and had to bite back a smile of pure feminine pride when she heard him catch his breath. "Ye search for them now. Let that be enough."

"It has to be, doesnae it?" He stroked her back, certain that he would never get enough of feeling her smooth, soft skin beneath his hands. "I think I may have found two of our Lost Ones."

"Aye, I begin to think ye may have. Is that what ye call us? Lost Ones?"

He looked at her face and frowned slightly. "It seemed to be a fitting name. Ye dinnae seem to be verra sure about wanting to carry MacNachton blood. I thought ye had accepted what I am."

She gave him a quick, hard kiss. "I have accepted what ye are. Never doubt that."

"But ye dinnae wish to be of my kind."

"Ah, Berawald, that isnae what troubles me. I have spent my whole life hiding what I am, fighting to conceal all that is different about me. Ye have lived amongst your clan, concerned about what ye are only when ye left it, something ye did as rarely as possible. Hiding what I am, feeling the scorn and fear of others and the threat of that, has taught me that being different isnae safe. Being different cost the lives of both of my parents. Now ye tell me that I may be e'en more different from those I lived amongst than I thought I was. It shall take me some time to accept that without fear and I am so verra tired of being afraid."

"Ye can be safe at Cambrun. Ye can live amongst those who are like ye and David and ne'er have to hide again."

Before she could ask him what he meant, he kissed her. Evanna felt the hint of desperation in his kiss and immediately wanted to soothe him. When he began to make love to her again, she welcomed his every touch, his every kiss. The way he made her burn should have frightened her, but she reveled in it. Confusion dimmed her passion for one moment when he urged her over onto her hands and knees. Then he entered her with one swift thrust and she cried out each time he thrust again. This time when she felt his teeth against her neck she did not even tense. The pleasure and pain of his bite sent her tumbling headlong into desire's sweet abyss. A small part of her mind heard Berawald growl out her name as he joined her in that delirious fall, and knowing he was with her only sharpened her pleasure.

"I think we need some sleep," Berawald murmured as, once he had freshened them both with a cool damp cloth, he rejoined her in his bed.

She was in his bed, he thought as he pulled her into his arms, and he grinned with a satisfied pleasure that came straight from his heart. This was where she belonged. The heady taste of her blood still lingered on his tongue, and even though he had taken only a small sip or two, the way it filled his body with need told him that she was his mate. Berawald did not know that much about women, but he felt certain that getting her into his bed did not ensure that she would stay with him.

He bit back the urge to demand that she swear herself to him. It was not a good time for that. She was still reeling slightly from all he had told her even though she had accepted him for what he was. Once her enemies were vanquished, he would tell her that he wanted her to stay with him as his wife, as his mate, and, if God blessed them, as the mother of his children. He would take the time until then to woo her and to try to gain a place in her heart as he had gained the precious gift of her desire.

"Berawald, ye can see the spirits, too, cannae ye?" Evanna asked, needing to know despite the sleep weighting her body and her eyelids.

For a moment Berawald was reluctant to answer that question, not wishing to burden her with yet another thing that was strange about him. Then he realized that she had said *too*. She was, in a word, confirming all he had suspected. This time it was Evanna who sought assurance that he could accept a gift of hers.

"Aye. I have been able to see them since I began the change from boy to mon," he replied. "I see them and I hear them in my head. I can e'en see when the spirit finally leaves. For the ones who are good, they simply walk away and disappear into a light that begins to shine as they walk toward it. Some wait a long time before they do that."

"Why do ye think they linger here?"

"I am nay sure. My belief is that some linger to watch o'er a loved one, such as a child, or there is something left undone, some crime done to them that they need to have resolved. The spirit that insisted we go to David is of a woman who was murdered by her lover, tossed into the burn when it was running high and fast. Tossed in with the child she had borne him."

"How sad. Is the child's spirit still here?"

"Nay, I suspicion he was quick to go to that light. I believe she stays because she waits for her lover to pay for what he did to her and her child. I fear I may never be able to help her and hope that someday she will simply leave to be with her child."

"Do the bad ones linger? The spirits of the evil?"

"I have seen none, but I dinnae go verra far from here, do

I? The few I have kenned and seen die were claimed by hell verra quickly. Something dark rises up from the ground the moment death is certain and grabs hold of the spirit. I have heard it scream as the darkness closes round it and takes it down. To hell, I suppose."

Evanna shivered. "I pray my sight and David's are never that precise. We dinnae hear voices in our heads all the time, either. 'Tis rare that we hear them at all."

"That is because there is something about ye and David that strengthens the wall between the living and the dead."

"Truly?"

"Truly." He ran his fingers through her thick, soft hair and knew she would soon be asleep. He could hear it in her voice. "Since ye have joined me here I have kenned a peace, a quiet, that I havenae kenned since I became a mon."

"I am glad. Ye need your rest."

Berawald felt her grow heavier against him and knew she had finally fallen asleep. Her voice had been tantalizingly husky, but there had also been the hint of a slur to her words. She badly needed to rest. He knew he should sleep but his heart was too full of hope and pleasure. His mind was also too full of plans to make her love him, to make her and David his family.

He thought about his laird, about Jankyn, and about the others who had found their mates. Berawald had not fully understood the bonds they appeared to share, but he had felt the pinch of envy at times. He had envied them the pleasure of having a woman in their bed every night, of having one that was more than just a bedmate to ease an itch, and he had certainly envied them for the children they had. Now he understood what else they had found. He understood the depths of the bonds he had seen, how they twined around a man's heart, mind, and soul. He felt all of that with Evanna and desperately wanted her to feel the same.

How to accomplish that was the question. Berawald's experience with women was not much to brag about. He was often so lost in the world of the dead, his mind so clouded by the voices he heard day and night, that he did not even think about women and the bedding of them. Although he knew that the way Evanna's presence silenced the noise and cleared his mind was not all that bound him to her, he did not want to lose that. He did not want to lose her at all.

Closing his eyes and reaching out for sleep, Berawald prayed he could learn the trick of wooing a woman's heart. He needed Evanna as tightly bound to him as he was to her. Precious as her passion was to him, he craved her love. If it became necessary, he would swallow his pride and seek advice from Jankyn about how to woo a woman. His pride would be a small price to pay if it meant he could keep Evanna at his side.

Eight

The men are coming.

Berawald was jolted awake by that sharp voice, his heart pounding with alarm. He looked around but saw no one except the spirit who had urged them to go after David, and he realized the voice had been in his head. It took him a moment to clear the last vestiges of sleep from his mind. She had forced herself into his head, urgency cracking the wall that now sheltered his mind from the constant chatter of the dead, and he was not sure he liked that.

"Where are they?" he asked, hoping she would give him a reasonable, clear answer, something spirits were not usually very good at.

They are near the outside opening. They will find it soon. Save the lad.

"How many of them are there?"

More than ye can fight. Save the lad, she urged again before she faded away.

As he leapt from the bed and began to dress, Berawald suddenly realized what was holding the spirit of the woman here, or at least part of the reason she lingered. She had been unable to save the life of her own child. Guilt was but one of the tethers holding her in the land of the living. He hoped that by helping to save David's life she would finally find some peace, but he began to doubt it. She had already saved David's life once and yet she remained, haunting him.

Grabbing up Evanna's clothes, he shook her awake. "Get dressed. Our enemies are close to finding this place."

"Ye have seen them?" she asked as she took her clothes from his hands and hurried to dress herself.

"Nay, our ghostie told me. She watches over the lad." After buckling on his sword, he grabbed her by the shoulders and gave her a brief, fierce kiss. "Gather a few of your things and wait for me at that passage I showed ye. I will get David."

Evanna nodded, forcing herself to obey as he ran from the room. It was hard to leave David's safety in someone else's hands, even Berawald's. Every part of her cried out to run to her brother and get him to safety herself, but she resisted that call. She would only get in the way, and, even more dangerous, slow them down in their attempt to escape. Having become painfully knowledgeable about the need for a swift escape, she knew Berawald's orders were the ones she had to follow. It did not stop her from praying for success with every step she took, however. She also promised herself that if she heard even the faintest sound of trouble before David and Berawald joined her, she would go to help them. When Berawald had first shown her the way out, he had told her that no matter what else was happening she was to get herself to safety and never look back. That was an order she knew she could never obey.

Berawald was not surprised to find the ghost at David's bedside. She looked both frightened and frustrated. He suspected she was cursing her inability to just pick up the boy and run. He did not care to think of the many ways she might haunt him if he did not get David away from the men about to invade his home.

"David, wake up," he said, gently shaking the boy. "We must leave now."

The speed with which the boy woke, fear darkening his eyes, pinched at Berawald's heart. He knew life was hard for nearly everyone, that one could not always keep the innocent safe from death, pain, or hunger, but he wished he could banish the fear in David's eyes. He would, however, make the ones who put it there pay dearly.

"Have the bad men found us?" David asked as he climbed out of bed and began to dress.

"Aye, I fear they have," Berawald replied as he shoved a few of David's things into his small bag. "I had thought that I had hidden the other bo—men—weel, but something has brought their companions here."

"Mayhap they came looking for the other men."

"Verra likely. Ready, lad? We have to move quickly and quietly."

"I can be quick and verra quiet."

Berawald suspected he could be and that thought made him sad. As he led David out of the small bedchamber he had given him, he pretended not to see the boy wave farewell to the ghost. At some time David would have to learn the truth about him and the MacNachtons. Berawald could only pray that the boy took the news as well as his sister had.

"I think we need to move faster," whispered David. "I can hear the men in the passage coming this way."

Sharp hearing, Berawald mused. Yet another MacNachton trait. "They willnae find us, lad. Trust me."

"Aye, I do." The moment David saw Evanna he ran up to her. "They have found us again, Evie."

"I ken it. Be brave, lad," Evanna said, quickly hugging her brother and kissing his cheek. "Berawald has a way for us to get out of here unseen. They willnae get us."

"Ye and the lad go first," Berawald said, keeping an eye on the entrance to the tiny room they now stood in. "I will take up the rear. There are no turnoffs so ye dinnae need to fear ye will take a wrong turn or get lost if I fall behind and cannae tell ye where to go. Just move quietly and carefully. There are loose stones upon the path that could trip ye and a few low spots."

Taking David by the hand, Evanna moved to the far end of the little room where the bolt-hole was cleverly hidden by the angle of the walls and Berawald's supplies. "Dinnae fall too far behind," she said, and then slipped into the passage that would lead them away from their enemies.

Berawald waited until he was certain the pair were well inside his escape route. He then began to quietly back toward it himself. He was just inching into the opening when he heard the men enter his great hall. Holding himself as still as the stones surrounding him, he fixed all of his attention on their voices and hoped he would hear something useful before he had to flee. Any hint of what the men sought, planned, or knew could prove helpful.

"Curse it!" bellowed one man. "They arenae here!"

"But where could they go? This is a cursed cave," growled another man. "They didnae come by us as we came in."

"They cannae do that, can they, Duncan?" asked yet another man, unease creeping into his slightly boyish voice. "They cannae make themselves like the mist or the fog, can they?"

"Dinnae be any greater fool than ye already are, Will," said the first man who had spoken, one Berawald assumed was Duncan. "There has to be another way out of here. Start looking."

"But where could they go?" asked Will, repeating the question the second man had asked. "He is one of them. Ye saw what he did to our men. Jesu, Duncan, he ripped out poor Robbie's throat. He must be one of the stronger demons, one of them MacNachtons."

"Of course he is, lackwit. I am nay surprised the women wouldnae be as strong as the men. Women are weak by nature. And the wee lad isnae grown yet. I mean to see that he ne'er reaches his manhood. And that lass has to pay for cut-

ting me. I dinnae mean to let the bitch die easy once I get my
hands on her."

It took all of Berawald's willpower to stop himself from
rushing out there to confront Duncan. That man was definitely the leader and the greatest threat, but most of Berawald's rage was because of what the man had threatened to
do to Evanna. When a man said he would not let a woman
die easy, there was only one thing he could mean. Duncan
meant to debase Evanna, to force himself on her, and for that
thought alone he would die.

"Are ye sure she is even still alive? Ye caught her good
with your sword, nearly gutted her."

"Nay good enough, for she kept running with the lad, didnae she? Weel, soon she will have too many wounds to heal
from, just like her cursed mother had."

"There may be others of their ilk on this land."

"Fine, then we will be able to cull the herd. Find that cursed
bolt-hole! Now!" he yelled at the men Berawald could hear
moving around his home.

Berawald slipped farther into the passage and then hurried after Evanna and David. As best he could judge from all
the sounds and voices he had heard, there were at least twelve
men tearing apart his home. There would be others standing
guard outside, perhaps even a few searching the area all around
for signs of a bolt-hole. Far too many men for him to deal
with. The wisest thing he could do now was to get Evanna
and David to Cambrun. Then his kinsmen could help him rid
their lands of this scum.

"The ghostie is with us," whispered David.

Struggling to move as swiftly and silently as she could,
Evanna glanced behind her. The ghostly woman stayed close
behind David. The spirit was obviously trying to protect this
child as she had not been able to protect her own. Touched
by that though she was, Evanna would rather have seen a

broad-shouldered Berawald with his sword and all those knives she had seen him tuck into his clothes.

"Aye, I see her. She frets o'er ye, I think," she said.

"I wish Berawald would hurry."

"So do I, loving. So do I. If only because the only place he told me to go after getting out of here is Cambrun, his clan's keep. I have ne'er been there and dinnae ken them at all."

"They would help Berawald if he was in trouble."

"Which is exactly why I will do just as he told me to." That and the fact that David was still in danger, but she would not add to her brother's fear by saying so. "Now, we had best hush."

"But we are talking verra softly."

"E'en a whisper can carry a long way in places like these."

Evanna kept leading David along, thanking God that they could both see so well in the dark and wondering just how long this passage was. At times it narrowed and at other places she had to bend down to clear the low ceiling. She suspected Berawald nearly had to crawl through such places and that might be why he had not yet reached them. Such things would also slow down any enemy who followed them into the passage. They were also slowly climbing upward, which meant that they would come out somewhere above Berawald's cave. She could only hope there were none of her enemies waiting up there for them.

"The lady says someone is coming," whispered David.

Even as she turned, drawing her knife from the sheath she had strapped to her arm, she asked, "Ye can hear her?"

"Aye. I decided to let her talk to me and so she does. She whispers in my head. She says Berawald comes."

"Thank God. I had begun to fear he had decided to face those men on his own."

A moment later Berawald appeared and Evanna sighed with relief as all the tight fear inside her eased. It was foolish, for they were still in a lot of danger, but seeing Berawald alive and unharmed gave her the strength to keep the fear of their enemy at bay. She idly wondered if David noticed how Berawald eased his body past the ghost, but the boy just smiled at him.

"There are near to a dozen men searching for our wee bolt-hole," Berawald said, keeping his voice soft. "With so many looking they may weel find it soon. We must keep moving."

She nodded and started moving along the passage again. Compared to how silently Berawald moved, Evanna began to think she sounded like a herd of oxen stomping over the rocky floor of the tunnel. He did not urge her to be any quieter, however, so she decided she must not be doing as poorly as she had feared.

"Do ye think there are more outside the cave?" she asked.

"There is a verra good chance there are, but we will worry about that if and when we meet up with them," Berawald replied.

"The sun hasnae set yet."

"I ken it, but it is close to the time it does so. If no one is outside when we reach the end of this passage, we will judge how bright the sun is before we step outside. We may have to hide in here for a wee while. After all, we gain naught by going out into it too soon and making ourselves too weak to run or fight."

"True enough. Is it Duncan?"

"Aye. Ye didnae tell me ye had given him a good wounding. He was complaining about that."

Evanna grimaced. She could tell by the hard anger shading Berawald's voice that Duncan had been bellowing out his usual threats. Trying to fulfill them had been his downfall the last time he had grabbed her. It had allowed her to stab him. Unfortunately, after being in the sun for so long that day, she had been too weak to take swift advantage of that and it had given him the chance to cut her with his sword.

"He nearly caught me that time," she said, "but he was alone so I still had a chance to save David. I took it."

Berawald could all too easily picture what had happened and it made him ache to kill Duncan. He admired Evanna's courage and her skill with a blade, but he did not want her to have to depend on either for her safety. Not anymore. Whatever else happened, he would make sure that Duncan did not survive this time.

When they finally reached the end of the passage, Berawald cursed. Even with all he had placed in front of the opening to hide it, the light seeping in told him that the sun had at least an hour before it had set enough for them to go outside. He could tolerate that last half hour of sunset without becoming too weak to fight, but he would become almost useless if he spent a full hour in it. He had been hoping that they would at least discover some thick, dark clouds had swept in to cover the sun.

He moved as close to the opening as he dared and listened carefully. Assured that no one waited outside their bolt-hole yet, he waved Evanna and David back into the deep shadows. For a moment he considered sending Evanna and David ahead, for they could endure the late afternoon light, but he quickly cast that idea aside. The sun might not weaken them as it did him, but it would make them both all too visible to their enemies. He sat down, his back to the wall, and silently signaled for them to do the same.

"How long do we wait?" Evanna asked as she sat down next to do him.

"I can venture out in a half hour or so, when the sun is but peeking o'er the horizon," Berawald replied, silently cursing the weakness that held him back and put them all in danger.

"Then we will wait." She took his hand in hers and closed her eyes, slowly caressing David's soft curls when he settled down beside her and put his head in her lap. "I dinnae understand why they come now or came last night when they are so certain that we avoid the day because we are demons."

"Either they dinnae ken how the sun affects us, that it actually could be used as a weapon against us, or they are fools."

"'Tis probably a wee bit of both."

"Aye, and when Outsiders fight Outsiders, attacking in the dead of night can give the attacker a big advantage. These men may nay be able to change their ways."

"What will happen if they follow us to Cambrun?"

"My kinsmen will kill them."

Evanna winced but did not protest. It would be a bloodbath if all of his kinsmen fought as Berawald did, yet she could feel no true remorse for what she might be leading Duncan and his men into. They had killed her parents and wanted to kill her and David. The only way to stop them was to kill them. She just hoped she did not have to watch.

Nine

"I think they have found the passage," David whispered into Berawald's ear.

Berawald looked at David but did not ask the boy how he knew that. He could see the ghost pointing at the doorway out of the passage, silently ordering him to move. It took only one glance toward the opening to know the sun had not yet fully set, but he had no choice. He had to get David and Evanna away from here as soon as possible. He shook Evanna awake.

"We go now," he said as he helped her to her feet.

"'Tis too early. The sun has nay set," she protested as she tried to shake free of the weariness that gripped her so tightly. "Ye cannae go out there."

"I can and I must. 'Tis close to the time that it would be safest for me and we arenae so verra far from Cambrun."

"They have found your bolt-hole."

"Aye, and I willnae risk ye and David by trying to stand and fight or buy myself a wee bit more time ere I have to leave here. We leave now."

Evanna did not bother to argue with him. If it was just herself at risk, she would urge him to wait until the sun set or their enemies were too close; she would even fight as his side. There was David to think of, however. He could not fight and his life was as much at risk as hers and Berawald's.

She stood holding David's hand as Berawald carefully but swiftly removed the brush and rocks from the opening and then looked around for any sign of their enemy. She winced as they all stepped outside and her fear for Berawald's safety returned in full force. Although she and David could bear standing in the sun when it was so low in the sky, she knew that every minute Berawald stood in it his strength ebbed. There was not even a cloud in the sky to help shelter him. She all too clearly recalled how it felt to have the strength slowly leave your body, and shuddered.

They began to make their way down the small hillside. Evanna helped David over the uneven ground and kept looking toward the trees. At least there Berawald would be able to find some shelter from the sun, and she was determined to get there as quickly as possible. At this time of day any shadow, any piece of shade would be enough to give Berawald some protection and help him hold on to enough strength to fight if he had to.

By the time they reached the shelter of the trees, Evanna was not sure she had the strength to go on, and this had nothing to do with the rapidly waning light of the sun. She was tired, tired to the bone. As she leaned against a big tree, she watched as Berawald stared up at the opening of his bolthole. She could barely see the place where it should be but knew that his eyesight was much sharper than hers.

All her differences, the ones she had struggled to hide all her life and had caused the death of both of her parents, were pale shadows of the ones he had. Now, as they tried to outrun an enemy intent on killing them, she could see how those differences could easily be considered a gift. Right now those differences could very well be all that kept them alive.

"There they are," muttered Berawald, his hand tightening on the hilt of his sword. "Bastards."

"Do ye think they will ken which direction we are going

in?" she asked as she straightened up and struggled to gather what few scraps of strength and willpower she had left.

"I think it would be wise to assume that they do or can easily guess," he replied. "Come, I ken ye are tired, but 'tis just a wee bit farther."

"I am nay so tired that I will do anything to let those men catch me, nay e'en a wee stumble."

Berawald nearly smiled at her words, for she was swaying on her feet, but he knew she meant what she said. "Good. If we move fast we can be safe inside the walls of Cambrun before they even discover which path we took."

Evanna truly doubted that but did not disagree. She could see that the hearty words had given David some much needed strength and courage. Still fighting to find enough of her own to keep on moving and fulfill her boast, Evanna started off in the direction Berawald pointed her in. She ignored the icy chills on the back of her neck that told her Duncan Beaton was stalking her. She suspected she would feel that chill even if Duncan were skipping through the vineyards in France and just happened to glance toward Scotland. Until the man was dead, she doubted she would ever feel truly safe.

"There is Cambrun," Berawald said nearly an hour later.

Evanna stumbled to a halt and stared at the huge, dark castle. It appeared as if it had risen straight out of the solid rock that seemed to cover all the ground around it. She had not *seen* many castles in her time, but she had the suspicion that Cambrun had to be one of the most threatening ones in all of Scotland, perhaps in several other kingdoms as well. This was to be her haven? Safety and kindness were not the first things that leapt readily to her mind at the sight of that dark, foreboding pile of stone.

"There is an awful lot of open ground to cover ere we reach the gates," was all she could think to say.

"Aye, but my kinsmen have sharp eyes and can move verra fast."

"So cry out verra loudly if ye think we are about to lose this race?"

"A verra sound plan. Ready?"

"As ready as I can be. I am a wee bit tired."

Berawald smiled at her and brushed a kiss over her forehead. "As am I. As is poor David. I will carry him from here on," he said even as he picked David up into his arms.

Evanna almost said something in protest of that plan, but one look at David made her bite back her words. The moment Berawald settled the boy in his grasp David rested his head against his broad shoulder and closed his eyes. He was exhausted and even though Berawald would be hindered some by carrying him, it was better than being slowed down even more by dragging a completely exhausted little boy along by the hand. She felt a little guilty for not noticing how weary the child had become, but her own blind determination to keep on going no matter how tired she was had held all of her attention.

They had just reached the edge of the cleared area around the keep when a cry rose from behind them. Evanna turned to look behind her in horror as men began to rush at her and Berawald through the trees. She recognized the brutish figure of Duncan Beaton and reached for David. To her surprise Berawald shoved the child into her arms and pushed her in the direction of Cambrun.

"Berawald, we must run," she said.

"Ye run and get the boy to safety," he said, arming himself with a sword in one hand and a knife in the other.

"But e'en with all your strength and speed ye cannae beat so many men all on your own."

"I willnae have to. I only need to hold them back until ye and the boy can get to safety. My kinsmen have already seen us and will soon join me."

"But—"

"Trust me, Evanna. I will nay be alone for long. Now—run."

She gave him a fast, hard kiss and then began to run. It astonished her that she could find the strength to do so, but suspected it was the feel of her little brother's trembling body in her arms that gave her that strength. He was terrified and this time he was too exhausted to try and run and hide without her assistance.

The gates to Cambrun were close enough for her to see the heavy carvings on their iron-banded surface when she felt as if she could not run another step. Her whole body shook from the effort it took to keep on moving and she knew that at any moment her legs would simply collapse beneath her. When the gates to the keep opened and a horde of dark men rushed out, her mind told her to run in another direction, but her body simply did not have the strength to obey. She had the chilling feeling that she had just run from one death right into the arms of another.

She tensed and held David more tightly when a tall, impossibly handsome man with golden eyes stopped right in front of her. Evanna had the wild thought that there did not appear to be such a thing as an ugly MacNachton. When he reached for David, she staggered back a step and drew her knife even though she knew she did not have the strength to stop him from doing whatever he wished to.

"Be at ease, lass," he said in a voice that was as golden and smooth as honey. "I mean ye no harm. I am Jankyn, Berawald's cousin. He has told ye about me?"

Relief swept through her and she almost fell to her knees. "Aye. Berawald needs help."

"Oh, he is getting quite a lot of it at the moment."

She shuffled around just enough so that she could look back to where she had left Berawald. One look was enough. Duncan and his men would never escape alive. All she cared about at the moment was that Berawald still stood, alive and apparently unharmed. She turned back to Jankyn.

"That is good, for I really am too tired to go back and

help him," she said, and knew she was tired when the man's beautiful smile did nothing at all to her.

"Let me take the lad," Jankyn said.

"Thank ye. He almost made it here on his own."

The way the man took David into his arms and gently brushed a lock of hair from the boy's brow made the last of Evanna's doubts about him disappear. She was about to thank him for his help when he glanced behind her and began to reach for her. Even as his hand touched her arm a fiery pain ripped across her back. She clutched at his arm, hearing a chilling scream from behind her as she fought to stay on her feet. A little wildly she decided that Jankyn MacNachton had an admirable skill with curses as she heard him spitting out a whole river of them.

"Curse it, lass, I should have seen him coming up behind ye," he said. "How bad is it?" he asked the man who was standing behind her.

"'Tisnae pretty. He swiped that cursed sword clear across her back. If I hadnae been already trying to pull him back he would have cut her in two."

The words being said in the deep raspy voice did not really sink into Evanna's mind. She heard a movement behind her that told her whoever the man was, he was about to move away from her back. If the wound was bad, Berawald would be able to see it from where he was and she could not allow that, not when he was in the midst of a battle.

"Nay, dinnae move," she said. "Dinnae move away from my back."

"I was going to lift ye up so we can take ye inside and see to that wound."

"Dinnae do that, either. Is Berawald still fighting?"

"Aye," replied Jankyn. "He is facing some hulking brute he is cursing and calling Duncan. He is the one that tried to cut ye in half from the front, is he?"

Jankyn, she decided, was one of those men women probably adored even while they wanted to slap him. "Aye. Ye cannae let Berawald ken that I am wounded, nay while he still fights someone."

"Berawald could defeat that fat fool with both hands tied behind his back."

"Nay if he is distracted because he sees that something has happened to me. He had to walk in the sun for longer than he liked today. We had to leave the safety of his bolt-hole ere it had fully set and it took us a while to make it to the shelter of the trees. He may nay be at his full strength. E'en if he was, it wouldnae be a good idea to let him see that I am wounded until all of our enemies are dead or disarmed."

"Oh, there willnae be any disarming," Jankyn said in a voice that sent chills down her spine and briefly interrupted the searing pain she was fighting against.

"Then help me to walk into the keep and, whoe'er that is behind me, ye walk so that none can see what has happened to my back."

"'Tis Raibert," came the raspy voice, "and we had best get moving then or ye willnae be able to get inside ere one of us has to carry ye."

Jankyn moved to her side and wrapped his arm around her waist. The strength he revealed as he nearly carried her to the door that way astonished Evanna. All the while they walked along as if she was not leaving a trail of blood along the ground, she heard him murmuring soft, comforting words to David. Her brother had obviously seen that she had been hurt and Jankyn appeared to be doing an excellent job of calming him down.

The moment they stepped inside the keep and Evanna heard the heavy doors shut behind her, she felt the last shred of her strength give out and she began to collapse. Strong arms caught her up against a huge chest. She glanced up and through a fog of pain saw yet another dark, handsome man.

A little wildly she thought it might be best for the women of the world if the MacNachton men continued to stay hidden behind the walls of Cambrun.

"I need to be cleaned up ere Berawald comes looking for me," she told him as he carried her up a flight of stairs.

"Ye worry too much o'er the mon."

"Nay, ye see he will blame himself," she whispered, and finally gave in to the pain and weakness that swamped her.

Jankyn stared down at the woman in Raibert's arms and shook his head. "She kens our Berawald verra weel. He will blame himself. Let us get some women up here and a healer and then go and make sure that fool hasnae gotten himself killed."

By the time Jankyn and Raibert reached the battle it was over. The bodies of the hunters were already being taken away to be hidden or destroyed, whichever was easier. Jankyn frowned as he saw a rather pale Berawald slumped against a tree.

"Have ye gone and injured yourself?" he asked as he walked up and crouched down in front of his cousin.

"A wee bit," said Berawald. "It wasnae a good time for me to fight. Nay enough sleep and too much sun. But I won and I will heal." He winced as Raibert knelt by his side to look at the wound there.

"He still bleeds," said Raibert and, without another word, bent his neck toward Berawald.

"Are ye certain, Raibert?" Berawald asked, deeply touched by the gesture.

"Aye, ye are going to need your strength."

It was not until Berawald had taken all he needed from Raibert and was sitting back letting the magic of MacNachton blood do its work that the words his friend had said finally sank into his mind. "What did ye mean when ye said I will need my strength?" He saw the serious expression on the men's faces and tensed. "Evanna?"

Jankyn caught him and held him still when he jumped up

and would have raced to find Evanna. "Where is she? What has happened to her? And where is David?" He suddenly realized that it was strange that neither of them had come looking for him now that the battle was over.

"The boy is clean and fast asleep in a soft bed," Jankyn said.

"And Evanna?"

"She was wounded."

Berawald cursed. "How? She should have been far away from the battle."

"She was. She was just a few feet from our gates when one of those bastards somehow managed to escape the melee, get up behind her, and slash her with a sword." Jankyn watched all the color fade from Berawald's face. "Dinnae swoon on me like some frail lady; she isnae dead. Badly wounded, aye, but nay dead. She made us walk her into the keep and be sure ye didnae see that she was hurt, for she feared it would distract ye and mayhap put ye in danger as ye were in the midst of a battle."

Berawald could still hear the venom that had poured from Duncan Beaton's mouth as they had fought. Even as his men had died screaming all around him, Duncan's eyes had continued to gleam with hatred and fury. Berawald knew that, even a little weakened from the sun, he could have disposed of the man in a few quick moves but he had wanted to make him sweat. He had gained a few bloody wounds from the battle, but in the end he had been able to see that insane gleam turn to fear and then he had finished it, doing to the man all he had so feared. He had fed from him. Not enough to heal his wounds, for he had found the taste of the man foul, but enough to have Duncan screaming in terror before he snapped his neck. The price of that grim enjoyment now seemed too high. While he had played his game with Duncan, Evanna had been nearly killed.

"He is doing just what she said he would," murmured Raibert.

Scowling at his friend, Berawald demanded, "What are ye talking about?"

"She said ye would blame yourself when ye found out she was hurt," said Jankyn, easing his hold on Berawald but keeping one hand on his arm. "If it is anyone's fault it is mine. I wasnae watching for an attack so close to the verra doors of the keep and I didnae react fast enough when I saw the mon swing his sword."

"Nay, I—"

"Ye were in the midst of a battle and had sent her to our doors where she should have been safe. She wasnae. Now, we can all stand here and decide who is most at fault or accept that it was just one of those things ye can ne'er plan for and get ye inside and cleaned up."

"I have to see Evanna."

"Ye will as soon as the women are done doing whate'er it is they do. It would also be best if ye were looking less like ye were cut to ribbons when ye do."

Berawald knew it would be a waste of time to continue to argue with Jankyn, so he followed his cousin into the keep. He bathed and put on clean clothes, even had something to drink, before he made his way to the bedchamber where Jankyn had said they had put Evanna. Afraid of what he would find, he entered the room slowly.

Evanna was lying in a huge bed, pale and asleep. He nodded at Efrica and moved to the side of the bed to brush his hand over Evanna's forehead. She felt cold, and after listening closely, he realized her heart was not beating with the strength it usually did.

"She is verra weak," he said.

Efrica moved to his side and handed him a goblet half-filled with wine. "Ye ken what she needs, Berawald. We felt ye wouldnae want another mon to give it to her, nay after we saw the mark ye left on her neck."

"She isnae going to like this."

"If ye dinnae do it, someone else will, for I fear she will die without it. And none of us will allow that. She is of MacNachton blood, Berawald. Her and the lad. I have nary a doubt about that."

"So this should work," he said even as he bit into his wrist and added his blood to the wine.

"Like a charm."

"She still isnae going to like this."

"I am sure ye can make her see the need of it."

Berawald just snorted with a mixture of amusement and resignation as he lifted Evanna up enough so that she would not choke on the wine as he poured it down her throat.

Ten

Evanna slowly opened her eyes. She frowned, for she had expected to awaken to pain as she had the last time she had been wounded, but there was none. Cautiously, she reached around to touch her back and felt only the remnants of a scar. Had she slept through the healing?

"So ye are finally awake?"

The way that deep, smooth voice made her feel told her exactly who was there and she turned her head to look at Berawald. He sat sprawled in a chair pulled up to the side of the bed and had his arms crossed over his chest. The fact that the very sight of him looking handsome and unharmed had her wanting to yank him into the bed with her, made Evanna realize that she did not even feel weak. She just felt as if she had had a very good night's rest.

"How long have I been asleep this time?" she asked.

"Just one night." Berawald waited to see if she would guess what had happened to make her recover so swiftly.

"One night? How can that be? There is naught but a rough scar on my back and I was cut verra badly."

"Ye were cut more than verra badly. Yet again someone

tried to cut ye in half. Ye werenae only because Raibert had already started to pull your attacker away."

"Then how am I so weel healed? I have ne'er healed that quickly and I dinnae e'en feel as weak as I did from my last wound." She suddenly noticed that there was a look of unease in his eyes. "What was done to me to make me heal as quickly as ye do?"

He sighed and leaned forward to take her hand in his. "I gave ye some of my blood."

"Ye made me bite ye?"

"Nay, I put some in a tankard, mixed with wine, and poured it down your throat. Efrica, Jankyn's wife, said that ye would die without it. Ye were cold as death, Evanna, and your heart was fluttering like some wounded bird. Efrica also said that, if I didnae do it, someone else would and she felt ye would prefer it to be me."

She could not argue with that. "And just a wee drink of your blood in wine was enough to make me feel as if I had ne'er e'en been wounded?"

"It appears so. Can ye sit up on your own?"

Checking to be sure she wore clothes and deciding the white linen night rail she had on was decent enough, Evanna braced herself for any pain and sat up. There was not a twinge aside from a slight sense of stretching skin on her back. Shocked, she slumped back against the pillows. Then she suddenly wondered what else drinking some of his blood might have done to her. "It only healed me, right?"

"Ah, I see what has ye frowning now. Aye, it only healed ye. Ye willnae grow very long, sharp teeth like I have, although"— he idly rubbed his shoulder and grinned when she blushed— "I think your teeth are sharp enough already." The way she scowled at him almost made him laugh, and he knew some of that was from sheer relief that she had recovered so well. "Do ye want something to drink?"

"Just a wee bit of cider, aye. Thank ye."

As he fetched her some cider, Evanna considered the miracle of her rapidly returned good health. She knew without even testing it that she could get up as if it were any other day and not suffer for it. It was no wonder the MacNachtons lived for a very long time if their blood was so powerful.

"I cannae believe it," she said as she accepted a tankard of cider and had a long drink. "'Tis as if there is magic in your blood."

"Your blood, too," Berawald said as he sprawled on the bed beside her.

"Weel, we cannae be sure of that yet."

"Aye, I think we can. Efrica said it was so and she has a way of kenning such things. Also, the way just a wee bit of my blood caused ye to heal almost before our eyes was more proof. An Outsider can be helped in the same way, but it ne'er works as swiftly as it did with ye. Jankyn will still search for the true connection in all of his ledgers and scrolls, but none here doubt that ye and David are Lost Ones who have returned to the fold, so to speak."

For a moment she was overwhelmed with the knowledge that she and David were not alone, but then hard, cold reality set in. She could not stay here when Berawald lived so close at hand. Nor could she live with him just because he felt some passion for her and a sense of responsibility. Now that Duncan was dead it was probably time to cut Berawald loose from the chains of responsibility she had wrapped him in. She did not need to go far away, just off on her own enough so that she did not have to see him every day and know how much she had lost. Or, if she was very lucky, close enough so that he could come and woo her if he felt he wanted to.

"Then I gather it is time for David and me to let ye have your freedom back. We can find a wee cottage near Cambrun. I think it would be good for David to grow up near ones who understand and accept him, dinnae ye? There may be some work I can do to support us as weel. Perhaps ye will allow David to come and visit ye from time to time as he has grown verra fond of ye and—" She shut up when he clapped a hand over her mouth.

Berawald stared at her. When she had first begun to speak of leaving he had felt as if his heart had simply stopped beating. Then he began to listen to her and realized several things. She was babbling and she was not looking him right in the eye. Hope started his heart beating again as he began to think that she was just doing as she thought she ought to. That was followed by annoyance over what he saw as her idiocy. Could the woman not even guess at his feelings for her?

"Do ye truly wish to go away and live on your own with David?" he asked but did not remove his hand, for he wanted a simple yea or nay answer and she could do that by nodding or shaking her head.

Looking into his eyes, Evanna thought she saw something there, something far more than a sense of responsibility or simple manly desire for a woman in his bed. Bracing herself for the possibility of pain, she decided to take a chance that she was right, that he did feel more for her. Slowly she shook her head. One should have the courage to grab for what one truly wanted.

"Good, then ye and David can stay with me," he said as he removed his hand from her mouth.

Evanna rolled over and pressed him down onto the bed, rather pleased with her strength. It was as if none of the last few weeks of pain, fear, and exhaustion had ever happened. She stared into his eyes and caught that glint of uncertainty she had come to know so well. Berawald was no more sure of himself than she was of herself. Someone had to take a firm stand to untie the knots they were so busily tying. She was in the mood to be the one. By the time he left this bedchamber he would either be pledged to her or he would be finding her a cottage where she and David could live in peace and she could try her best to mend her crushed heart.

"Berawald, tell me why ye want me and David to come and live with ye."

"I want ye to be my family," he said quietly, and began to stroke her back, unable to keep himself from touching her.

"That is verra nice, but there is a lot more to being a family than the sharing of a home."

"There is this," he whispered, and kissed her, trying to tell her with his kiss all he could not seem to put into words.

"Also verra nice," Evanna said, not surprised to hear the huskiness in her voice, for that kiss had curled her toes and left her fighting the urge to stop talking and start tearing his clothes off.

Berawald sighed. "Evanna, I am nay verra skilled with women. I havenae had that many in my life and none that I have wanted to come and live with me."

"And I am heartily flattered by that, but it still doesnae tell me why ye want me to share your home. Is it only for a wee while until ye decide ye cannae abide the company anymore? Is it because David and I give ye peace from all the ghosts? It certainly cannae be because I can cook, as ye dinnae need the food I make. So why, Berawald? If I am to give ye my life, put myself and my brother in your care, I need to ken why."

"Because I need ye. Because I cannae bear the thought of nay seeing ye when I wake or holding ye as I sleep. Because I want to teach David so many things and listen to ye laugh and hear your voice and hold ye when ye feel sad. Because I love ye."

Although her eyes stung with tears, Evanna forced them back, for she knew Berawald would not understand that she could cry simply because she was full to bursting with sheer joy. "That wasnae so verra hard to say, was it? I bet it didnae hurt a bit."

"Nay, but it might start to if I dinnae hear something similar from your lips."

"Fool." She kissed him. "I think I have loved ye from the moment I woke up and saw ye. That was why I stayed nay matter what ye did or what ye told me. I am three and twenty and have ne'er had a mon. Did ye think a woman like that would bed down with a mon just because he is beautiful? Of course I love ye."

She was not surprised to feel him tremble faintly as he held her tightly in his arms. She was trembling as well. Such strong emotion, the baring of one's heart, should have a profound effect on a person.

"How healed are ye?" he asked in a thick voice.

"I feel as if none of the last few weeks have ever happened. I am rested and strong and there isnae a twinge of pain in my entire body."

"Good."

Evanna was not sure who started taking whose clothes off first, but they were soon strewn all over the room. The loving was fierce and fast and Evanna reveled in it. When Berawald ceased his loving on her body and thrust inside her, she nearly screamed out his name. She did it again when her release swarmed over her and she felt that fleeting pain of his bite that only sent her higher. The bellow in her ear told her that he was flying right alongside her.

Berawald stayed deep inside her until he softened so much he slipped out. Still holding her in his arms, he rolled onto his back. He felt the unmanly urge to weep with the sheer joy he felt. Never would he have believed it if anyone had told him that he would find a mate like Evanna. She was passionate, loving, and beautiful. He suddenly grinned. And she could bite almost as well as he did.

"I am sorry for this," he murmured as he ran his fingers over the long scar on her back.

She lifted her head from his chest enough to frown at him. "Ye have nothing to be sorry for. Ye werenae the only MacNachton there and yet the fool still managed to get to me. Everything we did once we saw Duncan and his men coming was right. Things just go wrong sometimes."

"That is what Jankyn said."

"Weel, he is right. Ye must cease to blame yourself for all

that goes wrong, Berawald. Sometimes ye can plan and plot each move until your head aches and something still just goes wrong. Everything that has happened to us since we met has brought us here, together, ready to make a future. Surely, it couldnae have been all wrong."

"The fact that such danger brought ye into my arms is something I shall never regret. There is one thing I have to tell ye now," he said, and lightly stroked the mark on her neck.

"Another difference?"

"Mayhap. This bite I gave ye the first time we made love?"

Evanna touched his fingers where they lay across the faint mark. "'Tis odd that it hasnae healed as the others ye gave me did, but I think that may be because I was still a wee bit weak after being wounded and chased halfway across the country."

"Nay, that isnae why the mark stays. 'Tis what we call the mating mark." He nodded when her eyes widened. "I could-nae believe I bit ye the first time. We all have better control than that and I had just fed enough to last me for a verra long time. But there is one time when that control can slip and 'tis when we find our mate. Everything within us pushes us to mark our mates."

"So ye kenned from the first that I was your mate?"

"Obviously."

"Why didnae ye tell me?"

"I didnae want ye to come to me because ye felt gratitude or even some obligation or mayhap even just the need for somewhere to live. I wanted ye to come to me because your heart demanded it."

"Then we are where we are supposed to be, my brave dark hero." She grinned when he blushed. "So easily undone by flattery."

"I am nay a hero, Evanna. I stepped wrong so many times and both ye and David nearly lost your lives whilst I was supposed to be keeping ye safe."

Evanna shook her head and then kissed him. "The word

to note in that humble speech is *nearly*. We are both alive and I willnae hear ye demean your part in accomplishing that again. So, do ye mean to marry me, then?"

"Aye, as soon as we can drag a priest here."

"Nay too soon as I mean to have a bonnie dress ere I stand before a priest."

"Ye would look verra pretty in sackcloth."

She felt herself blush and lightly swatted his arm. "Ye are getting verra good with pretty words, sir."

"Good. Ye deserve them. I am about to make ye share my life in the shadows, more shadows than ye and David have ever lived in."

"I would share anything with ye, Berawald, and be happy. I can still see the sun if I have a mind to. Although I will grieve a wee bit that ye arenae by my side when I do."

"Dinnae grieve, my Evanna. I dinnae need the sun. I hold all the sunshine I need right here in my arms."

Evanna felt tears clog her throat and knew she had two choices. She could weep like a bairn over those beautiful words or she could thank him for the sentiment by making love to him until his eyes crossed. Knowing full well what her dark hero would prefer, she kissed him.

Bride of
the Beast

Adrienne Basso

One

The swirl of wind was steady, yet not too strong. The light mist of rain that had been falling for the past week had finally stopped, but even at this early hour of the morning the clouds hung dark, low, and heavy. Thirteen-year-old Bethan of Lampeter stood on the highest rampart on the south edge of the timber castle, her mother at her side, her eyes pinned to the scene below.

The view down to the fortified bailey was unobstructed and Bethan watched with growing puzzlement as her stepfather, Sir Agnarr de Bellemare, walked among the hundreds of prisoners, barking out orders and separating them into groupings.

"Whatever is he doing?" Bethan questioned, leaning forward to get a closer look.

"I suppose he is arranging them into new squads of workers," her mother speculated. She pulled the windblown veil away from her face and tucked a lock of honey-colored hair beneath it. "He told me yesterday the foundation of the new castle has finally been completed, so the stones must be moved in order to begin construction on the lower half."

"All he thinks about is building his wretched castle," Bethan grumbled. She looked beyond the wall that surrounded the village and the dwellings protected within those walls to the acres of cleared land stretching between the forest and the manor. "A portion of those men should be working the soil. We are already weeks behind. The fields need to be plowed and planted now or else we shall all go hungry this winter."

"There are some furrows awaiting seed," her mother replied, pointing to a small section where mounds of dirt sported neatly dug rows.

"'Tis a pittance," Bethan countered. "I see but one oxen straining mightily to pull a single plow and less than a dozen villeins toiling behind. If this does not change soon, we shall once again be racing against time and weather to harvest whatever meager crops reach maturity."

"Goodness, Bethan, such gloomy thoughts. When I was a girl of your age I thought only of my needlework, my prayers, and my future husband."

"I have not that luxury, Mother," Bethan replied with honesty. "Nor would I wish for it. I want only to see our people safe and prosperous."

"As do I," her mother whispered, a tremble of emotion in her words.

Guilt instantly washed over Bethan and she silently cursed her wicked tongue. She had not meant her remarks as a criticism. She knew there were many within the walls of Lampeter who blamed her mother for inflicting de Bellemare and his iron-fisted rule upon them all. Life, while never easy in this harsh, rugged climate and wild countryside of Wales, had been good for nearly everyone when Bethan's father had been alive.

To the surprise of many, within days of her husband's death Lady Caryn had married Sir Agnarr de Bellemare, a man who spoke the Norman French of England's noble class, yet fought with the ferocity of his Viking given name. For the past three years, discord, discontent, and fear were the predominate emotions among those who lived within these walls.

The soldiers, tradesmen, even some of the peasants thought Lady Caryn a weak female, frail in figure, spirit, and mind. In their eyes she did little to stop her husband from his often abusive behavior toward them.

But others knew the truth, including Bethan. Lady Caryn had no choice in the matter. If she had not accepted de Belle-mare he would have laid siege to the castle and taken it by force. Many would have died; all would have suffered horribly.

"Come, Mother. Let us walk out to the fields and see what crops are being sowed today. The fresh air will do you good."

Taking hold of her mother's arm, Bethan led her slowly down the winding staircase. Lady Caryn's thin frame seemed more frail and fragile this morning, the burden of her swollen belly almost too much for her to carry. The constant sickness she had experienced since first quickening with child had weakened her previously strong constitution. Each day she seemed to wilt more and more.

Bethan worried about her mother, resenting this unborn child for myriad reasons. The very last thing she wanted was a blood tie to a whelp of de Bellemare. Still, Bethan was astute enough to realize there were times when it was only the promise of the child her mother carried within her body that kept them safe from the worst of her stepfather's wrath. The knight had made no secret of his desire to have a son and heir, regardless of the toll it took upon his wife's health.

When Lady Caryn had miscarried two other infants, de Bellemare's anger had been felt throughout the castle, but he saved the majority of his displeasure for his wife. Though she never spoke of it, Bethan knew her mother feared what would happen if she could not successfully deliver the son her husband demanded.

As they strode through the large wooden front doors of the keep, Bethan saw her stepfather heading in their direction, the captain of the garrison at his side. She quickly steered her mother out of his line of view, hoping to escape an encounter.

Unfortunately, de Bellemare stopped before entering the keep. Bethan braced herself for his comments, but he apparently did not take notice of them, for he turned his back and spoke directly to the captain.

"Kill them," he commanded in a deep, emotionless tone. "Start with the group on the left and finish with those I have placed in the center. I want them all dead and buried by tonight."

"But my lord, we need these men to move the stones," the captain protested.

"I culled out the larger men for that job. They will carry the stones and begin building. The rest can be eliminated."

The captain frowned. "Moving the stones is an enormous task. All these men are needed."

"If you need more workers, then press more of the villeins into service."

The captain frowned. "We have already recruited every able-bodied man on the estate. There are none left who are strong enough to do the work. Grumblings have started among the people because there are no fit men to till the fields and plant the spring crops."

"I do not give a damn about the peasants' complaints!" De Bellemare dragged his hand through his hair and cursed loudly. "I will grant you this day to complete the moving of the stones. Tomorrow morning I want those men killed."

The gasp of shock and horror that Bethan had struggled to contain burst forth and squealed from her throat. At the sound, the men turned toward her. The gleam of annoyance in de Bellemare's eyes was unmistakable. The unsettling feeling prickling in Bethan's belly deepened, but she did not lower her gaze.

She could not allow this to happen. She could not! Helplessly, Bethan cast her eyes beseechingly toward the captain of the guard, hoping for support, a voice of reason to state an objection. He cleared his throat, then lowered his eyes, avoiding her imploring gaze.

She next turned to her mother. Lady Caryn's eyes were wide with distress, her hand lowered to hover protectively over her swollen belly. She licked her lips in obvious distress, yet remained silent.

"Please, my lord, I beg of you to show mercy. You cannot possibly kill all these men," Bethan cried, fearing her protests would fall upon deaf ears, yet unable to stop herself. "'Tis unthinkable."

"These men are prisoners, captured after I defeated them in battle," de Bellemare snorted, clearly unfazed by her reaction. "Their fate is in my hands."

"But they are innocent of any crime. You have no right to slaughter them."

"Innocent? They are my enemies. They are *your* enemies. You would hardly call them innocent if they pulled you from your warm bed in the dead of night and raped you repeatedly before gutting you through with a knife from belly to neck, now, would you, little Bethan?"

Dismissively, he turned and stepped around her, stalking away. Fear and revulsion coiled in Bethan's belly at the image of such a brutal act against her, yet she would not be deterred. True, warfare existed between the Welsh tribes. And those living along the border fought long and hard against the Normans and their English allies, defiantly resisting invasion. But even those captured warriors were not treated with the kind of savagery her stepfather intended.

Bethan had not missed the tension surrounding de Bellemare's features, the annoyance at her interference. Common sense told her to let the matter drop. And yet her feet propelled her forward.

"Please, please, my lord, you must reconsider," she begged. Racing ahead, she slumped to her knees in front of him. Tamping down the fear that rose to choke the breath from her lungs, she forced herself to confront him. "'Tis a grave sin to shed so much blood in such a fashion. I fear this atrocity will bring us all great suffering."

"Thor save me from feebleminded women and their meddling ways," de Bellemare growled.

Bethan ignored the mockery in his tone. Lifting her chin, she stared at his face, schooling herself not to react as his pale, soulless eyes pierced her own. Inexplicably she remembered the first time she had seen him. He had been sitting atop an enormous horse, leading his soldiers through the gates of Lampeter, a broad-shouldered knight with wind-tousled, overlong hair that gleamed as dark and glossy as the richest fur.

The women around her had sighed and giggled, exclaiming over his handsome face with its strong dark brow, blade-sharp cheeks, and stern jaw. But for some unknown reason the sight of him had sent a shiver of distress through her entire body.

"My father would never have ordered such a barbaric act." Bethan spat the words at him without thinking, desperation clearly overtaking reason.

The light blue of de Bellemare's eyes first flashed with astonishment, then darkened with anger. "Your father is no longer here to make these decisions. The last time I recall seeing him, he was lying on a battlefield in a puddle of his own blood, a lance planted squarely in the middle of his chest."

Bethan remained perfectly still as she absorbed his goading comment. She thought herself used to his ever-growing cruelty, yet he so often proved he still possessed the power to wound. But she refused to allow him to see he had upset her. Instead of tears, she permitted the indignity she felt to flair within her.

How dare he speak so ill of her beloved father? De Bellemare was not fit to wipe his boots. She rose to her feet, squaring her shoulders in a pose of confidence she was far from feeling. "My father was a great warrior. He labored hard to keep this land, and his people, prosperous and safe, secure in times of trouble. He inspired love from his family and loyalty and admiration from his people. A feat few men can claim, especially you, my lord."

At that instant lightning flashed and thunder cracked. The menace in de Bellemare's eyes glowed red hot. She saw his gloved hand reach for the gleaming hilt of his sheathed broadsword and Bethan knew she had pushed him too far. Thinking he might strike her, she braced for the blow. But it never came.

She realized then that her mother had stepped forward, placing herself between them. Lady Caryn's face was pale as whey, save for the dark patches beneath her eyes. "Forgive her wicked tongue, my lord. She is but a young, tenderhearted female who knows nothing of the ways of the world, understands nothing of the business of men. We all know 'tis you who keep us safe, you who provide us with all that we need, and we are all most grateful."

"Your daughter's opinion is of no consequence to me," de Bellemare proclaimed, yet Bethan believed her barb had stung him more than he wanted to credit. "But her insolence is something I will not tolerate. If you know what is good for you both, keep her from my sight."

His eyes burned into Bethan and she felt her knees begin to tremble. In anger, de Bellemare was a menacing expanse of muscle and ruthless power. Her breath quickened as she struggled to stay calm and expressionless, knowing her stepfather would take great amusement in her fear.

"You are needed on the practice field, my lord," the captain of the guard interrupted.

Lord Bellemare grunted his acknowledgment of the message. Throwing her a final dark scowl, the knight turned and stormed away.

"Whoreson," Bethan cursed under her breath, the moment he was beyond her hearing.

"Bethan!" Lady Caryn pulled frantically at her daughter's arm, fearful her words might have carried on the wind.

"Saints preserve us, would you anger him further? You put us all at grave risk with your wicked tongue."

Bethan's answer was an embarrassed silence. Her mother was right; 'twas sheer madness to provoke her stepfather, especially when his ire had already been pricked.

Hanging her head, Bethan meekly followed her mother. The rain had steadily increased, so it was no surprise Lady Caryn elected to go indoors. They retired to her mother's solar, where Bethan diligently plied her needle to the small garments her mother was crafting in anticipation of the baby's birth.

She later accompanied her mother uncomplainingly to evening Mass, where she prayed sincerely for forgiveness and guidance. She spoke not a word during the evening meal, taking her customary place on the dais beside Father William, the manor's resident priest.

She tried all day to push the incident from her mind, yet as she lay in her bed that night, sleep would not come, for her mind would not rest. The fate of the condemned men weighed heavily on her conscience and as each hour passed the need to take some sort of action pressed against Bethan's heart.

A few hours before dawn she made a decision. Dressing quickly in her warmest wool gown, Bethan stepped over the elderly maid who slept on the pallet in front of her bedchamber door and crept from the room. She met no one as she moved through the dark corridors, arriving quickly at her destination. Isolated from the rest of the castle, the small room where her father had gone over the estate accounts was no longer used, but the cupboard where he had stored a second set of keys remained.

Snatching what she needed, Bethan retraced her path, but instead of returning to her chamber she went down to the great hall. Moonlight crept in through the high windows and she blinked several times to adjust her eyes to the dimness.

Sleeping servants were stretched on pallets against the far

wall, their even breaths telling her they were deep in slumber. After a careful scan of the room, Bethan was relieved to find no dogs among the prone forms, knowing they would never have allowed her to enter the room unchallenged.

With great care, she crept slowly along the outer edges of the great hall, her steps muffled by the clean, herb-scented rushes on the floor. Luck was on her side when she saw the young soldier guarding the door was dozing, his head lolling against the wall. Moving with as much stealth as she could muster, Bethan maneuvered around him and then slowly, carefully opened the heavy wooden door that led to the lower depths of the castle. Being a slender girl, she needed but a few inches of space to squeeze herself through.

After three attempts she was able to light the torch she had brought. Taking a deep breath, she quickly recited a simple prayer before descending into the castle depths.

Though she had hoped to do more, Bethan was well aware that it would be true folly indeed to attempt to release a great number of the condemned prisoners. Which was why she had chosen this path. It led to a small, isolated cell carved deeper underground that was sectioned off from the other dungeon.

Given the vast numbers of prisoners her stepfather had taken and now housed, it seemed likely this cell would be occupied. As she moved forward, the stench of unwashed bodies and damp earth suddenly filled her nose, letting her know her assumptions had been correct.

Heartened, Bethan pressed on, one hand holding the wall of solid earth on her left to keep her steady on her feet, the other hand raising her lit torch higher, illuminating the way. Thin snakes of smoke curled up from the flame gathering on the arched corridor of the shrinking ceiling, and she soon realized she would have to bow her head if it got any lower.

After a few minutes, she reached the bottom. Ten steps forward and she found what she had been seeking. A single cell with long iron bars stood in the damp corner of the small, nearly airless space. Inside the cell were six, perhaps eight men. The light from her torch caught their attention and slowly they turned to investigate.

The stillness in the air changed to something tense and dangerous. Bethan instinctively took a step back.

"My, my, what do we have here? Have you come to poke at the animals in the cage, little miss?" one of the men asked.

"Get close enough and I'll give you a right proper poke," another mocked, and several men grunted with lecherous amusement. "One you won't soon forget."

Bethan's feet faltered. Her stepfather's dire predictions of rape and murder echoed through her head as the nagging flaw in her plan crystalized in her mind. Freeing these men could very well place her own safety, her own life, in grave danger. She closed her eyes, fighting back the sickening queasiness in her stomach as the jeering grew louder, the comments cruder.

"Be quiet. All of you."

The sound of a commanding voice from the shadows instantly silenced the jeers. When it was quiet, the speaker stepped to the forefront, into the circle of firelight cast by her torch.

To her surprise, Bethan saw a man far younger than the rest of the prisoners, a lad probably only a few years older than herself. A handsome lad, with short dark hair, gray eyes, a jutting nose, and a strong jaw. It seemed impossible that he was their leader and yet he exuded an air of power and command that far exceeded his years.

"Why are you here?" he asked.

"I have come to help you escape," Bethan proclaimed breathlessly.

Instead of the surprised excitement she expected, the men hooted with laughter. All except the younger one, the one who had posed the question. He was silent, watching her with studied interest, his gray eyes hooded, revealing nothing of his emotions.

"Why would you do such a thing, *demoiselle?*"

Bethan swallowed. As much as she wanted to reveal the truth, she worried at the men's reaction if she told them they were to be executed in the morning. "Do you wish for your freedom, sir? Or shall I journey to the dungeons on the north side and find others who would be grateful for my assistance?"

"Is that what you seek? Gratitude?"

"No. I seek justice."

"A strange quest for the daughter of de Bellemare," the lad retorted.

"He is not my father!" Bethan's face flushed with emotion.

"Aye, the lass speaks the truth," one of the men concurred. "I heard the guards speak of how de Bellemare took this place a few years past without any bloodshed. He married the widowed Lady Caryn. The girl is too old to be his get."

Those piercing gray eyes grew thoughtful. "So this is an act of revenge against your stepfather?"

Bethan shook her head vehemently, denying the charge, though inwardly she admitted there was some measure of truth in the question. She *did* want to strike back at de Bellemare, but she also felt a great need to try and prevent some of the senseless violence he seemed so intent on inflicting.

"Lampeter was a joyful place before Agnarr de Bellemare arrived. Releasing you is but a small attempt on my part to restore some of the dignity and honor my stepfather has stripped from us."

The leader was silent, his face pensive. But the others were most vocal with their doubts and suspicions.

"'Tis a trap, I say! A trap! We shall all be gutted the moment we climb those stairs." The prisoner who spoke, a large brute of a man with thickly muscled forearms, wiped his mouth, then gave Bethan an amused smirk. "We'd be fools to trust her."

"Or fools to so easily scoff at her offer." The leader looked at each of the men in turn, then returned his gaze to Bethan. "Agnarr de Bellemare does not need the excuse of escaping prisoners to kill us. He can order our deaths at any time."

Bethan inwardly flinched, amazed at how he had correctly deciphered the truth. Though she willed herself to remain expressionless, she must have done something that revealed her true emotions. The leader's expression changed, his voice grew urgent. He stood up, drew closer, his expression alert.

"Is that it, lass? Is he planning to kill us?"

"Aye. You and nearly a hundred others."

The cell became very quiet. A few of the men seemed angry, others concerned, while one gave her a skeptical look. Yet to a man, they turned to the lad for guidance.

"What is your name, *demoiselle*?"

"I am Bethan of Lampeter."

"And I am Haydn of Gwynedd." He inclined his head in a gesture of courtly gallantry. "How can you aid us?"

Bethan's fingers curled around the heavy iron key she had hidden in her pocket. Slowly she withdrew it, holding it out so the light spilling from her torch would illuminate it. "I have the key that will unlock your cell."

There was a hiss of an indrawn breath, along with a whistle of excitement. The men began to press forward against the iron bars. Choking back the cry that lodged in her throat, Bethan dug her heels into the hard-packed dirt floor and stood her ground.

"How many guards are there aboveground?"

"There is but one soldier standing guard at the entrance to this passage."

"One!" a man exclaimed. "We can easily overtake him."

Bethan shook her head. "No. Once outside that door, you must pass through the great hall in order to exit the castle. 'Twas difficult enough for me to manage the task. With your numbers, you will never slip through undetected."

"Then we will have to fight our way out. Can you get us some weapons, lass?" the largest man asked.

Bethan's eyes widened in alarm, but before she could answer another of the men spoke. "Don't be daft, man. Eight men against a garrison of de Bellemare's soldiers? We'd be cut down before we reach the castle walls."

A murmur of agreement went through the men. Bethan waited a moment, then spoke. "I know of another way out."

Once again, her words produced an instant silence.

"Another way?" Haydn asked.

"There is another passage, one that leads to a trapdoor in the stables."

"Then that is our route of escape," Haydn declared. "Will you lead the way, Lady Bethan?"

She nodded. Bethan fumbled with the key, her hand shaking noticeably as she tried to fit it into the lock. Behind the bars, the men were pacing in the cell like beasts on a leash. With freedom so near, their agitation was palpable.

But palpable also was Bethan's fear. Faced with the reality of the reckless act she was about to commit, she trembled with doubt. The men could easily attack or kill her once they were free.

As if sensing the warring thoughts within her mind, the leader reached through the bars, closing his hand over hers. She gasped and looked up. His eyes gleamed in the frail light.

"You have nothing to fear from us," he assured her. "I give you my word that you will be safe."

A sad smile tugged at the corner of her mouth. "My fate is in God's hands now."

Once unlocked, the cell door swung open easily. The men pushed forward, eager to be free. Bethan felt a hand at her elbow and was relieved to see it was Haydn. He had placed himself protectively between her and the other men. Slowly, she exhaled.

"Which way?" he asked.

She lifted her chin to indicate the direction. "The passage is very low and narrow. We must form a single line and be very, very quiet."

With a confidence she was far from feeling, Bethan led them along the shadowy corridor. Mice and rats scurried over their feet, cobwebs caught on their hair and faces, but no one uttered a sound.

Finally they reached the base of a narrow, wooden staircase. Regretfully, Bethan extinguished her torch, plunging them into total darkness. Biting her lip, she started the slow climb up the stairs, but was quickly pulled back.

"Let me go first," Haydn commanded. "You do not know what you will find above us."

It took two tries to dislodge the trapdoor. Once it was pushed aside, Haydn easily pulled himself through. After he had successfully cleared the opening, Bethan followed, poking her head out. The smells of straw, horses, and manure let her know they had reached the stables. Blinking hard, she reached up and allowed Haydn to help her out. The rest followed quickly behind her.

"We would be harder to catch on horseback," one of the men suggested as he stroked the back of a sleek mare who stood contentedly in her stall.

"No!" Haydn ordered. "If we try to ride out we will alert the guards and be pursued. Our best chance is to escape on foot."

"He is right," Bethan agreed. "You can slip over the wall on the south end. From there it is but a short run to the forest, and freedom."

They left the stable under Bethan's guidance, avoiding the watchtower, keeping to the darkest shadows of the buildings. The ground, wet from the recent rain, was soft beneath their feet. They came to the south section of the wall and Bethan halted. The moon, low in the sky, cast a few weak rays through the primeval forest that loomed just beyond, the tops of the dark, thick trees lashing in the wind.

Silently, the men hoisted themselves over the wall, until only young Haydn was left. He turned to face her and Bethan felt her breath catch.

"I owe you a debt I fear I can never repay. But have a care, Bethan of Lampeter. If de Bellemare ever learns of your part in all this . . ." His voice trailed off.

Bethan swallowed hard as she acknowledged his warning. She saw the sincerity in his eyes, heard the genuine note of concern, and felt vindicated in her actions. This young man did not deserve the cruel death her stepfather had decreed and she was pleased she had been able to save him.

"I will be careful," she replied. The rain began, a steady drizzle that quickly soaked her gown. "Godspeed, Haydn of Gwynedd. I shall pray for your safe deliverance from this place of evil and I shall pray even harder for the rain to cease and bright sunshine to greet the day."

"Sunshine?"

"Aye, sunshine. I do not know why, but 'tis the one thing that always keeps de Bellemare indoors. If he learns of your escape, he will give chase, leading his men until you are found. He is vengeful, ruthless, and possessing of powers beyond mortal men. He will not return without you. Or your mutilated bodies." She swallowed hard. "But if there is sunshine tomorrow, he will send his soldiers out alone and if you have run far and covered your tracks, you might yet succeed in eluding them."

He nodded, though she worried that he did not fully understand the danger her stepfather presented.

"Farewell," he whispered.

Then to her utter astonishment, he executed an elegant bow, vaulted over the wall, and headed toward the open fields. Bethan scrambled on top of an abandoned oxcart and watched, her heart thumping with fear. She could see the other men had fanned out through the fields, all scurrying in different directions, hoping to increase their chances of survival if they were pursued.

Yet it was so open, so bare. If any were sighted, they would be easily captured. And most likely tortured before they were killed.

Bethan shuddered with revulsion, but knowing there was nothing more she could do, she climbed down from the cart. Carefully, silently, she made her way back to her bedchamber, her mouth moving in prayer with each step she took.

Haydn ran through the clearing toward the thick grove of trees. He pushed himself until the burning in his lungs became a constant, unbearable pain, but he did not slow until the tall trees and dense thickets had swallowed him. Still keeping a steady speed, he glanced over his shoulder, relieved to see no one.

The scent of spicy pine drifted around him, normally a comforting scent but the tension inside him seemed to crackle in the air. Panting, his breath coming in deep gasps, Haydn allowed himself a moment of rest. He strained, listening for the sound of horses's hooves, the baying of dogs, the thundering rhythm of marching men in hot pursuit. But he heard nothing. Only the groaning of the trees as they fought the wind and in the distance, the hooting of an owl.

He picked up the pace, his leather boots slipping on the wet pine needles that carpeted the forest floor. Rain fell in torrents, splattering Haydn's face, making it difficult to see. He lowered his head and thrust himself forward, determined to make progress, knowing if he reached the outer edge of the forest it was but a short sprint to the base of the rugged hills.

He ran for hours, until every muscle in his body ached, every bone jarred. Blinking against the pelting drops, he lifted his head. Lightning forked in the sky and thunder boomed through the forest, illuminating the mantle of darkness. And then he saw them. The stark, bare, stone hills.

Freedom.

Rain lashed from the sky, pummeling the ground. But Haydn barely felt it. With renewed strength, he pushed his wet hair from his eyes. For the first time since he had been captured two long months ago, he smiled.

They would not be able to track him once he began to climb, even if de Bellemare led his soldiers on the hunt. He remembered the earnest expression on Bethan's face as she told him she would pray for sunshine so her stepfather would not pursue him.

As for Haydn, well, he would pray for light rain and a dense fog. Bethan knew only that de Bellemare was reluctant to be in the sunlight, freely admitting she was unaware of the reason.

But Haydn knew. He knew that once bathed in sunlight de Bellemare would burst into flames and burn until he was consumed. He knew de Bellemare was cursed. He was not alive, nor was he dead. He was undead. He could breathe, his heart beat, he ate, drank, slept, but most importantly he could not easily die.

De Bellemare was a vampire. He could live forever, with his amazing strength and cruel, evil countenance, as long as he had blood. Human blood.

Haydn knew that de Bellemare could go mad with bloodlust, killing humans as well as other vampires. Haydn believed that was what had happened to his parents—de Bellemare had gone on a rampage, had broken a taboo held for centuries among his kind and slaughtered every creature that drew breath within Haydn's family manor.

Haydn knew this, understood this, because he too was a creature of darkness, a vampire. A twist of fate had saved him from sharing the same gruesome end as his family. He had been away from the manor at the time of the attack. He had tracked those responsible for the carnage and been caught and imprisoned.

The need to avenge this evil wrong, to destroy his sworn enemy was the force that drove Haydn. Much as he wanted to, he knew it was madness to challenge de Bellemare now. Haydn was young, his abilities not yet fully developed. Therefore he knew he must wait, he must build his strength, harness his powers, and in due time, gain his revenge.

Thanks to young Bethan of Lampeter's courage, he would have that chance.

Two

Ten years later, early spring

"I have decided that you shall marry within the month, Bethan," Sir Agnarr de Bellemare decreed. "I am done with your paltry excuses and maidenly foolishness."

The self-proclaimed Lord of Lampeter made his announcement as the evening meal was being served. The hall bustled with activity, people, and noise, but Bethan felt several pairs of eyes turn to her. She imagined her stepfather had raised his voice intending to be overheard, intending to demonstrate yet again that he, and he alone, ruled this land and all who resided within it.

Bethan clutched her hands together in her lap so no one, especially de Bellemare, would see them tremble.

"Precisely who am I to marry, my lord?" she asked cautiously, trying to force a light, uncaring note into her voice. "'Tis over a year since any acceptable men have presented themselves to me as potential suitors."

"The fault for your lack of suitors does not lie with me," he spat out.

To her dismay, Bethan flinched. His words had struck a

chord. At three-and-twenty she was well beyond the age when most women married. As she matured, there had been some interest, but any man that she was willing to consider quickly changed his mind when he tried to negotiate a bridal contract with her stepfather.

In the end, Bethan had not been too despondent, for she knew the one characteristic she required in a husband, above all others, was his ability to stand up to the Lord of Lampeter. Unfortunately, that man had yet to be found.

"I have been far too lenient about this matter," de Bellemare announced. "I will select the groom myself and you will be pleased with my choice."

"Your choice?" Bethan said in a clear voice that easily reached the end of the hall. "I agreed to an arranged marriage, my lord. Not a forced one."

"Damn your insolent hide!" Lord Lampeter slammed his fist upon the trestle table so hard his goblet of wine shuddered, tipped, and fell over. The rich red liquid ran like a river to the edge, then trickled over the side.

Bethan straightened her shoulders. "Three years ago you agreed, sir, that I would have the final choice as to which man becomes my husband. Surely, you do not mean to break your promise to me, an oath sworn before God and our people?"

He glowered at her and Bethan felt a rising fear. 'Twas not prudent, or safe, to push his temper beyond a certain point, but she had to reestablish her rights in this process in front of witnesses. It was her only chance.

"You know your stepfather is a man of his word," Lady Caryn said quietly. "He would never dishonor himself in such a fashion by breaking his promise."

Bethan turned to her mother in gratitude, grateful for the support. The answering smile of encouragement she received nearly broke her heart. The once lovely Lady Caryn was thin to the point of gauntness, her complexion pale, bloodless. She was in so many ways a shadow of her former self, but her instinct to protect her daughter remained strong.

"I need no defense from you, lady wife," de Bellemare grunted in disgust. "If you had given me a son, a proper heir, this matter would not be of such grave importance."

Cowed, Lady Caryn bowed her head. The Lord of Lampeter never missed an opportunity to berate his wife over her failure to produce the requisite heir. Bethan felt it was especially unfair, since her mother had literally tried for years to bring forth a living child, becoming pregnant nearly every spring, and either miscarrying or burying a stillborn babe by fall. So much sadness and difficulties, both physical and emotional, had taken a toll on her health and spirit.

For a time Bethan thought he might put aside Lady Caryn and take a new wife, but surprisingly that had not come to pass.

Without a son to inherit, Bethan was heiress to Lampeter, a vast property of sizeable wealth. But de Bellemare had no intention of letting control of the property slip from his grasp any time soon. Though he left his true motivation unspoken, even a fool knew that Lord Lampeter meant to mold her bridegroom into his image, intending to train him to do his bidding.

Would they never escape this dreadful tyranny?

Bethan's blood ran cold at the thought of spending the rest of her life joined to a man like her stepfather. Arrogant, violent, aloof, cruel. She would be better off dead. Or in a convent.

For a moment she let her mind wander as she contemplated life as a nun—serene, reflective, safe. It was tempting. Though she freely acknowledged she had no calling to do God's work, the prospect of spending the rest of her life out from under the thumb of Agnarr de Bellemare held enormous appeal.

It was also a dream, a selfish dream. She could not abandon her mother, nor turn away from those who depended on her. De Bellemare was a harsh taskmaster. He slaughtered not only the soldiers he fought, but many of the innocent people they protected. He routinely burned villages, defiled women, cared not one wit when famine swept through Lampeter.

It was only through Bethan's intervention these past years that so many of her own people survived. If she abandoned them now, they might all perish. Though it meant personal sacrifice, she knew she must do whatever she could to protect them.

That promise brought her mind to the book that awaited her in her bedchamber. Through means he would not divulge Father William had smuggled the missive to her and begun teaching her to read it. As a woman, she had not been given the benefit of learning, but the situation was so dire Father William could not refuse her pleas.

The book was an ancient tome, containing knowledge of pagan rights, the dark arts and the mystical, unholy creatures who performed them. There were accounts of men who could change their humanly form at will into an animal of prey such as a wolf; men who became glowing red-eyed monsters when the moon was full; others who possessed the upper body of a man and the lower body of a winged serpent.

There were tales of witchcraft, sorcery, and demons who made pacts with the devil. It fascinated and frightened Bethan, but she continued to study the volume each day, for what she sought was knowledge. Knowledge to understand her stepfather's strange habits.

She was convinced he was not a man of this world. A witch perhaps? Or a wizard? 'Twas the only explanation for the things that could not be explained or understood. Nearly everyone in the castle feared de Bellemare too much to pay close attention, but Bethan had observed him for years.

While others had started to show the passage of time on their face and form, the Lord of Lampeter had not aged a day.

Instead of declining, his physical strength had increased. Bethan had witnessed on several occasions his peculiar and disturbing ritual of drinking the warm blood of an animal he had just slain.

He was noticeably restless, edgy, and even more prone to strike out at others when the moon was full. He claimed the sunlight caused a pain in his eyes and thus avoided it, staying indoors on the rare days the sun shone brightly. But on such a day Bethan had been the only witness to a most bizarre event.

She had been tucked away in the corner of her mother's solarium, enjoying a few moments of quiet solitude. Her stepfather had entered the chamber. Not finding what he sought, he turned to leave. But as he strode from the room he stepped too close to the window, passing his hand through a shaft of sunlight. The exposed flesh of his fingers had burst into flames.

Frightened, shocked, horrified, Bethan had curled herself into a tight ball, hiding herself behind the stone archway, praying she had not been seen. Cursing, de Bellemare had left the solarium. When he appeared at the evening meal, all traces of the wound were gone.

"We shall speak no more of your marriage," de Bellemare ordered in a menacing voice, and the sound of his raised tone brought Bethan back to the present. "Since I gave you my word, I shall put forth two of my own knights as your potential bridegroom, so you may *choose* your husband. But mark me well, girl, you shall be married before the last crop has been planted on my lands or suffer the consequences."

Though she vowed to remain impassive, Bethan was having trouble breathing. She knew from experience that once he had reached a decision, Lord Lampeter did not change his mind. There would be a wedding within the month, even if she had to be brought kicking and screaming to recite her vows.

She knew there was only one way to avoid a match to a

man of her stepfather's choosing. She needed to find herself a husband. Quickly.

There were many times in the past ten years that Bethan firmly believed God had forsaken her. The Almighty had delivered evil—in the form of Agnarr de Bellemare—on their doorstep and done little to keep it in check.

But a skirmish on the southern borders called her stepfather and his most loyal troops away and Bethan knew her prayers for a miracle had been answered. With Lord Lampeter otherwise occupied, she now had the chance to find her champion.

It had not been easy, but with a heartfelt plea and a touch of guilt, Bethan was able to persuade Sir Colwyn, the hardened soldier who had loyally served as her father's garrison commander, to escort her on her quest.

They had traveled north on horseback with a handpicked contingent of soldiers, making only brief stops for food, water, and rest. They met few travelers as they climbed the mountains, the roads slick with mud from the constant rain, the forest blanketed with spindly trees not yet awakened from their winter sleep.

Bethan made no complaints as she lolled with exhaustion in her saddle, grateful that she had been given this chance. Sir Colwyn had been most skeptical indeed when she revealed her plan to find Lord Meifod, the man they called the Warrior of the North. He was said to be a bold, self-assured man, a battle-seasoned warrior with unrivaled fighting skills. She believed he was the one man in all of Wales who could protect her, and her people, from Agnarr de Bellemare.

"What will you do when we meet Lord Meifod?" Sir Colwyn had asked.

"I will convince him to take me as his wife."

"How do you know he does not already have a wife?"

"I have never heard any tales of a Lady Meifod."

Colwyn snorted. "Perhaps she is a dull maiden, not worthy of a troubadour's tale."

"Hmmm, perhaps." Bethan offered him a scant smile. A wife was but one of the many obstacles she faced, but she was not about to voice any of the nagging doubts that tormented her. Her only chance of escaping her stepfather's ruthless domination was to strike a bargain with her future husband.

They rode another two leagues through a steep mountain pass and then Colwyn announced, "We are here, my lady."

Teetering with exhaustion, Bethan was instantly revived by the knight's words. She squinted at the castle perched high upon the crest of a hill, inordinately pleased to discover the impressive structure was constructed of timber, in keeping with the Welsh tradition.

The rain had stopped, the gray mists of the morning had burned away, leaving a rare afternoon of bright sunshine. Bethan nudged her horse forward. Her guard surrounded her on all sides, engulfing her in a protective ring as they joined the scattering of men, women, and children on the road to the castle.

There were wagons filled with casks of ale, carts pulled by oxen loaded with bags of grain. Women carried baskets of eggs and young spring vegetables, one lad hauled a pail of fish, another an armload of firewood.

"Are you certain we are at the right place?" Bethan asked. "'Tis said that Lord Meifod prefers solitude. This hardly appears to be the dwelling of a recluse."

"Lord Meifod lives in the castle, my lady. Not the village," Sir Colwyn replied.

Sir Colwyn kept his eye squarely on the castle looming ahead while Bethan took a moment to inspect the rest of the area. The village was set within a valley of rolling hills with steep mountain ranges on all sides that provided a natural defense.

She noticed a few fat cattle grazing in a nearby field,

while a second meadow accommodated a substantial herd of sheep. The sounds of honking geese, clucking chickens, squealing pigs, and yapping dogs filled the air, along with the occasional shout of a child at play.

They were not challenged entry by the soldiers that stood sentry around the perimeter, yet all normal activity seemed to cease, as the villagers stopped whatever they were doing to turn and stare as they went by.

"I suspect they have few visitors, my lady," Sir Colwyn commented.

"No doubt they have never seen such a fine and handsome escort," Bethan teased as she offered a smile to a pretty, pregnant woman carrying a large basket of laundry under her arm. The woman returned the smile shyly, then lowered her head and hurried away.

The blacksmith, leatherworker, weaver, and potter all had shops disbursed among the cottages and each appeared to be doing a brisk business. Bethan was surprised and impressed by the obvious prosperity of the village. The buildings were in good repair, the merchant stalls stocked with a variety of goods, and the people examining the wares looked hale and hearty.

Once through the village, Sir Colwyn quickened their pace. A shout of warning was heard from the castle, long before they reached it. When they did arrive, the sentry standing high on the watchtower assessed them with a furrowed forehead. Bethan's soldiers tightened the protective ring around her further as they halted in front of the large, closed oak gates.

"State your business," the sentry called out.

"I am Lady Bethan of Lampeter. My guard and I seek shelter for the night."

The sentry snorted, then said something to his companion, who took off at a run. Bethan straightened her back and tried to quell the nerves that had started fluttering in her stomach.

"Hardly a friendly greeting," Bethan exclaimed wryly to Sir Colwyn, her eyes fixed on the archers lining the walls.

"The men are well trained," Sir Colwyn commented, his voice echoing approval.

"'Tis hardly necessary. Our numbers are too small to pose any sort of threat to a fortified castle of this size," Bethan protested.

"A soldier who underestimates any potential threat quickly loses his position," Sir Colwyn added. "And often his life."

They continued to wait, the warm sun beating down on their heads, until an order was given granting them entry. Slowly the portcullis began to rise. Bethan and her guard moved together in synchronized step as they passed through the large gatehouse and across the outer bailey.

Bethan immediately noted that the calm serenity and cheerful atmosphere so prevalent in the village was clearly lacking within the castle walls. Armed knights patrolled the low battlements, while the archers lining the walls had shifted their attention inward, their notched arrows at the ready. There was no doubt that this was the home of a warrior, a mighty stronghold meant to keep others out.

They passed through to the inner bailey and here everyone seemed in a hurry, bustling quickly from task to task. The armorer was pounding out metal into swords, the carpenter repairing the door on the stables, the carter fixing a broken wheel on a large oxcart. Bethan watched for a moment, then realized with a startled surprise why it seemed so strange. There were no women. Those hauling the firewood, tending the kitchen herb garden, and hanging the laundry were all male servants.

A tall man wearing a long, hooded mantle emerged from behind a pile of wine casks and hurried toward them. Though the material of his garment was costly, Bethan did not think he was Lord Meifod. He seemed too slight in stature, too refined to be known as the Warrior of the North.

"Welcome, my lady." He bowed, his eyes moving over her

with interest. "I am Frederic Bonvalet, steward of the castle. I am pleased on behalf of Lord Meifod to offer you and your men shelter for the night."

"I am Lady Bethan. We gratefully accept His Lordship's kind offer of hospitality."

Bethan smiled and with the steward's assistance, dismounted. She fell in step beside him as they walked into the hall. Sir Colwyn followed at a respectable distance while the rest of the men saw to the horses. They crossed the wide expanse of the great hall and Bethan's stomach rumbled as the scent of freshly baked bread and rich spices tempted her appetite.

"We will be serving the evening meal shortly," Frederic remarked.

Bethan blushed. "Will your master be joining us?"

"No."

"Oh. Is he away from the castle?" she asked, voicing a fear she had not anticipated. "Will he be gone long?"

"Lord Meifod is too busy to attend to any unexpected guests."

"But I wish to express my gratitude for his hospitality to your lord in person, as any well-bred lady ought."

"I will convey your thanks to him myself."

"You do not understand."

"I understand far more than you think," the steward replied, not unkindly. "There are many who wish for an audience with Lord Meifod, but few are granted. And never to a woman."

Bethan felt the blush on her face deepen as her cheeks heated with embarrassment. She had not meant to sound so desperate. "I am afraid I was unclear. I have traveled a great distance to speak with His Lordship concerning an urgent, personal matter. Surely he can spare me a few moments?"

The steward glanced at her impassively. "I will convey your request to Lord Meifod, but caution you not to hold out hope." He cocked a brow. "I notice you are traveling without a maid. We have no female servants at the castle, but I can send for a woman from the village to attend you, if you wish."

"Thank you, no. I can manage very well on my own."

They had reached another door, which the steward opened. Bethan entered the bedchamber, hardly glancing at her surroundings.

"I will send a servant to fetch you when dinner is served," Frederic said, bowing gracefully.

Though she smiled pleasantly, inside Bethan was nearly shaking with disappointment. *So close!* She had overcome so much to get here, and then to be so easily dismissed was a bitter, painful pill to swallow.

Her fingers gripped the base of the ewer set on the table near the canopied bed. Itching to lift it and hurl it across the room, Bethan instead forced herself to take several calming breaths.

All was not yet lost. She had found her way inside the castle. Somehow she would find a way to see Lord Meifod. She had not come this far to be denied.

Haydn stood well back from the deadly rays of sunshine and stared out the window of his bedchamber. With growing annoyance he watched the progression of the small troupe of soldiers as they wound their way through the village and started on the path to his castle.

"Hellfire and damnation!" Haydn cursed, curling his hands into fists, when he spied the female rider in the center of the pack.

"My lord?"

His steward, Frederic Bonvalet, appeared in the doorway.

"Grant them one night of shelter," Haydn commanded, knowing the answer to the question before it was even asked. "No more."

The steward bowed and hurried away. Not surprisingly he returned within the hour.

"The lady wishes an audience with you," Frederic said.

"Did you tell her that I refuse?"

"I did. Several times. But that did not appease her." The steward cleared his throat. "She claims 'tis a personal matter of great urgency."

"Ah, great urgency. For women 'tis always urgent when it comes to getting their own way."

"She seems especially desperate, my lord. Would you not consider making an exception this one time?"

Haydn's mouth twisted in irritation. She must be a real beauty or a particularly fine actress to have influenced the loyal steward to plead her case.

"My answer remains the same. And it would behoove you to remember that your allegiance is to me, Frederic, not some flighty noblewoman with a pretty face and a heaving bosom."

The steward wilted under Haydn's disapproving gaze. "Forgive me."

Haydn dismissed Frederic with a wave of his hand, but his thoughts remained on the mysterious lady.

She was hardly the first to come and beg for his assistance. For years, women had flocked to his castle, seeking something from the Warrior of the North. They flattered him, pleaded for help, even coyly offered him sexual favors.

At first, he was polite, yet firm with his refusals, trying to cushion the rejections. Still, they came. So after a time, he ceased meeting them. In his experience, mortal women of noble means brought nothing but trouble.

Haydn moved to the window and released the heavy linen curtain, plunging the chamber into blackness. Dark as pitch, he waited for the calm to settle his agitation, but it eluded him. Haydn's jaw tightened. It was the woman. Her presence within his castle walls had stirred the air, had created a tension that would not leave until she departed.

Perhaps it was time for him to consider returning to the fortress where he had lived with his parents. He had seen it three years ago, a dark and deserted ruin, blackened by fire, overgrown with brambles. The locals claimed it was cursed, a sinister place, fit only for the devil.

He could reclaim it, repair it, make it comfortable for himself, but even restored, he knew no humans would willingly reside there with him. He closed his eyes, wondering if he was ready to embrace that life.

He lived here in solitude, but had come to appreciate the occasional company of those who lived under his command. They accepted him because they knew not what he truly was, a vampire, a creature of darkness who hunted in the dead of night, thirsting for blood.

The villagers worshiped him from afar, because he kept them safe. His soldiers, in awe of his battle prowess, were loyal to him, the male servants who worked at the castle were content, because he treated them fairly.

He was pleased with the life he had created for himself, yet never far from his mind was the purpose of his existence, the need to plot his revenge against his bitter enemy, Agnarr de Bellemare.

His gut still burned every time he thought of de Bellemare's treachery, but Haydn had learned to leash his anger, to harness the demons that clamored in his head. He knew he would have but one chance to annihilate his enemy. He knew also that if he failed he would suffer the same grim fate as his parents.

The afternoon sunshine eventually gave way to the dusk of evening, but Haydn did not leave his chamber. He sat in the dark. He sat in silence. He sat alone and pondered his future.

"They want us to depart within the hour, my lady," Sir Colwyn told Bethan the following morning.

"But we cannot leave! I have yet to see the Warrior of the North and made my proposition."

Colwyn shook his head. "Bonvalet was most adamant in his instructions. I suspect we will get our innards spilled all over the great hall if we remain much longer."

Bethan rubbed her temples to alleviate some of the pain that was throbbing over her eyes. Her initial worry of having her proposal soundly denied by Lord Meifod seemed like a ridiculous concern, considering that she was finding it almost impossible to even present that plan.

"Tell him that I am ill," she said.

"My lady—"

Bethan held up her hand to silence Sir Colwyn's protests. "Tell the steward that I am ill, unable to rise from my bed. Explain this is a usual occurrence, one that happens each month to me."

"Each month?" Sir Colwyn's bushy brows drew together in confusion, and then a blush of red heated his cheeks.

"Precisely." Bethan paced between the window and bed, trying to release her nervous energy. "I am hoping the hint of womanly difficulties will embarrass the steward enough to buy us another day inside these walls."

"But what good is another day? Lord Meifod has refused to see you."

"True, he has refused me a formal audience. But a casual meeting will serve me just as well. Today you must discover the location of the master's chambers and plot a route from my room to his. I shall wait until the castle sleeps and then go to him in the dead of night to plead my case."

"Lady Bethan, you are a maiden! You cannot present yourself to this warrior in his bedchamber. Whatever will he think of you?"

"He will think I am serious," she retorted. "And desperate. Both of which are true."

"I cannot allow it," the knight declared. "I am sworn to protect you and this plan puts you directly in harm's way."

Bethan threw back her shoulders. She knew Sir Colwyn was right. Her unexpected, uninvited appearance in Lord Meifod's bedchamber would put her in a very precarious position indeed.

But she had little choice. Time was running out. Her tale of a womanly illness would not work beyond today. She must see him tonight or else forever lose the chance to save herself, to save her people.

"No arguments. Just find that bedchamber, Sir Colwyn."

The hallway was dark, cast in shadow by the few lit torches scattered along the wall. Bethan had spent the past two hours memorizing the directions Sir Colwyn had given her and she was grateful to have committed the details to memory, for her nerves were making it difficult to think. Tamping down her doubts, Bethan allowed her feet to carry her forward, through one corridor, then up a steep set of stairs to the next level and chamber where Lord Meifod slept.

She felt the goose bumps rise on her skin and she sent up a hasty prayer that she would find him soon. Biting her lip, she hurried onward into the darkness. She took but two more steps before the hair on the nape of her neck rose in warning, giving her the heart-stopping sensation that she was being watched.

"Hello? Is anyone there?" she whispered.

Icy silence was the only reply. Bethan drew herself up, paused, and listened. She froze, allowing her senses to sharpen; then slowly pivoting her head, she studied the shadows behind her, half expecting someone to materialize and confront her.

But there was nothing.

Shaking her head at her foolish nerves, she continued, until suddenly from out of the darkness came a dark figure, large and imposing. Bethan gasped and took a step backward, nearly stumbling over her clumsy feet.

The noise catapulted the figure into action. The shadow moved, so swiftly she was unsure she could trust her eyes that it had in truth been real. Then suddenly a bulky arm came out of the shadows and snaked around her waist. Before she had a chance to utter a sound, a second hand clamped over her mouth, snuffing her cry of alarm.

For the space of a heartbeat, pure terror pounded through her veins, rendering her immobile. Her captor dragged her down the hall and Bethan came to life. Kicking, thrashing, and twisting, she fought to escape the iron bonds that held her prisoner.

Oh, why had she not listened to Sir Colwyn? It was utter madness to put herself in such grave danger by wandering the hallways of a strange castle in the middle of the night. Tears of frustration came to her eyes when she realized she might very well pay for her foolishness with her life.

"Cease your struggles at once or else you shall wake my guards."

The voice that spoke was low and arrogant. Bethan winced and tried to calm herself, knowing this must be the man she sought. She remained perfectly still and he removed his hand from her face. But the other arm, strong as steel, remained around her waist.

Bethan could barely breathe, was terrified of moving. Yet slowly she turned and looked up at her captor, straining to see the features hidden within the hooded cowl of the man's mantle, but it was too dark.

"Who are you?" he demanded.

His tone was menacing and angry. The panic tightened in her breast. Bethan tried to summon a smile, but her lips trembled so forcefully she knew the effort was a failure.

Stay calm. Keep your wits. "I am Bethan of Lampeter. My men and I arrived yesterday afternoon."

"There are no guest chambers in this section of the castle. What were you doing here?"

"Looking for you."

A rumble of displeasure rose from deep within his chest. "Well, now you have seen me. I bid you good night, my lady."

He released his grip and turned to leave. Bethan felt despair tear at her soul. "Wait! Please, I must speak with you on a matter of grave importance. Is there somewhere private we may converse?"

"Private?"

"Your bedchamber, perhaps?"

He shifted and his hood fell from his head, revealing his face. Bethan was almost afraid to look, worried he might be hideously scarred or disfigured. But her fears were unfounded. The Warrior of the North was an uncommonly handsome man. Black hair, silky thick and straight, hung to his shoulders. The arch of his brow was noble, his cheeks chiseled, his jaw square and strong and perfectly symmetrical. His eyes were pale and silver, alert and intelligent.

For one brief, fanciful instant she thought there was something familiar about him, but knew that was impossible.

"There is but one reason for a woman to come to a man's chambers in the middle of the night."

"I just want to talk," she muttered.

"That's what they all say." A menacing smirk quirked one corner of his mouth. "Come."

Bethan stared at him, sensing it could be dangerous to trust him, yet all the while knowing he was likely her only hope of defeating her stepfather. Her breath rasped out of her lungs in thin puffs. She swallowed hard, her courage dwindling for a moment. Then burying deep the fear that choked her throat and robbed her of speech, Bethan held out her hand and let the volatile stranger lead her away.

Three

Haydn kept his stride purposefully long, but the woman kept up despite her smaller stature. Her breath came in panting puffs and he felt a brief flash of sympathy, but he did not slow.

Though he had not shown it, he had been startled when she revealed her name. Bethan of Lampeter. He remembered well the young girl who had risked all to save him from de Bellemare's butchery. 'Twas difficult to believe that this beautiful woman, with long golden hair that cascaded over her full bosom and a face boasting delicate, feminine features and luminous green eyes, was one and the same.

Why was she here? What did she want from him?

He shut the door to his bedchamber and faced her. With the curtain pulled aside, the light of the half-moon shone brightly through the window, more than sufficient for someone with his keen eyesight. His gaze moved over her once more, marveling anew at her delicate beauty. He waited in silence, watching her shift uncomfortably from one foot to the other.

"You are in my bedchamber. As you requested. Speak."

The pallor on her face increased. "I have come seek . . .

seeking . . ." she stopped, stumbling over the words. "Forgive me, but I have the strangest sensation that we have met before."

"We have met, my lady." His gaze softened on her. "You knew me once as Haydn of Gwynedd."

Bethan's eyes widened. "You survived! I always wondered. And the others?"

Haydn shook his head. "I know not of the other men. We broke apart and each went our separate way, hoping to increase our chances of escape. Did the guards or de Bellemare give chase?"

Her eyes lightened with amusement. "My stepfather never knew you had escaped. The guard that watched the door to your cell changed at dawn. The new guard was brother to the first, so when they came to take the men from your cell to be executed, the second guard insisted you had already been moved. He knew if my stepfather discovered there had been an escape, both brothers would have been tortured and killed."

"It seems that fate smiled upon us all that night."

"Indeed." A victorious grin stretched across her lips.

"Tell me, why have you come all this way, Bethan of Lampeter?"

"I need a husband."

"You are a comely lass. 'Tis hardly necessary to travel such a great distance to find a man willing to marry you."

"I need a man with the courage and skill to defeat my stepfather, to free us once and for all from his savage brutality." She moved closer and placed her hand over his. "I believe you are that man, Lord Meifod."

In the depths of her eyes, Haydn could see her haunted sense of desperation. Her agony. Yet he forced himself to ignore it. With this offer came trouble—he could feel it deep in the marrow of his bones.

"I have no need of a wife," he answered. "I desire peace in my life, not vexation."

"Peace?" Her eyebrows arched. "A strange word for such a skilled warrior."

"I do not seek battles. I do not make war. I merely defend my own."

"I also wish to defend my people. But I cannot do it alone. Please, will you not aid me?"

Her simple plea touched him in a way he had not thought possible. More than anyone, he knew precisely the kind of evil that surrounded de Bellemare. She had survived it for years, but her strength was ebbing, her fear increasing.

He took a step closer, surprised by the sudden, savage need within him to protect this proud woman, this lovely mortal whose eyes glimmered with an odd mixture of desperation and strength. Haydn's gut clenched and he silently called himself a witless fool as his hand reached out to touch her face.

Lord Meifod's nearness produced a most unexpected effect on Bethan. With one hand he skimmed his knuckles over her cheek, a touch so gentle it turned her insides to knots. Fighting to quell the clamoring of her heart, Bethan smothered the impulse to turn her face into the caress.

She swallowed against the dryness in her throat. "Do we have a bargain?"

"I told you, I have no interest in acquiring a wife."

Bethan bit her lip in frustration. "Lampeter is a rich property. Our villeins are honest and hardworking, producing some of the finest goods in all of Wales. Once you defeat Lord Lampeter it will belong to you. As ruler, you will be a very wealthy man."

"I have no need of great wealth. My lands provide a more than adequate life for me."

"Is there nothing I can use to barter?"

The look he sent her made her heart skip a beat. "You are a lady. I will not dishonor you, tempting as it might be."

Bethan's cheeks stung with heat. That was not precisely what she meant, though in truth he had a mesmerizing, sensual presence that she found most appealing. Shockingly, she admitted if he had demanded she give herself to him in exchange for his aid, she would not have protested too hard or too long.

"You misunderstand, my lord. I know my—"

He curled his knuckles beneath her chin and slowly tilted her face to his. Their eyes locked. She read the passion simmering in his eyes and waited for whatever was to come.

"You saved my life and thus deserve my gratitude. For that reason only, I will journey to Lampeter and see what I can do to help you. I cannot promise marriage, but will seek another course." His voice was low, lulling. Heat, like scalding flames, crackled through the air. "Now go, before I do something dishonorable that we shall both regret."

A frisson of fear raced through her. Turning on her heel, Bethan scurried from the room. As she neared her chamber, her steps quickened, until she was practically sprinting. She yanked open the heavy door, ran through, then shut herself inside.

Bethan's breath blew out in short pants. Flattening her palms against the wooden door, she leaned into it for support. As her breathing came under control, she pressed her ear to the heavy wood. She could hear no footsteps, no sounds at all.

She was safe. For now.

A week later, as the mist swirled and the steady rain pounded, Haydn, flanked by a contingent of his most loyal, skilled knights, rode through the gates of Lampeter. He had sent a rider ahead, announcing their arrival and asking for shelter, ensuring that he would be admitted.

They were greeted in the courtyard by the castle steward, a man who had perfected a subservient, bowing manner that was distinctly annoying. He led Haydn and his knights into the great hall where de Bellemare awaited them.

"Lord Meifod."

"Lord Lampeter." Though it cost him much, Haydn bowed graciously.

"I bid you welcome. 'Tis an honor to meet the man they call the Warrior of the North."

De Bellemare did not rise from his seat on the dais, but instead looked down at Haydn, his arrogant expression revealing his belief of the power he held over everyone and everything around him.

"'Tis I who am honored to meet you, my lord."

Haydn attempted a smile, but failed. The need for vengeance against his bitter enemy burned through his veins and pounced with an ache in his skull, but he restrained himself. The six guards flanking de Bellemare were all large, muscular men. Even with the element of surprise, he would never be able to successfully strike at him.

Haydn noted that two were pale and not as alert as the others. He surmised de Bellemare had most recently feasted upon those two. Though it was something he did not do, 'twas a common practice to keep a close contingency of mortals around to ensure a steady supply of fresh blood upon which to feed. That he took the risk of using his personal guards spoke of de Bellemare's arrogance. But he was not a fool. The fresh blood kept his powers sharp, his strength nearly unbeatable.

Haydn sighed with genuine regret. When he agreed to journey here, he knew it was the perfect time to seek his revenge. He had hoped to do so without directly involving Bethan. But now that he had assessed the situation, he knew he would not be able to destroy de Bellemare as quickly as he had hoped.

He would have to stay, study de Bellemare's movements, then plan a surprise attack. There was no other way. In order to stay, Haydn would have to marry Bethan.

"Tell me, Lord Meifod, was there a specific purpose for your visit?"

"I hear you have an unmarried daughter."

"I do." The eyes that assessed him were unblinking, hard and ruthless. "Do you wish to meet her?"

"I have no interest in her face or figure. I care only about her dowry. And forming an alliance with you."

"I will not deceive you. She is not much of a woman; willful, outspoken, at times almost unruly," Lord Lampeter remarked.

Haydn shrugged. "Even the most difficult creature can be beaten into submission."

De Bellemare laughed, his eyes smoldering with delight. "You!" he barked, pointing a finger at a young servant, who paled with fright at being noticed by his master. "Bring us wine. I have important business to discuss with Lord Meifod."

Bethan paced her bedchamber anxiously, waiting for a summons from her stepfather. She had seen Haydn riding proudly into Lampeter, his back straight, his chin raised, his banner of blue and gold snapping in the rain. But that had been hours ago. Surely by now something had been resolved?

The door opened and Sir Colwyn poked his head inside. "Your stepfather has ordered you to stay in your chambers tonight. If you behave, I can fetch you something to eat. If you complain, or disobey, I was told to lock you inside and guard the door."

"But what about Lord Meifod? Is he still here? What is happening?"

"I know not." The old knight shook his head. "Meifod is here, cozing up to de Bellemare like a calf suckling from his mother's teat. There are rumors flying that he has asked for your hand in marriage, but nothing has been announced."

Bethan's lips quivered with agitation. Her stepfather and Haydn thick as thieves? The image did not sit well in her mind. Though she would dearly love to storm the great hall and discover what was going on, Bethan feared Sir Colwyn would be punished if she disobeyed her stepfather's orders.

"I shall wait here. Please, promise you will bring me word the moment you learn anything?"

The knight agreed. Left alone for the next few hours, Bethan fought to control her worry. She paced the floor of her bedchamber until she had worn a path in the rushes. Finally, when she thought she would go stark raving mad, there was a knock at her door. She opened it, then gasped with surprise.

Lord Meifod stood framed in the doorway, his expression grim. "I need to speak with you."

She glanced hastily down the corridor, thankful no one was in view, then yanked him inside and slammed the door.

"Our wedding will take place in two days," he announced without preamble.

"So soon?"

Haydn's somber gaze held hers for an unsettled moment, his gray eyes glowing in the flickering candlelight. "If you have changed your mind about the marriage, I shall tell de Bellemare I do not want it. 'Tis your choice."

"I will marry you." She moved close and touched his sleeve. "I am grateful for your help, but surprised at your decision. When we spoke at your castle, you seemed most set against marriage."

"There is no other way. De Bellemare is surrounded by his personal guard. It will take time, planning, and luck to find an opportunity to strike at him." Haydn's eyes flashed with emotion. "However, I shall stay only until he is destroyed and you are free from his tryanny. No longer. Do you understand?"

Bethan pulled her hand back and frowned. "Once he is dead, you expect me to leave here, to live with you in your castle in the north?"

"No! I will be here but a brief time. And when I leave, I will never return. I will never see you again."

"Oh." Bethan bit her bottom lip as a confusing riot of emotions turned over in her heart.

"Is there a way for you to dissolve the marriage after I have gone?" he asked.

Bethan exhaled sharply. "Divorce? Is that what you demand?"

He raked a hand through his dark hair. "I will not be here as a husband to you, Bethan. In fairness, you should have the chance to choose another."

The image of spending the rest of her life alone, without the joy of a good husband and the comfort of children, brought a lump of anguish to her throat. But she willed it away. She had to be strong, had to accept that this was her destiny.

"A second husband is the very least of my concerns. However, there is something else I must tell you." Bethan's gaze shifted away for a second, her mind searching for the right words. "My stepfather will not be easy to destroy. There is true evil in him, something . . . unnatural."

A cold grin stole across Haydn's handsome features. "I can handle de Bellemare."

"Does this revelation not disturb you?" she asked, surprised at the complacent expression on his face, worried he did not understand the magnitude of this problem. "His powers give him a great advantage."

"I am not afraid. All things can be destroyed, Bethan, including evil."

His harsh, arrogant tone sent a shiver done her spine. His attitude was confusing, for he did not seem to be dismissing her warning, but rather embracing it. She had the distinct and uncomfortable feeling he was keeping something from her, something very important.

"Has my stepfather announced our marriage?"

"Not yet. I think he plans to do so in the morning. I advise you to look none too pleased when you are given the news. I believe it will give de Bellemare great joy to see you miserable."

"Aye."

Haydn lingered in her chamber for another moment, his

keen gaze rooted on hers. "There is still time to change your mind. If you do so, send word to me through Sir Colwyn."

Bethan nodded, but she knew there was no going back. He bowed his head, then left. Slowly, she closed the door, then leaned against it. She had orchestrated this entire chain of events. It was what she wanted, and yet Bethan admitted a part of her was afraid of Haydn. The darkness, the violence, the isolation that seemed to cling to him like a shroud was fearful and disturbing.

But another part made her want to hope. To dream. To dare to believe that he was the one man who could defeat her stepfather and set them all free.

But at what price? Bethan shuddered. Wearily, she lifted her hand to her brow. God help her, what had she done?

Bethan stood beside Haydn outside the church doors. Feeling too nervous to look at her groom, she instead glanced down at the royal-blue gown she wore. The dress had been a surprise gift from her mother, the long cuffs lovingly embroidered with golden flowers and vines, the shade matching the silken lining of the garment. Tight-fitting, it was fastened around her waist with an intricately twisted gold belt. In addition, she wore a long, finely woven veil that had belonged to her grandmother. It covered her shoulders and hung down to her feet, concealing her hair, which had been plaited and decorated with pearls.

She felt pretty in her bridal finery, pleased that she had gone to the effort, especially after a quick glimpse of her groom. His strong legs were encased in dark hose, his feet in soft leather boots. His scarlet surcoat was made from the finest material and his coat-of-arms, a mighty griffin with its wings outstretched, was embroidered upon it with precious stones, leaving no question as to his wealth.

In keeping with tradition, the bride and groom exchanged their vows outside the church doors. The chapel at Lampeter was squat and round and crafted of simple stone. Not as pretty or grand as the churches that boasted stained glass, high steeples, and beautiful statues, it was nevertheless a place of true sanctuary for Bethan, for it was seldom used by her stepfather.

Bethan was proud that her voice did not waver as she spoke her vows, nor did Haydn's. She meant every word as she vowed to have and to hold from this day forward, for better, for worse, for richer, for poorer, in sickness and in health, till death did them part, if the holy church would ordain it. She reasoned God would forgive the prior agreement she had made with Haydn if she kept those promises to remain a true wife.

Entering a marriage when she knew her husband had no intention of living with her for any length of time might be considered dishonest by some, but Bethan had every intention of honoring her commitment to be faithful and true to him for the rest of her life. She hoped fervently that God would understand.

With the vows exchanged, the newly married couple bowed their heads for the priest's blessing. At that moment, a thick fog rolled in, encircling them in an eerie, mystical cocoon, separating them from the rest of the guests.

She heard murmuring behind her that this was a sign, an omen of sorts. Good or bad? Bethan could not hear the determination, but she chose to believe it was a good sign.

Father William efficiently calmed the crowd and invited everyone inside the church to celebrate the nuptial mass. Though she tried, Bethan had difficulty concentrating. Her mind wandered as she twisted the ring she now wore on her finger, a gold band with a dark jewel of bloodred that shimmered with fire.

At the conclusion of the Mass, Father William invited the groom to kiss his new bride. Haydn took her face in his hands, framing the delicate bones of her cheeks. He angled his head and swiftly kissed her closed lips. Bethan barely had time to savor the sensation because it was over so fast. Swallowing back her disappointment, she smiled at her groom, then turned to face the crowd.

They retired to the great hall, to indulge in the feast that had been prepared. For the first time since the day began, Bethan risked a glance at her stepfather. He sat in his chair on the dais, his arms crossed, frowning with displeasure.

Her mother had mentioned that de Bellemare was annoyed with the expense of the wedding feast, but faced with her groom's obvious wealth had little choice but to provide a suitable celebratory meal. The servants had been thrilled to have the opportunity to show their love and gratitude toward Bethan, and their efforts were much appreciated by her.

Fresh herbs and bunches of wildflowers had been hung from the rafters of the great hall above the rows and rows of trestle tables. On the dais the table was set with a white linen cloth, and gold plates and goblets had been placed in front of every chair. Rose petals were strewn along the edge, adding a touch of color and a pleasing scent.

The tables fairly groaned under the vast array of food that was hot and ready to eat. Platters of veal dressed with vinegar, baked trout, tarts filled with spicy pork, stuffed roasted boar, goose in a sauce of grapes and garlic, stewed cabbage flavored with cinnamon and cloves, and thick crusty bread flavored with ale were soon emptied and fresh food brought out.

Ewers of ale, mead, and spiced wine were quickly emptied and refilled as various toasts of goodwill and happiness were offered to the bride and groom. Minstrels filled the air with the sounds of harp and lute, which blended with the tinkling sounds of laughter. Bethan could not remember a time when the great hall had been filled with so much boisterous life and merriment.

Midway through the meal the contingency of soldiers seated below them started pounding on the wooden trestle tables with the edges of their swords. Within minutes, the sound grew deafening. Bethan stole a glance at her husband. His brow was furrowed in confusion.

"They want you to kiss me," she whispered as she leaned closer. "For luck."

His silver eyes narrowed. "If they demand it, then I suppose we must."

Bethan licked her lips in preparation, expecting another quick, almost impersonal kiss similar to the one he had bestowed upon her at the church. But just as Haydn was about to lower his head, a deep voice rang out from the crowd.

"Kiss her like you mean it, my lord!"

The words stopped him cold. A new determination ignited a glint in his eyes as a salacious, challenging smile curved his mouth.

One large hand slipped behind Bethan's neck at the same moment the other curled around her waist. Haydn pulled her off her feet and into his arms, holding her so tightly she almost couldn't breathe. Bethan's heart began to race as she felt her breasts crush against the solid wall of Haydn's chest, but she ignored the rush of embarrassment, concentrating instead on the tingling anticipation. This was her second kiss and despite the audience she intended to make it a private moment.

She thought she was ready, yet Bethan felt a startling shock as he brought his mouth down on hers. His lips were supple but insistent, almost commanding. Warm, firm, and expertly sensual, his kiss awakened a sudden yearning deep within her soul. At the urging of his tongue, pressing boldly against the seam of her lips, she opened to him.

The nature of their kiss changed. He was no longer gentle, and oddly that pleased her. Haydn tilted his head and pressed a little harder, his mouth hot and hungry as it captured hers. She breathed in and smelled his skin, spicy and inviting.

Her knees wanted to give way, her heart pounded harder and faster. He stroked her lower lip with his tongue and the desire within her shot into flame. Bethan raised her hand and wrapped her arm around the back of his neck. Haydn responded by pulling her closer. Now their bodies touched. Everywhere.

Heated arousal swirled down her spine. The rumbling noise of tankards being banged on the wooden tables, hoots, hollers, and whistles gradually penetrated her mind. Slowly Bethan opened her eyes. A blush of embarrassment colored her cheeks as he let her slide slowly down to her feet. She buried her face in his neck for a few seconds, struggling for composure, then lifted herself away and looked at him.

Haydn appeared as stunned as she felt. His touch lingered on her face for a moment longer, firm and warm. She parted her lips, but could not catch her breath to speak.

The noise in the hall grew louder. Haydn flashed a wicked smile at her, then exhaled sharply through his teeth. Turning toward the frenzied crowd of screaming men, he lifted his goblet of wine skyward and shouted loudly, "A toast. To my bride, whose beauty and courage are beyond compare."

Four

The wedding celebration went on into the wee hours of the morning, but at midnight Lady Caryn, along with two older serving women, escorted Bethan from the hall. She was grateful that Haydn had refused to allow a formal bedding ceremony, reasoning it would be easier if they were alone.

When she entered her room, she hardly recognized the chamber. Her small, narrow bed had been replaced with an enormous canopied one. Against the far wall stood a wooden wardrobe, large enough to house clothing for her and Haydn. Candles had been lit and placed on a trestle table; dried herbs and scented flowers had been mixed into the clean rushes strewn about on the floors.

Bethan deliberately kept her mind and expression blank as the women helped prepare her for her bridal bed. Carefully they undressed her, reverently folding the fine garments of her wedding outfit. After a brief wash, Lady Caryn herself pulled the simple night rail of white linen over her daughter's head. Then taking a comb, she brushed Bethan's golden hair to a fine sheen, placing a wreath of wildflowers on the crown of her head when she was done.

"For luck," she whispered in Bethan's ear. "And fertility."

The room was eerily quiet after they left. Bethan wondered if she should leave the privacy provided by the dressing screen her mother had thoughtfully provided and await her husband in bed. Nervously, she twirled a strand of hair around her finger as she considered her predicament.

The door opened, then closed. The butterflies in Bethan's stomach fluttered so violently she thought she might become ill. She waited a long moment, unsure of what she would find when she stepped from behind the screen. Would he be standing there, waiting? Unclothed, perhaps? Or would he already be in the bed?

Taking a deep breath, Bethan emerged. Haydn was seated on the only chair at the small table near the fire, a goblet of wine in his hand. He silently offered her a drink, but she declined by shaking her head, fearing her voice would tremble.

Biting her lower lip, Bethan turned her gaze upon him. He smiled, though he said nothing, watching her expectantly as he drank from a goblet of wine. He had removed his tunic and shirt, but still wore his hose and boots. The firelight danced on the naked flesh of his upper torso, illuminating an impressive expanse of hard muscle and lean lines. A dusting of dark hair spread across the planes of his wide chest, tapering to a single line across his corded belly.

"Goodness, wife, you look pale as a ghost. Do you fear that I shall ravish you on the spot?"

She attempted a smile. And failed.

"Though I am far older than most brides, I am still an untouched maid," Bethan responded, tilting her chin for courage. "My mother has explained the act, though I confess to being unprepared."

"Preparation is the man's job. If you desire it."

"Sir?"

"I have never laid an unwanted hand on a woman before," he said mildly. "And I most certainly do not intend to start now."

"I am your wife. 'Twould be a sin for me to refuse you."

"I give you leave to refuse me, wife."

He turned from her and slowly poured more wine into his goblet. Bethan's body began to quake as she realized he meant it. The decision was hers. What did she truly want?

Her heart began to race as she pictured herself kissing him. Not just on the lips, but everywhere. His chiseled jaw, the pulse beating sensually at his throat, against the dark hair on his chest down to the flat stomach below.

No matter what happened tomorrow or the next day, or the day after that, Bethan knew with all her heart that she wanted this to continue. With this man.

"Teach me how to please you, husband."

Bethan's voice pulled Haydn into the moment. He lifted his head and turned to face her, and the pleasant speech he had prepared vanished from his mind. He was caught in her stare as though she held him in a spell. Her lanky frame was silhouetted by the orange glow of the fire that blazed behind her. Her long golden hair was unbound and draped about her shoulders like a veil. Somehow he knew it would feel as soft and silky as it looked and he imagined his fingers wandering through that glorious mass.

Images flashed into his mind, each more lurid than the last. He closed his eyes, remembering the kiss they had shared in the hall. The feel of her lips and tongue and soft, supple body had easily shattered his defenses.

She moved closer. Haydn reached out and caught her hand. Holding it to his mouth, he placed a kiss in the cradle of her palm.

"I want there to be no misunderstanding between us," he declared. "I will stay with you only until I have accomplished my task and freed you all from de Bellemare's tyranny. If tonight you wish to be my wife in truth, I will gladly accommodate you, but I make no promises beyond our bargain."

"I expect no more," she replied.

Haydn barely caught the laugh of irony that formed on his lips. "Mortal . . . ahh . . . women are known for changing their minds about this sort of thing."

The dreamy, faraway cloud of emotion in Bethan's eyes vanished. "I am a practical woman who knows that my survival, and that of my people, rests on one thing. De Bellemare must be destroyed and I wholly believe you are the man who can accomplish that task. You are my champion and that is all I shall ever demand of you, Haydn."

Bethan's gaze bored into him. Unfamiliar emotions he could neither name nor identify assailed him. It took every ounce of discipline he possessed to stop himself from pulling her into his arms and kissing her senseless.

"I will be your champion," he proclaimed.

He gently placed a sensual kiss on the delicate inside of her wrist, feeling her pulse leap as his lips tasted her flesh.

A sweep of color rose to her cheeks, but she did not lower her eyes. "You are also my husband and I very much want to be your wife. In all things. For as long as you are here with me."

Hellfire!

Desire, long simmering, rose to the boil. Primal male instinct, no longer in check, assumed control. Haydn shifted forward in his chair and pulled Bethan into his lap. She came to him with a startled yelp.

It had been far too long since he took a woman, Haydn told himself. Or perhaps it was the kiss they had shared in the hall earlier that had stirred his passion to such heights. For an instant he wondered if the intense desire he had felt had been a fluke, an emotion and passion brought on by the heat of the moment.

Haydn bent his head, intending only a gentle kiss. Yet the moment their mouths met, Bethan opened to him with a small gasp, parting her lips and reaching up to him. With a groan, his tongue entered, finding, then stroking hers, darting deeper, then withdrawing.

Lust swept through him like a hot wind. In that moment he admitted the truth, acknowledged that he wanted to lose himself within her. Only her. Only Bethan.

His hard gaze unable to conceal his desire, Haydn let his free hand trace a gentle pattern along her delicate jaw and neck. She trembled under his touch, her breathing shallow.

He stood suddenly, holding her in his arms, knocking over the chair. She gave a startled cry when he dumped her in the middle of the bed, then lifted the edge of her night rail and swiftly pulled it over her head. Eyes pinned to her now nude body, Haydn tore off his hose and boots.

Naked, almost painfully aroused, he paused a moment to look at her. Her skin was the color of fresh milk, her breasts firm and full, the rosy peaks aching for his touch. Her legs were long and well formed, her waist slender, her hips curved. A blush colored her cheeks at his intense scrutiny, but she made no move to cover herself.

"I like it when you look at me," she confessed in a wicked whisper.

"You are a very beautiful woman," he rasped.

"I am your woman."

She arched upward, offering herself. Her sensual abandon intoxicated him far more than any of the spirits he had consumed that day. He leaned in and kissed her, trailing his hands over her bare back, then moving forward to her front. He teased her with his tongue, with gentle nips of his teeth, and she gave a shuddering moan in response.

Excited by her response, he ran his fingers lightly across her breasts. She gasped when he squeezed the hardened nipples. Taking a shuddering breath, he bent down, replacing his fingers with his tongue. He kissed her, lapped her, teased her, suckled her. She made a small noise in the back of her throat and lifted her hips.

Smiling with savage determination, Haydn reached between her legs, sliding his hand up her smooth thigh. His thumb rubbed and circled and teased. Within moments she was swollen and wet and writhing on the bed.

Passion nearly blinded him. He shifted, moving down her body, spreading the plump folds that guarded her womanhood, exposing the perfect pearl inside. Bethan cried out, arching her back, lifting herself off the mattress. Haydn never hesitated. He moved between her silken thighs and placed an open-mouth kiss on the very heart of her.

She stiffened. Shocked? Frightened? Embarrassed? The reasons were unimportant to him. She had said she wanted to be his in every way and this was one of the ways. His fingers clutched her hips, lifting her closer. His tongue slid between the curls and settled against her swollen, sensitive flesh. He continued to feather his tongue over her, gently laving, then sucking.

She cried out again, helpless in her pleasure, her hands grasping at his shoulders. His tempo increased to match the frantic thrust of her hips, his tongue stroking rhythmically over that one magical spot, until she gave a sharp gasp and her entire body began to shudder.

Her climax unleashed the devil within Haydn. He grabbed a pillow from the head of the bed and shoved it under her hips, tilting her upward. Desire consumed every inch of his flesh, passion coursed swiftly and heatedly through his veins. He felt on fire, fully aroused and nearly trembling with need. Knowing he could wait no longer to possess her, Haydn nudged her legs farther apart with his knee, covered her fully, and thrust inside.

She screamed as he filled her, a strangled moan of equal parts pain and pleasure. He paused, his desire faltering. He had not realized that breaking through her maidenhead would be so painful.

Her face was buried against the side of his neck. He heard the muffled sound of her voice and nearly yelled out with frustration. Awash in an agony of pleasure, he moved his hand to cup her skull, holding her so he could look into her eyes.

"Are you stopping?" she asked. "Is it over?"

He saw the confusion, the frustration in her eyes. Her fingers clutched at his hair, tugging hard. He was unsure what she wanted. "Are you in pain? Do you want me to stop?"

"No!"

He might have laughed, had not his passion been so deeply aroused. It pleased him to know that she was not afraid, that she wanted to continue. Propping himself up on his forearms, Haydn stared down to where they were joined. It was an obscene, tantalizing sight to see himself swallowed inside her body. An unexpectedly emotional and humbling experience not being able to determine where he ended and she began.

"I am still with you, Bethan."

He felt her move and realized she was also looking.

"We are one," she whispered in awe. "Oh, Haydn."

His control crumbled. Withdrawing but a few inches in a slow, measured stroke, Haydn brought her legs around him and then thrust forward, filling her again. He reached between them to stroke her as he moved within her, then felt her body soften, relax.

It was heaven. He was buried inside her to the hilt, her softness surrounding him. Gritting his teeth, Haydn set a steady rhythm, holding back his release as he pumped into her. His patience was soon rewarded as her soft cries and murmurs intensified and she began to undulate beneath him, her movements mirroring his thrusts.

He felt the first shudder radiate from her body into his, heard her strangled cry. She trembled, her inner muscles tightened around him as the convulsions overtook her, her shout of delight echoing throughout their candlelit chamber.

Her climax gave him his. He grew harder, thrust deeper, then savagely filled her womb with the sudden, hot rush of his seed.

Thoroughly sated, limp with exhaustion, Haydn pushed himself into a kneeling position, pulled out of her, and slid to the edge of the bed. Bethan lay sprawled wantonly on her back, her thighs slightly parted, her eyes closed, her skin flushed, her hair a golden tangle among the rumbled bed linens. Her expression was one of utter contentment, bringing him a stab of masculine pride, knowing he had done that to her.

She mumbled and shifted her legs. He could see streaks of pink on her inner thighs and the covers beneath. Marks of her recently lost virginity.

The sight pleased him. He had never before lain with a virgin and it gave him an odd sense of possession and ownership knowing he had been her first.

He had done his duty by her and in the process brought them each great pleasure. But now it was over. Every instinct coursing through his veins told him to walk to the other side of the room and sit by the fire, calmly drinking another goblet of wine until she fell asleep. Given her state of pure contentment and exhaustion, it would not take long.

Yet he found that he could not bring himself to leave her. Crawling forward, Haydn snaked his arm around Bethan's waist and slowly pulled her into the center of the large bed. He stretched out beside her, adjusting their positions so that their bodies were pressed close.

Bethan let out a small sigh of contentment and curled into him. Her skin was unbearably soft. Idly, Haydn stroked her shoulder, marveling at how the trusting yielding of a woman's body could bring him such a strong measure of peace. It made him realize how alone he had been for so very long, how desperate he had been for the warmth of another's touch.

Shaking his head at such weak, fanciful thoughts, he pulled the furs over them. Trying to ignore the strong sense of possession he felt toward this woman, Haydn listened to the gentle cadence of her breathing. Then gradually he, too, allowed sleep to claim his weary body.

* * *

Bethan awoke with her cheek nestled on Haydn's bare chest, her body pressed against his, one of her legs settled between his thighs. The room was bathed in an eerie glow of sputtering candles and glowing embers from the low-burning fire in the grate. No sunlight, nor moonlight for that matter, invaded the chamber.

Puzzled, Bethan glanced at the window on the far side of the room and realized it was covered with a dark swath of material. Haydn's cloak? She shifted her weight, intending to investigate, but the movement woke her slumbering husband.

"Is it morning?" he inquired huskily.

She shook her head. "I am uncertain. I think 'tis still night." She moved herself into a half-reclining position, staring intently at the hidden window. "Why did you place your cloak over the window?"

"To ward off the chill," he explained.

Her brow rose in confusion. "I had no idea you were so affected by the cold."

"'Tis a grave secret that I shield from others." He sighed with exaggeration. "Truth be told, I have a most delicate constitution."

Was he jesting with her? Startled, she gazed down at his fit, muscular body, then up to his face where the merest hint of a smile curled his lips. The Warrior of the North was teasing her? The notion produced a sudden, almost painful tug on her heart.

Uncertain how to interpret this unexpected, playful side to his character, she huddled down beside him. Her hand rested on his chest. When he moved, she felt the ripple of hard muscle under her fingers and the steady, heavy thump of his heart.

"It must be night," she muttered. "All is quiet and still inside the castle."

"Sleep. I am certain you are exhausted."

"No, not really. The small nap I just took has revived me."

She ran her hand over the knotted contours of his arms and chest. His physique was beautiful, the skin sleek and smooth. "You have no scars, no wounds at all. 'Tis strange for a warrior of your experience."

He opened one eye and stared at her. "And what do you know of warrior's scars, wife?"

Bethan smiled. She liked hearing him call her wife. "I have seen the soldiers on the practice field. When it gets too warm, they often remove their tunics and continue the training bare-chested."

Haydn snorted. "Saints preserve us all from curious maidens. No doubt the men worked harder to build up a sweat, knowing you were ogling them."

Laughing, she turned toward him, pressing her mouth to his chest, impishly sending her tongue across his nipple.

Haydn went perfectly still. Curious, Bethan did it again. He groaned, softly. Encouraged, she swirled her tongue around the turgid peak, then pulled it into her mouth and sucked. Hard.

He muttered a few words and she continued. Featherlight, her fingers slid down his belly, across his firm stomach. She smiled as his penis sprang up against her hand. The air grew sultry with need.

"More," he rasped.

Bethan's heavy-lidded gaze followed the path of her fingers. Thick and hard, his penis thrust out from a thatch of dark hair at his groin. Her hand looked very small as her fingers closed around the width of him.

She felt him shudder. Bethan drew her hand up the stiff length of him, then repeated the motion going down to the root. He moaned, flexing his hips. The response delighted her. It made her feel wanton, womanly, in control.

He caught at her hand, clamping his large one over hers, holding it immobile. Bethan, fearing he would pull it away, protested instantly. "No, let me."

For a minute he used her hand to stroke himself. Eagerly, Bethan followed his instruction. When he let go she continued the movements he had taught her, using her thumb to spread the silky bead of liquid that leaked from the tip all around the jutting head.

He pressed himself more firmly against her, grinding his hips madly, then with an oath falling from his lips, pulled away. Dismayed, Bethan reached for him, but he held himself out of her reach.

"'Tis late. You should sleep."

His words angered her. She was restless, edgy, filled with a need that only he could fulfill. And he wanted her to sleep? "I can sleep anytime, husband. I have but one wedding night to indulge myself."

He stared down at her, his silver eyes fierce. "I rode you hard, my little virgin. You will be sore," he warned.

"Probably." She shrugged. And waited. And when he made no move, she reached out with both hands and curled them around his still hard penis.

He sucked in a sharp breath. Quick as a flash of lightning, he flipped her onto her back, pulled her close, and covered her mouth with his. The heat from his body warmed her, the press of his lips and tongue delighted her. With a sigh of excitement, Bethan wrapped her arms around Haydn's neck, giving herself completely to the moment, and the man.

The next time Bethan awoke, the chamber was empty. Noting the hour was far later than usual, she summoned her maid. After a quick, thorough wash, she selected a deep red gown, delicately embroidered with silver thread around the scooped neckline and tapered cuffs. She plaited her hair, leaving one long golden braid down the center of her back, then added a short, simple linen veil.

Bethan descended the winding stairs to the great hall

with a heart that felt lighter than it had in years. As she reached the bottom of the stairs, she spied Haydn rising from his seat on the dais.

Eagerly she started toward him, feeling a blush of color warm her cheeks as she remembered their ardent love-making. Yet the shy smile of greeting died on her lips as Haydn brushed past her with barely a glance, not even a nod of acknowledgment. For an instant Bethan was too stunned to react. But her hurt was soon pushed aside, replaced by a crushing sense of anger. How dare he treat her so?

"My lord! My lord!"

She trailed after him, running to catch up. He ignored her cries, but she quickened her pace. Somehow she was able to grab the sleeve of his tunic, forcing him to stop and turn to her. Yet before she could speak, Haydn clamped a fist around her upper arm and pulled her close.

"Slap me," he whispered in her ear.

"What?"

"Slap me! Hard. Your stepfather is watching."

Angry enough to oblige him, Bethan swung her open palm at his handsome face. But he was too fast for her. Capturing her wrist, he twisted her arm up over her head. She jerked and kicked, trying to break free, but he slammed her against the stone wall, immobilizing her with his hips.

"What are you doing?" Her breath came in gasping pants.

"Keeping you safe." Slowly, deliberately, he ran one finger down her throat, lingering on the wildly beating pulse at the base.

The sound of raucous laughter reached her ears. Bethan jerked her head to the left and saw several grinning knights watching the exchange. Behind them, with a smug smile of satisfaction on his lips, stood the Lord of Lampeter.

"Come, Lord Meifod. We have important matters to attend," de Bellemare shouted. "You can *play* with your wife later."

"Forgive me." Haydn spoke barely above a whisper, studying her, his face expressionless. Then without a backward glance he released her, and strode away.

Her hands shook as her heart clamored in her chest. Though he appeared to be doing it for her stepfather's benefit, Bethan was horrified at the way her husband had treated her. Humiliated, embarrassed, angry, and hurt, she tried to go about her business as if it did not matter, but the day had been ruined, the hope within her dashed.

The next three days were among the most miserable of Bethan's life. Haydn spent all his time in the company of her stepfather. If he happened upon Bethan during the course of his day, her husband either ignored her or made a crude remark.

Though a logical part of her mind realized it was necessary for Haydn to get close to de Bellemare, to understand his enemy before he could defeat him, it was nevertheless a painful time. Her bed remained empty at night, her heart lonely and frightened during the day.

Rumors reached her ears of raids with neighboring villages, sport with other women. She tried to stifle the concern building inside her, yet these tales worried her, made her feel guilty. Each day, the knowledge that she had brought the Warrior of the North to Lampeter, had welcomed him into her bed and into her life, tore at her heart.

On the afternoon of the fourth day, Bethan reached a decision. She could not go on like this, speculating as to Haydn's motivation, not fully understanding his actions. She knew she must confront her husband, must hear from his lips precisely what he was planning.

Her mood sour, Bethan walked briskly through the courtyard, trying to decide how best to approach Haydn, when a shout rang out. Villeins began running and she was swept up in the moving crowd. They stopped short at the edge of a solid wall of people and Bethan found herself jostled toward the front.

Excitement charged the air and Bethan soon realized the reason. Two knights were fighting and it was quickly apparent this was not a practice drill, but a personal argument. Bethan froze as she recognized Haydn as one of the combatants. The men were equal in height, but Haydn was pure muscle, giving him the clear advantage.

They fought with their fists, not swords, and truth be told 'twas not much of a fight. Haydn ducked and swung, landing blows, yet receiving none. Frustrated, the knight lowered his head and charged, but Haydn easily smashed his face into the wall of a nearby building with a resounding crack that made her cringe. The man screamed as blood spouted from his nose and mouth.

Pulling him up by the collar, Haydn hit him in the jaw. The knight collapsed at Haydn's feet. As he lay on the ground, Haydn pulled his sword from its leather scabbard, then lifted his arms high over his head.

"Stop! For God's sake, stop!"

Bethan screamed in distress, but Haydn never hesitated. She cringed, trying to avert her eyes but she was too slow turning her head away. To her horror, she witnessed the final blow, as Haydn swiped his blade smoothly across his opponent's throat. There were gasps from the crowd, along with several shouts of approval. With a sickened stomach, Bethan scurried from the scene, her eyes nearly blinded by unshed tears.

Minutes later, Haydn found her in the chapel.

"Bethan?"

She swallowed hard and prayed for strength as she rose slowly from her knees. He took a step forward and she gasped, recoiling.

"You are afraid of me?"

Tightly fisting her hands to keep them from shaking,

Bethan squared her shoulders and tried to prepare herself for this confrontation. "Should I not be afraid? You have become little more than de Bellemare's lackey, spending your days and nights by his side. The castle buzzes with rumors of your actions, tales of your cruelty."

"'Tis merely gossip."

"Perhaps. But with my own eyes I have witnessed your brutality."

"Are you speaking of the man in the courtyard?"

"There are others?" Bethan covered her face with her hands, the fatigue and grief overwhelming her.

Without another word Haydn turned and left the chapel.

A sob escaped from her throat as Bethan fell back to her knees and began to pray.

Haydn returned, but this time he was not alone. Beside him stood a young girl. The lass looked no more than ten and was in a sorry state. Dressed in little more than tattered, filthy rags, she was pale and emaciated. Ugly bruises and lacerations marred her cheeks. Her right eyelid drooped half-closed, puffy and discolored, and her lower lip was split open in several places.

"Tell her," Haydn commanded the girl. "Tell her about the man I slayed in the courtyard."

The girl shivered, looked at him, helpless, afraid. "I . . . I . . ."

"You are safe now." Haydn's voice was soft, gentle. "Tell Lady Bethan what happened to you."

The girl hesitated a moment more; then her voice came out in a rush of emotion. "He beat me, my lady, when I would not do as he asked. I should have let him, for he took what he wanted anyway."

"He raped you?" Bethan asked softly.

"Aye." Her head lowered and a tear slid down her face. "Several times. He was going to do it again, but this time I screamed and Lord Meifod heard and came to my aid."

"Oh, you poor child." Bethan reached out a comforting

hand and laid it on the girl's head. "You must go to the kitchen and ask for Anne. Tell her I sent you. She will have salve for your bruises and hot food for your belly."

"Thank you, my lady." The girl curtsied, then sniffed, wiping her nose on the sleeve of her dirty gown.

With one final glance of worshipful eyes at Haydn, she left. Once they were alone, Bethan had difficulty meeting her husband's eyes.

"I owe you an apology, my lord," she said primly. "It appears this knight was a man who deserved killing."

"Indeed. 'Tis why I chose him." The candlelight fell on his face, revealing a surprising mix of emotions—confusion, concern, guilt. "I want you to know that while I have been much in de Bellemare's company these past few days, 'tis not something I have enjoyed. Far from it."

She nodded. "I was praying that your behavior was only because you needed to prove yourself to him, to prove your skill, your worth. Yet I confess it has been most painful for me to watch, and equally hurtful to be treated so shabbily by you."

"Forgive me." He placed his large hand over her small one. "I did not realize you would be so upset. I should have told you, should have explained what I was doing with de Bellemare. I am sorry if I caused you worry and pain. 'Twas never my intention."

She turned her hand over and gave his a squeeze. "Thank you for explaining. I feel honored to be in your trust."

"I do not give it lightly."

For the first time in four days, Bethan smiled. "Nor do I."

He put his other hand on her shoulder, then gently turned her face to his. "I have missed you, wife."

She studied his angular face and her heart thumped with emotion. "Will you come to our chamber tonight?"

His eyes widened, his lips curved. "Yes."

Haydn leaned closer. Their mouths met with no hesitation, in a short, openmouthed tender kiss that held a sweetness tinged with a hint of longing.

Haydn spent the remainder of the day as he had these past three, at de Bellemare's beck and call. By the evening meal he was ready to scream with frustration, having more than his fill of the older man's plans and schemes.

Yet what bothered Haydn most was that a part of him was drawn to this savagery. He and de Bellemare were of the same kind. He possessed the same primitive instincts as his enemy, was capable of the same brutality.

Haydn shuddered as a wave of self-loathing engulfed him. He saw the possibility of his future. He saw that if he did not learn to harness his power, if he could not learn to control his lust, to suppress the savagery of his nature, he would become like his enemy. A creature with no conscience, a being who existed in a crimson haze of bloodlust.

Haydn's thoughts were troubled as he climbed the stairs. He wanted to destroy his enemy and leave this castle as soon as possible, but it was proving far more difficult than he thought to challenge de Bellemare. The older man was clever; his guards were around him at all times. Haydn needed to find a vulnerability and exploit it or else he would never accomplish his task.

Bethan was awake when he entered their bedchamber. His eyes met hers and for a moment something passed between them. He was glad they had talked earlier in the chapel. It had cleared the air between them, but more importantly had united them in a shared purpose, a shared burden, a shared trust.

"I have something to show you," she said. "'Tis a book Father William has given me."

"It can wait." Haydn closed the distance between them in three strides. He took her in his arms and clutched her tightly to his body, breathing in her warm, intoxicating scent. "I need you, Bethan of Lampeter. I need to bury myself deep inside you, where there is goodness and joy. Will you welcome me in your bed?"

Her eyes softened. "Always."

Five

Haydn's footsteps quickened with anticipation as he cut through the alley behind the village tavern. He had spent far more time in the armorer this evening than he had intended and was anxious to return to the castle, to his chambers where Bethan was waiting for him.

Their relationship had taken a significant turn after they had spoken in the chapel a few days ago. Though still cautious, they were more relaxed and open around each other.

Each agreed that the burdens and worries of the day had been far easier to bear now that their nights were spent in each other's arms.

"Stop!" The bulky shape of a tall, brawny man suddenly stepped from a shadowed doorway, blocking the path.

"Who goes there?" Haydn peered at the figure through the darkness, trying to get a look at his face.

"Hand over your money," the brute demanded. The blade of a broadsword flashed out of the man's cloak, the tip pressing against Haydn's chest.

The sudden, unprovoked attack triggered rage inside him. Quick as lightning he turned, knocking the sword away, then grabbed his assailant around the neck. The man screamed and thrashed, trying to free himself. Muscles straining, Haydn shoved him hard against the wall, hearing a distinct crack when his head connected with the stone. The man went limp.

Panting with breath, Haydn shifted the man's bulk, rolling the body onto its back. He stared at him for a long time, a war of conscience raging in his head. It had been three days since he last fed, over a year since he had tasted human blood. Animal blood provided the sustenance he required, though vampire lore decreed human blood gave one true strength, enhanced power.

Walk away. The voice shouted in his head, but the rage of the attack still pounded through his veins. With a growl, Haydn sank to his knees and buried his teeth into the man's throat, feeding in a frantic, possessed manner, gulping blood, savoring its warmth and sweetness.

Sated, he sat back on his haunches, staring down at his victim. The brute's eyes were closed, his body spread at an awkward angle. Haydn reached beneath the man's cloak and felt the beat of his heart. At least he had been able to stop before the man was completely drained. He would awaken with a clouded mind and a thick, pounding head, but no memory of the attack. With time, the bite marks on his neck would heal and fade, leaving no lasting effects.

Haydn shuddered with regret, angry that he had allowed himself to follow his most primitive instincts. He yanked the heavy leather purse hanging from the belt at the thief's waist. With a final glance of regret, Haydn walked away. He would leave the purse on the church altar, but even knowing that Father William would use the coins to help those most in need gave Haydn little comfort.

"You really should read this, Haydn," Bethan admonished. "This knowledge could mean the difference between defeat and victory over de Bellemare."

Haydn paused, looking up. He had been carefully checking his chain mail for tears or bent links, a task normally done by a squire, but one he had always preferred to do himself.

"I assume you are referring to your magical book?"

"Yes. And stop teasing me about it."

She lifted the tome in her hands and walked over to him. Clad only in a simple white shift, she looked ravishing. Though they had spent the past hour making passionate love, Haydn's pulse quickly stirred at the sight of her.

Pressing the book practically beneath his nose, she waited with an expectant air. Knowing he would get no peace until he looked at the damn thing, Haydn reluctantly put down his chain mail. He carefully began turning the pages, marveling at the delicate parchment, fine scrollwork, and vivid illustrations.

"This must have cost you dearly," he commented as he skimmed the contents.

"I appreciate the beauty, but it is the knowledge that it contains that marks its true value." Her brow suddenly furrowed and she gave him a questioning look. "Can you read it?"

"Aye." Haydn smiled. "Though I am not sure 'tis necessary. You pore over that tome constantly. I imagine you can recite most of the pages without looking at the words."

She lowered her gaze and blushed. "There are certain sections I have studied harder than others. Here, let me show you."

Having decided to indulge her, Haydn had no recourse but to read the pages she indicated, though secretly he knew that whatever half-truths and nonsense written there would be of little use to him. Haydn already understood far too well the type of creature de Bellemare was and was very aware of his superior powers and artful cunning.

He knew that Lord Lampeter had dark magical powers, that he could morph his human form into mist or become a wolf or a large bat. He knew that de Bellemare treated everything as a conquest, that he craved the hunt, delighted in plotting the strike, and reveled in the victory.

Nevertheless, he read the section that Bethan had indicated, surprised at the amount of accurate information, his thoughts distracted as he pondered who had acquired and then compiled this knowledge.

"You believe de Bellemare is a vampire?" Haydn asked, taking a perverse sense of pleasure in her intelligence for discovering the truth.

"I do."

"But it says here that vampires fear all Christian relics and symbols. I have seen de Bellemare in the chapel."

"I know." He handed her the book and she set it carefully on the table. "There are a few other claims that seem a bit far-fetched, but too many of the characteristics hold true. My mother has been pale and weak ever since de Bellemare became her husband. I believe he feasts on her, draining her of blood, which he needs to survive. And look, here it says a creature of the night cannot get a child off a human female. That could explain why my mother was never able to birth an heir for him."

"Yet he persisted in trying. Would he not have realized it was a fruitless possibility?"

Bethan pursed her lips. "De Bellemare believes he is invincible. I'd wager he thought he would be the one of his kind who would succeed. It cost him nothing to try. 'Twas my poor mother who suffered all those years."

Haydn nodded, agreeing with her theory. It was actually more of a myth than a proven fact that the males of his kind could not impregnate a mortal female. De Bellemare certainly had the arrogance to test it.

"It says a vampire often keeps a hidden lair under ground to ensure a place of total darkness. Do you know of such a chamber?" he asked.

Bethan shook her head. "There are many passages and chambers in the depths of this structure, but I know of none that are exclusively my stepfather's domain. Yet since the castle was built to his specifications, I think 'tis fair to assume one exists. Should we try to locate it?"

"Aye. It could prove useful." Haydn picked up the book and turned the page. "There is not much here that speaks of how to destroy these demons."

"I have found a few clues." She took the book from him and searched through the pages, reading aloud when she found the proper passage.

"Vampires are cursed. They are not alive, but they are not dead. They are undead. They possess amazing strength and are extremely difficult to kill. Once defeated in combat, a stake of wood or metal must be driven through its heart, thereby pinning it to the ground. Then the head must be severed and either buried separately from the body or both parts can be burned to ash. Fire can also kill a vampire, but the creature must be burned to absolute dust."

Haydn regarded her silently. It was chilling to hear the words of destruction fall from her sweet lips with absolute accuracy. Saints above, how would she react if she knew the truth about him?

Swept up in a sudden maelstrom of conflicting emotions, Haydn felt an almost compulsive need to blurt out the truth. To reveal that his kind were neither innately bad nor innately good. That they were like mortals, varying widely in character, possessing flaws and strengths in equal numbers.

He wanted her to understand this truth, yet he also wanted her to accept him. He wanted her to know that even though he was a vampire, he was not a monster like de Bellemare. He was capable of goodness, of kindness, of love.

Yet love could never flourish with such a secret between them. Was that what he really wanted? The chance to truly love this woman? A strong breeze wafted through the window, the sudden chill recalling his senses. What fanciful thoughts! He was thinking with his emotions, not his mind.

A lasting relationship between them was an impossibility.

Haydn closed the book with a resounding thud. Bethan turned and smiled at him, her expression open and trusting.

Haydn returned the smile, yet his heart felt heavy. His secret would be kept, the barrier between them intact. It was the only prudent decision, as he grimly acknowledged that some things were best kept hidden. For everyone's sake.

Bethan paced the confines of her chamber, her mind in turmoil as she waited for her husband. The evening meal had been a particularly trying one, with de Bellemare taunting her mercilessly and Haydn customarily ignoring it. She knew it was imperative that he keep his distance from her, especially in front of de Bellemare, but it was distressing nonetheless.

Their bedchamber door opened and Haydn entered. He was wearing leather breeches, boots, and a linen shirt. It was open at the neck, the laces loose and dangling, exposing his wide, muscular chest. As always, the power and confidence of his presence struck her anew.

"Why did you leave the hall so suddenly?" he asked. "Did you feel ill?"

"I could not tolerate another minute of my stepfather's snipping at me." She put her arms around her waist, trying to hold herself together.

"It seemed no different than his usual behavior."

Disgusted, Bethan shook her head. "Was the light that bad in the hall this evening? Could you not see him glare at me with enraged and bloodshot eyes?"

"I did not notice," Haydn replied. "Yet even if he did glower, you were in no real danger."

She shuddered and turned her face away. "'Tis easy for you to talk, when you are not the one on the receiving end of those cold, menacing stares."

"You must trust me, Bethan. I know how to handle de Bellemare and keep you safe."

She put her hand to her chest and sighed. It was so difficult to trust, to hope, to believe she would finally be free from her stepfather. Yet if anyone was capable of accomplishing the task, it was her husband.

Haydn came up behind her. He began smoothing her hair, stroking her scalp and neck. The tension in her body fled. She turned, relaxed into his touch, tilting her head. Accepting the invitation, Haydn pressed his mouth against hers, his tongue sweeping inside her mouth.

Bethan surged toward him, softening her lips, then parting them, seeking his tongue. She cradled his face in her hands, rejoicing in the intimate contact. He was large and hot and the power seemed to glow out of him and into her.

She felt his hands on her breasts, his fingertips stroking her sensitive nipples through her gown. Then he moved his hand and began to tug at her gown. With a wicked smile he pulled it higher and higher until it slid over her hips.

Bethan felt the chill air blow over her exposed bare skin, but she made no move to cover herself. His eyes raked possessively over her glowing flesh and she thrilled at the fierceness of his expression. She wanted to belong to him utterly, woman to man. She wanted to lose herself in his heat and strength, revel in his passion and desire.

She ran her hand over the hard tendons in his forearm, then boldly reached down and caught his stiff penis in both her hands. He was thick and hard and fiercely aroused.

Deep inside, her body pulsed insistently in response.

She put her mouth to the base of his throat and kissed it, then pulling away, blew heavily on his wet skin. She smiled at his shiver. Keeping her hands busy, Bethan rubbed his stiff penis furiously up and down, reveling in his moans as she ran her finger down to the heavy sacks below.

Glancing up, she saw his head was thrown back, his eyes shut, lost in the sensations she was creating. She lowered his breeches, and his erection sprang free. Bethan sighed with excitement, in awe of his strength and beauty. Pressing a kiss against his flat abdomen, she moved lower and touched her tongue to the tip of his rigid penis.

He jerked and teasingly she did it again. She looked up. His eyes were open, staring down at her, heavy lidded with desire and passion.

"Shall I finish what I have started?" she whispered.

She thought he laughed, though it might have been a groan. Bethan went down on her knees in front of him. He arched his hips forward and she opened her mouth, encircling the head of his penis with her lips. He ran his fingers through her hair, tightening the grip on her scalp. The moment was so decadent, so beautifully sensual, tears formed in her eyes.

Bethan explored him with restrained excitement, licking and teasing with her tongue and mouth. His erection was rock hard and it shivered and throbbed under her ministrations. She quickened her rhythm, eager for a taste of his seed, but just as she felt him begin to climax, he suddenly lifted her off her feet. With a grunt, he propelled her backward until the table set beneath the window struck the middle of her back.

Surprised, Bethan teetered, almost losing her balance. Haydn caught her, spun her away from him, and once again lifted her skirts. Bethan found herself bent from the waist, her hands gripping the sides of the smooth wood.

"I have not had you this way," he whispered. "I know you will like it."

Bethan shivered as he moved close against her back and pressed her down. His mouth was warm and hungry on her neck as his lips traced a line of wet kisses along the sensitive nape. Her body pulsed, tightened. Heat and wetness collected between her legs and desire burned through her blood.

There was a rustling of clothes as he stepped out of his lower garments. She felt him reach between her legs, probing for entrance. She arched her back as his hardness slid deep inside her, the urgency of his mating making her dizzy.

Haydn griped her hips, holding her in place to receive his

deep thrusts, pounding into her again and again. He was buried so deeply it was shocking, yet even more arousing. She felt him pulsing inside her, almost inside her womb, and felt her own throbbing response.

"Come for me," he commanded, reaching down to stroke her.

For a moment, her mind and body hung suspended in time and then her body obeyed, the sensations bursting hotly into an explosion of bliss.

When she floated down from her pleasure, she realized he was still hard and thrusting inside her. She relaxed her body, then tightened her inner muscles. He cried out and she felt the hot rush of his seed flood her womb, his shout of contentment carrying through the small chamber.

Sated, he collapsed on top of her and she felt comforted by his warmth and weight. Harmony and contentment stole over her and she forgot her earlier distress.

He turned her onto her back and smiled down at her. His face was flushed, his eyes sparkling wildly. Bethan grinned back at him, feeling sly and wanton, empowered by her womanhood.

He caressed her gently with his fingertip, trailing a path across her face to the corner of her lips, then back to her ear. "You appear more content, more relaxed."

"I am." She reached up to touch his cheek, running her fingers tenderly over the dark, rough stubble on his jaw.

He moved closer, joining her on the table. She wondered idly if it would hold their weight, then realized with a laugh that she didn't much care. All that mattered was being with him.

Bethan nestled against his warmth as he wrapped his arms around her and brought her into his embrace. In the perfection of that moment Bethan realized she had finally found the safe place she had always feared she would never find. Here, in Haydn's arms, the possibilities of her life seemed endlessly joyful. Because she loved him.

Deep within the secret of her heart she longed for the day when he would return that love. Ever practical, ever realistic, she knew that day might never come.

She felt a sharp stab of sadness, but shook it away. No matter what happened, she knew she would always love him. And no one could ever take that away from her.

Bethan frowned as she entered her bedchamber. Her thoughts were on the hall moot to be held tomorrow, where local issues would be decided. She worried that she would be unable to sit calmly, passively as her stepfather sat in judgment of the villeins. Perhaps she should ask Haydn to intervene, even though it would be difficult for him to express an opinion contrary to de Bellemare. Still, something needed to be done to protect her people from the Lord of Lampeter's barbaric sense of justice.

She was so preoccupied with her troubles that she was at first unaware of her husband's presence in the chamber. He stood in the far corner of the room, his back toward the door. She opened her mouth to call out a greeting, but before she had a chance to speak she saw him lift the object he held in his hands and raise it to his face.

A strange, forbidden sense of danger washed over her. In silence, she crept forward, peering closer for a better look. A rabbit. Haydn held a rabbit in his hands. But why?

Her uneasiness grew and then suddenly, shockingly Haydn pressed the wiggling animal to his mouth and sank his teeth into the hare's neck. It squealed, twitched, then shook, struggling to break free.

Terror clutched at Bethan's heart. For a long moment she stood and stared in dumbstruck silence, refusing to believe what her eyes and ears revealed. Haydn was suckling the blood from the animal while it still lived, swallowing every drop.

Bethan closed her eyes, slowed her breath. She fought the pain, but was unable to hide the truth from herself. She had read a description of this very act so often it was vividly committed to memory. Witnessing it now was a verification of a truth she could hardly believe, was loath to accept.

Haydn was a vampire! A vampire!

Her heart was pounding so hard the sound thundered in her ears. She stumbled backward, but must have made a noise, for his head turned sharply in her direction.

"Bethan?"

His voice sounded rough, gravelly. He looked the same and yet . . . her gaze was pulled to the small, dark red smear at the corner of his mouth.

"Blood," she whispered. Her right hand moved and she hastily made the sign of the cross.

Haydn wiped his mouth with his sleeve, then tried to disarm her with a smile. But as his lips parted, she saw the fangs of his teeth, stark white except for the hint of blood that clung to the tips.

"My God, don't come near me!" Bethan screamed. She lifted the pitcher of wine she held in her left hand and with all her might threw it at him. It hit the stone floor and shattered, splattering wine everywhere.

"Bethan, calm down."

Haydn stepped over the mess on the floor and moved toward her. Dazed, she took a step back. Only one, for she was too astonished, too horrified by what she had discovered to command her limbs.

"Unnatural beast! You lied to me! You betrayed me!" She let out a broken cry, hurting from the depths of her soul. "I trusted you! I believed you would help us finally break free of de Bellemare's cruelty. But you are just like him. An unnatural creature of darkness and evil."

Haydn paled slightly. "No! You misunderstand. I am not like de Bellemare."

"There is no misunderstanding. I saw you bite that hare, I heard you suckle the blood from the wound you made like a babe drinks milk from his mother's breast." She spoke in a trembling voice, laced with pain and anger. "My ears have not deceived me. My eyes have not deceived me."

She had trusted him. She had confided in him. What a fool! She should have been wiser, smarter, less innocent and foolish. She had given him her affection, her body. She had given it all willingly, joyfully, and with utter abandon.

She had loved him. And he had betrayed her. Bethan's muscles began to shake and she felt her legs threatening to give way beneath her. Haydn grabbed her and pulled her close. For a second she allowed his strength to keep her standing. But she was no longer fooled by his expression of concern.

She backed out of his embrace as though it burned her to feel his touch. "Are you going to kill me?"

"Kill you?" His silver eyes narrowed. The pupils shifted and for an instant, his eyes flared with red. "I could. Or I could turn you, and make you as I am. Which frightens you more, I wonder?"

Her eyes began to water, but she refused to give in to the tears. She needed to think, to plan, to somehow make this right. But all she seemed capable of doing was to stare at Haydn in despair. "It feels like I have walked into a hideous nightmare from which I shall never awaken."

"Bethan," he muttered, reaching out to her. "You have nothing to fear from me. I am the same as I was before you discovered this truth. It changes nothing." His breath hissed between his teeth. "Christ's blood, there is no need to stare at me as if I were a monster."

A sob twisted out of her throat. "But you are a monster, a soulless villain, no different from my murderous stepfather."

"I am not." His voice was low and taut. "I do not prey on humans as he does, I do not gain pleasure by showing cruelty to others, I do not revel in another's pain and suffering."

"Does he know that you are one of his kind?"

"No." Haydn shook his head, his gaze locked on hers. "He knew of my parents and killed them because he feared they would try to stop him from building his empire of power. I was not at the manor on the night he attacked. I think he suspected I might have been taken as a prisoner. I believe that is why he ordered so many killed when you rescued me. De Bellemare wanted to make sure I was destroyed."

"So that part is true? You came here for revenge?"

Something fierce leapt in his eyes. "Yes. I never promised anything else. I agreed to marry you because it was the only way to stay at Lampeter within de Bellemare's presence. From the beginning, I informed you I would not stay after my task was completed."

"And bedding me?"

"That was your choice."

The bitterness of that statement made her lift her chin and stare into his eyes. "I never would have allowed it if I had known the truth."

"Are you certain?"

Bethan stiffened, her throat clogging tightly. It was unnerving to realize that though she might wish to hide it, deny it, her body had craved his, her desire for him had been strong and complete. Remembering the passion they had shared sent a wave of confusion through her, followed quickly by a stab of fear when she thought of the consequences. "What if I am carrying your child?"

He looked taken aback by her question. "There is hardly cause for worry."

"Not worry? Are you mad? How will I ever tolerate giving birth to an unnatural, evil creature?"

"You would hate an innocent babe?"

His words brought on more confusion, for the hurt in his tone was unmistakable. "I would fear it," she answered honestly.

"Then you must look to your precious book for answers. Amazingly, it does contain some correct facts. A full-blooded vampire is unable to produce a viable child with a human female. You have no cause to worry. Or fear."

She shook her head and almost grinned in nervous agitation. Nothing to fear! Saints above, she was so frightened she did not know what to do. Everything she thought she knew, thought she believed had just crashed and crumpled before her. She could feel the tears sliding down her cheeks, all the more powerful because they were silent.

She closed her eyes, flinching from the ferocity on Haydn's face. Why was he so angry? Clearly she was the one who had been wronged, deceived.

"I am expected on the practice field. 'Tis unwise to be late." He reached beyond her and picked up his sword. "We will talk of this later."

Temples throbbing, she walked to the window and stared blindly outside. She valiantly tried to analyze the situation with some calm, but her mind and body failed to cooperate. Feeling ready to collapse, Bethan covered her face with her hands.

The man she loved was a vampire. A demon. Something unnatural, unholy. How could she love such a creature, a monster?

Bethan's eyes burned as the tears continued to fall and the true extent of her emotions surfaced.

How could she not?

Six

For Haydn, the next two days passed in a haze of guilt and remorse. Bethan avoided him, speaking only when it was necessary, barring the door of their chamber at night, forcing him to stay elsewhere. He knew it would not help to brood over what could not be changed, but that did not ease his frustration.

In an odd way, it was almost a relief to finally have the truth revealed. He knew this was coming, had realized soon after he acknowledged to himself the depth of his feelings for Bethan that this was to be his fate.

He would forever love a woman who would never accept him. And what he was, an unnatural creature of darkness and evil as she so bitterly declared, could never be changed. Haydn admitted there was no one to blame but himself. He knew better than to allow himself to feed inside the castle, where there was a chance he might be seen. But he had grown complacent, comfortable within the walls of their bedchamber, and his carelessness had been his undoing.

In one way he hated that he had been caught, that his secret had been revealed in such a crude manner. Yet far worse, his mistake had caused Bethan great pain and for that he was truly sorry. It hurt remembering the agitation in her voice, the fear on her face. He could not change who he was, what he was, but he would have done anything within his power to spare Bethan this agony.

Seeing her pain had cut him in a way he had not thought possible. He had tried to apologize, but her agony was too raw, her sorrow too fresh for her to contemplate forgiveness.

Perhaps in time . . . ? Haydn let out a grunt of laughter at his foolish thoughts. The passage of time would make no difference, would bring no comfort. All he could do now was fulfill his promise to Bethan, to complete the task he had vowed to accomplish by coming to Lampeter.

He must destroy Agnarr de Bellemare. It was the least he owed his wife.

The sleepy guards at the town gates gave Haydn a passing nod as he rode out. The loneliness he felt at his estrangement from Bethan was especially acute tonight. Perhaps the solitude of the darkness would ease his pain, the thrill of the hunt in the thick woods beyond the castle walls would focus his restless energy on something besides his torment.

Securing his mount to a thick tree at the edge of the forest, Haydn continued on foot, sprinting through the dense foliage, his senses attuned to the life pulsing around him.

The hunt would serve two purposes, to occupy his mind and nourish his body. Fresh blood was necessary for him to build his strength, to keep his senses on alert for the coming confrontation with de Bellemare. And after being discovered by Bethan, Haydn had vowed never to feed again within the castle walls.

He slowed his pace, listened, sniffed, and caught the scent of a deer. Pleased with the discovery, he began to track his prey. A scurrying noise drew his attention to a dense thicket of bramble off to his left. A twig snapped and Haydn drew his bow, making ready to let an arrow fly. He would strike the deer in the leg, preventing it from swift flight. Once it was captured, he could feast at leisure on the nutritious blood, slowly, painlessly, draining it, yet stopping while the animal still clung to life.

He peered around the trunk of a large oak, poised to shoot, yet Haydn saw not a deer, but a young boy of eight or nine, a brace of rabbits clutched in his hand. Haydn shifted his weight from one foot to the other, then heard a sharp intake of breath as the lad discovered him.

With a frightened shriek, the boy turned and ran but after a handful of steps was forced to stop. The area was thick with underbrush on all sides, making it impossible to flee with any speed. Haydn stepped from behind the tree trunk, and the lad's eyes opened wide, darting nervously from him to the vast stretch of forest that surrounded them on all sides.

"You cannot outrun me," Haydn cautioned in a low voice. "'Twould be foolish to try."

The boy trembled with indecision. It was illegal to poach in the lord's woods, an offense punishable by death. At least if he ran, he might have a chance of escape.

Haydn could feel his tension, smell his fear. He quickly, too, became aware of the isolation of their predicament. It was within his power to dispense justice however he saw fit. No one would be the wiser and he doubted the lad would ever breathe a word of what had happened, fearing for his life.

But there was something else to consider. The tender blood of a human victim would bring Haydn added strength. The lad was young, his flesh, though dirty, would be sweet and pure. The additional strength of drinking human blood could make the difference in defeating de Bellemare.

Haydn lunged forward, then stopped, his hand on the trunk of the large tree. He took a long, deep breath. *Control.* He needed control, he needed the strength to discipline his urges.

"For . . . forgive me, my lord," the lad whispered, and then he burst into frightened tears.

The bloodlust inside him quickly faded as he mastered his urges. Haydn's lips twitched. "If I turn my back, then I cannot be a witness to one who steals from his master," he said casually.

Hoping the boy possessed the wits to understand, Haydn leisurely pivoted on his heel. There was a rustle of underbrush, followed by the snapping of several twigs. Haydn slowly counted to ten, then turned back. The boy was gone, the only hint of his presence the brace of rabbits set on the forest floor.

With a grim smile, Haydn retrieved the animals. They were still warm. Placing them near his mouth, he feasted on the blood, feeling the strength return to his body with each swallow. When he had drained them both, he walked to his horse and left the protection of the deep woods.

Riding back through the village, he dropped the now bloodless hares on the doorstep of the first cottage, knowing the inhabitants would be too grateful for the unexpected bounty to question their odd state. Then with a heavy sigh he returned to the castle and his lonely sleeping spot in front of the fireplace in the great hall.

The following morning Haydn arose with a new sense of purpose. After breaking his fast with a small piece of hard cheese and a tankard of ale, he went in search of his wife. She was quickly found, rushing from their chamber, her brow creased with worry.

At the sight of her, the air boiled with tension. Yet as he drew closer something inside him cracked and melted. She looked tired and sad. He wanted to reach out, to touch her hair, to soothe her hurts. Instead, he straightened, leaving his arms hanging by his side.

"I have spent this night pondering my next move," he told

her. "'Tis past time that I confronted de Bellemare. The longer I wait, the harder it will be. I must destroy him, before he destroys us."

Bethan nodded her head. "That is what I have come to tell you. I think I have found the entrance to his secret lair."

"Show me."

"We must act quickly. Sir Colwyn told me de Bellemare left the castle less than an hour ago. He is not expected back until later."

"He has probably gone outside to hunt for fresh prey," Haydn speculated aloud.

He saw her shudder and cursed his unguarded tongue, knowing his words were a stark reminder to his beloved exactly what sort of perverted creature her stepfather was—the same demon vampire breed as himself.

She stiffened her spine, but said nothing. Quietly he followed her, fully expecting to be taken on a strange, twisting route down long, winding corridors, but instead Bethan went through the great hall, then turned down a short side corridor. To the left was an unassuming door.

Surprised, he turned to Bethan. "Are you sure this is it?"

"Yes. 'Twas most clever of him to keep it in plain sight. I'm sure the door is hardly noticed by anyone, including me. The servants are so fearful of de Bellemare they would never dare to venture anywhere unless given specific permission."

"An element of surprise should give me the advantage." He reached for the latch.

"Wait!" she cried, covering his hand with her own. "What if we are wrong? What if de Bellemare is down there now?"

"If he is down there, he is alone, especially if he has brought a victim to feast upon. If not, I will lie in wait for him. Either way, I will have the element of surprise and the opportunity to confront him without his guards."

"And if you are wrong?"

Haydn's mouth twisted into a grim line of determination. "I cannot afford to be wrong."

He tried the door, not entirely surprised to find it open without protest, for he suspected it was well used by de Bellemare. Haydn took a step forward, then turned, sensing Bethan close behind.

"I am coming, too," she announced before he had a chance to question her.

"No!" he exclaimed, his heart jolting in his chest. "'Tis far too dangerous."

"I can help."

"You will distract me."

"I know I can help," she insisted.

"Bethan, I have never doubted your courage or your wisdom, but this is something I must do on my own." He reached out to smooth away a tendril of golden hair that hung across her brow. "Stay here."

Giving her no chance to protest, he walked through the door and closed it behind him. Worried that she might follow, Haydn waited for several minutes to ensure that she obeyed him. When he was certain she remained on the other side, he turned. Directly in front of him was a set of stone stairs.

He descended quietly, embracing the darkness, his sharp eyes focusing through the inky blackness. As he moved, he kept his attention on his surroundings, watching, listening. The warning signs that prickled his keen sense of danger grew stronger with each step. He took a deep breath and slowly drew his sword.

After several minutes, he entered a dank, musty, vaulted stone crypt and knew he was getting close. He could feel de Bellemare's presence, could sense that his enemy was near. He let his gaze roam the room, not liking the stillness of the place. Closing his eyes, Haydn trained his senses to search the darkness for his quarry.

But it was elusive. Perhaps de Bellemare was not here now, perhaps it was the essence of his evil spirit that clung to every stone that was causing these sensations. Frustrated, Haydn slowly opened his eyes and strained his gaze forward. He saw only shadows, until suddenly there was a slight shift of movement.

Too late, he realized his mistake. A wall of darkness rose before him a mere second before he felt the stunning blow of a heavy sword hilt smash into the side of his skull. He went down on one knee, struggling to remain conscious, trying to shake off the burst of pain and light that exploded inside his head, but to no avail.

His eyes opened one final time at the sound of chilling laughter and the last thing he saw was a gleam of satisfaction coupled with evil, black intent blazing in Agnarr de Belle-mare's eyes.

And then, nothing.

Bethan knew that Haydn was right. 'Twas best for her, safer for her to stay behind. Ten minutes passed, then twenty. She crossed her arms, uncrossed them, crossed them again. Tapped her foot, then began pacing, her strides quickening with each step. Stopping suddenly, she pressed her ear flat against the wooden door, but heard nothing. Perhaps if she opened it a mere crack . . .

Once the door was open, the floodgates of her anxious curiosity were breached. With small cautious steps, she went through, following the same path as Haydn.

It was dark as pitch. Bethan ran her hand along the wall as a guide, taking each step slowly, carefully. Gradually her eyes adjusted to the gloom, though she could see very little.

Finally she spied something promising, an open area that held a large stone crypt. Its perimeter was lined with thick pillars of stone, like some ancient pagan temple. Hovering in the shadows behind one of them, Bethan leaned forward, her eyes straining in the darkness.

It was then she noticed a prone figure lying in the center of the room. She whispered an earnest prayer, waiting to see if there was any movement, any sign of life.

"Haydn?"

She moved forward, then stumbled to her knees as something grasped her ankle.

"Ah, 'tis little Bethan. I was hoping you would come."

Stark terror seized her as she heard de Bellemare's voice and realized it was his hand that held her like an iron cuff. She shook her leg violently, wrenching against that biting hold, fighting to free herself, but was no match for his unnatural strength. He pulled her forward, the wretched sound of his laughter ringing in her ears.

Terrified, she renewed her struggles, her fingers scraping vainly at the hard stone floor, the nails breaking, the tips bleeding.

"Mother Mary, save me," she prayed tearfully.

"How quaint. You pray to your weak God to deliver you from evil."

He took her by the wrist and hauled her to her feet, his strong fingers gripping her so tightly they left bruises. She jolted back, but could barely move away. De Bellemare's eyes glowed with bloodlust, cruel in their intensity.

"What have you done to Haydn?" she asked.

"He is merely stunned. For now." He dragged his attention away from Haydn's limp body. "He fooled me at first, but not for long. I know what he is, who he is, and I know he must be destroyed."

"He is younger and stronger," Bethan cried. "'Tis you who will be defeated."

"Youth is hardly an advantage among vampires. Those with greater powers are the more experienced of our kind."

"His powers are far greater than you can ever imagine."

"Such lies, Bethan. I always did admire your spirit, however misguided your motivation. For a time I even considered turning you, so you could be my mate. Yet in the end I knew I would never be able to fully trust you. Pity, you, too, must be destroyed." He lifted his hand to touch her face and she flinched away. Her defiance seemed to amuse him. He gave her a wicked, leering grin, full of arrogance and malicious satisfaction.

Bethan's heart was racing, her breathing erratic and shallow. Yet she struggled to keep de Bellemare talking, knowing it was their only chance, knowing she needed to buy some time for Haydn to recover and come to her aid. Then miraculously, as if he'd heard her silent plea, Haydn's deep voice came from behind a pillar on the opposite side of the chamber.

"Leave her alone, de Bellemare! This fight is between you and me."

Bethan turned her head toward the sound, relieved to hear him, yet terrified of what would come next. The Lord of Lampeter laughed as he took a small step toward the center of the chamber. With a harsh shove, he pushed Bethan away from him and then quickly drew his sword.

He charged Haydn with a roar. In the space of mere moments, de Bellemare delivered five strong blows. Metal clashed on metal as Haydn caught de Bellemare's blade upon his, the hideous noise echoing through the cavernous chamber.

Bethan's nerves coiled into springs as she watched the two battle. De Bellemare fought with the frenzied strength of a demon, but Haydn steadily deflected the attack. They seemed evenly matched in skill and strength, though de Bellemare's larger, more muscular frame seemed to give him an advantage.

Haydn's face wore a strange, remote look, but his silver eyes glittered with fierce determination and resolve. Their grunts and heavy breathing soon filled the chamber as they sought to bring each other down. With a lightning move, Haydn leapt forward, striking a heavy blow that drove de Bellemare into the shadows.

Grunting and groaning, de Bellemare managed to parry

the attack, and then suddenly he turned, twirled, and struck from below. The tip of his sword caught Haydn's sleeve, tearing it from elbow to shoulder.

The red stain quickly appeared. Bethan's nostril's tingled with the coppery scent of blood. Seemingly unconcerned, Haydn flexed his shoulder, rubbed it, then wiped his bloody palm across his tunic.

"I have drawn first blood," de Bellemare taunted. "Next I will plunge my steel through your heart, and then I will delight in feasting upon it before I burn the paltry remains of your flesh."

"I suppose you can try," Haydn answered grittily.

He lifted his broadsword with both hands and swung it was such speed that de Bellemare barely caught it with his sword. Enraged, de Bellemare lunged forward with a piercing battle cry, raining blows that Haydn struggled to deflect.

Time and again, they engaged and retreated and Bethan could see they were beginning to tire. Sweat poured from their foreheads and dripped onto the floor and their breath came in heavy bellows. As Haydn angled his blade to deflect the next blow, de Bellemare suddenly whirled around and drove a knee into his groin. Haydn doubled over, then dropped to the floor with a leaden thud. The sword fell from his grip, clattering ominously on the floor.

"You see, I am the superior being," de Bellemare taunted as he slashed his sword over Haydn's thigh, cutting deeply into the flesh. Then he moved in for the kill, his teeth showing in a satisfied smile.

Her heart hammering with terror, Bethan saw Haydn twist on his side and reach for his fallen sword. Surging up to his knees, he grasped the handle and somehow positioned the weapon. As his enemy lunged forward, Haydn uttered a hoarse cry and thrust his blade upward, deep into de Bellemare's chest, directly piercing his heart. His evil face registered surprise as he twitched, then toppled over, landing on his back.

Bethan screamed. Running across the floor, she fell to her knees beside her husband. She was shaking so badly her teeth were chattering. Haydn might be the victor in this brutal fight, but he was badly wounded and bleeding profusely. She lifted her gown and ripped away the undertunic, using the material to stanch the blood that oozed out of his shoulder and onto the floor.

"My leg," he croaked.

"What?" He sounded as if he were being strangled. She leaned closer to hear him. "The wound on my leg is more serious."

Bethan glanced down and saw there was blood soaking his hose. She ripped the skirt of her overgown for a second bandage and attended to the wound. He grunted, groaned, but he did not jerk away from her.

It was painful to look at his face, to see his anguish and suffering. Tears sprang to her eyes. She dashed them away and continued. "There. I think I have stopped the bleeding. But we must get to our bedchamber so I may clean and dress the wounds properly. Can you stand?"

"Not yet."

She risked another glance at him. He was pale, sweaty, smeared with blood. She worried that there might be other injuries, ones that she could not see, ones that were even more serious. A helpless feeling of despair stole over her and the tears continued to fall.

"What should we do?" she whispered in anguish.

A muscle twitched in Haydn's jaw and it took a moment for him to reply. "You must act quickly and dispose of de Bellemare's body."

"How?"

"Bury him. In the deepest grave that can be dug. Find Sir Colwyn and give him the order yourself. It must be done before nightfall."

"Must we remove . . . remove his head?" she asked, her voice quivering.

"'Tis unnecessary. A blow struck with a blade directly in his heart has effectively ended de Bellemare's existence. However, you must not allow anyone to remove my sword. It shall be buried with him, with the silver thrust into his heart, or else he may rise again. Do you understand?"

Bethan nodded and struggled to force down the rush of panic that threatened to overtake her. "What of his guard? Will they try to stop us?"

Haydn shook his head. "No. His power over them ended when the fatal blow was struck."

"And my mother? Will she always remain weak and sickly?"

"She will improve over time. But she was a host for many, many years. She will never fully recover."

For one long minute, Bethan kept her gaze trained on Haydn. His eyes kept drifting closed, slower each time. She was terrified to leave him, yet knew she had to follow his instructions, had to finish what he had started and bury the body.

"I need to get Sir Colwyn," she said. "Will you be all right if I leave you for a few minutes?"

His eyes fluttered open. He cursed, then gave her a rueful smile. "If I did not know any better, I would think you were concerned about me, dear wife."

Bethan let out a choked laugh. Now was hardly the time to examine her feelings for Haydn. "I shall return," she said softly.

He let out a long sigh and closed his eyes. Knowing there was no more time to waste, Bethan gave him a final, reassuring touch. Then she stood and ran from the chamber.

Haydn recovered slowly. His wounds healed far more quickly than any mortal man's, yet they were deep and severe and it took over a week before he was able to rise from his bed.

Bethan was a constant presence. She tended his wounds,

brought him food, even procured the fresh animal blood he needed to survive and properly heal. She was polite and gentle, yet there was a distance in her eyes, a guarded, reserved edge to her manner.

He did not doubt that she cared for him, perhaps even loved him. But she also did not forgive him, nor did she understand what he had done and why he had done it.

Lying in his bed, with nothing to do but think, Haydn contemplated his future as he revisited his past. His victory over de Bellemare closed a chapter of his life, yet opened a new one. Would he now move forward with Bethan at his side?

He suffered no doubts that she was the most suitable female to be his mate. He respected her more than any other individual he had ever known. She was intelligent and kind, with an unmatched inner strength and courage. He admired her fortitude and resolve, he delighted in her beauty and grace.

She was his. Deep inside he knew it, though he also acknowledged staying together might be impossible.

As a misty gray light heralded the dawn, Haydn rose slowly from his bed, restless from spending too much time lying on his back. He dressed himself in a loose-fitting tunic and hose, then donned a pair of boots, securing a knife inside.

Silently, he walked the castle hallways, committing it all to memory. There were few servants about, yet the atmosphere was markedly changed. The dark, oppressive presence of Agnarr de Bellemare was gone, replaced with a palpable feeling of lightness and hope. Haydn experienced a sense of pride and accomplishment, knowing he was in part responsible.

There was more activity in the great hall, as the fires in the enormous fireplace were banked and the trestle tables were being arranged for the morning meal. He saw several women clustered together. Even with her back toward him, one in particular was most familiar.

Bethan.

Haydn waited for her to finish giving her orders. When she came toward him, he stepped from the shadows, until they stood toe-to-toe, with barely an inch between them.

"Haydn! Goodness, you startled me." She lifted her brow. "Is something wrong?"

"No. I wanted to speak with you. I have healed well, thanks to your devoted care. I shall be leaving in a few days."

"Are you certain?"

"'Tis time, Bethan."

She frowned. "We will miss you."

"Perhaps. But mostly I think you will be glad this is all over."

She was silent. He gazed into the pain and doubt in her lovely eyes, and finally admitted to himself that gratitude, devotion, and respect were not enough. Love was not enough. He could spend a lifetime trying to regain her trust, only to fail at the endeavor. And without trust, their relationship was doomed.

"I never once deliberately deceived you, Bethan," he said, compelled to make some kind of explanation.

She heaved an emotional sigh. "You omitted a most important fact, Haydn. One I still find difficult to comprehend."

"I cannot change who I am, what I am."

"I know." Her eyes were fathomless pools, yet he could read the sadness in them. Frustrated, he glanced away. It tore at his heart to witness her pain.

He felt her move and knew she was turning to walk away. Unable to stop himself, Haydn reached for her, pulling her into his arms. He dipped his head and kissed her as he had never done before, with a desperate, fierce, possessive wildness.

Aggressively he parted her lips and plundered her mouth, one hand tangled in her hair to prevent her escape. He could taste the passion on her lips, the desire, could feel the yielding of her body. But not the acceptance of her spirit.

Slowly, regretfully, he let her go. Bethan bit her lower lip as she pulled back from him, her eyes shining with unshed tears. Haydn's heart stilled. His eyes burned into hers.

"Whatever else you believe, Bethan, know this and know it well. I love you. I love you now, and will continue to love you for all eternity."

Then he turned and limped away.

Seven

"Sir Colwyn said that Lord Meifod will depart within the hour," Lady Caryn remarked as she pulled the scarlet embroidery thread through the cloth she held on her lap. "Are you going with him?"

Bethan's eyes widened in astonishment. "Of course I shall not go with him. Honestly, Mother, how can you ask such a thing?"

Lady Caryn shrugged her shoulders. "He is your husband. Your place is by his side."

"My place is here, with my family and my people."

"Though I am not as strong as I once was, I am perfectly capable of taking charge," Lady Caryn replied. "We have good, loyal soldiers who will keep us safe and hardworking people who are joyful at being freed from de Bellemare's tyranny. Lampeter is once again a fine place to live."

"'Tis not only to run things that I am staying." A muscle worked spasmodically in Bethan's throat. "You know what Haydn is, Mother. I told you everything. He is a vampire. A creature of darkness and evil, like de Bellemare. I am shocked you would dare to suggest that I go with him."

Lady Caryn sighed. "I confess to knowing very little

about his kind, but I do know one thing with great certainty. The Warrior of the North is nothing like Agnarr de Belle-mare."

"He betrayed me!" Bethan cried. "I can never trust him, never look at him without feeling a crushing sense of loss."

"'Tis not too late. He loves you, Bethan. And you love him. Go to him. Quickly, before he leaves."

Shaking her head vehemently, Bethan turned away, hugging her arms around her waist, trying to control the tremors of emotions that shook her body. "Our feelings do not matter. I can never be a part of his world."

"There is a way." Bethan looked over and saw a gleam of excitement in her mother's eyes. "Haydn can transform you, he has the power to make you one of his kind. I asked Father William to check the book and he said 'tis possible for an immortal to *turn* another."

Bethan's hands curled into shaking fists. She was well acquainted with the passage her mother spoke of, for Bethan had read it so many times herself she could recite the words from memory.

"I shall be eternally damned," she whispered.

"Perhaps. Perhaps not. I know not what to believe about God and salvation. I only know that while I was with de Belle-mare, I lived in hell while on earth. And your Haydn was the one who released me from that hell. Surely that must mean something."

"Do not romanticize it. 'Twas a fight, Mother, between two enemies. Haydn emerged victorious because he was younger and stronger."

"Or had more to protect," Lady Caryn insisted. "Agnarr de Bellemare fought to hold on to his power, but Haydn fought to keep you safe. Haydn fought for love."

Bethan shook her head. "It was revenge. De Bellemare destroyed Haydn's parents."

Yet even as the words left her mouth, she knew she spoke but part of the truth. Haydn had defeated the Lord of Lampeter to save Bethan and her people. He had done it because he loved her.

Lady Caryn reached for her daughter's hand and held it tightly. "Even as a child you had courage. How I admired your spirit, your strength. So often it gave me the will to carry on when I believed in my heart that we were all doomed. I beg of you, reach within yourself and find that spirit. If not, you shall end your days a sad and bitter woman."

The uncertainty of her future wavered in Bethan's mind. It was wrong, most likely sinful, to contemplate becoming an immortal and the very idea of it frightened her dreadfully. "How can I even consider consigning myself to such a fate, to willingly become a creature of darkness?"

"How can you not?" Lady Caryn gave her a trembling smile. "For so many years you have fought for me, fought for our people. Now 'tis time to think of yourself. He made you happy, Bethan. Think long and hard before you toss away this chance at happiness, this gift of love."

Bethan pushed the doubts and fears from her mind and contemplated the feelings of her heart. She envisioned her days without him, the bleak years of loneliness stretching before her. A single sob escaped and Bethan covered her mouth.

The aching in her heart propelled her feet forward, down the stairs, though the great hall, out the front doors, toward the stables. Rain began to fall, but Bethan ignored it, moving forward as quickly as her heavy skirts would allow.

By the time she was within sight of the stables, the curtain of falling rain was thick and pounding, nearly blinding. Yet Bethan pushed herself forward, ignoring the pelting raindrops and the wind whipping at her gown, searching through the deluge for Haydn.

Thunder rumbled and lightning split the sky and suddenly she saw him, in a blaze of light. He stood alone, in the open stable doorway. Powerful, proud, noble. Sensing her presence, he turned. Their eyes met and raw emotion seared her soul.

She would never love anyone as much as she loved Haydn,

would never want for anything, care for anything, need anything as much as him. Bethan swallowed hard, blinking back the tears she swore she would not shed.

Haydn remained as he was, standing still and silent, his handsome face an impassive mask, the raging storm swirling around him like a tempest. Waiting. Waiting for her to come to him.

"I want to hate you," she confessed, shouting to be heard above the storm.

He lowered his chin in the slightest acknowledgment. "You have the right."

"I want to hate you, yet I cannot. I deliberately avoided you and kept myself busy from dawn to dusk, feeling such exhaustion by evening that I could almost fall asleep standing on my feet. Yet when I closed my eyes at night, you were what I saw. No matter what I did, I could never escape it. And now . . . now far greater than my desire to hate you is the paralyzing fear that once you are gone, I shall never see you again."

"Come with me."

It took one small step to be in his arms. With a sob, Bethan clung to Haydn's powerful frame, burying her face in the crook of his neck, letting his strength seep into her. "I want to be with you always, Haydn, wherever you go, however you live. Please, make me as you are, my dearest."

He stroked her damp hair and held her close. "I know my days will be bleak and barren without you. But I cannot ask you to sacrifice your humanity for me."

"I do it because I am selfish, because I love you." Bethan lifted her hand, pressing her palm over his heart. "I do it for us, Haydn."

He sighed and leaned his head back. "Are you certain?"

"I am certain of nothing," she replied honestly. "Except that I love you. And that I need to be with you, to be a part of you. Though I have tried to deny it, you are so deep inside me, you touch my heart."

Haydn captured her face in his hands. "'Tis not what you have known, but we can have a good marriage, a solid partnership." His face drew closer until his lips brushed hers in a gentle kiss. "I will do all within my power to ensure that you never regret this choice."

Bethan leaned into him, pressing herself firmly against his side. "Do it," she urged. "Turn me now, before I lose my courage."

He pulled her inside the stable, toward a secluded corner, and she willingly followed. Shielded from any passing eye, Haydn gathered Bethan within the circle of his arms. His lips moved lightly across her skin and Bethan instinctively arched her neck to allow his mouth greater access.

She felt his breath over the artery in her neck and she tensed, but he nuzzled and kissed her gently. Bethan's fear began to fade and then suddenly she felt a sharp burst of intense pain at the base of her throat. Her body convulsed. She threw herself protectively forward, thrashing wildly, but Haydn had her locked in an iron grip.

Sweet Mother of God, Bethan thought, trying desperately to find her breath. 'Tis a miracle that anyone can survive such a thing!

The edge of her panic was distracted by the sound of an odd suckling noise. Slowly, the pain diminished and a languor descended over her entire body. She tried to reach up to touch Haydn's face, but her arm felt heavy as a stone.

"Is it over? I feel so strange," she croaked out weakly.

"Let yourself go, Bethan. I will keep you safe."

The sound of Haydn's voice calmed her. Bethan sighed, feeling the shadows and darkness flood into her vision. Her eyes closed. She knew then that she was drifting away, leaving this life and heading toward another. Sighing, she gave herself over to the sensations, trusting Haydn to make it right.

"Drink."

Responding to the command, she obediently swallowed.

The coppery taste of the warm liquid invaded her entire being, bringing forth a new strength and awareness.

Bethan's lashes fluttered, her eyes opened, and Haydn's handsome, smiling face suddenly appeared before hers. Amazingly, a single tear streaked down his face.

"Are you crying?" she asked as she reached out to brush away the moisture on his cheek.

"With joy," he assured her, staring deeply into her eyes. He gently stroked his fingers against the wound at her nape, then lowered his head to her lips for a slow, passionate kiss.

Bethan eagerly responded, kissing him back with all the love and happiness that swelled her heart.

Finally, she was at peace.

Kiss of the Vampire

Vampire

Eve Silver

One

Swirling fog and mizzling rain settled about Sarah Lowell like a shroud, clinging to her hair and skin and clothes, a faint damp sheen. Her boots rang on the wet cobbles, her steps sure and quick, her heart beating a rhythm in time to her pace as she ducked through the dim alleys and twisting lanes, past wretched houses and tenements, and rows of windows, patched and broken.

'Twas a dangerous route, one that carried her through the edge of St. Giles, north of Seven Dials—a route made all the more distressing by the dying moments of darkness and shadow that fought to stave off the first creeping fingers of the dawn.

A part of her was attuned to the street before her, the gloomy, faintly sinister doorways, the courtyards that broke from the thoroughfare. And a part of her was ever aware of the road behind, dim and draped in fog and menace. Beneath her cloak, she closed her fist tight about her cudgel, a short, sturdy stick that saw her from point to point in the place she was forced to live. She never left her room in the lodging house on Coptic Street without it. With good reason.

This was not a place for a woman alone, but she had no choice but to be here. Her choice lay in protecting herself. That she could do, though she had neither the means nor the inclination to own a pistol, and she had considered—and discarded—the possibility of defending herself with a knife.

So a cudgel would do, and she prayed she never found herself in a circumstance where she would be required to use it.

She suspected that surprise would be one thing in her favor should her prayers go unheeded. An attacker would have no expectation that she had strength in her small frame, but then, he would have no knowledge of the years she had spent by her father's side, honing her muscles lifting and turning patients who could not do so for themselves. With her wide hazel eyes and her straight dark hair pulled back in a knot at her nape, she had a delicate appearance that was deceiving. Her father had always said she was sturdy in both body and spirit. She wished it had not taken his death and the desperate turn of her life to prove his assertions true.

A muffled sound to her left made her spin and peer down the alley next to the darkened chandler's shop. Her heart gave a terrible lurch in her breast, and her fingers closed tight about the cudgel as she dragged it free of her cloak. With a moan, a man stumbled toward her, then veered away to lean, panting, against the wall. Muttering and cursing with a drunken slur, he fumbled at the flap of his breeches.

Turning away, Sarah paused but an instant to steady her nerves, then walked on, willing her racing pulse to settle. Perhaps it was the cold that made her shiver, but she thought it was unease that did the deed. More nights than not she felt as though unseen eyes watched her from the gloom, footsteps dogging her every move.

Now, in the early moments before dawn, it was no different. The feeling of being watched, being stalked, oozed across her skin like a slug. She never saw anyone, though she took care to look over her shoulder often. But when she looked, there were only the empty street and hollowed doorways behind her.

She quickened her pace and hurried on.

"Almost there now," she murmured, with yet another glance about. She dared not relax her attention, not even for a second.

Her destination was Portugal Street and the old St. Clement Danes workhouse that now housed King's College Hospital. There was talk of a new building, but for now there were some hundred and twenty beds split into several overcrowded wards that offered care to the sick poor.

No one of wealth and means would step foot in King's College. By choice, the rich would be seen to in their own homes, and because of it, they were more likely to survive. But the poor could not afford that luxury, and so they came to King's College, and often enough they died.

There were those who would argue that they would die regardless, and that the hospital offered some hope, however small. Sarah was inclined to favor that belief because, somehow, they did manage to save some.

Still, she found it a horrific irony that King's College was situated squarely between a crumbling graveyard and the abattoirs of Butcher's Row, and she had her own well-guarded opinion that some doctors and surgeons here might be better suited to work in the slaughterhouses.

At least there, death was the expected outcome.

As the cheerless building loomed before her, she paused and glanced about once more. A shiver chased along her spine. There, near the graveyard, she swore she saw a black-cloaked figure, painted in shades of pewter and coal and ash, clinging to the shadows. Watching.

Genuine fear touched her, with cold, slimy fingers that reached deep into her soul.

Each night, she felt the unnerving suspicion that she was being followed, but proof of her supposition was, for the most part, absent. This was only the second time that a form had actually materialized from the mist. Or had it? She stared hard at the spot, but could not be certain she saw anything more than a man-shaped shadow.

Regardless, she intended to exercise every caution.

She had come early for her shift this morn, determined to vary her schedule. Tomorrow, she would vary her route, as well.

Reaching the safety of the hospital, she hurried into the building and made her way first to the nurses' cloakroom, where she divested herself of her damp overgarment, then through the dim hallways to the women's sick ward. There was a patient here she wished to check on, a woman who was so ill she had not been able to eat or drink or even void for two days. It was as though her body refused to carry out the normal functions of life. Sarah hoped she had taken a turn for the better, though she knew in her heart that would not be the case.

She paused in the hallway near the ward. The only light was the eking dawn that filtered through grimy windows to steal across the floor in pale slashes. The sounds of suffering carried through the place, eerie moans and louder cries, a sob, the creak of a bed as someone shifted, then shifted again.

Moving forward, Sarah stepped through the doorway. She dared not breathe too deeply. No matter how much lime wash was slapped on the plaster, no matter how many scrubbings with yellow soap the floors took, the smell—the metallic bite of blood, the raw-onion stink of old sweat, the harsh ammonia of urine—never quite melted away. These small battles might beat back the wretched stench for a time, but in truth, the war was long lost. The sick ward was forever infused with the vestiges of human misery.

Her gaze slid over the beds. Each one was full. Some even had two patients crowded into a space meant to hold only one.

In the corner was the bed she sought. Little light inched that far into the gloom, and Sarah could see only the outline of pale sheets. She took a step forward, then froze with a gasp.

There was someone sitting on a stool at the far side of the bed, a man, garbed all in black, the pale ghosting of the patient's partially upraised arm a stark contrast against the dark background offered by his coat.

He held the woman's wrist. Sarah could see that now.

She must have made a sound that alerted him to her presence, for he raised his head. She saw only the faint highlight of his features, so deep was the gloom that surrounded him.

"Miss Lowell." His voice reached across the space that separated them, low, pleasant, and though he was wreathed in darkness and she could see almost nothing of his face, she knew the speaker.

Killian Thayne.

Her pulse jolted at the realization.

"Mr. Thayne," she acknowledged.

Neither said anything more, and Sarah remained where she was, frozen, strangely disturbed by the sight of the patient's white forearm contrasted against the cloth of Mr. Thayne's black-clad form.

A moan sounded from behind her, drawing her from her frozen state with a jolt. "Water," came a woman's plea. "I am so thirsty. Please, water."

Sarah glanced about, and saw the night watch nurse curled in a corner by the fire, sleeping. She could not help but feel pity for her, a widow with three small children who, after working the day as a charwoman, came to sit the night through for a shilling and her supper, leaving her little ones with a neighbor, and paying her in turn.

With a sigh, Sarah turned away to tend to the patient herself.

When she was done, she looked back to where she had seen the surgeon, Mr. Thayne, sitting in the darkness. University-trained physicians were addressed as *Dr.*, apprentice trained surgeons as *Mr.*, and there was a distinct barrier between

them, not only at King's College, but at any hospital throughout the city.

He was gone, the patient asleep, her head lolling to one
side, her arm hanging across the far edge of the bed.

Another patient called to her. Sarah hesitated, a feeling of
wariness sluicing through her. Stepping forward, she almost
went to the patient Mr. Thayne had been tending. Then she
wondered what she was thinking. What could she do for her
that he had not? The woman was sleeping now. Best to leave
her undisturbed.

Again, the patient behind her called out, becoming more
insistent. Sarah moved to her side and offered a sip of water,
and then noting the time, she made her way to the surgical
ward.

Only hours later did she learn that the patient in the corner had died in the silvered moments when night turned to
day, discovered by the night nurse when she roused from her
slumber.

Only then did Sarah hear the whispers that the woman's
wrist had been torn open, with nary a drop of blood spilled
to mark the sheets.

Mr. Simon, the head surgeon, determined that she had injured herself on a sharp edge of the bedstead, and in truth,
they found a smear of blood there that offered some proof of
the supposition.

But throughout that day and well into the night, Sarah could
not dispel the memory of Killian Thayne, swathed in darkness, his head bowed, and the woman's arm so white against
the black of his coat.

The bell tolled—once, twice, thrice—a solemn and sinister
peal that carried through walls of ancient, crumbling plaster
and floorboards of greasy, rotting wood.

Two weeks had passed since the woman had died in the
sick ward, her wrist torn open, her skin white as fresh-fallen

snow. Sarah's gaze slid to the bed in the corner. A new patient lay there now, moaning softly.

A shiver crawled up her spine, the memory and the hollow sound of the bell leaving her anxious and distressed. It rang out not to mark the time, but to summon the attendants.

She ought to be used to it by now, ought to have learned to slam the door against her horror and dismay. But she had not, and that was no one's failing but her own.

A moment later came the pounding of feet in the hallway. Summoned, they came, burly men in stained coats. The attendants. Their footsteps echoed through walls and closed doors, down the dim corridor toward the surgical ward, heavy and ominous.

She closed her eyes, imagined the scene as it would be, and felt a chill of horror. The attendants would hold the patient down and the surgeon would be quick, the blades sharp, the ligatures tight, but it would not be enough. It was never enough. The screams would come, the tears and pleas. And for all that suffering, by tomorrow or the next day, the patient was as like to be dead as not.

On a sharp exhale, Sarah opened her eyes and forced her attention to her task. She ladled porridge from the massive cauldron on the floor at her feet into small bowls, and lined them in neat rows on the tray atop the square table by her side. If she leaned in, she could detect the slightly acrid scent, as though the gruel had cooked on too hot a flame, or perhaps too long, and burned a little at the bottom.

One more unpleasant scent to add to the slurry.

The grimy windows let in little of the morning light, and what did filter through was browned and thinned by the filth. Bedbugs bit at the patients, and cockroaches scurried down the walls. Just last week, the matron had said they ought to hire a man like the one at Guy's Hospital to deal with the bugs. Sarah thought the plan meretricious. All the staff here gossiped about the state of the hospital; they had not the funds to pay such a man.

As she turned her attention back to her task, a sudden chill of premonition crawled across the back of her neck, raising the fine hairs at her nape. Or perhaps she heard a whisper of sound. She could not say with certainty.

Pausing in her actions, she raised her head, alert and cautious.

In the corners, the shadows breathed and waited.

Surreptitiously, she looked about, but saw nothing to cause her alarm. As for the occupants of the ward, the poor souls in their filthy, reeking beds focused on nothing but their own pain.

There was no danger here, unless it was the danger of human suffering and tragedy.

Turning her head, she glanced at the half-open door to the hallway just in time to catch sight of a black-clad form—broad shouldered, long limbed, sun-bright hair drawn back and tied at his nape.

That glimpse was enough. She knew him.

Killian Thayne.

Light in the darkness.

Her belly fluttered and danced, the sensation having nothing to do with ill ease, and everything to do with Mr. Thayne.

With her head cricked to one side, she leaned back, just a little, trying to see the last of him. But he was gone, and she was left with only the faintest echo of his boot heels on the floorboards.

Facing the room once more, she cut a glance through her lashes to see if any of the other day nurses had noticed her inappropriate interest in Mr. Thayne.

He was a mystery, a man who kept to himself, preferring the night and shadows over the daylight, and the company of his books to that of his fellows.

She found him both fascinating and frightening.

With a swish of her black skirts, Mrs. Bayley, a widow who worked with Sarah as a day nurse on the ward, approached.

She hefted the heavy tray and waited as Sarah set down her ladle.

"There are three on the list today," Mrs. Bayley intoned, jerking her head in the general direction of the surgical ward. "Bless their poor souls."

"Three?" Sarah asked as they moved between the beds, shoulder to shoulder in the narrow space. She knew that Mrs. Carmichael's two rotten fingers were to be cut away, and Mr. Riley's foot at the ankle. Both surgeries were to be done by Mr. Simon, the head surgeon. But she hadn't known of a third.

"Mmm-hmm. Mr. Scully's doing poorly. The blister on his stump burst, and he's been feverish the night through. Mr. Franks wants to cut away the rest of the leg at the hip."

"The hip?" Sarah repeated. Such a high amputation was fraught with danger. The patient rarely survived, and in this case, Sarah was almost certain he would not. A week past, the first surgery that had seen his leg taken just below the knee had almost killed him. A second such intervention surely would.

"Pity they must do their grisly work there on the ward," Mrs. Bayley said, stopping to let Sarah pass the bowls to the patients on either side. "My sister was at St. Thomas. In Southwark. For the cholera. Spent a week there, and glad she was for the mercury the doctor gave her. Do you know they have a real operating theater? Built in the old herb garret of the church. Imagine!"

"An operating theater? I cannot imagine," Sarah replied as she waited for the patient to haul herself to a sitting position using the rope that was strung between two tall poles attached to the bed, one fore, one aft. Sarah was heartened to see such progress, for the previous day the woman had been able to do little more than lie on her back and stare at the ceiling with tears creeping from the corners of her eyes.

With a smile, she reached down and drew the blanket smooth across the patient's legs.

"Feeling stronger today?" she asked.

"A mite," came the reply, accompanied by a wan smile.

After passing off the bowl and spoon, Sarah followed Mrs. Bayley and thought about the operating theater—a wonderful thing, in her estimation. King's College had no such luxury. Surgeries took place on the ward, with the surgical and apothecary apprentices gathered tight around the table, and all the other patients watching and listening in horror and distress as the attendants held the patient down.

Continuing along the row of beds, Sarah doled out her porridge to those well enough to eat it, and made silent note of those who were not, intending to return and assess their condition once she was done handing out the meal.

The situation was horribly frustrating to her.

She was a day nurse, in essence a domestic servant in the ward, charged with cleaning and serving meals and little more. The head nurse or the sisters under her supervision were responsible for direct patient care. On the surgical ward, the apprentices were often tasked with the care if it was a complicated case. It ate at Sarah that she was capable of doing more, wanted to do more, and she was prohibited.

Once, several weeks past, she had braved the office of the matron to request additional duties and chores. She had worked by her father's side—both in his surgery and at the homes of patients—for almost her entire life, and she wanted to do more than work as a char. Her father's training should not go to waste.

But the matron had reminded her that she was lucky to have a position at all, and that her presence here was suffered only on the memory of her father's good work and good name.

"I can finish this, Miss Lowell," Mrs. Bayley offered when the tray had been emptied twice and only a handful of patients remained to be fed. "You go on to the surgical ward."

With a nod, Sarah took her leave and moved along the

dim corridor, her black cotton skirt swishing softly as she walked.

She had not even passed through the doors of the surgical ward before she heard the argument already in full vigor.

"I say we cut just above midthigh," came the voice of Mr. Simon, his tone tight with anger. "We can do it this very morning, before the other two."

Pausing in the doorway, she glanced at the group who stood by Mr. Scully's bedside. The man had been brought in more than a week past. He had fractured his tibia and fibula in a fall, and the jagged shards had come through the skin. Open fractures were the most dangerous, the most prone to suppuration. Within two days Mr. Scully's limb had become infected, and he was left with only two options. Amputation or death.

He had chosen the former, and Mr. Simon had sawed off the limb below the knee.

For some days, Mr. Scully had done relatively well, but then his eyes had become glassy, his skin flushed and hot to the touch, and red streaks had begun to crawl up what was left of his leg.

Sarah had seen such an outcome many times before, and she knew it boded ill for the man's survival.

"And I say we must cut higher, closer to the hip," insisted Mr. Franks. "Do you not smell it? Sickly sweet? 'Tis not the rancid wet gangrene we deal with here, gentlemen, but the galloping gas gangrene. It will reach high into the healthy tissue and foul it as surely as I live and breathe."

There were murmurs of agreement from the group of gentlemen who hung on Mr. Franks's every word.

Sarah hovered in the background, listening to the discussion as she began to ladle portions from a fresh kettle of porridge that had been brought from the kitchen by a lad with a low, wheeled cart.

The gentlemen pressed together in a throng. Mr. Franks

was the peacock of the bunch, his black frock coat the single somber element of his attire. He wore buff trousers and a red waistcoat over his protuberant belly, and a bright blue stock high about his neck.

His appearance contrasted starkly with Mr. Simon, an extremely tall and gangly man, dressed all in black, his bony wrists sticking out beyond his cuffs, his hands milk white with long, slender fingers.

To his left was a young apothecary apprentice, his dark green frock coat and navy trousers covered by a white bib apron, the only one of the group who bothered in any way to protect his attire from the gore of the ward, or perhaps he sought to protect the patients from the unhealthy humors that might cling to his clothing.

Sarah's father had ever insisted that humors brought in from the street might create an unhealthy miasma for the patient. In her months working at King's College, she had seen much to support his theories.

"We'll take the midthigh amputation," Mr. Simon decreed with finality.

Sarah set down her ladle and angled closer to the bed, until she could peer around the press of bodies to better see the patient for herself. His skin was as pasty as freshly boiled linens with two bright, flushed spots, one on each cheek. His eyes were glassy, his breathing labored. She had no doubt that were she to have the opportunity to feel for his pulse, it would be rapid and wild.

There was a terrible odor coming from the stump of his leg. She could smell it even at this distance. Sarah disagreed with Mr. Franks on this. The smell was not sickly sweet, but the horrific stink of rotting flesh. Thick, rancid pus oozed from the stump, and the free ends of the ligatures draped across the sheet, leaving trails of yellow-green suppuration.

"The hip it must be," cried Mr. Franks.

"I beg to differ, sir. I must insist on midthigh," came

Mr. Simon's sharp reply. "You well know that the higher the amputation the greater the risk of death."

"His risk is great enough from the spread of the poison. Do you not see it, man, crawling up his thigh like a spider?" Mr. Franks turned and looked about at his supporters, who murmured agreement.

The patient, Mr. Scully, roused himself enough to look slowly back and forth between the doctors, his entire body trembling, his lips working but making no sound. Sarah wondered if he understood what they were saying, or if he was caught in a delirium brought on by the poison that was leaching through his body.

From the corner of her eye, she saw the attendants moving about, preparing the large wooden table for the operations to come, scattering fresh sawdust on the floor beneath to catch the blood that would drip down. There was only a curtain separating that table from the remainder of the ward.

On a smaller, low wooden bench were laid out the necessary implements. Sharp knives, some curved, some straight, designed to sweep clear through skin and muscle, down to the bone. An ebony-handled saw. Petit's screw tourniquets. Curved needles. Tenaculums to grab the artery and allow for the silk ligature to tie it off. A basin.

How many times had she stood by her father's side and handed him each item as he needed it, no words exchanged, no request necessary?

From him, she had learned how to tighten the tourniquet, tie a ligature, even the appropriate way to cut flaps of skin and allow for healing by first intention.

Of course, she had never done a surgery on her own, but she had worked at her father's side for years, never thinking about whether she liked the role, whether she wanted to be there. She was there because he needed her hands.

And then, abruptly, he was gone. Dead. He had left her alone and destitute, forced to take a position at King's Col-

lege as a day nurse, because there was no other option open
to her. Well . . . not unless she wanted to stand on a corner,
leaning against a post by the gin houses of Seven Dials.

Sarah was grateful that the physicians of King's College
remembered her father with fond respect, and so recommended
her to the matron for a position in the wards.

She had thought a great deal about her preferences since
then, and she had realized that though her emotions rebelled
against the suffering of the sick and injured, she yearned to
help them, to offer comfort and solace and what little healing she could. What had begun as a path followed in her father's footsteps had become her own inclination somewhere
in time.

The surgeons were still discussing the relative merits of a
higher versus a lower amputation, and Sarah sensed the patient's growing distress. With a cry, he reared up and peered
around the crowd to lock his gaze on the area being prepared
for his care.

Thrashing, he turned his gaze to Sarah, and she saw that
his eyes were fever bright. He began to moan, short sobbing
sounds, and she felt them in the marrow of her bones, in her
viscera. His gaze was locked on her, his attention complete.

She stood, frozen. All eyes turned in her direction, and she
was caught like a rabbit in an open field. Her heart twisted in
a tight, black knot.

All around her, other patients shifted restlessly, disturbed
by Mr. Scully's cries. Some called out, and some stayed stoically silent.

"Enough." A single word, spoken in a mellifluous tone.
And it *was* enough, for the sounds settled and somehow, the
tension in the ward seemed to ease.

Killian Thayne stepped from the shadows on the far side
of the bed. He was garbed all in black, the somber tone a
contrast to the bright glittering gold of his hair.

Slowly, he reached up to remove the strange bottle-green
spectacles she had never seen him without. Head bowed, he

folded the arms of the spectacles with meticulous care and placed them in the inside breast pocket of his impeccably cut coat. Then he raised his head and his gaze slid past each gentleman in turn, to the attendants setting up the operating table, and finally to Sarah herself.

The force of his direct stare made her gasp.

His eyes were gray. Not the soft color of a dove, but the rough, turbulent shade of a raging winter storm. A powerful storm.

He held it leashed, that power. She felt that as a certainty. And it made her shiver.

Two

Very aware of the scrutiny of the doctors and apprentices—and most assuredly of Mr. Thayne—Sarah shuffled away from the group, back toward the kettle of porridge. Lifting her ladle, she feigned absorbed interest in her task, and after a moment, they turned away from her once more.

She wondered what had possessed her to step up and insinuate herself at the edges of the group. 'Twas far better to avoid notice, to go about her duties like a wraith. Tipping her head, she watched through lowered lashes as the scene unfolded.

Mr. Thayne stared at her for a heartbeat longer, then looked down at the man in the bed, offering his full and undivided attention. Sputters and mutters came from the surrounding group, but none stepped forward to blatantly challenge his authority, though both Mr. Simon and Mr. Franks had seniority here.

"Mr. Scully, you have an infection in the flesh of your stump, and a poison in the blood," Mr. Thayne said to the patient, his tone calm, compassionate. "My companions suggest that if they do a second amputation, higher than the first, they might save your life."

The patient had ceased his moaning and restless thrashing the moment Mr. Thayne turned his attention to him. Sarah had seen this before. Killian Thayne ever had a calming effect on the sick and dying.

She wondered at that, wondered how a man who caused such upheaval inside *her* could so effortlessly smooth the emotions of those in physical torment.

"Mr. Simon argues for the thigh, Mr. Franks for the hip," he continued.

"I fear it will not save me," the patient said, his voice trembling. "I fear I will die regardless what they do now. I feel it. I feel the poison working through me, an evil humor. So you tell me . . . which will save me, the higher or the lower? Or do they propose the cutting only as a means to show these apprentices the way of things?"

"I say," interjected Mr. Simon, his tone outraged. Then he exchanged a glance with Mr. Franks, and Sarah read the truth in that. They *were* inclined to insist upon the surgery in order to offer the learning experience to their apprentices, for how were prospective surgeons to know the way of things except by observation of the operations in question?

Though she understood the logic, the thought of seeing Mr. Scully—or any patient—subjected to such horror merely as a teaching tool revolted her.

As Mr. Scully raised his hand from the mattress, the limb shaking wildly, Mr. Thayne grasped it, his gaze never leaving the man's face. Sarah held her breath, waiting for his answer, wondering what he would say, for she suspected that he thought as she did, that it was far too late.

Mr. Simon and Mr. Franks were spluttering and interjecting, but it mattered not. The patient's entire focus was on Killian Thayne's eyes.

"You say that you fear you will die regardless, but is it death you fear, sir?" His voice was low, smooth. Enticing. Luring the true secrets of the patient's deepest deliberations.

Sarah thought that should Killian Thayne ask *her* a question in that tone, with that intent look fixed upon her, she would surely bare the entirety of her heart and soul.

"Fear death?" Mr. Scully frowned, and pondered that for an instant; then he went on, speaking with unexpected eloquence for one who had been mired for days in the depths of delirium. "No. My wife has gone ahead of me, and my three sons. I've little left here, and I suppose"—he shot a glance at Mr. Simon—"that no matter where they make their barbarous cut, I shall die regardless. I can feel the weight of death's touch on my shoulder."

Sarah swallowed, strangely unnerved, for it was Mr. Thayne's free hand that rested upon the man's shoulder.

"Yes," Mr. Thayne agreed. "Death's touch is upon you."

The gaggle of murmuring apprentices fell silent at the low-spoken pronouncement.

"I do not want the surgery. Let death come," the patient said, vehement. "You asked if it is death I fear? Not at all. I fear they'll cut me in bits and pieces until there's no more of me to cut. But I am already dead. There's just the shell of me what's got to give up the spirit. I feel it inside me, the poison. I feel it."

His words were clear and certain, and again Sarah could not help but wonder at that, at his lucidity of the moment. He had been nothing of the sort for days now, instead rambling and moaning and insisting he saw his wife sitting at the foot of his bed, talking to her, though she had been dead these past four years.

She had the unexpected thought that it was Mr. Thayne—his touch on the man's shoulder—that steadied him. Rationality argued against the possibility, but Sarah could not discount it.

"You have no say here, Thayne," Mr. Simon interjected, spittle flying from his lips as his agitation spurred his words. "The patient is not yours, and I will thank you to mind yourself."

"And the *leg* is not *yours*," Mr. Thayne replied, unperturbed. His lips were faintly turned, as though he found Mr. Simon amusing or, perhaps, contemptible. "We both know that your proposed intervention is more likely to kill than to cure. The patient has said he has no wish for your further surgical involvement, and I am of the opinion that his decision is wise."

Mr. Simon made a sound of dismissal, but Mr. Thayne quelled him with a look.

"Were you the one dying on this bed, you would surely prefer the route of least pain rather than most," he continued. A silky threat. Sarah's gaze slid back and forth between the two; then Mr. Thayne made a smooth gesture of dismissal. "Offer him as much gin as he can swallow. Laudanum, if you have it. Dull the pain as best you can, and let him make this journey in whatever peace he can find."

With that, he returned his attention to the man on the bed, leaning low to say something near his ear. Sarah could hear none of it, and from the expressions on the faces of the group of apprentices and surgeons, they could hear nothing of the exchange, either. It irked them. That much was obvious.

Whatever quiet words Mr. Thayne offered, they had an immediate further calming effect on the patient, a lessening of visible agitation. Mr. Scully's eyes slid shut and the tension in his body eased.

Surprised, Sarah wondered if Mr. Thayne was a mesmerist.

Before his death, her father had taken her to see a public demonstration put on by the mesmerist John Elliotson. He had laid his hands upon a woman and sent her into catalepsy from which loud noises and even needles poked into her skin had not roused her. Now Sarah could not help but note the similarities between Elliotson's display and the way that Mr. Scully eased so completely from distress into relaxation.

Regardless of the reason, she was glad that Mr. Thayne's presence offered some relief for the patient's suffering, and she was glad, too, that he was here to speak against the futile amputation of the remainder of the limb. There was no hope for this man's survival, certainly no hope in further surgery. If he was destined to live, it would not be a mortal intervention that would decide it.

Again, Mr. Thayne's gaze slid to hers, and he made a small nod, as though he knew and understood her thoughts. As though they shared some sort of collusion.

Awareness shivered through her, an instant of connection. On several previous occasions there had been such moments in the ward, when Mr. Thayne walked his rounds and Sarah came to be in his path. To her befuddlement, he had deigned to speak with her, to ask her opinion of the patient's progress, to note her responses with interest and grave attention.

Once, he had even followed her suggestion, refusing to allow a patient with an open wound to be placed in a bed until the linens were removed and exchanged for clean ones. Thereafter, he had insisted on clean linens each time a new patient entered the ward, and Sarah had understood it was because he took her opinion as one of value.

It was a gift he offered her, one that meant a great deal.

In this moment, she thought that were it not for the mass of men and the likelihood that discourse with her would adversely affect her position here, he would ask her opinion of *this* case.

And he would find it in agreement with his own.

Losing interest in Mr. Scully when their efforts to bully him produced no result, Mr. Simon and Mr. Franks moved on, followed by their entourage.

Sarah took the opportunity to sidle closer.

Stirring a little, Mr. Scully opened his eyes and murmured languidly. "Sit with me for a bit, Martha. Sit with me for a bit and sing to me the way you sang to our babes when they were small."

He shifted restlessly and scratched quite vigorously first at his neck, then at his arm. "Itchy," he muttered, then made a watery laugh. "Sleep tight. Don't let the bedbugs bite."

She raised her gaze to Mr. Thayne and found him watching her with those amazing gray eyes. She had never before seen them unobscured by his tinted spectacles, never seen the myriad colors swirling in their depths, variegated shades of gray and silver and icy blue.

His eyes were as extraordinary and beautiful as the rest of him. She ought to have expected that.

"'Tis the fever that makes his skin itch," she murmured, compelled to fill the silence. "Or the bedbugs."

Slowly, his gaze slid across her features, and his straight, dark gold brows drew together, as though he puzzled through some particular matter. She felt undone by that look, felt that with it he reached beyond her skin and looked deep inside her heart and soul.

With a faint smile, he inclined his head.

"I leave the patient in your most competent care, Miss Lowell."

His words shimmered through her, and she wondered if he knew how much she valued that, his acknowledgment of her competence. To have her work recognized was a warm and pleasant thing.

In that instant, the man on the bed lurched up and caught hold of Mr. Thayne's frock coat, fisting his fingers in the material so tightly that his knuckles showed white.

"Please," he begged, his voice slurred, as though he had already been dosed with the gin and laudanum Mr. Thayne had recommended. "Please do it for me. Do it quick. With poison or a knife. This is a terrible suffering, and we both know they'll only come again. What if you are not here to speak for me? What if they drag me to that table and hold me down and cut my flesh? I do not want to die that way, sawed into sections like wood for a fire." He paused, and then said in a clear, ringing voice, "Kill me and be done with it."

In that instant, Sarah felt the heavy hush that fell on the ward. She glanced about and saw that many eyes watched the scene unfold and many ears listened. A chill of premonition crawled across her skin, and she jerked her attention back to the scene before her.

Mr. Thayne held the man's gaze for a moment, his expression ruthlessly neutral. Then he reached into his pocket, withdrew his bottle-green spectacles, and slid them on to hide his eyes.

A mask, Sarah thought. A wall.

At length, Mr. Scully loosed his hold and dropped his hand back to the sheets. It slid down to hang at an uncomfortable angle, and Sarah moved forward to set it back on the bed.

When she looked up once more, a single shaft of light broke through the grime of the window to cut across the floor exactly where Mr. Thayne had stood.

But he was gone. Disappeared. His passage silent as the mist.

Early the following morning, well before the dawn, Sarah arrived at the hospital. The chill of the night air clung to her clothes and a strange wariness churned in her belly, though her walk from Coptic Street had been calm and undisturbed, with no hint of someone watching her from the shadows.

That was a boon to her frayed nerves.

As she made her way down the corridor, shadows and moonlight crept across the floor in an alternating pattern of light and dark stripes. Her steps were quick and sure as she made her way directly to the surgical ward, anxious to check on Mr. Scully. He had clung to life throughout the previous day, growing increasingly ill, feverish, and lost in a world of his own making, crying out, moaning. Each time Sarah had looked in on him he had not recognized her, and had mistaken her for his dead wife.

Now she wondered if he had lived through the night.

Reaching the surgical ward, she paused in the doorway,

her gaze sliding to Mr. Scully's bed. She took a single step, then froze and made a startled gasp.

There, outlined on the far wall, was a looming shadow in the shape of a man, his height and breadth exaggerated and magnified.

Her blood chilled and her gaze skittered about the room, returning in horrified dismay to the shadow cast upon the wall.

A shadow with no source.

She was the only upright person in the ward. Everyone else was supine on their beds.

A shiver crawled along her spine. She whirled to look to the windows at the far end of the ward, then turned once more to face Mr. Scully's bed and the wall beyond.

Her heart jerked and danced an uneven jig.

The shadow was gone, disappeared.

But the fine hairs risen at her nape and the clammy fingers oozing across her skin made her certain that she had not imagined it, and that whoever—whatever—had cast the dark silhouette yet hovered, unseen, in the gloom.

Pressing her palm flat against her breastbone, she tried to will both her racing pulse and her galloping imagination under control.

"Mr. Scully," she whispered, walking forward. "Mr. Scully, how do you this morn?"

He lay quiet and still, his head lolling to one side, his arm hanging over the far side of the bed.

Alive still? She did not think it, and that came as no shock. But there was *something* about the way he was arranged on the bed . . . something both macabre and familiar.

Breathing too fast, she crept forward, closer to the silent, still man.

A patient called out to her, but she did not so much as turn her head, for her entire focus was on the sight of Mr. Scully's form, a lump beneath stained and frayed sheets. Not moving. Not breathing.

The smell hit her first, a heavy slap of urine and excrement.

Dead. He was dead. Released from his pain.

She reached the bed and stared down at him. His eyes were closed, his arms arranged in an odd position, hanging over the edges of the mattress. And his wrist was torn open, a jagged, gaping wound.

For a moment, she could not breathe, could not think, and then she forced herself to sharpen her attention, to determine exactly what it was that gnawed at her with vicious little teeth.

There was no blood.

Despite the torn edges of the hole at his wrist, there was not a single crimson drop upon the sheet or the floor beneath.

Slowly, she walked all the way around the bed, aware that the patients on the ward were stirring, asking for water, for food, for a moment of comfort. Soon, someone else would hear the commotion, and they would come, they would see . . .

What? They would see what?

The body of a man who had been destined to die? Only, the manner of said death was both bizarre and disturbing.

And it was the fourth such death here at King's College.

She shivered.

"Miss Lowell? Is aught amiss?"

She heard the voice as though through a long, narrow tunnel.

Turning, she faced him, Killian Thayne, tall and broad and unsmiling. He stood close enough to touch, dressed all in black, like a shadow.

"He is dead," she murmured, her tongue like leather in her mouth. "Mr. Scully is dead."

"An expected outcome"—he paused—"yet you are distressed by his passing."

"By the *mode* of his passing," she whispered in a rush, then wondered that she could be so foolish.

Someone had been here earlier, beside Mr. Scully's bed.

She had seen the shaded outline of his silhouette cast against the pale wall.

And here was Killian Thayne standing before her, just as he had been there by another patient's bedside on a morning two weeks past—another patient who had died with the same strange and inexplicable wounds.

"Let me see." Mr. Thayne stepped around her and then around the bed to the far side. He stared at Mr. Scully's sprawled form for a long moment.

Wrapping her arms about her waist, Sarah turned and watched him. His expression was unperturbed, his posture relaxed, but something felt off. Then she realized his lips had drawn taut, as they had the previous day when he confronted Mr. Simon. That was the only sign of his displeasure.

"Fetch a stretcher," he instructed, his voice ever soft. "I shall wrap him in a sheet."

"I can summon one of the other nurses to help me." She wondered why he offered to do this chore himself. Surgeons were not responsible for wrapping the dead.

Only for killing them.

She shuddered at the thought. What was it about Mr. Thayne that made her mind travel such a path? She knew that the physicians and surgeons at King's College did the best they could, that their efforts were based in genuine desire to cure, to save lives. That more than half the surgical patients died was a fact indisputably assigned to every hospital in the city.

But as she looked at Mr. Thayne where he stood looming over Mr. Scully's pale form, she wondered how it was that he had been present at two such similar deaths. No . . . not two. Four. He had been present when all of the four patients had been found with their wrists torn open, and the bloody pool that ought to have accompanied such injury inexplicably absent.

What was she thinking? He was a healer. She had witnessed his care and kindness to many patients in the months she had worked these wards. Was she now to imagine that he had killed four people by slashing their wrists? To what purpose? What end?

And where was the blood?

Confusion buffeted her, and she was appalled by her own thoughts, disdainful of them. She could not think why she allowed her mind to travel such a path.

Sarah steeled her nerves, wanting to ask him all manner of questions, but in that instant came a shocked cry that made her turn quickly toward the sound.

"Oh my word. Another one with his wrist looking like he's been chewed by a beast," Mrs. Bayley exclaimed, bustling closer and leaning in to peer at Mr. Scully's lacerated flesh. She reared back and looked about, her gaze pausing first on Sarah, then on Mr. Thayne. She paled as she looked at him, and blurted, "You were here. When Mrs. Moldaver died, and again when Mrs. Barr's body was found. . . ."

"I was, yes." He made no effort to disagree, his tone calm and even. "I am a surgeon in this hospital"—he made a small, sardonic smile and cast a glance at Sarah—"and am expected to attend on occasion."

She wondered that he took no umbrage at the woman's accusations, that he bothered to explain himself to her at all.

"But you were there each time. No one else. Only you," Mrs. Bayley whispered in horror, and the patients in the neighboring beds began to pick up the words and repeat them anew.

For an instant, Sarah felt a dizzying disconnection at the oddity of the situation. Here they stood among beds that held people whose limbs had been hacked away, yet the sight of a torn wrist elicited such horror and dismay.

Because there *was* something sinister about Mr. Scully's wound. It was not clean. As Mrs. Bayley had said, it *did* look as though an animal had chewed it open and lapped up all the blood before going on its way.

Uncertain from where she dredged her temerity, Sarah turned her gaze to Mr. Thayne and said, "Please do not let us delay you, sir. Mrs. Bayley and I can see to Mr. Scully. I am certain you have other things to occupy your attention."

One straight brow rose in question, and again, his lips curved in a hard, sardonic smile. He inclined his head and strode away, his long limbs eating the distance to the door. Sarah could not stop herself turning her head to watch him go.

And all around her, the whispers continued.

Leaving Mrs. Bayley to wrap the body, Sarah went to fetch a stretcher. When she returned, she found both Mr. Simon and Mr. Franks standing by the edge of the bed, along with the matron. All three were involved in an intense whispered discussion with much gesticulation and wary glances cast about. Mr. Simon rounded the bed, lifted Mr. Scully's savaged arm, and spoke in a low, fervent tone. The content of his comments was lost to Sarah's ears, obscured by the general hubbub of the ward.

Her movements made awkward by the stretcher she carried, she inched closer to the small group.

"'Tis Thayne's doing," Mr. Simon insisted, the words resonating with tension. "We all know it. He attended each of the four deaths, and we had words over the care of each of the four victims. Does no one else wonder at the strange coincidence?"

"What do you suggest, sir?" asked Mr. Franks. "That he bled the man dry? For what purpose? To what end?" His voice lowered still more. "Do you accuse him of murder?"

Sarah stifled a gasp, the sound faint in comparison to Mrs. Bayley's huffing exclamation of dismay.

"I make no accusation." Mr. Simon offered a sneering, ugly smile. "I state only facts. Thayne disagreed with the treatment of each patient. He insisted that there was no hope for recovery, and that death was the definitive outcome." He paused dramatically, and looked about at the neighboring beds as though attempting to be circumspect. A carefully structured ploy, for had that been his genuine intent, he would have taken this discourse to a more private venue. "I postulate that Thayne was the last to see this man alive, and that it is well past time for us to summon the authorities."

She could not say what possessed her in that moment, but Sarah stepped forward as though in a trance, and spoke in Mr. Thayne's defense.

"Sir," she said, "I was here when Mr. Scully died. Mr. Thayne arrived only later." Not precisely the truth, but not exactly a lie, either. Mr. Thayne *had* arrived later . . . at least, she thought he had, for she could not say whose shadow she had seen. And as to her assertion that she had been here when Mr. Scully expired, well, she had likely been on the premises somewhere, though not at his bedside. Gently bending the truth was a far cry from breaking it. "And perhaps his wound might be explained by the bugs."

They all stared at her.

"He was . . . That is . . ." She wet her lips.

"What place have you in this discussion, miss?" Mr. Simon demanded with enough force and fury that Sarah almost silenced herself.

Drawing her courage about her like a cloak, she forced herself to continue in a calm and even manner. "Mr. Scully was complaining yesterday that his skin itched. He said it was bedbugs, and perhaps the added distress of the fever made him scratch. Could the injuries to his wrist be excoriation?"

She felt the urgency of her defense, as though she was driven to offer an alibi for Mr. Thayne. Something inside her would not let them mark him as a murderer.

Because he was not.

She felt that certainty to her marrow.

"You suggest that all of the four patients tore at their own skin, driven mad by the itch?" Mr. Franks scoffed.

"Matron said we ought to hire a man to see to the bugs,

the way they have at Guy's Hospital." Sarah cut a glance at the other woman, who nodded her agreement.

"But to tear the skin clean through? And the blood vessels, as well?" Mr. Franks folded his hands across his ample belly and peered down his nose at her.

Sarah bit her lip. The possibility was ludicrous, but she had set herself on this path and now saw no clear way to proceed. Her thoughts skittered this way and that as she tried to summon an appropriate reply.

"Let us examine his body for signs of excoriation," came Mr. Thayne's low voice from close behind her. Gasping in shock, she spun so quickly that she nearly unbalanced herself.

He had arrived just in time to save her from her attempt to save him.

Calm and steady, his gaze met hers for an instant, his green-tinted spectacles nowhere to be seen. She almost wished that he were wearing them, for they offered some protection from his piercing, too-knowing gaze.

"Yes, let us examine for such signs," snarled Mr. Simon, and with little care for propriety or respect, he reached down and yanked aside the neck of the nightshirt that covered Mr. Scully's pale torso. Deep runnels were gouged in his chest from where he had, indeed, scratched himself raw.

His face a mask of shock, Mr. Simon jerked back and let go his hold on the cloth. "It means nothing."

Mr. Franks shook his head from side to side. "It means a great deal."

And Sarah was immensely glad of Mr. Franks's contrary nature. If Mr. Simon claimed the sky was blue, then Mr. Franks would argue that it was green, simply because he could not help himself. A boon, under the circumstances, for it offered her an unexpected ally.

With everyone's attention locked on this new evidence, Mr. Thayne leaned in and spoke for her ears alone.

"My champion, Miss Lowell?" He sounded amused.

She shook her head. "Only the voice of reason," she whispered in return. "They were ready to name you a ravening beast."

When no reply was immediately forthcoming, she glanced back at him over her shoulder, and found him far too close for either propriety or comfort. Too tall. Too broad. Too male.

Golden stubble dusted his jaw and a lock of his sun-bright hair had come free of its queue to fall across the sculpted line of his cheek.

"A ravening beast," he mused, and his lips curved in a dark smile. "Perhaps the descriptor is fitting."

His eyes glittered, gray and brooding as a storm-chased sky, myriad emotions reflected in their silvered depths. Dark emotions.

She turned forward once more to stare straight ahead at Mr. Simon and Mr. Franks, who bickered back and forth like two boys in short-pants.

Buffeted by both confusion and dismay, she heard not a word of their discourse. In that moment, with the heat and the leashed threat of Killian Thayne so close at her back, she had the strange thought that he was not like other men, that there was something inside him, something dangerous and barely restrained.

That perhaps the label of beast was most apt.

Three

With Mr. Scully wrapped in his sheets and removed from his bed, Sarah went off to fetch fresh linens. Another poor soul would arrive soon to take that bed, to lie moaning in pain, or stoically white-lipped.

That was the part she found difficult. She had little enough to offer the patients save for a cool hand on their brow or a cup of gin. The physicians doled out laudanum with a miserly fist, for the cost was dear and the stores low. So the patients suffered, and that suffering wore at her. She longed for a way to alleviate it.

She paused only long enough to carefully wash her hands in the basin at the side of the ward. She knew that others watched her with suspicious interest, wondering at her obsession with cleanliness. Mostly, the nurses washed not at all, and the surgeons only after a messy surgery to clean away the blood and gore. But Sarah's father had thought it important to wash both before and after patient care, so she did as she had been taught, and wished that others might learn by her example.

A mouse scurried in the shadows as she made her way along the wide corridor, the noise and clamor of the wards fading behind her. Slowing her pace, she turned down a narrower hallway and, finally, stepped into a small, dark alcove that housed the storage closet. The door was an ill-fitting slab of wood that stuck fast until she pulled hard, and then it scraped along the floor with a grating rasp.

She stared into the interior of the closet, and thought that she ought to have brought a candle, for though the day was bright, the closet was set in a dim corner. There were no windows in the alcove or in the short, narrow hallway that led to it. The only light filtered from the windows of the wider corridor, and it was far enough away that paltry illumination strayed this far.

The pale linens were easy enough to see, set on the middle shelf, a low stack of oft-mended, yellowed cloths that had been scrubbed and boiled time and again, and still bore the stains of many uses.

Sarah stepped into the storage closet, then held herself very still, an eerie sensation tickling the fine hairs at her nape. Heart racing, she spun and peered into the gloom, but saw nothing more than dust and shadows.

Feeling foolish, she turned back to her task, stacking sheets and choosing several tallow candles to add to her pile. She paused, then added a stack of torn strips of cloth to act as bandages, for she had noticed that the stores in the ward were quite depleted.

Something alerted her. The faint scent of citrus. A whisper of sound. She could not say, but eerie conviction coalesced inside her, and she sucked in a startled breath, certain now that she was not alone.

Certain that Killian Thayne was directly behind her.

Her heart thudded hard in her breast and the walls of the small closet seemed to move closer still. There was a flicker of fear in her heart, true, but there was something else as well, something bigger and stronger, a stirring excitement that raced through her veins, dangerous and alluring at once.

Resting her hands on the shelf, she swallowed, struggling

to gather her wayward emotions. He was here, behind her. If she turned, he would be only a hand span away, and she would . . . What? Dare to touch him? To lay her hand on his arm and know the strength of him?

'Twas one thing to dream it in her secret heart, in the dark of night while she lay in her cold, narrow bed. Quite another to be faced with the reality.

Strange how this moment so closely resembled a thousand others. The difference was, *those* moments had taken place in her dreams, or in the waking daze as she broke from slumber's embrace, alone in her bed, her thoughts focused on imagined shared moments when Killian Thayne came to her as a lover would.

The touch of his hand on her cheek. The scent of his skin. The feel of his lips, warm, soft, as they brushed hers. Those were the secret, naive imaginings of a girl who had never been courted, never been kissed.

But standing here, in the dark little closet, with Mr. Thayne at her back, blocking her way, was a far different thing, entirely.

Slowly, she turned, her heart pounding in anticipation, a wild, untrammeled rhythm, her mouth dry, her cheeks hot.

Did he know? Could he tell that she had dreamed of him and watched him and fantasized about him for as long as she had been employed here at King's College? Foolish, girlish dreams, because he was beautiful and mysterious and far more intriguing than any other man she had ever met.

She saw now that he was not so close as she had first anticipated, and she did not know if she was disappointed or relieved. He was standing in the alcove beyond the door, the insubstantial light that leaked from the main corridor creating a faint nimbus about him, leaving his features obscured by shadow.

"Miss Lowell," he greeted her, so polite, his tone low and smooth.

"Mr. Thayne." The words came out a cracked whisper,

and she dropped her gaze to the tips of his polished boots. Always polished. His trousers always neat and pressed. His clothes impeccable and obviously expensive.

An enigma.

While physicians to the upper class might earn quite a respectable income, a surgeon was less likely to do so, and was definitely a rung below on the social ladder. All the more so a surgeon who practiced in a poor hospital such as King's College.

Rolling her lips inward, she swiped her tongue across the surface, and waited, wondering what he was doing here. He had followed her. She could have no doubt of that, but the reason for such action escaped her.

"You defended me," he murmured. "I would like to know why."

He asked only why she defended him, not why she lied for him. The differentiation did not escape her.

Was there some import, some key relevance to his choice of words?

She wondered if it *had* been his shadow she had seen earlier, or just a trick of the light. She could not say with certainty, could not state unequivocally that in defending him, she had not lied for him.

From the open doorway of the little closet he watched her, the shadows and his ever-present darkened spectacles masking his eyes and any secrets his expression might reveal.

"I defended no one. I merely pointed out possible explanations for what had occurred, and since no one came forth with any other, it appears my suggestion was given full merit"—she paused—"though I suspect this is not the end of the inquiry, nor the end of supposition and accusation."

His lips curved in a ghost of a smile, and she found herself staring at his mouth, the hard line of it, the slightly squared, full lower lip, so incredibly appealing. She could not seem to look away.

He had not shaved. She noticed that now, and realized that more often than not, his jaw was shaded by a day's stubble. His grooming was otherwise impeccable, but he eschewed the razor. She wondered if there was a particular reason for that, or merely that he found it a bother.

There was no question that she liked it. Liked the look of his lean, squared jaw with the faintest hint of a cleft at the front of his chin. Of its own volition, her hand half rose, and she stopped the movement with a tiny gasp, wondering what she thought she had meant to do. Touch him? Lay her fingers against his jaw and feel the golden hairs beneath her fingers? She wondered if they would be soft or scratchy, and she could not suppress a small shiver.

"No, I suspect it is not the end of the inquiry," he agreed, and she wondered at his calm amiability. He seemed not at all distressed by the observation.

Suddenly reckless, she dared ask, "*Were* you there this morning? Before I arrived? Was it you that I saw?"

His fine humor dropped away, and his expression turned cool and blank. "What did you see?" A harsh demand.

"I—" She backed up a step, put off by the sharp change in his tone, but the shelves were at her back and there was nowhere else for her to go.

He prowled a step closer. Her heart slammed hard against her ribs and she stared at him, afraid and appalled and tantalized all at once.

"Whom did you see, Miss Lowell?" He moderated his tone now, made it gentle and smooth. But he did not step back. He held his place, close enough that she had to tip her head far back to look into his eyes.

"Do you crowd me on purpose, sir?"

His teeth flashed white in a brief smile, and despite her words and tone, he made no move to step away. "And if I do?"

"Then I would ask you to stop."

"I like being close to you," he murmured, his words warming her blood and leaving her dizzy. "Your hair smells like flowers."

He left her at a loss, breathless and warm and so aware of his assertion that it hummed in her blood. Her hair *did* smell like flowers. She bathed every other day using scented soap. The soap was her one excess, her baths her sole luxury, one she worked hard for, heating water and dragging it up the stairs to the hip bath she set up in her chamber. Her landlady and the other lodgers in Coptic Street thought her mad.

Dipping his head until his cheek brushed against her hair, he inhaled deeply. She stood very still, her pulse racing, her breath locked in her throat and all manner of strange and bright emotions cascading through her like a brook.

Only when he eased back did she dare to breathe, and even then it was only a short, huffing gasp.

"Tell me what you saw," he coaxed.

"I am not certain." She was grateful for the change in topic and the tiny bit of space he allowed her. Her heart raced too fast; her nerves tingled with excitement. He made her lose her common sense, and she did not like that. "Perhaps I saw a shadow cast through the windows. Perhaps nothing." She paused and lifted her gaze, but found only her own reflection in the dark glass of his spectacles. "Perhaps I saw *you.*"

"If you think that, then why did you defend me?"

Humor laced his tone, and she was not certain if she was relieved or dismayed. He confounded her, made her wary, and yet he fascinated her.

"I never said I thought it. You asked what I saw, and as I truly do not know, I offered a variety of options."

She told only the truth. She could not say why she had leapt to his defense. She only knew that she could not find it in herself to believe that he had ripped open the wrists of four patients at King's College and drained their bodies of blood.

Even standing here in the gloomy little closet with the

height and breadth of him—the *threat* of him—blocking her path, the possibility that he had done murder seemed absurd. She had seen him work far too hard to save patients' lives to believe that he would choose to kill them.

He reached up and slid his bottle-green spectacles down his nose, then dragged them off entirely, leaving his gaze open to her scrutiny. His eyes glittered in the darkness, and the shadows only served to accent the handsome lines and planes of his features. The slash of high cheekbones, the straight line of his nose.

For a long moment, he studied her, saying nothing, the only sound the escalated cadence of her own breathing. He was so focused, so intent.

Again, she wondered if he was a mesmerist, for she found she could not look away. Had no wish to look away.

Her limbs felt heavy, languid, and her blood was thick and hot in her veins.

Raising his hand, he laid his fingers along the side of her throat, and her pulse pounded harder, wilder.

"Sarah." Just her name, spoken in his low, deep voice. The sound thrummed through her body, leaving her limbs trembling and her thoughts befuddled. "Such a wise and brave creature you are."

Wise. Brave.

He could not know her thoughts or he would not say such things to her.

Her pulse was racing like a runaway cart, but the emotion that suffused her was not fear. Her skin tingled, her nerves danced, and she was aware of Killian Thayne's every breath, of the sweep of his dark gold lashes as he blinked and the thick, bright strand of hair that had worked free of its tie to fall against his lean cheek.

A sound escaped her, a breath, a sigh. He leaned closer, until their breath mingled and the faint hint of citrus on his skin became more discernible. She wanted to rest her nose against the strong column of his throat and simply breathe him in, but she held her place, paralyzed by incertitude and inexperience.

He would kiss her now. She wanted him to kiss her now.

Her lips parted.

Voices carried to them from the main corridor, laughter and the murmur of conversation. The moment dropped and shattered, fractured into a thousand bits. Sarah felt the loss like a physical blow.

With a rueful smile, Killian Thayne drew his thumb across her lower lip, the brief contact making her shiver. Then he stepped away, leaving her body aching in the strangest way, as though her breasts and belly were pained by disappointment.

She closed her eyes, drew a deep breath, and when she opened them once more, he was gone and she was alone. Alone with the shadows and the dark and the memory of the way he had looked at her. Focused. Appreciative.

Hungry.

Five days passed, with Sarah coming to work before dawn each day, and walking home each night long past dusk. The sun she saw only through the grimy windows of the wards or the corridors.

She had grown wily, careful to vary her route between her room in Coptic Street and the hospital, which meant she could not help but skirt the dangerous edges of St. Giles. The sensation that someone stalked her had not abated. In fact, the certainty that she was followed had grown and solidified until she trusted it without question.

Twice more, she had seen a man standing in the shadow of the gravestones, watching her as she entered the building. He never approached her, never made any truly menacing move, but he was there, always there, and his presence unnerved her.

Yesterday, she had dared to turn in his direction and take

a step toward him, intending to call out to him from across the way. Her attention had forced him deeper into the gloom. Clearly, he had no wish to entertain her company, only to watch her from a distance.

A menacing conundrum.

Now Sarah turned her attention to Mrs. Bayley, who stood by her side holding a stack of clean bandages to replace the blood and pus-stained cloths that Sarah had just unwound from a dressed wound. The patient was stoic, lips pressed together in a tight line, eyes dull with pain.

Adept at changing dressings and bandages, she worked with calm efficiency. Her father had shown her the way of it when she was twelve and she had had much practice in the intervening years.

She turned her full focus to her task, glad to be trusted with this duty, for it was usual that only the sisters or a surgical apprentice would be allowed to bandage wounds. But today, two sisters were sick with the ague, and one apprentice as well, which meant that the day nurses were set to do what needed to be done, for the surgeons were occupied elsewhere.

With a quick glance about, Mrs. Bayley stepped close and asked, "Do you think he done it? Killed them in a mad fit?"

Sarah sighed as she continued bandaging the patient. There was no question that Mrs. Bayley was asking about Mr. Thayne. The entire hospital had been buzzing with conjecture and whispered supposition for days.

A mad fit. The question nearly made her laugh. She had never seen Killian Thayne less than composed and controlled . . . except for a single moment in the closet when she had thought he might kiss her. There had been a fleeting instant there where she thought she challenged his control.

"I think Mr. Thayne is an extremely competent surgeon," Sarah replied, avoiding the question altogether, for whatever response she offered could only fuel the fire.

Mrs. Bayley made a huffing sound of displeasure when Sarah failed to snap at the bait.

"An officer was here yesterday," she confided, "from Bow Street."

Sarah murmured a wordless reply, for she already knew of the officer's visit, but Mrs. Bayley was undeterred by her lack of enthusiasm for the topic.

"He spoke with Mr. Simon and Mr. Franks, and after that with Mr. Thayne, but in the end, he left. I thought he might like tea, so I went after him and asked about that." Mrs. Bayley shook her head. "He very politely declined the tea, saying he found the place off-putting."

"I can't imagine why . . ." Sarah said, and exchanged a glance with the other woman, a shared commiseration. "If it wasn't the bleak and sad atmosphere, then surely the smell had done."

Mrs. Bayley snorted. "He did share enough conversation that I can tell you he was called in to investigate by Mr. Simon, and that he will not be back." She unfolded another bandage and handed it to Sarah. "It seems that the officer holds the opinion that people die in hospitals, and without further evidence, he cannot think there is foul play afoot."

Something in her tone made Sarah pause in her work and turn her head to offer her full attention.

Mrs. Bayley tapped her foot on the wooden floor, a rapid patter. She pursed her lips, and after a moment continued. "But I wonder. I do. I worked at Guy's Hospital before I came here, and in all the years, I've never seen the like of that wound, ripped open and not a drop of blood shed."

Sarah stared at her for a long moment, having no words, but so many thoughts. Because she *did* wonder, not just about the wound, but about the shadow she had seen the morning Mr. Scully died, and about Killian Thayne's presence beside the bed of the woman who had died two weeks before that.

Wetting her lips, she shook her head. "We need more bandages, Mrs. Bayley," she said, her voice soft, her heart heavy, for she did not want to wonder about him. She wanted to believe that he was exactly the man she conjured in her dreams.

The trouble was, she had learned in the months since her father's death that the boundary between dreams and nightmares was wont to blur.

Sarah drew her frayed and much-mended cloak tight about her shoulders. The night was very cold and very clear, the stars winking bright and pretty against the dark blue-black sky, a sliver of moon offering pale, cool light. Her gaze strayed to the graveyard. There was nothing there save old stones and a single ancient tree, its gnarled branches casting creeping shadows along the ground.

Still, she shivered, in part from the chill, and in part from the certainty that he would come, the man who watched her, and he would follow her through the wretched, twisted streets and alleys of St. Giles. She sighed. The night was so cold, and the temptation to take that route so strong, for it halved the distance. But it was not safe, and so she would take the longer route and hope the crowds kept him away.

She began to walk, her cudgel gripped in her fist beneath the material of her cloak. Her steps were quick and sure, her senses alert. She heard nothing, felt no creeping certainty that she was being watched, but she had come to understand that the streets were far from safe and she was yet far from home.

Home. Such a strange word to apply to the tiny, cramped room where she slept each night. She had grown up in a pretty house with fine china and chocolate every morning. They had not been wealthy, but they had made do quite nicely, she and her father, a physician who saw to the health needs of merchants and tradesmen. Not the upper class, but not the poor, which meant her father had always been paid moderately well.

She had never thought beyond her pleasant life.

But then, inexplicably, her father had changed drastically, his temper fraying, his thoughts and actions growing irrational. After months of frightening and unusual behavior, he was alive one night and dead the next morning, fallen in the Thames, his body never found. It was a terrible and tragic culmination of months of descent into what she suspected was opium addiction.

Sarah had found herself without funds, evicted from her home, without relative or friend. She could not say how that had happened. She had never thought her father the type to squander his money, but in the weeks before his death, he had spent it on something that defied her understanding.

A cure, he had insisted. He was searching for a cure.

She could have told him that the only cure was to stop taking the drug. She thought now that she *should* have told him that.

Well, it mattered little, she thought now as she passed small, cramped houses that backed onto the slaughterhouses, the smell of death and old blood always heavy in the air. Come morning, there would be children running in the street next to a herd of pigs, with inches of blood flowing beneath their feet. A terrible place, really. Before her father's death, she had never imagined the like.

She kept her head down as she hurried past. It was too late to change what he had done, what he had become—an opium addict. She must only find a way to go on.

Turning left on Queen Street, she was confronted by light from the streetlamps and sound and a tight press of bodies that she navigated with care. Near Drury Lane, the public houses spilled their patrons into the streets. To her left, two men engaged in fisticuffs, dancing about to the taunts and calls of their fellows. To her right, three women were screaming like harpies, pulling and yanking on an old dress stretched out between them, none of them willing to relinquish their grasp.

The next street was narrower, with fewer people, and the

street after that narrower and less crowded still. Now her route brought her to a place where she could no longer avoid the dimness and the shadows. There was only one working lamp on the street, and tonight it was unlit, so perhaps it was working no longer. She quickened her pace and ducked down an alley.

A staircase ascended the outside of the building and a man, bowed and bent, slogged up the steps, a sack of cabbages slung over his back. He would peel the outer leaves off on the morrow and take them to sell as fresh, though they were likely already several days old.

Sarah scanned the shadows and moved on, unease trickling through her now. This was the part of her trek she liked the least.

Again, she turned, this time into an alley narrower than the last.

Almost there. Her boots rang on the cobbled pavement; her heart pounded a wild rhythm.

She was walking very quickly now, the wind tunneling down the alley to sting her eyes, her cheeks, and behind her, she heard footsteps. Not ringing like her own. Shuffling, sliding.

He was behind her. The man who watched her and harried her each day. He was there, behind her. She could *hear* him.

Her breath came in ragged harsh rasps, and she dragged her cudgel free of the draping material of her cloak, holding it before her at the ready as she quickened her pace even more.

There was nowhere safe, nowhere she could turn.

The courtyards that fed off the narrow alley held their own dangers, for she knew not what manner of men, or women, might lurk there. In this place, poverty forced even women and children to toss aside morals and do what they must to survive. Calling out for help was therefore not an attractive option.

Ahead of her loomed a dark shadow, and she skidded to a stop, horrified to realize that a large wooden cart blocked her path.

From behind her came the sound of cloth flapping in the wind, and she whirled about, the open palm of one hand pressed to her chest, her cudgel clutched tight in the other.

The light here was so dim, there was only charcoal shadow painted on shadow, but she knew what she saw. The shape of a man loomed before her, some twenty feet distant. He was draped in a dark cloak that lifted and fanned out in the wind like the wings of a raven. His features were completely obscured by a low-crowned hat pulled down over his brow.

He was tall and broad and menacing . . . familiar somehow, his height and the shape of his shadow . . . similar to the shadow she thought she had seen on the ward the morning Mr. Scully died.

Trembling, she clenched her teeth tight together to keep them from clacking aloud. If she dared cry for help, she might bring down a dozen worse creatures on her head.

Taking a step backward, and another, she pressed against the wood of the cart, her legs shaking so hard, she knew not how they yet bore her weight.

Run, her mind screamed, and she dared a rapid glance in each direction. To her right was a courtyard, to her left, another alley.

The man before her took a single step forward, menacing. Terrifying. He was done toying with her. He was coming for her, as she had always known he would.

Still clutching her cudgel, she snaked her free hand behind her back and groped for the wooden cart. It was high-wheeled, and she could feel the lower limit of it at a level with her waist.

There was her best choice.

Sucking in a breath, she held it and dropped to the ground, rolling beneath the cart.

She heard a sound of surprise. For the briefest instant she

wasn't certain if it was a hiss, or her name—*Ssssarah*—but she did not pause to look behind her. Bounding to her feet as soon as she reached the opposite side of the cart, she grabbed her skirt with her free hand and hauled it up to her knees, then ran as fast as she could, her legs pumping, her breath rasping in her throat.

The cobbles were caked with years of grime and refuse, and her feet skidded and slipped on the sludge. Once, she slammed hard against the wall, nearly falling, but she pushed herself upright and ran on, weaving through the alleys, taking any turn she recognized, not daring to take those that were less than familiar.

The only thing worse than being chased through this warren would be running blindly without having a clear concept of her location.

Twice, she dared look behind her. She saw nothing to make her think she had been followed.

Finally, she ducked into a shadowed niche beneath a narrow wooden stairwell. Her lungs screamed for air, and she huddled as deep in the gloom as she could, pulling her body in tight to make herself as small as possible. Her ears strained to hear the sound of footsteps pounding in pursuit, but there was nothing.

From the window above her came the discordant noise of an argument, a man's voice, then another, deeper voice in reply, and a moment later, the dull thud of fists on flesh and a cry of pain.

Panting, she struggled to satisfy her desperate need for air.

She waited a moment longer, then crept from her place. Staying close to the wall and the sheltering gloom, she made her way clear of the labyrinth of alleys to New Oxford Street. There she crossed and then continued north to the small lodging house where she rented a room from Mrs. Cowden.

The building was old, musty, her chamber very small and dark and damp, but it was inexpensive and it was located not in St. Giles, but in Camden, both high recommendations as far as she was concerned.

She made her way quickly along the street toward the front door of the tall, narrow house. She had almost reached the place when she drew up short and stumbled to a dead stop. A man lounged against the lamppost several houses away.

A tall man, garbed in a long, dark cloak.

Four

The lamppost obscured the man's face, and Sarah's heart skidded to a stop, then set off at a leaping, bounding pace as the wind caught his long black cloak and set it billowing like a sail. She froze, uncertain whether to run for the door of her lodging house, or flee down the empty street.

He shifted, and the light from the lamp spilled down, glinting off the metal rims of his spectacles and highlighting the sun-bright hair that framed his angular face in thick, shiny waves.

She knew him then.

Emotion slapped her, anger and uncertainty and fear.

As though aware that any sudden move might send her into frenzied flight, he watched her for a moment longer. Then he straightened, lifting his shoulder and the weight he had rested on it from the post, his breath blowing white before his lips.

His head was uncovered. Her gaze dropped to his hands, searching for a low-crowned hat like the one her pursuer had worn. But his hands were empty, his skin bare. He did not wear gloves, though the wind was bitter.

Had he followed her? Had Killian Thayne been the one stalking her—hunting her—in the dim alleys?

She shook her head, bitterly confused and distraught. If he had followed her, how had he come to be here before her, standing leaning against a post, waiting, while she fled through the poorly lit streets, her lungs sucking great gasps of air, her heart pounding a frantic rhythm?

If he was the one who had been behind her in the alley, then she did not think he could be standing so relaxed before her now unless he had taken to the skies and flown like a bat.

"Sarah," he said, his brow furrowed in concern as he strode toward her. Not Miss Lowell. *Sarah.* The way he said her name in his incredible melted-chocolate voice made her heart twitch. "What is it? What has frightened you?"

He paused a foot away from her, making no move to touch her or accost her in any way. She knew not what to think, what to feel, what to say. Her emotions cavorted and danced from fear to elation. In that moment, she did not know herself.

"I was—" She glanced over her shoulder, almost expecting a second tall man to materialize behind her, one with black gloves and a black hat. When she saw no one there, she turned to face him once more."—followed. Someone followed me from King's College."

Raising his head, he looked beyond her to the empty street. She felt a strange disorientation overtake her. The night was dark, save for the twinkling stars and a thin sliver of moon. The shadows were darker still. Only one lamp shone on this street, casting a bright glow in a circle some ten feet across, then fading away to nothing at the periphery.

Yet Killian Thayne—with his sight further dimmed by the dark glasses he preferred—perused the night-wrapped street as though he could see things that were veiled from her sight.

He said, "He is not there now."

No, he was not. But he had been. She did not doubt her own perception of that.

"I cannot imagine that you can discern anything wearing those," she murmured.

From a distance, a faded cacophony of laughter and shrieks carried to them through the cold air. He tipped his head a bit toward her, then away.

"I see as well with them as without. Better, in fact." He shrugged, the casual gesture out of keeping with his normally reserved manner. "My eyes are sensitive to light."

She stared at him, thinking his comment a jest. But his expression showed him to be in earnest.

"It is full night. There is very little light to be sensitive to," she said.

A moment longer, he studied the street, and then he turned toward her and smiled. Despite everything—her breathless run, her fear, her disorientation—that smile touched a place inside her, making it crackle and flare like a spark roused to flame.

His gaze dropped to her hands, and she realized then that she was turning the thick stick she carried over and over in nervous inattention. Reaching out, he eased it from her cold and numbed fingers, then tested the weight of it on his open palm.

He seemed not at all surprised to find she carried a weapon.

"Why not a pistol?" he asked.

"I would need to learn to shoot it with accuracy, and such knowledge comes only with a great deal of practice."

"Ah." He handed the stick back to her, and she sucked in a breath as their fingers touched, hers gloved, his bare. Even through the wool of her gloves she felt the warmth of his skin. She frowned, stared at his naked hands. They should be cold, not warm.

"Why not a knife, then?" he asked.

Her head jerked up and she studied his face, wondering at

this odd conversation they were having in the middle of Coptic Street on a sharp, frigid night. She could see that he asked the question out of genuine interest, that he expected a reply. "I am small. My assailant might be large. It would be too easy for him to twist a knife from my hand and turn it upon me."

"Ah," he said again, and his straight brows rose above the limits of his spectacles. "But you feel confident to wield your stick?"

"Confident enough. No one would expect me to have it, and I have a good chance at landing a solid blow to the underside of the chin or across his shins before an attacker could know my intent." Her landlady, Mrs. Cowden, had kindly shown her the way of it the day after Sarah moved in.

He was startled by her words. She could read that in the slight stiffening of his form and the way his brows rose even higher.

"Wise and brave," he murmured, and she knew then that he was not only startled, but impressed.

She felt uncharacteristically unnerved by that. Yet also warmed by it, and pleased.

"What are you doing here?" she asked, aware that her responses to him were neither logical nor appropriate.

His smile widened. White teeth. An attractive smile that was somehow less than reassuring. "Waiting. For you."

"Why?"

The wind picked up, snatching at her cloak, her hair, making her shudder. Mr. Thayne took note of that and glanced about, his attention turning to the lodging house. "You are cold. Perhaps we might take this conversation inside to the parlor. You will be more comfortable."

She laughed at that, though she noticed that he made no mention of his own discomfort in the chilly night. "The parlor?" Oh, that he thought she lived in such a fine place—the expectation of a parlor—was both funny and sad. "On the ground floor are the kitchen and the dining room and the landlady's rooms. The first and second floors are all to let. There is no parlor."

Reaching up, he drew off his spectacles, and she was struck again by the beauty of his eyes, pale against the thick sweep of dark gold lashes.

"Then we may take this conversation to the room you rent."

"I take a very small room from Mrs. Cowden," she demurred, struck by the image of him, tall and masculine, filling the tiny space of her chamber. Standing beside her narrow bed. The thought made her breath catch. "There is not even a sitting room. I cannot have you come in at this hour of the night, Mr. Thayne."

"Killian," he murmured absently, his gaze sliding to the front of the house. The brick was dirty and the yard ill kept. Mrs. Cowden was anything but house proud, her fondness for gin overtaking her fondness for anything else, save money.

Sarah felt absurdly unveiled to have him study the house with such careful regard.

"You must call me Killian."

Killian. She dared not say his name, lest he read her secret longings in the way her lips shaped and caressed the syllables.

"I am going inside now, where it is warm"—an untruth, for though it would be sweltering hot next to the kitchen fire, the remainder of the house was bound to be little warmer than the brutal climes she was subject to outdoors—"and where I hope Mrs. Cowden has kept a plate for me. Whatever you wished to discuss will have to wait for the morrow. At the hospital." She frowned. "How *did* you find me?"

Again, he looked to the street, his gaze alert. The focused intensity of his perusal was enough to stoke the embers of her unease.

"Does it matter?" He returned his gaze to hers. "I am here now."

It did matter, but she knew enough of men and their ways to understand he would offer nothing further. To understand, too, that his alert posture and the way he positioned himself between her and the street meant that he yet felt the threat of whoever—whatever—had followed her.

Deciding that she was destined to lose any further argument, she turned and led the way to the front door. Modesty, propriety, her good name . . . she might have presented any of those as reasons he must not come inside. But, in truth, what was the point? The other lodgers in the house on Coptic Street would have no care if she brought a man to her room. She knew for certain that one of the girls did exactly that on a regular basis and slipped Mrs. Cowden an extra shilling each week so that she would turn a blind eye.

Pausing at the door, she looked back at him over her shoulder. *Killian.* He bid her call him Killian, as she had a thousand times in her dreams.

"You are safe with me, Sarah."

No, she did not think so.

But she knew he meant to reassure her that he was not the one who had chased her through the alleys, and *that* she thought was the truth. "You have no hat."

His eyes narrowed slightly at her observation. "Does the lack offend?"

Sarah made a soft, chuffing laugh that hung in the air with a nervous aftertone. "Taking offense at some nicety of fashion is a luxury I have no use for." She pressed her lips together. "It was only an observation."

"Because your pursuer wore a hat, and you want to be certain that I am not he."

"No, I—" At his cool, assessing look, she shook her head. "Yes."

"I am not he. Had I chosen to hunt you, Sarah, you would not have known I was there." He paused, his lips curving in a dark smile. "And I would have caught you."

Yes, she believed that, and it gave her a twisted sort of comfort to know it.

Had I chosen to hunt you. An odd turn of phrase. A chill crawled up her spine, one that had nothing to do with the wind or the cold.

Seeking to alleviate the fraught tension of the moment, she said, "I shall be lucky if Mrs. Cowden kept a plate for me this evening, but if she did, I will be glad to share my meal with you."

At her words, some indecipherable emotion flickered in Killian's eyes. "Your offer is most kind, but I have . . . already dined."

The slight hesitation did not go unnoticed, and she wondered what his words masked. After a moment, she sighed and turned back to unlock the door.

She led him inside. The hallway was dark, musty, the paint yellowed and flaking, the floor a tiled geometric pattern of gray and black. Sarah thought that once, many years ago, the pattern might have been white and black, but layers of accumulated grime had altered the shade. The hallway was so cramped that they could not stand side by side, and Sarah went in first with Killian close behind.

Turning back, she was confronted by his cloak-draped form, so broad and tall. He unnerved her. Drew her. Appealed to her on some level she could not explain.

Suddenly, she felt glad that she was not alone.

No, more than that, glad that *he* was here. It was a dangerous and inappropriate gladness that bubbled and danced inside her like the effervescent spring water her father had insisted was good for the health. Killian's presence made her feel safe. How long since she had felt that way?

Hoping that her expression betrayed none of her inappropriate thoughts, she reached around him to draw the door closed, an action that brought them far closer together than they ought to be. He was so warm, the heat coming from him beckoning to her. She did not understand how he could be. It was bitingly cold outside, and he had been in the wind just the same as she.

He was looking down at her. She sensed that, but dared not raise her gaze to his.

Stepping back, she undid the fastening of her cloak, but did not draw the garment off. The hallway was barely warmer than it was outdoors, and she was loath to forfeit whatever heat the cloak offered.

Directly ahead lay the rickety staircase with the faulty third stair, the one with the poorly nailed board that would pop up and bang the unwary person sharply on the ankle bone if he were not careful. She knew that now, and she knew to be careful. There was room enough for one person to go up or down, but not enough for two to pass. She had learned to pause at the top or bottom and call out to see if someone was coming in the opposite direction before she began her ascent or descent.

There was no light coming from the dining room, and none showed under the crack of the door that led to Mrs. Cowden's chamber. Sarah was glad of that, for it meant there was none about to beg explanation for Mr. Thayne's inexplicable presence here.

"I will be but a moment," Sarah said, and hurried beyond the stairs to the small kitchen at the back of the house. No candles were lit, but the hearth held a faltering flame, and Sarah moved close to warm her hands. Closing her eyes, she let the heat sink through her.

He made no sound, but she knew he had followed. Stepping to the side, she glanced at him over her shoulder. The glow of the dying embers danced over his features, painting him gold and bronze and more beautiful than any man had a right to be.

"Here," she said, beckoning him closer. "There's room enough for both of us. The night is so cold, you must be frozen clear through."

"No." He made a small smile, looking handsomer still because of it. "I am not cold."

"Oh, how can you not be? The wind cuts right through a person."

"I do not notice such things. Not the cold in winter or the heat in summer."

"You are an adaptable fellow."

"That is one way to describe it." He glanced about the tiny kitchen, his gaze lingering on the covered plate set on one side of the small table. "You must be hungry."

She shook her head. She wasn't. The fright of earlier in the evening had left her insides shaking still, but she would take the plate up with her and eat a bit later.

"Where are your rooms?" he asked.

"Rooms?" she echoed, and made a humorless laugh. "Only one, I'm afraid. But it suits well enough. I'm on the second floor."

She took the plate and led the way from the warm kitchen back into the frigid hallway, up the stairs to the landing on the first floor, then up another flight to the second.

"How many rooms up here?" Killian asked, his voice hushed, the sound incredibly appealing.

"Three. And three on the floor below." She unlocked the door of her chamber and pushed it open. "I have the smallest of these. 'Twas the frugal choice." Why had she said that? It sounded small and petty.

Setting the plate on the little tulip table in the corner near the door, she then took up a lucifer match, struck it to the sandpaper, and lit the stub of tallow candle that sat in the small porcelain dish, one of the few possessions she had salvaged from the shattered remnants of her old life.

The flame flickered and danced, barely denting the darkness. She turned to face Killian Thayne, who filled the doorway like a shadow.

What to do now? Invite him inside? There seemed no help for it, but she felt so odd to be in this situation, to have him here in this dim and crowded room. He had been here before, but only in her mind, her dreams, her fantasies.

The reality of him was overwhelming.

"Come in," she said, suddenly incredibly weary.

He did as she bid, stepping inside and pulling the door shut behind him. He filled the space, so tall, so broad. His eyes locked on hers, glittering in the dancing candlelight, and her heart beat so hard, she thought it might fly apart. She dropped her gaze and toyed with the remnants of the match; she could not look at him, did not dare to look at him, for so many twined and knitted reasons.

"You are cold," Killian observed, stepping closer, and before she could protest he had his cloak off his own shoulders and over hers, still warm from the heat of his body, smelling faintly of citrus and man.

His action highlighted exactly the reasons she admired him so. Because he would do something like that for her. Because he offered so many quiet kindnesses to so many people. She saw it time and again on the ward with patients, and even with staff. Though his tone was usually cool and analytical, his treatment choices unaffected by emotion, there were small things he did that showed the warmth beneath his icy facade.

She knew he had given Mrs. Bayley warm coats for her two growing sons, saying they no longer appealed to him, though they were brand-new and never worn and far too small to ever fit on his broad-shouldered frame. And she had seen him slip coins in the night nurse's apron while she slept, a shilling or two, enough to buy shrimps and tea and butter.

He was a cold, cold man with a flame inside him that he hid behind a heavy screen.

She stood staring up at him, feeling foolish and overwhelmed and so grateful for this small kindness. Tears pricked her eyes and that made her angry. She had no place in her life for self-pity, and after crying for three days straight when she found out her father was dead, she had thought herself moved past such a childish waste of time.

"Tell me why you came here tonight," she said, pushing aside her maudlin thoughts and pitching her voice low so as not to carry through the thin walls.

"Let us sit, Sarah." So reasonable. So calm.

His words made her anxious. Sit where? On the low bed? Uneasy, she cast a glance exactly there, and for a moment, she could not understand what it was she saw on her pillow.

Then she *did* understand and fear curdled in her belly.

On her pillow was a small box of chocolates tied with a bow and beside it, a length of lavender ribbon.

She gasped and stumbled back, the very familiarity of those things making them all the more sinister.

Someone had been here. In her room. Someone had left these unwelcome gifts.

Distress ramped through her, closing a tight fist about her heart.

"What is it?" Killian asked sharply, drawing near. "You've gone white as the belly of a dead fish."

Sarah's gaze jerked to his, and she could not help the startled chuff of laughter evoked by his words, despite the unease that gnawed at her.

"An appealing image." Dead fish. She shuddered, thinking of her father, his body never fished from the Thames. Never found.

The shudders would not stop, though she willed them to.

Killian closed his hands about her upper arms, and he held her, just held her. She wished he would draw her closer, not just clasp her arms, but clasp her body tight against his own.

Sinking her teeth into her lower lip, she pondered what to say. Her thoughts and suspicions burbled like a witch's brew, noxious and vile. It was possible that Killian had brought the box and the ribbon, but if he had, why not simply hand them to her? Why sneak into her chamber and leave them on her bed, then sneak back outside to await her arrival?

And if he hadn't . . . then how had they gotten here? Who were they from?

"My father used to bring me candy and ribbons sometimes, before he . . . became ill."

Killian's gaze flicked to her pillow, then back. "Ill?"

Her chin kicked up a notch. "He became addicted to opium. By the end, he clung to the shadows and eschewed the light. Sunlight made him cry out in pain. Lamplight made him wince. He took no food, and his complexion took on a terrible grayish cast." There had been no more money, for he had been too ill himself to see patients. He had spent his days abed in a darkened room, and his nights prowling the streets, or perhaps in opium dens. One night, he had fallen in the river and drowned. More than ten witnesses had seen it, and though she had no body to bury and mourn, she had their testimony, the gruesome truth of it.

"My father is dead," she continued, "so he could not have set those things on my pillow." She turned her head and looked back toward the ribbon and chocolate, the memory of the man who had followed her terrifyingly clear. An icy chill slithered through her. "Someone was here, in my chamber. But I locked the door when I left and it was locked still when I returned."

"Perhaps the landlady . . ." Killian offered the suggestion, but his tone implied that he himself did not lend it credence.

She shook her head. "She turns a blind eye to quite a bit, but she is not so unscrupulous as to let a stranger in my room. No, he came in by some other means."

She realized then that he yet held her, his strong fingers clasped around her arms, and she had to battle the urge to lean in against him, to rest her cheek against his chest and let the sound of his heartbeat ease her worries. Instead, she forced herself to step away from him. The backs of her legs brushed the spindly chair in the corner as his hands dropped away.

She sank down and stared up at him, her thoughts a muddle of wary confusion.

There was no sense in any of this. Not in the pursuer who dogged her every step. Not in the gifts left on her pillow. And not in the attention shown her by Killian Thayne.

She yet had no idea why he was here.

"I think you should go," she said, and lifted up enough to drag his cloak from about her and hold it out in offering before sinking onto the seat once more. His brows drew together as he took the cloak from her and draped it over his forearm.

"That request poses a slight problem." His hard mouth curved up a little. "I am afraid that my damnably chivalrous nature precludes my leaving you here alone tonight."

For an instant she made no reply, her thoughts spinning through a thousand remembered dreams where he had been in this room with her, his lips on hers. She took a slow breath and forced herself to speak. "What are you suggesting?"

"Ah, there is the question. I can remain here with you—"

"You cannot—" She shook her head from side to side.

"—or you may accompany me to my home—"

"I cannot—"

"—and I beg you to cease interrupting my every word."

"My apologies," she offered acerbically, not bothering to mask the fact that her words were insincere. "You cannot simply step into my life and tell me what I may and may not do. I do not answer to you, sir."

"No, you do not," he murmured, and shot her an indecipherable look. "I wonder if you have ever answered to anyone."

The words wounded, though she thought he had not meant them to, for there was a measure of admiration in his tone. She was not certain how she felt about that.

"There was a time that I relied on my father's decisions to guide my life. Then he began to make only bad decisions, and finally, none at all, and so I learned to chart my own course."

She rose and crossed to the bed, where she scooped up both the ribbon and the box. She strode to the door, opened it, and set both out on the landing near the stairs, then closed and locked the door behind her.

Turning to face him once more, she rested her back against the wooden door and made a noisy, rushed exhalation.

"Well," he said, his tone laced with humor, "that was a solution."

"The best I could conjure at the moment."

"You are ever resourceful." Again, the whisper of admiration. It made her feel as though he *knew* her, saw the practical, intelligent part of her and valued that.

The moment spun out, thin and fragile, her thoughts battling within her. A part of her wanted him to step closer, to gather her in his arms, press his lips to her hair, and a part of her was appalled by those thoughts.

She sighed in both relief and disappointment when he tossed his cloak on the bed and moved to the far wall with its two tall, narrow windows. He checked the latch on the first, then drew the frayed and moth-eaten velvet curtain across it. With a step to the right, he faced the second window and tested the latch. It slid free and the pane swung open, letting in a swirling blast of frigid air.

He did not so much as blink as the wind hit him, but Sarah huddled deeper in the folds of her cloak.

With careful attention, he closed the window and again tested the latch, then played with it a moment until it clicked into place. It was merely temperamental, not broken.

His gaze sought hers. "I am staying."

The temptation to sink into the safety of his presence and simply thank him and let him do as he wished was a succulent lure. But she refused to be beguiled.

"While I appreciate your kind offer, there is no need for you to remain here. I have spent many nights alone in this place, and I awaken each morning with my heart yet beating and breath in my lungs. Tonight will be no different. I think it best if you go."

Eyes the color of a storm-laden sky pinned her and held her in place. "I will sit on that chair, or I will take you to my home and you may spend the night there. The choice is yours."

"You cannot spend the night in this room."

"As you wish," he agreed amiably, and grabbed the chair from the corner. He dragged it to the door. "I shall spend the night on the landing outside your door."

"There is no need," she insisted once more, skirting around him to pick up his cloak from her bed. "I shall be perfectly safe here with the windows latched and the door locked."

"I beg to differ. There are creatures of the night that even the best locks will not hold at bay."

The way he said that, soft and menacing, set a shiver crawling up her spine.

"You cannot sleep in the hard chair." She stepped forward and laid her hand next to his on the chair back.

"I need little sleep." The smile he turned on her was languid, and it made her pulse trip. "I will stay the night through and leave at the first hint of dawn before the house awakens. No one will know I was here, and you will be safe in the light."

She held her place, held his gaze, her heart racing a wild, heady pace. "Safe in the light? I do not understand."

"I know. And I am not yet ready to explain." His smile dropped away, and he took a slow deep breath, his chest expanding, his gaze gliding over her in a lazy caress, lingering on her lips in a way that made her pulse pound hard and fast. "I hear your blood rushing in your veins, Sarah."

How could he possibly hear that? And yet it sounded as though he spoke the truth. She made a stunted, nervous laugh, low and breathy.

His hand shifted on the chair until it covered her own. Warm skin. Firm flesh. She could not think, could not breathe.

"Is it for me that your heart races?" he whispered, his voice warm and rough.

For him. Yes.

He leaned in, his cheek almost touching hers.

"I have watched you for so long, Sarah. I have longed to touch you, to hold you. I had not planned it, this fascination. But here it is"—his cheek brushed against her hair, and her heart stopped, her breath stopped—"and I find myself glad of it, though reason argues it is unwise."

Her senses hummed with her awareness of him, with the warm glow that swelled at his words and the wild ache that spread through her limbs.

Oh, her mind was not her own, her body so heavy and hot.

She wanted him to kiss her. Wanted to know the feel and taste of him. She was hungry for him, her lips tingling, her belly lit from inside with a heat that bordered on pain. Even in her inexperience, she recognized the feeling for what it was. Attraction.

It was lovely, this feeling, lovely and frightening and thrilling. She thought that if only he would press his mouth to hers, she would understand, would *know* secrets that hovered just beyond her reach.

He turned to her then, his movement quick, and she fell back a step, her back pressed to the wall.

Both hands shot out and Killian laid his palms flat on either side of her shoulders. She held herself still, her heart thudding, her gaze locked on his mouth, and he smiled, a dark, dangerous curving of his lips that bared a flash of white teeth for but an instant.

"You crave my touch." Not a question. She was glad. She had no breath left to form an answer.

Taking his weight on his outstretched arms and flattened palms, he leaned in and brushed her lower lip with his, so soft, so gentle. Their bodies touched nowhere but their lips and she was undone by that caress.

She was so focused on him that the world beyond faded away to nothing.

His tongue traced the seam of her mouth, and when she gasped in shock, he pushed inside, his tongue *inside* her, tasting her, touching her.

She moaned, stunned by the wild kaleidoscope of sensation, endlessly wondrous.

Winding her arms about his neck, she tunneled her fingers in his hair, enjoying the sensation of the thick, silky strands running through her fingers like rain. She kissed him back, following his lead. Tentatively, she touched her tongue to his, then grew bolder, stroking him and learning the feel of his mouth.

His weight came down on her, the lush heat of his body making her blood rush and her belly dance with a low, humming ache. She rose on her toes, driven by instinct to mold herself to him, to fit every ridge and edge of him in the soft swells and dips of her body, his thighs hard against her own, his belly and chest taut where hers were soft. She found exquisite pleasure in the feel of him heavy upon her.

He kissed her jaw, her neck, his mouth lingering on the pulse that beat there, his breathing ragged. Arching back, she offered herself, loving the sensation of his lips at her throat, his teeth grazing the tender skin.

With a groan, he tensed, then drew back, his eyes gone dark, the pupils dilated.

Panting, she stared up at him, understanding neither herself in that moment nor the wild, turbulent emotions rolling about inside her like heavy charcoal-limned clouds in a storm.

He meant to turn away. She sensed that. Meant to block out the wonderful connection that spun out between them like a glittering thread.

"I feel as though I stand on the edge of a cliff, the wind whipping my cloak behind me, and if I can only find the will and courage to leap, I will fly," she whispered. "Kiss me again, Killian. Make me fly."

She felt drunk on the taste of him, the feel of him, unlike anything she had ever experienced.

The look he turned on her was feral. Hungry. She thought he would plunder her, take her, drag her against him and kiss her in ways she was too untutored to imagine.

Yearning sluiced through her, fever bright.

And she thought her heart would break when he stepped away, mastering himself with visible effort, his cool mask sliding in place to obscure the burning heat she knew she had not mistaken.

"Sarah," he rasped, his gaze locked on her throat, hot and dark. Slowly, he raised his eyes to hers. "I must not—"

He shook his head, and she felt lost, barren, already missing the connection that melted away. He brushed his thumb along her cheek and she ached to fling herself against him.

Rooted in place, she watched as he took a step toward the door, then paused to look back at her over his shoulder, his eyes gone flat and dark, fathomless, mysterious, too many secrets reflected back at her. She was so attuned to him in this impossible moment, she *felt* the leashed tension inside him.

There had been a thrilling edge of desperation in that kiss, coupled with swirling emotion. A heady blend. She ached to untether the bonds he set about himself, to follow where that desperation and emotion might lead.

A perilous path to tread; a most dangerous thing to want.

Five

Looking back at her over his shoulder, Killian held her gaze a moment longer, his hands fisted at his sides, his control clearly in place, if somewhat tattered. Sarah recognized that she affected him—deeply—and that pleased her. The realization was disconcerting.

"Lock the door behind me," he said, his voice taut. He broke the connection, turning his face toward the door, his thick golden hair sliding across his shoulders, bright against the black cloth of his coat.

She had no wish to lock the door against him. She had no wish for him to leave at all. Her lips felt warm, swollen from his kiss, and she wanted only to kiss him again, to press her mouth to his.

"If I lock the door, how will you come to me should I call out?" Such a reasonable question, despite the unreasonable circumstance. She could not imagine calling out to him, could not imagine him sitting out there all night on the small, stiff chair. Why would he do that for her?

His shoulders tensed, but he did not look at her again. "There is no door that could stop me if I wanted to be at your side, Sarah. Remember that. Remember that I . . ." He made a slow exhalation, as though he struggled with the words, and after an instant, he continued in a low, ragged tone. "I am not like other men."

No, he was not. A part of her recognized that with soul-searing clarity. He was like no one she had ever known. She could sense a hidden part of him, held in careful check just beneath the surface, and she did not doubt that he spoke the truth, that no lock, no door could hold him. It was a strange and frightening comfort.

He walked toward the door, past the small table with the candle and the plate of food, and he paused there, his attention snared. She thought he meant to insist she eat, and she knew that she could not. Her stomach was alternately in knots and dancing and twisting like a thousand butterflies struggling to get free.

"What is this?" he asked, lifting the old and yellowed copy of *New Monthly* magazine that lay open beside the plate. He read aloud the title of the short story she had pored over so many times that she could recite it by heart. " 'The Vampyre' by John William Polidori"—he glanced at the date—"April 1, 1819."

His voice had grown eerily flat, devoid of inflection.

"My father was obsessed with that story before his death. He read it again and again, studying and dissecting the words as though they held the secret mysteries of life." She shook her head. "I have read it myself so many times that I can recite it in its entirety. A sad and horrid tale, but I do not see what agitated my father so greatly. There are no secrets hidden there."

"Are there not?" He cast her a veiled look. "May I take this to read while I keep watch?"

Keep watch. Over her. When was the last time she had felt safe? Months. Perhaps years. But tonight, with Killian guarding her door, she was safe.

She knew not how to place that fact in the twisted uncertainty that had become her life.

What was it about him that made her firm in her conviction that she would come to no harm whilst he was near? He was a doctor, a healer. But he was also a formidable man. She shivered. "Yes, please do. Perhaps in your reading you will find the secrets that I missed."

"Perhaps. Tell me, in the end, is the vampire revealed for the monster he is?"

"Yes, how did you know?"

"A guess. Are vampires not always fiends?" The thread of irony in his tone gave her pause.

He dipped his head, drummed his fingers in a slow roll across the tabletop, and she had the feeling that he argued a silent debate within himself, as though he meant to say something more. In the end, he only inclined his head and exited her chamber, closing the door behind him with a soft snick.

She hesitated, then went to the door, pressing her palms against the frame. She could not say how she knew it, but she did; she knew he waited, listening, until she turned the key in the lock.

Her hand trembled, and she held it out flat, watching the fluttering movement, feeling the reflection of that quaking in her soul. With a sigh, she rested her forehead against the cool wood and imagined that on the far side of the door, Killian leaned in and did the same.

A moment later, she heard the creak of the chair as he sat, and it was only then that she recalled there was no light on the landing, and Killian had taken no candle.

She wondered how he would read the story of "The Vampyre" in the dark.

The house was still and silent when Sarah awakened the following morning. Pale fingers of light stole through the crack where the ancient, frayed curtains met. Recalling all that had passed the previous night, the fear of being hunted, the thrill of being kissed, she gathered her resolve and crossed to the door. Throwing it open, she found Killian gone from the hallway, and her magazine resting on the chair.

He must have left with the dawn as he had warned her he would. She was both disappointed and relieved by that. Relieved, too, because the chocolate and ribbon were gone from the landing. He had taken them away, a small but welcome kindness.

She washed and dressed with haste, for the hour was later than she preferred. Soon, she walked briskly along Portugal Street toward the hospital, her thoughts consumed by recollections of all that had passed between her and Killian, her emotions in a terrible state of confusion. Questions scurried about in her mind like the mice in the hallways of King's College. She had run the gamut last night from abject terror as the unknown man chased her through the alleys, to absolute bliss as Killian kissed her, his mouth hot and hungry on her own.

His kiss had aroused both her body and her mind, weaving her in a spell of delicious wonder. His abrupt withdrawal had left her adrift, uncertain what to think, what to feel.

One thing she did know was that, oddly, last night she had slept better than any night since her father's drowning, and she was grateful to Killian for that. After the terror she had endured on her panic-scored flight to Coptic Street, it was only the knowledge that he guarded her that had allowed her to sink into sweet slumber, and once there, she had dreamed of him.

There was danger in allowing herself to succumb to the lure of his protection, for who would watch over her tonight and in the nights to come? Only herself, as it had been only herself for so many months now. She was proud of that, of her ability to find solutions and care for herself in a city that was far from kind to a woman alone. Still, the luxury of allowing herself to be protected for a single night had been a sweet and wonderful balm.

And a distraction.

In the end, she had never learned why Killian waited for her outside Mrs. Cowden's house, the question of that forgotten in the muddle of other concerns and the heady lure of his kiss.

She was left wondering about that this morning as she made her way along the street, about his reasons for seeking her out last night.

Reaching the hospital, she hurried inside, out of the biting wind. After hanging her cloak away, she went to the sick ward and found Mrs. Bayley there ahead of her, setting out bowls on the tray.

"Have you heard?" the widow exclaimed, her eyes wide and round. "There's been another death. This one worse than the others. The victim's throat was torn open, and still not a drop of blood to be found. Explain that by bugs and fever and excoriation, if you can."

Reeling with the horror of Mrs. Bayley's words, Sarah stood frozen in mute dismay. A greasy knot of dread congealed in her gut. Finally, she managed to croak, "Where?"

"Surgical ward. Mr. Simon found him perhaps an hour past."

"What was Mr. Simon doing here so early? He usually comes in past ten."

"He said he had concern for the patient he trephined yesterday. Wanted to see how he had weathered the night."

Sarah held very still, sensing the answer before she even asked the question. "And how had he weathered the night?"

"Oh, he's the one who is dead."

The words scratched at Sarah's composure and sent a whisper of foreboding curling through her veins like ice.

Mrs. Bayley darted a quick glance about and dropped her voice. "Yesterday, Mr. Simon and Mr. Thayne had words over that patient. Mr. Thayne said that the man had been insensate for over a week since he fell from the roof of the Bull and Mouth Inn, said he wasn't likely to get any better if Mr. Simon drilled a hole in his skull. But Mr. Simon said there was no way to know for certain and so he went ahead and did it anyway."

"And today the man is dead."

"Not just dead." Mrs. Bayley pressed her lips in a tight line. "Murdered."

Horror clawed at Sarah then, from inside and out, the whisper of unease coalescing into chilling certainty that something terrible was about to take place. Without another word, she spun and ran down the hall to the surgical ward, skidding to a halt just inside the doors. She stood, trembling, her heart hammering, her palms damp.

A group of men huddled around a bed in the middle of the large room, among them Mr. Simon and Mr. Franks, and two men she thought must be from Bow Street. One of them— dark haired and swarthy—seemed familiar, and she wondered if he was the officer who had attended the ward before, the one who had declined Mrs. Bayley's offer of tea.

"I tell you, sir, that I saw Mr. Thayne lurking about when I left last night," said Mr. Simon.

"And what time was that?" asked the constable.

"Just before midnight. I know it because as I walked through the front doors, I heard the clock strike the hour."

"And did you speak with Mr. Thayne at that time?"

"I did not. But I believe it was he that I saw."

"You *believe* it was he?" the second constable asked. "Did you see him or not?"

Mr. Simon's lips thinned, and when he spoke his voice was high with irritation, his cheeks flushed red. "I did not see his face clearly, but I saw enough of him to determine his identity. His height and build are distinctive."

The dark-haired constable cocked his head to one side, and said, "You and he are of a similar height."

"I tell you the culprit is Mr. Thayne," Mr. Simon insisted. "He has been on this ward each time someone died of the strange and inexplicable wounds perpetrated upon their bodies. He and I had words over the care of each of those patients. And—"

"And I would like to know exactly what you accuse me of," Killian said in a ringing voice as he stepped through the second doorway on the far side of the ward. His gaze slid to Sarah, lingered in an instant of connection, then slid away. He scanned the faces of the men assembled around the corpse. "For if I was here each time, so were you. Does that bring you under equal suspicion, Mr. Simon?"

Killian stepped deeper into the room, holding to the shadows, out of the spill of morning light that came through the window.

"It does not." Mr. Simon's words fell like drops of burning acid. "As to what I accuse you of, the way of it is clear enough. Five dead bodies. I accuse you of having a hand in that."

"Ah." Killian raised a brow. "And when exactly did this patient expire?"

"Last night," snarled Mr. Simon. "I saw you here."

"Did you?" Killian did not appear particularly perturbed by the assertion, but Sarah noted the constables studying him with wary assessment.

He prowled closer, avoiding the dappled light leaking through the grimy windows, his dark garb blending with the gloom, his bright gold hair the only pale thing about him. There was grace and power in the way he moved, and suddenly, Sarah wished there was not. She wished he were ungainly and gangly. Less masculine. Less threatening.

Her gaze slid to the constables. Of a sudden, she saw Killian exactly as they must, as a powerful man who would surely emerge the victor in almost any altercation. All the more so if he chose to attack a sick and weakened patient.

He would never do that. She knew it. There was no question in her mind or in her heart.

In time, an explanation of these repulsive acts would

surely come to light, and that light would *not* shine on Killian Thayne.

But the constables did not know it, and they had stepped toward him into the shadows, flanking him on either side as though to block any possible escape. They began throwing questions at him like darts.

The drone of their voices buzzed as they challenged and prodded and Killian answered each sally with calm equanimity. But with both Mr. Simon and Mr. Franks interjecting, the constables were increasingly disinclined to believe him. Their doubt was written on their faces.

For the third time, one of the constables asked him, "And exactly where were you at midnight last night, Mr. Thayne?"

For the third time, he answered, "Occupied elsewhere."

He sounded amused, and Sarah thought his attitude only further inflamed the officers, inclining them to believe the worst of him.

"I am afraid that will not do, sir. I need details of your whereabouts, and witnesses who can attest to your activities during the time in question."

Sarah held her breath, her throat tightening, horror and fear congealing in a sickening knot. They believed that he had done this thing. They were convinced that he had killed this man in a hideous, unthinkable manner. No, not just *this* man. Many people. They thought Killian was responsible for all the questionable deaths on the ward.

Killian's gaze met hers, and he made a small jerking movement of his head, as though willing her to leave. She understood then that he meant to protect her, even to his own detriment.

"I must insist that you accompany us to Bow Street, where we can finish this discussion in a more appropriate venue," said the taller of the two constables as he exchanged a quick look with his companion.

Her fear magnified. She had heard about the interrogation rooms beneath the offices at Bow Street, heard about fists and cudgels and the manner in which suspects were *encouraged* to answer questions and admit their guilt. Anyone who lived in this parish had heard the horrible tales. The thought that they might carry out such brutality on Killian, the image of him beaten and bloodied, made her ill.

Before she could ponder ramifications and consequences, Sarah stepped forward and said, "He was with me. I am your witness. He was with me"—her chin came up, and she finished firmly—"all night."

Killian swung his gaze to her, pewter and ice, and she read his shock that she spoke in his defense.

"He was with me," she said again, louder, firmer. "So he could not have killed anyone because he accompanied me to my lodging and remained there with me from ten o'clock last night until dawn."

She heard gasps and murmurs, and only then did she realize that Mrs. Bayley and the matron and the other nurses had all gathered in the hallway just beyond the door, that the surgeons and apprentices and patients all leeched on to the exchange.

Their censure hung in the air like a foul smell.

Of course, she had known it even before she spoke. In saving Killian Thayne, she had doomed herself. A woman of loose moral character was not a woman to be respected and offered the opportunity of advancement on the wards.

Once before, the day Mr. Scully died, she had stepped forward in Killian's defense. That day, he had saved her from herself. But today, she was not so lucky, for so speedily had she forged into battle, there had not been a moment for her protector to stand before her.

"You assert that Mr. Thayne was with you the entire night?" the constable demanded.

"I do," she replied.

"The *entire* night?" The second constable stepped between her and Killian, using his physical presence to sever any influence that proximity might have over her answer.

She held his gaze and waited for uncertainty to creep to the fore on little rat feet. In truth, she could *not* swear that Killian had sat in the chair every moment of the night, guarding her door while she slept. He had been gone when she awakened, and he could have left at any time after she closed the portal and locked it.

Her gaze dropped to the dead man on the bed. This time, the killer had ripped open the victim's throat. And still, there was not a drop of blood spilled.

I hear your blood rushing in your veins, Sarah. Killian's words echoed in her thoughts. How could he possibly hear her blood? How? And why had he said such a thing at all? *I am not like other men.*

His own softly spoken admissions were rife with macabre possibilities.

With a shudder, she looked away from the corpse, her gaze lifting to meet Killian's over the constable's shoulder.

The silence hung heavy, like a thick, cloying fog.

"Miss Lowell," Killian said, his attention focused upon her, and she knew he meant to say more, to sacrifice himself for her honor, to ensure that her name not be besmirched by her assertion that he had remained at her side the night through.

"Killian Thayne never left my side during the hours between ten o'clock and dawn," she said again, her tone steady and sure. She *knew* it for the truth. He had told her he would guard her and keep her safe, and he had meant it. Whatever beast lurked beneath Killian's skin, it was not a beast that had done this murder.

She turned her attention fully on the dark-haired constable and stared him down, though her legs trembled beneath her skirt, and her pulse pounded so heavy and fast it made her temples throb. She must find a way to make these men understand that they were looking for their monster in the wrong place.

"He is not your killer, regardless of what Mr. Simon believes he saw. In fact, Mr. Simon"—she turned her head toward the man in question and found him watching her with narrow-eyed rage—"I believe you said that you saw the patient alive sometime close to midnight, a full two hours after Mr. Thayne left King's College. With me."

All about her were gasps and murmurs and she knew what they thought. That she had lain with Killian. That she had allowed him liberties of a base nature.

She almost laughed. Why did their attention focus on the salacious, rather than on her implication that Mr. Simon's proximity to the patient was equally suspicious, if not more so?

Killian's eyes met hers, and she read confusion and awe, as though he expected anything but her defense of him. As though her support was a treasure of infinite value. In that instant, she wanted to stride to his side and take his hand between her own, and decry their vile suspicions.

In that instant, she wished she were guilty of all the lascivious acts they suspected. She wished that she *had* allowed him those liberties, that she deserved the horrified looks they cast her way.

The truth was, she might well have allowed them, if he had only asked.

Because . . . oh, sweet God . . . her heart twisted and she felt the blood drain from her cheeks. She was in love with him.

The magnitude of that realization left her reeling.

She was in love with Killian, despite—*and because of*— all his secret layers and hidden depths, all the mysteries and shadows that dogged him.

She was in love with a man they suspected of murder.

Sarah turned the corner onto Coptic Street a little over an hour later, her feet moving one before the other, a mechanical tread that carried her to the hovel that had become her home. Her heart was heavy, her thoughts bleak and twisted.

The constables had drawn Killian off to a separate room

to question him further, but they had not taken him to Bow Street, and for that she was grateful. Still, she was consumed by worry and fear, tormented by the overwhelming knowledge of how deeply she had come to care for Killian, by the danger that surrounded him, and by her own tenuous circumstance.

The early morning's sun was gone. A thick fog had rolled in, heavy and damp. Caught in the gray blanket of cloying mist that clung to her skin and obscured the way, she could see little of what lay ahead.

Sounds echoed about her, the creak of a wheel, the jingle of a bridle. She stumbled, then righted herself, glancing about as though waking from a daze.

Continuing on, she passed a mangy dog that sniffed at the gutter; then she jerked to a stop as Mrs. Cowden's house materialized from the mist, ghostly tendrils wrapping about the crumbling chimney and sagging fence. The sight of the house, fog-shrouded and shabby, drove deep the vile desperation of her circumstances.

With sneering antipathy, Mr. Simon had dismissed her from her post. She no longer had her position at King's College, and she had little hope of finding another. There was no chance that she might receive a recommendation from anyone at the hospital. She had effectively slammed that door when she had spoken in Killian's defense.

Tears pricked her eyes, and she dashed them away with the back of her hand. There was no value in tears of frustration and anger, fear and hopelessness. They would only serve to leave her nose red and her lids puffy.

They would neither change nor solve anything.

In the end, she would still have three days left until her rent was due once more, with no means to pay it.

And she would still be in love with Killian Thayne.

At this moment, she could not say which of the two quandaries was fraught with the greatest uncertainty.

Her options at the moment were so narrow and frayed,

she was having a difficult time seeing them at all. And despite that, she knew that if faced with the same choice in the same setting, she would again do exactly as she had done. Because she could not let them take him.

The sound of wheels clacking on the cobblestones and the clopping of horses' hooves made her head jerk up and her gaze dart along the street. As though teased apart with the edge of a knife, the fog gradually parted to reveal four great black beasts and, behind them, a gleaming black coach. Instinctively, she stepped back, only to find the carriage rocked to a halt several paces away, before Mrs. Cowden's lodging house.

A prickling sense of expectation bloomed, for she had no doubt as to the owner of the carriage. She had known by his dress and his mode of speech that surely Killian was from a different world than the other surgeons at King's College—a different world even than the comfortable one she had been raised in. But this coach, with its gleaming finish and beautifully matched horses, spoke of wealth beyond what she could have imagined.

The sight of it was both welcome and worrisome, for Killian's presence here created a labyrinth of complexities and enticements.

A footman climbed down and stood by the carriage door. He wore a smart green and gold livery, as did the coachman on the bench.

Feeling as though she slogged through a bog that mired her every step, she walked the last dozen paces to the coach.

"This way, miss," the footman said, indicating the door on the far side.

Wary of the horses that snorted and pawed the ground, she offered them a wide berth as she rounded the carriage. The footman opened the door. She blinked and peered into the dim confines. Killian sat in the far corner, wrapped in shadow and mystery.

The collar of his cloak was raised high, and his hands

were gloved in black leather. She frowned, certain there was some significance to that, but unable to place exactly what.

"Come inside please, Sarah," he said. "I wish to speak with you."

A request? An order? She could not say. But since she had much she wished to ask him, much she wished to say, she took the footman's offered hand and allowed him to help her inside the coach.

Settling herself in the corner opposite Killian, as far from him as the small space would allow, she waited in silence as the footman closed the door, leaving them alone. She could see only the gleam of Killian's hair and the hint of highlight on his brow, his nose, his chin. The blinds were pulled down over the windows, and wishing to have a clear perspective of his expression, Sarah reached to draw one up.

He moved quickly, leaning forward to trap her wrist, his gaze intent, and she thought she ought to be afraid. But she was not. For some inexplicable reason, when she was with Killian, she felt safer, more secure, more confident than she ever had in her entire life. She felt as though he opened a dam and let her soul dance free, let her be exactly who she was.

Strange thoughts. Mad thoughts.

"Leave it," he said softly. "The light is too bright."

She thought he spoke in jest, but a glance disabused her of that notion. He found even this fog-shrouded day too bright for his comfort.

For a flickering instant, she had the terrible thought that he was as her father had been, an opium addict whose eyes were pained by even modest illumination. Yet Killian evinced none of the traits associated with that malady. Her father had been lethargic, his pupils ever constricted, his speech slurred. He had shown no interest in his appearance or grooming. In the end, she had barely known him, for his mannerisms and behavior were so drastically altered.

By contrast, Killian was alert, his clothing impeccable, his intellect sharp and clear.

Perhaps he simply disliked the sun. Perhaps. But wariness unfurled inside her, and she thought otherwise.

"Are you cold?" he asked, cutting the silence.

It was only then that she realized she was trembling.

He did not wait for her answer, but loosed his hold on her wrist and spread a thick blanket over her legs, then used the toe of his boot to push a warming brick along the floor. "Drape the blanket over top and the heat will rise to warm you."

"Thank you," she murmured, touched by his consideration.

He settled back in the corner and studied her for a moment, leaving her strangely uncomfortable and disconcerted.

But no longer cold. The blanket and the brick saw to that.

"It seems you are ever leaping to my defense, Sarah." He dipped his head, toyed with the edge of his glove, then looked up once more, his expression intent. "Why did you lie for me?"

She sucked in a startled breath. *Lie.* Had she lied? Had he left his place at her door and returned to the hospital at midnight? She did not believe he had, and that made her either very intuitive or very foolish.

"They were going to take you," she said, her voice low. She dropped her gaze to the tips of his perfectly polished boots. "The constables. They were going to take you to the interrogation rooms at Bow Street. They would have hurt you." The thought of that horrified her.

She raised her head and saw that he watched her with complete attention, his expression one of bemused wonder. Her heart leapt at the emotion she read there, the fact that he clearly was both puzzled by and appreciative of her defense of him.

"I would rather that than any harm befall you," he said flatly. "I wish to see you safe, Sarah. Safe and protected."

The warmth that flooded her at those words, at his implied affection, was delicious.

"Then you must understand that I could not bear for them to hurt you," she whispered. "And they would have . . . to make you confess to a crime you did not commit."

He made a small smile, faintly sardonic. "And you know that I did not commit it?"

"I do." She nodded, feeling fierce and certain. "I know you could never do that, never harm someone weak and ill."

He appeared taken off guard by her ferocity.

"Do not paint me with gilded righteousness. There are things you do *not* know of me, Sarah. Things I did many, many years ago when I was a different creature than I am today."

"Creature?" She laughed, the sound hollow in her own ears. "You say the word as though you are some ravening beast. You are a man."

"I am many things. I have been many things." He trapped her hand between his own, the action making her breath lock in her throat and her pulse leap wildly.

Leaning forward to rest one elbow on his knee, he released her and feathered the backs of his gloved fingers along her cheek.

Oh, the sweet sensation of his touch. It poured through her like rich, red wine. She read such longing in him, such pain, as though he was desperate for that contact. As desperate as she.

She ached for him to kiss her and hold her so tight against him that she could feel his heartbeat.

"Whatever you have been, whatever you are, I know you, Killian. I *know* you."

He said nothing for a moment, then spoke, very softly. "I wanted to grab him by the throat and slam him against the wall when I heard from Mrs. Bayley that he had censured you."

Mr. Simon. He spoke of Mr. Simon, who had sneered at

her in a most demeaning manner after the constables had drawn Killian away.

Stunned by the ferocity of the sentiment, she could summon no reply, and so they sat for a moment in silence while she tried to gather her thoughts and emotions into some semblance of calm. Her world was coming unraveled at the seams, and she was not certain how to drag the edges back together. She was not even certain she wanted to.

He made a vague gesture toward the closed door of the carriage. "Would you prefer to wait while I have Jones pack for you, or shall we proceed and I shall send someone to fetch your belongings later?"

"Pack? I don't . . ." *I don't understand.* But she did. Killian meant to take her away from here. To bring her . . . where?

He lifted something from the seat beside him and extended his hand. She saw then that he held the pretty porcelain saucer that had been hers since childhood. He must have been in her room. How? She knew she had locked it when she left.

"How did you know that I would want this?" She took the dish from him and cupped it in her palms. "Of all the things in my chamber, this is the one that means something to me."

"I know much about you, Sarah. It is there in every subtle glance, in the way you breathe, in the delicate sweep of your lashes. If I watch you, I see it all. And I do love to watch you. You are endlessly fascinating to me."

His words made her heart race, and she had no need to wonder if he knew it, because he said, "I can hear each precious pulse, Sarah, feel each beat of your heart."

Impossible. Surely he could not. But somehow she believed him. Believed he did feel her and hear her. Believed he *knew* her.

"Where do we go?"

He smiled at her question, obviously reading her acquiescence in her words. "We go home. My home, now yours."

And all the arguments that tumbled to her lips died as he turned his gaze upon her.

"I offer you the world, Sarah. Anything you want."

She believed him in that as well. "What do you demand in return?"

"Demand? No, I only ask. I ask for you. Your company. Your smile. Your eyes, dancing and pleased as they look to mine. Your intellect. Your valor. But mind me well, Sarah, you will need that valor. I am not an easy . . . man."

The hesitation hung in the air, a warning, but not a surprise. She had seen from the start that he had depths like a roiling ocean in the midst of a storm. She sensed he meant it as a warning of something deeper, something greater. But he was not ready to tell her. Not yet.

He shared something of great import here, some secret that shimmered between them and slid away from her like smoke. She tried to clasp it, to see it clearly, but the meaning dissipated, and she was left with the certainty that his words revealed something she did not quite grasp.

"Well, I suppose that I am neither meek nor submissive, which makes me a somewhat difficult woman, wouldn't you say?"

He made a soft laugh, his eyes glittering in the dim light.

"I would have you only as you are, and no other way. The thought of having you by my side, of sharing the world with you is a heady temptation. You are a balm to my loneliness, Sarah." His tone turned muted and dark, his eyes bleak. "I have been alone for a very long while."

She swallowed, mesmerized by the heat in his gaze. "I understand loneliness," she whispered.

Again, that fleeting, dark smile, as though her words both amused and saddened him.

He reached down and lifted something else from the seat. The yellowed magazine that held the story her father had found so fascinating. Polidori's "The Vampyre."

Offering it to her, he held her gaze, and she sensed that

unlike her candle dish, he had not retrieved this out of care and kindness, but for another reason entirely. Cautious and watchful, she took the pages from him, her pulse speeding up, her thoughts tumbling to and fro as a strange expectation suffused her.

Something clicked inside her, a key in a lock.

No. What was she thinking? It was not possible.

"The Vampyre."

The smoky ideas that had eluded her a moment past coalesced, and she was left speechless and overwhelmed.

Impossible. And not. It explained so much.

He stared at her, unsmiling, severe. She had the thought that he knew the direction her suppositions traveled. That he *wanted* them to flow toward that impossible conclusion.

Her breath stuttered to a stop, trapped in her lungs, and she stared at him, suddenly certain. Certain of the impossible, the terrible, the mad.

Inexorably drawn, her gaze dipped to the magazine once more. The seconds ticked past, protracted and sluggish.

"You did not kill those people at King's College," she whispered, the words so soft she wondered that he could hear her at all. When he made no reply, she raised her head and realized that he waited only for that, that he wanted her to look at him as he made his response.

"No, I did not kill them." His eyes, liquid mercury, gleamed in the dim light, boring deep inside her.

"But you could have." She wrapped her arms about her waist and held herself tight. "You could have because . . ."

There was both sorrow and resignation etched on his face as he finished the thought that she dared not speak aloud. "Because I am . . ." He paused, and she waited, her breath stalled in her chest, then he shook his head and finished. "I am not like other men."

And suddenly, that assertion was laced with a multitude of subtle inferences and implications that she was not yet ready to drag into the light.

In that moment, though she knew not its source, she felt his suffering as her own.

Whatever his tormented secrets, she recognized in him like to like, knew that whatever horrors he had known and seen, whatever mysteries lurked in his heart, he was even more alone than she.

That he needed her as she needed him.

Six

At his instruction, the coach set off. Killian closed his eyes and rested his head back against the velvet squabs, baring the strong column of his throat. Once, Sarah stretched out her hand, almost brave enough to succumb to the urge to lay her fingers against his neck and feel the steady, solid throb of the pulse that beat beneath his skin. In the end, she dropped her hand and contented herself with letting her gaze roam his features and her heart swell with the knowledge that he had come for her.

He had cared enough to come for her.

She concentrated on the wonder of that rather than the multitude of questions that their cryptic dialogue had skirted.

Mindful of the light, she leaned close to the window and peeked through the lifted edge of the blind as the carriage rocked to a halt before Killian's town house in Berkeley Square. His was the last in a row of very large, very tall houses. There was a black ironwork fence surrounding the entirety, with a break at the stairs that ascended to the front door, and another that descended to a servants' entry.

Sarah counted four floors, each with three large rectangular windows across the front, save for the ground floor, which had two windows to the left of the door.

After a moment, the liveried footman opened the carriage door and waited as Sarah gathered her candle dish and the magazine. She caught her lower lip between her teeth, staring at the curled and faded pages . . . wondering . . .

Raising her gaze, she found Killian watching her, his expression bland and cool.

She turned away, and let the footman hand her down from the coach. Killian descended behind her. She glanced back to see that he had put his spectacles in place to shade his eyes. He kept his head bowed, his thick, honey gold hair falling forward to veil his features.

Without a word, he offered his arm, and she sensed that any questions she had would be better spoken indoors rather than out here, for even this dim, cloud-filtered light was uncomfortable for him.

They ascended the stairs and he did not wait for a butler or maid to open the door, but opened it himself and gestured for Sarah to precede him inside. The hallway was dark, but beautiful. Paneled walls of rich gleaming wood. A semicircular console table just inside the entry with a vase of deep red roses. There was thought and artistry in the presentation.

The scent of beeswax left a faint signature in the air, topped by the breath of the roses. Killian drew off his gloves and tossed them on the table, then swung his cloak from about his broad shoulders and handed it to a maid, who stepped forward and curtsied before taking the garment from his hands.

Sarah caught her breath as Killian stepped around behind her to stand close at her back. His breath fanned her neck, sending shivers of awareness dancing across her skin.

"May I?" he murmured, and she nodded, wordless. Boneless. Nearly swooning at the heat of him. She could feel it through all the layers of her clothing and his as he took her cloak. How long since she had been warm? Truly warm? Body, heart, and mind. She had been frozen for so long.

He twined his fingers with hers and led her through the house, up carpeted stairs with banisters of gleaming polished wood, through hallways lit only by lamplight, the heavy draperies pulled across the windows. The lighting here seemed to please him, for he had taken off his spectacles, and when he looked at her, his cool gray eyes sparked with a secret flame.

At last, they reached a heavy double door, and he threw it open, then drew her inside.

"My lair," he murmured, and a trickle of apprehension crawled through her at his choice of words.

She hesitated, then stepped deeper into the chamber. The walls were covered in blue paper that had a subtle texture, like velvet. A thick, soft carpet of darker blue with a design of green and yellow birds covered the floor. There were two large chairs before the fireplace, each matched with a low footstool. A spacious room, handsome in appearance.

"You like fine things," she observed.

"I do."

"Yet you work in one of the poorest hospitals in the city."

An instant of silence. Then, "Because they do not have fine things. I dislike the imbalance."

She recalled the way he tucked shillings into the night nurse's apron, and realized that she had already known this about him, though she had not defined it in such a pared-down manner.

Emotion bubbled to the surface, and she turned away lest he read it in her gaze. The feelings she had for him were too new, too raw. She was not ready to explain, perhaps to have them rebuffed. She did not think she could bear that.

Pressing her lips together, she shifted closer to the fireplace. Above the oaken mantelpiece was a large painting of a river. The dominant colors were blue and aqua and yellow and gold. She gazed up in mute wonder, drawn into the beauty and brightness of the watercolor.

"Turner," Killian murmured from behind her. "Some call him the painter of light."

It was true. The painting embodied light, captured it and set it free, pure and brilliant. And Killian hung it in his chamber, he who clung only to the shadows.

The thought made her sad.

"Do you long for it, for the sunlight? For the warmth of it on your skin?" She could not tear her eyes from the painting. She felt as though the sun's rays poured from the canvas to touch her face.

"No, I do not long for it. The moonlight has a cool and wonderful beauty, the night its own sweet music." He moved close behind her. She could feel the heat of him. "I remember the sunlight with a vague and hazy fondness, but I do not long for it. 'Twas a small sacrifice in exchange for all I have gained. I have learned to love the night."

His words brought so many questions to her lips, questions she dared not ask, for she was not yet certain what she would do with the answers. She closed her eyes, every sense tingling with awareness, with the knowledge that he was so close. All she had to do was reach out and she could know the answers to untold mysteries. About him. About herself.

If only she dared.

Dipping his head until his nose grazed the skin of her neck, he breathed in, his nearness and his action combining to set her heart racing. She ached for the stroke of his hand, the feel of his lips.

He uncurled her fingers from about her porcelain dish and set it on the mantel, beneath the painting of light. The magazine, he took from her and tossed on one of the chairs. For an instant, she thought to cling to it, to ask him about subtle hints and meanings, and then she thought not. Whatever secrets Killian held, he would share them when he willed.

Closing her eyes, she leaned back a little into his embrace.

"Be certain, Sarah," he whispered against the side of her

throat, sending a tinkling cascade of sensitivity dancing through her.

She knew all he meant with those softly voiced words. Be certain it was this she wanted, *him* she wanted. The unconventional life he offered. She did not know where he meant this to lead, but she could not imagine he offered her forever.

"I am certain," she whispered. She had no wish to cling to her past, had no idea of her future. In this moment she was changed from the woman she had always been. In this moment, she wanted only to *live*, to allow herself that luxury, that beauty. To know Killian's touch, to offer him her love, even if this day was all she ever had of him, all they ever shared.

Tomorrow would come regardless, and it would hold the same fears and uncertainties whether she indulged her heart or not. So for one shining snippet of the unfurling ribbon that was her life, she would grab hold of what she wanted and take what she could.

Reaching up, she pulled the pins from her hair and let it fall about her shoulders and down her back.

"Your hair is beautiful, a sleek, dark curtain with just a whisper of wayward curl at the ends." He stroked his palm down the length, emphasizing his point. That touch made her mouth go dry and her pulse jerk about like a skittish colt.

"You are beautiful, Sarah." His words, and the rich, lovely cadence of his voice mesmerized her. "The pink flush of your skin"—he drew his thumb along the edge of her jaw—"the lush curve of your lips"—his fingers slid to her lips, rubbed, and stroked, and as her mouth opened on a gasp, the tip of his index finger dipped inside—"you are so lovely to me."

On instinct, she licked his fingertip, then closed her teeth on him and bit down.

His sharp intake of breath stabbed through her, sinking to her breasts, her belly, her trembling legs. Because she knew she ignited him. There was a lush and heady pleasure in that.

"You bite," he murmured.

She hesitated but an instant, then whispered, "As, I suspect, do you." There. She had done it. Acknowledged the secret that hovered between them. On some level, she understood. And she knew that he would not hurt her.

He pulled her around to face him then, taking her mouth in a hungry kiss, his tongue tasting her, his teeth nipping lightly at her lips. Pleasure spilled through her blood like a tide, making her breath rasp and her pulse race. Her skin felt too tight. Her clothes were unbearable fetters, and she hissed a sigh of relief as he loosened them and slid each piece from her, kissing and caressing every inch of skin he bared.

Modesty demanded she blush and protest. Desire demanded that she open her mouth and taste him as he tasted her. The flavor of his kiss was heady, more wonderful than the finest wine she had ever sampled.

The cool air in the room touched her, making her shiver. The sheets of his bed were even cooler as he guided her there and pressed her back against them, his fingers splayed lightly across her throat. She could feel her pulse drumming against his fingertips.

With a groan, he traced his tongue along her jaw, her throat, his mouth coming to lie against her pulse. He kissed her there, his mouth open, insistent. She arched her neck, the graze of his teeth making her gasp, sending spiraling tendrils of need winding through her veins.

Feeling weightless and dizzy and wonderfully alive, she lay back and watched as he dragged off his coat, then his shirt, pulling the cloth over his head and down his arms. He bared the wonderful mystery of his chest, covered in dark gold hair that tapered to a thin line down the middle of his taut belly.

"You are lovely," she whispered. He was. But she had expected that, expected the lithe, lean lines and sculpted edges. She studied him in open curiosity, awed and amazed, and he laughed, a low wicked chuckle that stroked her senses.

His eyes never left hers as he prowled closer to rest his knee between her own on the mattress.

Her body arched of its own accord, instinctively seeking his touch as he trailed his fingers down her neck, along her collarbone, to the swell of her breast above the thin cotton of her chemise. Feeling like a bow drawn taut, bent to its limit, she waited to see what he would do next.

A gasp escaped her, and it became a purr as he closed his hand about the soft flesh of her breast, stroked his thumb over her tight nipple through the thin cloth of her chemise. The sensation was like fire and ice and fireworks exploding in the sky, only the explosion was inside her, inside her blood, an aching need that spread. Heat. Liquid heat.

"Please." She knew not what she begged for. But he knew.

Reaching down, he closed his fists in her chemise and tore it open, baring her to his gaze, his touch. His features were hard, hungry, and the way he looked at her made an answering hunger rear inside her.

He let his weight down full upon her, wonderfully heavy, holding her and freeing her, the hard ridge of his arousal between her thighs. She had never felt anything more breathtaking, more sensual. Longing burgeoned and swelled, and she cried out as he closed his mouth on her nipple, offering sweet kisses and gentle bites until she was panting and writhing beneath him.

Running her hands along his shoulders and down the hard planes of his chest, she explored the feel of his smooth skin, taut over lean layers of muscle. He was wonderfully masculine, wonderfully appealing.

His mouth moved again to her throat, his hands skimming her waist, and lower, dipping between her thighs to touch her sex. She moaned, lost in sensation.

She had never imagined this. Never. It was like a tempest inside her own body, a magnificent tempest that lured her to fling herself into the storm with untrammeled abandon.

Her body stirred, her hips rolling in a way she did not deliberately intend. But the movement felt so good, so right. She felt as though he led her to a place she had always known and never even thought to look for. Hot and quivering, sensation poured through her. She was alive, so alive.

Between her thighs, his arousal was thick and heavy, pressing against her sex. Again her hips rocked up, and she felt a slick pressure, there, between her folds. She opened to him, sliding her heels along the smooth, soft sheets, shifting to an angle that increased the incredible feelings he stirred.

Cupping her breast, he stroked her and rocked his hips to bring himself tighter against her. There was a tautness, a pressure; then he slid a little inside her, and she gave a shocked cry at the intrusion, the foreign sensation of being stretched and entered.

He held himself back. She could feel that in the leashed tension of his body. A press; a release. Just a little of his erection easing in to fill and stretch. It was alien and frightening and beguiling all at once, and she could not help but catch his rhythm and move with him. Again and again until she was panting, half in apprehension, half in wild abandon.

What a mad slurry of feelings. She wanted him, ached for him, but could not help but be a little afraid of the unknown.

And then it was unknown no longer. He pushed harder, the stretching so powerful and strange, she cried out. A sharp instant of discomfort, a burning, an ache, and then he was inside her, deep inside her.

She lay there panting, a little dismayed.

As though he knew everything she felt, he simply stayed as he was, allowed her to understand the feeling of his body joined with hers, and then he began to move, a shallow thrust, a retreat. He slid his hand down her belly to her soft curls, to a place so sensitive it made her moan, and he caressed her with lazy gentle swirls of his fingers until she gasped and arched up to meet each shallow thrust. Wanting more. Needing more.

With a little cry, she reached down and locked her fingers

around his wrist, holding his hand exactly where it was, aching for something she could not name.

Too much. It was all too much. She could not bear it, could not hold fast to the spiraling pieces of herself.

She twined her fingers through his hair, felt him thrust deep and hard, his breath ragged as he turned his face into the crook of her elbow.

Hot and sharp, she felt his bite, there on the soft skin at the inside of her elbow.

"Killian—" She cried out, and tried to make him understand, but it was too late. The sensation of his fingers sliding along her wet sex, and the feel of his erection moving inside her . . . She was flying apart, a thousand shining bits of her all flying apart.

And he was with her, flying with her, his release coming an instant after her own as he thrust deep one last time, throbbing inside her, spilling himself inside her.

She clung to him, floating, and finally drifting back to herself.

Panting, bewildered, wonderfully replete, she lay there and stared up at the gilded ceiling, one arm draped across Killian's broad back, the other flung free across the sheets.

He kissed her neck, her cheek, and finally roused himself to lift his weight from her and roll to the side. She missed it immediately. The weight of him. The heat.

She snuggled against him and smiled as he slid his arm about her and drew her close. Slowly, she lifted her lids, and languidly eased her arm across his chest.

Frowning, she stared at the golden expanse of his skin, and it took her a moment to understand what she saw.

Blood. She had left a smear of blood when she moved her arm over his skin.

With a cry, she jerked to a sitting position and stared at the crook of her elbow. Her veins traced blue beneath her skin, and there were two small gashes there and a small smear of her blood.

He had bitten her. Tasted her. The thought was both ap-
palling and fascinating.

Her gaze jerked to his, and she found him watching her,
his lips drawn taut, his eyes pinched.

"Killian," she whispered, a question, a plea.

His gaze never leaving hers, he reached out and traced his
index finger across the blood on her arm, then brought it to
his mouth and drew it across his lower lip.

On some level, she knew she ought to be repulsed, horrified, but the sight of him—the smear of crimson on his lips,
the trace of his tongue as he licked it, the look of pleasure on
his face as he tasted her—was incredibly sensual.

She stared at him, thinking she ought to feel disgusted,
horrified, afraid. But all she felt was love. Acceptance. Blood
held no mysteries or horrors for her. How could it? She had
mopped up buckets upon buckets in her time at King's College, not to mention the years she had worked by her father's
side.

"Have I shocked you beyond bearing?" he asked.

Wetting her lips, she took a second before she answered,
and then she offered the truth.

"Shocked me? Yes. I am shocked, but not so much by
what you did, as by the way I feel about it." She paused, and
he gave her the moment, gave her time to collect her thoughts.
"I am neither horrified nor repulsed, and *that* is the shocking
thing. I found it . . ." She shook her head, trying to understand her own emotions. "Is blood essential to you? For your
survival?"

"Yes. But that was not for survival. I did not feed from
you, Sarah. It is a"—he made an absent gesture—"for my
kind, it is a form of connection."

Somehow, she understood that. She *had* felt connected to
him, as though for a single glittering instant, they were one.

"But you do feed?"

"Occasionally." He made a small smile. "Not often. And

the bowls of blood the physicians bleed from their patients ought not go to waste."

She felt her lips twitch in an answering smile, and she wondered if she ought to be horrified by that. Her father had always deemed the practice of bloodletting to be both dangerous and barbaric. She could hardly fault Killian for putting the folly of others to a beneficial use.

Suddenly, the magnitude of their discourse overwhelmed her, and she fell back on the sheets to stare at the gilded ceiling. "That story in the magazine . . . You are—"

"Nothing like the monster in the story," Killian offered. "But, yes, I am a vampire, Sarah."

He leaned in as though to kiss her, but held himself inches above her, hovering just beyond reach, his gaze locked on hers.

She understood then. The choice was hers. To deny him or to clasp him to her, press her mouth to his, accept him for all he was.

To accept that he was a vampire.

What did such a thing entail? Did he mean to make her what he was? Was such a thing even possible?

"What we just shared . . . was it an act of love for you, the taking of my blood?"

His lashes swept down, veiling his thoughts.

"An act of connection," he reaffirmed, his voice ragged. "I have lived alone for more years than you can imagine. I dare not let myself love." He looked at her then, his expression so bleak that her heart broke for him. "To love means to lose, Sarah. I cannot. I dare not. 'Tis a path to madness for one such as me." He made a muted groan. "I think that in the years of emptiness, I have forgotten how to love. But I can keep you safe. I can make you happy. Those things I can offer you."

Tears welled, and she made no effort to stem their flow, but let them trickle from the corners of her eyes and across her temples.

Then she raised her head and pressed her mouth to his.

She could taste the faintly metallic hint of her own blood on his lips, and she could taste his torment and pain.

"Sarah—"

"Shh." She pressed her fingers against his lips, then kissed him again. "It matters not, Killian. I have enough love for us both. I *do*. I will share my love with you, and it will be enough. I swear it will be enough."

With a groan, he took her mouth in a hungry kiss. He made love to her once more, languid caresses and leisurely care, no part of her untouched. No part of her unloved.

But beneath his gentle care, she sensed his demons, tightly leashed. Sensed his pain.

And when they were both sated, the sheets rumpled and mussed, her heart thudding in the aftermath of passion, she stroked his hair and asked, "How long, Killian? How long have you been alone?"

His chest expanded on a deep breath, and she thought he would not answer. There was sadness for her in that, in his refusal to share any part of himself. Then he surprised her, his voice low and deep.

"Long ago, I loved, and it was an indescribable torment to watch each of them age, or sicken and die. I was alone. Ever alone. And in time, I learned not to love, not to care, to stand at a safe distance and watch mortal lives unfold, to extricate myself when it threatened to become apparent that I never grew a day older." His voice dropped to a rough rasp. "Three hundred years, Sarah. I have been alone for three hundred years."

The enormity of that slapped her, and she gasped. She could not imagine it, could not think how he had borne it.

"In all that time, you never took a companion, never shared yourself with anyone?"

"Physically, yes. I have taken many lovers. But not a companion. None knew what I am. I have shared my truths, my secrets, with no one . . ." He paused. "Until you."

She held herself very still, those words humming through

her mind like a symphony. And then she understood that he
did love her; he was only not yet ready to know it.

Hours later, Killian sat propped on the pillows, feeding
Sarah slices of apple dipped in honey. The sticky liquid
clung to her lips, and when he leaned in and kissed her, it
clung to his as well. He popped a slice in his mouth, chewed,
and swallowed, and Sarah watched him with unabashed curiosity.

"You eat," she observed.

He laughed. "Yes."

She laid her palm flat against his chest. "Your heart beats."

"It does," he agreed, amused. "Despite the stories and mad
suppositions, Sarah, I am not undead. My heart beats. My
body craves food. I sleep when I must, usually a handful of
hours each week. Blood is only one form of necessary sustenance for me, and I take it as I require, far less often now
than in the early years."

She nodded, and dipped her finger in the honey, then
smeared it over his lips. Tipping her head, she kissed him,
tasting honey, tasting him.

Then his words triggered a thought, and she drew back to
study him. "How often did you require it in the early years?"

"At least once each week. It was like a madness, a thirst
that could be assuaged no other way."

"The killer at King's College," she mused. "He takes the
lives of those who are dying, those who suffer terrible pain.
I think he believes it a mercy. But he does it often. Does that
mean he is . . . new? That these are the early years for him?"

Killian blinked, and sat straight. "A newly made vampire.
Yes. That makes sense. And he is making an effort to turn his
thirst to the good, to find a way to control it."

"Did you control it?" she asked, not quite certain that she
wanted to know.

He swung his legs over the side of the bed, planting his

bare feet on the carpet, and he turned his face to her, his expression somber.

"Not at first. At first, I was careless and greedy, drinking where I would. I did not murder indiscriminately, but I cannot swear that none died." He raked his hand back through his hair, and took a slow breath, as though deliberating how much to reveal. "I would have you know the truth, Sarah, though it paints me in a less than perfect light. I was no monster, but I was no saint. I fed from murderers and thieves, but I was not overly cautious about draining them. I fed, and I left them, and if they died, I neither knew nor cared."

"But the vampire who hunts at King's College does know," she pointed out. "He kills on purpose, and he chooses to drain those who are suffering a horrible death."

"A strange form of morality."

"Killian, I think the vampire follows me. I have seen him in the graveyard, sensed his presence behind me in the alleys. He dogs my steps." She shook her head. "It is the same man, Killian. The man who stalks me is the same as the one who moves like a wraith through the wards, stealing lives."

Killian studied her for a moment. "He moves about only in the darkness," he said. "His pattern indicates he is too new to have built up any sort of tolerance of the light."

"That is why you told me I would be safe in the light. You sensed that my pursuer was a vampire." And as she thought about it now, she realized it was true. She had never felt the sensation of being watched, being followed, in the daylight. Only in the hours between dusk and dawn. "But *you* can move about in the light."

He smiled at her then. "I can move about in the light, if I am careful and my skin covered, but I am centuries older than he."

Centuries. Her breath locked in her throat. She was not accustomed to that yet. Hundreds of years, alone. She could not imagine it, could not imagine how he had borne it. "What happens if you are exposed to the light?"

"Much the same as what happens if *you* are exposed for too long. My skin pinkens, then reddens. Blisters form. There is discomfort, then pain. It is not deadly, merely unpleasant. But for a newly born, it is far more than unpleasant. It is an agony that can lead to a debilitating condition that may last for months, even years."

"Will the light kill him?"

For a moment, she thought he would not answer, would hold fast the secrets she longed now to know. Then he made a huffing exhalation and said, "No, it will not kill him. There is very little now that can kill him." His lips drew taut, and after a pause he finished softly, "Another vampire could do the deed."

She shivered, reading his meaning in the things he did not say. "You will kill him, this newly made creature, if he does not agree to cease murdering people."

"Yes, exactly. Mortals, as a whole, are not ready to know of creatures such as me." He made a soft sound. "Even small children suspect that monsters exist. But suspicion is far different than certainty. I cannot leave him free to dart about and kill indiscriminately, leaving proof that we exist."

"But only if you are forced to. You will only kill him if you are forced to." Her heart pounded in apprehension and horror.

"Yes."

"Is there danger, Killian? To you?"

"No." She heard the smile in his voice as he replied. "He is newly made, and I . . . well, I am not."

"I can help," she said, and rushed on as he turned his head toward her, intending, she was certain, to argue. "He will not know that I no longer work at King's College. He will expect me to walk home this evening to Coptic Street, and that is exactly what I will do."

Her heart thudded as she waited for his reply, waited to see if he would recognize the value of her plan.

A slow smile curved his lips, and he curled his fingers round her nape and drew her close for a hard kiss.

"A brilliant plan. You will walk to Coptic Street"—he cast her a sidelong look through his lashes—"and I will follow in your shadow."

In that moment, she was both pleased that he valued her proposition, that he saw the importance of her participation, and faintly uneasy by the menace she sensed lurking just beneath the surface.

He shifted so his lips moved against her ear as he whispered, "I am what I am, Sarah. No matter how civilized, how controlled the veneer, beneath it all, I am the hunter."

Seven

That night, Sarah walked slowly past the graveyard, searching for some hint of the man who stalked her. The place was silent and still. No shadow, no sound, no movement. He was not there. She was a little surprised, for she had been so certain he would come. But there was still time. He might yet show himself at any point along the route.

A thick, damp blanket of fog clung to the tombstones and the surrounding buildings. She braved a glance over her shoulder toward the slaughterhouses. The fog veiled them from sight, though she knew they were behind her, for the air was stained with the scent of blood and butchered meat.

Beneath her cloak, she carried her cudgel, and her fingers curled tighter about it now. Killian had grinned when he saw it.

"What will you do with that?" he had asked with a low chuckle.

"I shall cosh him on the head if need be."

"Yes, I believe you will." He had caught her to him and kissed her, and held her against his chest, his laughter rumbling through them both.

The sound had poured through her like chocolate, luscious and warm. She made him laugh. She brought him joy. There was such pleasure for her in that.

Now she walked on, quickening her pace, the chill of the night, or perhaps unease, making her teeth chatter. She resisted the urge to peer about, to search for some sign of Killian. She knew she would see no hint of his presence. He blended seamlessly with the night.

The hunter. She shivered as she recalled his words, uncertain how she felt about that. He would do what he must to keep humans safe from one of his kind, but what did that make him? And what did it make her that she loved him nonetheless?

She turned onto Queen Street and continued toward St. Giles. They had determined that she would take the quickest way to Coptic Street this night, through alleys and courtyards, for that was the darkest route, the most isolated, and their best hope to draw out the man they sought.

Summoning the memory of her previous encounter with him, she recalled that he was tall, draped in a flowing black cloak, his hands gloved, his face shadowed by a low-crowned hat. There was little enough to hint at his identity, but for some reason, she thought of Mr. Simon. Of his height and the fact that, while he attempted to lay suspicion on Killian, he, too, had been present on the ward on the day of each murder.

But that was the conundrum. The *day* of each murder. If Mr. Simon was a newly turned vampire, how then did he manage to stand in the light?

A sound distracted her, and she whirled to see a group of dark, furry bodies nosing at the gutter. Rats. Twitching her skirt aside, she made a soft exhalation, then walked on.

Keeping a wary watch on her surroundings, she passed the darkened chandler's shop, and the black windows of the stores that dealt in all manner of birds and small animals. Between the buildings, the alleys and courts darted in all directions, made chilling and menacing by the impenetrable fog.

In the distance, a dog began to howl, a solitary, mournful cry. Shivering, Sarah hesitated and looked about, the hair at her nape prickling and rising. She could hear the sound of her own breathing, harsh and loud.

Drawing her cloak tight about her, she walked on, daring a glance over her shoulder that revealed nothing save darkness and mist. But she sensed him, the man who stalked her. He had come. And with him came her fear.

The sound of footsteps rang hollowly on the cobbles close behind her.

She froze, attuned to the faintest noise.

The footsteps stopped as she stopped, and when she began her trek once more, the echo of booted heels hitting the stones resumed.

A sharp trill of fear cut her, and she prayed Killian was behind her, for she had no wish to confront the man—the *vampire*—on her own. No sooner did the thought coalesce than the rising tide of her fear dissipated somewhat. Killian *was* watching, blanketed by the night. She had no doubt of that.

Faint sounds carried from the surrounding streets and buildings, raucous laughter, a woman's sobs, a baby's frantic cries. But all she could focus on was the ringing steps of the vampire that followed her, his steps matched to hers, neither falling back nor drawing near.

Just as she and Killian had planned, she turned down the same alley where the murderer had cornered her before. Up ahead, the wooden cart was angled to block the way exactly as it had been the last time she walked this route. The thick vapor swirled around the wheels in ghostly embrace.

She kept her steps even until she reached the wagon; then she spun to face the length of the alley, her back pressed against the rough wood, her pulse hammering a frantic rhythm.

She felt isolated here, the fog building a boundary between her and the rest of the world.

Before her, tendrils of mist stirred and parted, and she gasped as a dark shape emerged. Her heart slammed about in her chest like a bird desperate to fly free.

She saw him then, the vampire, there before her, a handful of steps away. His cloak hung about his tall frame and the low-crowned hat was pulled down on his brow as it had been when last he hunted her. Panic clawed at her, though she knew Killian was near, knew he would let no harm befall her.

Her breath rushed in and out in short, panting gasps. Her arms trembled as she raised her cudgel, her full attention focused on the man who moved toward her, one step, another, bringing him closer and closer still.

Slowly, he raised his hand toward her. Her heart leapt to her throat.

The sound of cloth flapping in the wind carried to her, and a dark shape plummeted down from above, black cape rising like wings. She gasped and jerked back as Killian landed neatly on the balls of his feet, directly behind her pursuer.

With a hiss of surprise, the man began to turn, but Killian was on him, his lips peeled back in a feral snarl, his arm coming tight around the stranger's throat, holding him fast.

With his hands clasped about Killian's forearm, the man struggled to break his hold. His efforts were in vain. Regardless of how he twisted and clawed, Killian held him.

In the tussle, the stranger's hat knocked free. Shaggy, dark hair tumbled across his brow and his gaze jerked up to lock with Sarah's. Her vision narrowed to a tight black tunnel and she swayed where she stood, overwhelmed.

Shock and disbelief slapped her, and she sagged against the wooden cart as Killian slammed the man against the wall of the alley.

Her cudgel slipped from her hands to clatter against the stones, and she pushed herself upright, stumbled forward.

"Killian, no," she cried. "He is . . . dear God . . . he is my *father.*"

The two men stood frozen, each staring at her.

She was dizzy under the onslaught of emotion that buffeted her. A thousand words tumbled to her lips, but she could manage only one.

"Why?" she cried, her gaze locked on her father, her nerves frayed and twisted in a Gordian knot.

"Daughter," he said, then pressed his lips tight and said nothing more.

"Why did you let me believe you were dead? Drowned?"

"No, I—" He brought his hands up before him, a gesture of despair.

"How could you—" She broke off and simply shook her head, too confused, too overcome by hurt and betrayal to formulate the slurry of her thoughts into any semblance of coherent speech.

Killian stepped back.

"Do not leave, Mr. Lowell," he breathed as he strode to Sarah's side. "Do not move. Certainly, do *not* force me to stop you." He dragged her against him, wrapping her in the haven of his embrace.

She could not say how long they stood thus. Perhaps only seconds, perhaps far longer. At length, she felt her control return. Drawing a shaky breath, she stepped free of the shelter of Killian's wonderfully safe embrace, her gaze lifting to meet her father's tormented stare.

"I thought you were an opium addict. I thought that under the influence of that foul drug you fell in the Thames and drowned." She paused as the implication of his presence clarified in her thoughts. "You *let* me think that."

"I did. And I am sorry." Her father held his hand out to her, tears glittering on his lashes. Even in the paltry light, she could see his pallor and the deep black circles beneath his eyes. He had suffered, and it hurt her to know it. "I was never an opium addict, Sarah. I wanted you to think it because it was the only way to shield you. The symptoms you saw were . . . it was the *hunger*. It only grew stronger, a gnawing pain that ripped me to bits until I dared not be near you, dared not trust myself. My God, you have no idea what I have become. I *did* want to die. I tried. Flung myself in the Thames. Only . . . my kind do not die." He drew a great shuddering breath. "My God, I have missed you so."

He lurched forward, as though to take her in his arms. Moving so fast he was little more than a blur, Killian insinuated himself between them, using his body as a shield.

"And you trust yourself now, Mr. Lowell?" he asked, darkly soft.

"She is my daughter," her father said, trying to shove Killian aside.

"She is my light, and I will let nothing harm her," Killian replied, unmoving.

Overwhelmed, Sarah looked back and forth between the two. Her lover was a vampire, and her father had returned from the dead. She was engulfed by the enormity of all that had transpired.

"How were you turned to a vampire, Papa?" she asked. "How did you become what you are?"

"You know about vampires? You *know*?" he asked, his brow furrowed in confusion.

"I do. And I need to understand how you became what you are."

"The patient from France. You remember? The friend that Mr. Montmarche begged me to see." His mouth twisted and his tone turned to a sneer. "My kindness was repaid by betrayal. He was a vampire, burned by the sun. His skin was blackened and falling away, and he was desperate for blood. He drained me nearly unto death."

Sarah shuddered at his words, for the images they conjured were ghastly. She recalled the dead patients at King's College, their wrists torn open, bloodless.

"No," she gasped.

With a sigh, her father reached out and laid his hand on her cheek. Beside her Killian tensed, ready to leap to her protection.

To protect her from her father.

"You cannot know," she whispered to Killian. "I thought him dead, and here he is. Alive. Touching me." She swallowed against the lump that clogged her throat. "I thought I would never see him again. I never even had a body to bury." She paused. "I thought I was alone."

Laying his hand against her back, Killian said nothing, but she could feel the tension that pulsed beneath the surface, sense the beast he had warned her lurked beneath the thin veneer. He did not trust her father, and she understood that, understood his need to hold her safe.

She reached back and took his hand, twined her fingers with his as she turned back to her father.

"You say he drained you nearly unto death, but how is it that you became what he was?"

"Montmarche's friend . . ." Her father made a dull laugh. "You know, I never did learn his name. Well, he gave me the choice. To die, or to take his blood and live. I chose life. But I did not understand. Not until I woke with the thirst." He exhaled sharply through his nostrils. "He was long gone by then, and I was left with the thirst and a thousand questions."

Killian made a small sound of disgust. "The newly made making more newly made. A dangerous folly. And he did not teach you how to drink without killing?"

Her father turned quickly in Killian's direction, shock chasing across his features. "You know these things? How? How can you—" He broke off and stumbled back, looking between Sarah and Killian, shaking his head from side to side as though trying to clear a noise from his ears. "You said she is your light." His tone was edged with horror. "You are *with* my daughter, yet you are like me? A vampire?"

"I am vampire," Killian confirmed.

For a moment, the three of them stood in an awkward, motionless tableau, and then her father turned to her and held his hand out in supplication.

"Sarah, my darling, I would not have left you alone had I a choice. But I have watched you from the shadows. Guarded you as best I could. I dared not be near you, for I was afraid both of what I might do to you, and of what you might think of the aberration I have become. But . . . you already know. You—"

"Mr. Lowell," Killian interjected. "Have you been killing patients at King's College?"

With a gasp, Sarah shook her head, only then recalling exactly why they had lured him to this place. Because of the murders. *Murders.* And Killian meant to end the string of deaths by terminating the killer.

"What? King's College?" Her father scrubbed his palms over his face. Dropping his hands, he glanced first at Sarah, then Killian. He seemed to sink into himself as he made a gesture of futility. "Yes. I saw no other course, no way to slake the hunger. I took only those who were suffering. Only those who would die regardless. You know, I can sense that now. I can feel death clinging to every breath. I know who will not survive, no matter what medical machinations are offered."

"So you chose with care." Killian's lips turned in a faint smile, and his tone was one of understanding. "I admire both your restraint and your compassion. It is common that the newly turned feed in a mad frenzy without thought or care. That you held yourself from that is admirable."

Something in his tone made Sarah's breath catch. Something dark.

He would kill her father.

She could not let him. But, oh God, her father was himself a murderer.

Her gaze jerked to Killian's, and she found him studying her, his eyes flat, his expression ruthlessly neutral. There was a sinister side to what he was. He had warned her of that.

"Killian," she whispered, even as her father said, "Sarah—"

Killian's gray eyes gleamed in the darkness, holding her trapped, breathless. He had told her this. He had told her of the murderers and thieves that he had fed from. Was her father to be his next victim?

"No, love. That is not the way of it."

Love. She drew a sharp breath, stunned by the term. Killian would not use it lightly.

"In three centuries, I have never made a vampire. The responsibility of that was too great to consider." He cast a sidelong glance at her father. "And now I go from being completely alone, to having a complete family." He made a wry smile. "There is a certain dark irony in that."

Her thoughts whirling, Sarah could only gape at him, trying to understand his meaning.

Killian inclined his head to her father, and said, "If you would afford us a moment of privacy, sir?"

Without waiting for a reply, he took her hand and drew her off into the shadows.

"He will need to live with us, at least at first, until I teach him the way of things," Killian said. Then his gaze grew somber, and the teasing glint disappeared. "Do not answer me, love, only listen to what I offer. I want to turn you."

"Turn me?" Even as she echoed the words, his meaning became clear. He wanted her to be as he was. "Killian—"

"Please"—he pressed his fingers to her lips—"hear me out. I want to share eternity with you. To show you the world. To never see you grow a day older than you are now. But there is a price. Both your father and I were turned without know-

ing the full extent of what we would become. If you choose
this, love, if you choose me, I need you to make that choice
with full understanding.

"So say nothing yet, my love. Make no hasty decision."
He pulled her against him, and brushed his lips across hers.
"Stay with me, Sarah. Be my light, my love. And when you
are ready, only then give me your answer."

Epilogue

One year later

Sarah snuggled close against Killian's side, languid and replete in the aftermath of their lovemaking. Reaching up, she dragged her fingers through the thick golden silk of his hair, loving the feel of it.

Loving him.

A year they had been together, and each day was a gift, a treasure. And in that year, he had shown her what it meant to be a vampire. The joys, the beauty, the freedom. The burden, the loneliness, the temptation.

Nothing ever came without a price.

But he had never again voiced the offer to make her what he was, and she had never asked.

Until now.

Rolling so she lay atop him, she stared into his eyes, his beautiful pewter and ice eyes, then leaned down and pressed her mouth to his.

"It is time, Killian." She drew her long hair to the side, baring the column of her throat. "It is time, my love."

He smiled, and dragged his fingers along her pulse where

it throbbed beneath the fragile skin of her throat. "You are certain?"

"I am. I would know the cool and wonderful beauty of the moonlight, the sweet music of the night," she whispered, offering back to him the words he had shared so long ago. "You are no longer alone. I would be with you always, Killian. Always and forever."

Please turn the page for an exciting sneak peek of
Hannah Howell's HIGHLAND SINNER!

Scotland, early summer 1478

What was that smell?

Tormand Murray struggled to wake up at least enough to move away from the odor assaulting his nose. He groaned as he started to turn on his side and the ache in his head became a piercing agony. Flopping onto his side, he cautiously ran his hand over his head and found the source of that pain. There was a very tender swelling at the back of his head. The damp matted hair around the swelling told him that it had bled but he could feel no continued blood flow. That indicated that he had been unconscious for more than a few minutes, possibly for even more than a few hours.

As he lay there trying to will away the pain in his head, Tormand tried to open his eyes. A sharp pinch halted his attempt and he cursed. He had definitely been unconscious for quite a while and something besides a knock on the head had been done to him, for his eyes were crusted shut. He had a fleeting, hazy memory of something being thrown into his eyes before all went black, but it was not enough to give him any firm idea of what had happened to him. Although he ruefully admitted to himself that it was as much vanity as a reluctance to induce pain in himself that caused him to fear he would tear out his eyelashes if he just forced his eyes open, Tormand proceeded very carefully. He gently brushed aside the crust on his eyes until he could open them, even if only enough to see if there was any water close at hand to wash his eyes with.

And, he hoped, enough water to wash himself if he proved to be the source of the stench. To his shame there had been a few times he had woken to find himself stinking, drink, and a few stumbles into some foul muck upon the street being the cause. He had never been this filthy before, he mused, as the smell began to turn his stomach.

Then his whole body tensed as he suddenly recognized the odor. It was death. Beneath the rank odor of an unclean garderobe was the scent of blood—a lot of blood. Far too much to have come from his own head wound.

The very next thing Tormand became aware of was that he was naked. For one brief moment panic seized him. Had he been thrown into some open grave with other bodies? He quickly shook aside that fear. It was not dirt or cold flesh he felt beneath him but the cool linen of a soft bed. Rousing from unconsciousness to that odor had obviously disordered his mind, he thought, disgusted with himself.

Easing his eyes open at last, he grunted in pain as the light stung his eyes and made his head throb even more. Everything was a little blurry, but he could make out enough to see that he was in a rather opulent bedchamber, one that looked vaguely familiar. His blood ran cold and he was suddenly even more reluctant to seek out the source of that smell. It certainly could not be from some battle if only because the part of the bedchamber he was looking at showed no signs of one.

If there is a dead body in this room, laddie, best ye learn about it quick. Ye might be needing to run, said a voice in his head that sounded remarkably like his squire, Walter, and

Tormand had to agree with it. He forced down all the reluctance he felt and, since he could see no sign of the dead in the part of the room he studied, turned over to look in the other direction. The sight that greeted his watering eyes had him making a sound that all too closely resembled the one his niece Anna made whenever she saw a spider. Death shared his bed.

He scrambled away from the corpse so quickly he nearly fell out of the bed. Struggling for calm, he eased his way off the bed and then sought out some water to cleanse his eyes so that he could see more clearly. It took several awkward bathings of his eyes before the sting in them eased and the blurring faded. One of the first things he saw after he dried his face was his clothing folded neatly on a chair, as if he had come to this bedchamber as a guest, willingly. Tormand wasted no time in putting on his clothes and searching the room for any other signs of his presence, collecting up his weapons and his cloak.

Knowing he could not avoid looking at the body in the bed any longer, he stiffened his spine and walked back to the bed. Tormand felt the sting of bile in the back of his throat as he looked upon what had once been a beautiful woman. So mutilated was the body that it took him several moments to realize that he was looking at what was left of Lady Clara Sinclair. The ragged clumps of golden-blond hair left upon her head and the wide, staring blue eyes told him that, as did the heart-shaped birthmark above the open wound where her left breast had been. The rest of the woman's face was so badly cut up it would have been difficult for her own mother to recognize her without those few clues.

The cold calm he had sought now filling his body and mind, Tormand was able to look more closely. Despite the mutilation there was an expression visible upon poor Clara's face, one that hinted she had been alive during at least some of the horrors inflicted upon her. A quick glance at her wrists and ankles revealed that she had once been bound and had fought those bindings, adding weight to Tormand's dark suspicion. Either poor Clara had had some information someone had tried to torture out of her or she had met up with someone who hated her with a cold, murderous fury.

And someone who hated him as well, he suddenly thought, and tensed. Tormand knew he would not have come to Clara's bedchamber for a night of sweaty bed play. Clara had once been his lover, but their affair had ended and he never returned to a woman once he had parted from her. He especially did not return to a woman who was now married and to a man as powerful and jealous as Sir Ranald Sinclair. That meant that someone had brought him here, someone who wanted him to see what had been done to a woman he had once bedded, and, mayhap, take the blame for this butchery.

That thought shook him free of the shock and sorrow he felt. "Poor, foolish Clara," he murmured. "I pray ye didnae suffer this because of me. Ye may have been vain, a wee bit mean of spirit, witless, and lacking morals, but ye still didnae deserve this."

He crossed himself and said a prayer over her. A glance at the windows told him that dawn was fast approaching and he knew he had to leave quickly. "I wish I could tend to ye now, lass, but I believe I am meant to take the blame for your death and I cannae; I willnae. But, I vow, I *will* find out who did this to ye and they will pay dearly for it."

After one last careful check to be certain no sign of his presence remained in the bedchamber, Tormand slipped away. He had to be grateful that whoever had committed this heinous crime had done so in this house, for he knew all the secretive ways in and out of it. His affair with Clara might have been short but it had been lively and he had slipped in and out of this house many, many times. Tormand doubted even Sir Ranald, who had claimed the fine house when he had married Clara, knew all of the stealthy approaches to his bride's bedchamber.

Once outside, Tormand swiftly moved into the lingering shadows of early dawn. He leaned against the outside of the

rough stone wall surrounding Clara's house and wondered where
he should go. A small part of him wanted to just go home and
forget about it all, but he knew he would never heed it. Even
if he had no real affection for Clara, one reason their lively
affair had so quickly died, he could not simply forget that the
woman had been brutally murdered. If he was right in sus-
pecting that someone had wanted him to be found next to the
body and be accused of Clara's murder, then he definitely
could not simply forget the whole thing.

Despite that, Tormand decided the first place he would go
was his house. He could still smell the stench of death on his
clothing. It might be just his imagination, but he knew he
needed a bath and clean clothes to help him forget that
smell. As he began his stealthy way home Tormand thought it
was a real shame that a bath could not also wash away the
images of poor Clara's butchered body.

"Are ye certain ye ought to say anything to anybody?"

Tormand nibbled on a thick piece of cheese as he studied
his aging companion. Walter Burns had been his squire for
twelve years and had no inclination to be anything more than
a squire. His utter lack of ambition was why he had been
handed over to Tormand by the man who had knighted him
at the tender age of eighteen. It had been a glorious battle
and Walter had proven his worth. The man had simply refused to be knighted. Fed up with his squire's lack of interest in the glory, the honors, and the responsibility that went
with knighthood, Sir MacBain had sent the man to Tormand.
Walter had continued to prove his worth, his courage, and his
contentment in remaining a lowly squire. At the moment,
however, the man was openly upset and his courage was a
little weak-kneed.

"I need to find out who did this," Tormand said, and then
sipped at his ale, hungry and thirsty but partaking of both
food and drink cautiously, for his stomach was still unsteady.

"Why?" Walter sat down at Tormand's right and poured himself some ale. "Ye got away from it. 'Tis near the middle of the day and no one has come here crying for vengeance, so I be thinking ye got away clean, aye? Why let anyone e'en ken ye were near the woman? Are ye trying to put a rope about your neck? And, if I recall rightly, ye didnae find much to like about the woman once your lust dimmed, so why fret o'er justice for her?"

"'Tis sadly true that I didnae like her, but she didnae deserve to be butchered like that."

Walter grimaced and idly scratched the ragged scar on his pockmarked left cheek. "True, but I still say if ye let anyone ken ye were there ye are just asking for trouble."

"I would like to think that verra few people would e'er believe I could do that to a woman e'en if I was found lying in her blood, dagger in hand."

"Of course ye wouldnae do such as that, and most folk ken it, but that doesnae always save a mon, does it? Ye dinnae ken everyone who has the power to cry ye a murderer and hang ye and they dinnae ken ye. Then there are the ones who are jealous of ye or your kinsmen and would like naught better than to strike out at one of ye. Aye, look at your brother, James. Any fool who kenned the mon would have kenned he couldnae have killed his wife, but he still had to suffer years marked as an outlaw and a woman killer, aye?"

"I kenned I kept ye about for a reason. Aye, 'twas to raise my spirits when they are low and to embolden me with hope and courage just when I need it the most."

"Wheesht, nay need to slap me with the sharp edge of your tongue. I but speak the truth and one ye would be wise to nay ignore."

Tormand nodded carefully, wary of moving his still-aching head too much. "I dinnae intend to ignore it. 'Tis why I have decided to speak only to Simon."

Walter cursed softly and took a deep drink of ale. "Aye, a king's mon nay less."

"Aye, and my friend. *And* a mon who worked hard to help James. He is a mon who has a true skill at solving such puzzles and hunting down the guilty. This isnae simply about justice for Clara. Someone wanted me to be blamed for her murder, Walter. I was put beside her body to be found and accused of the crime. And for such a crime I would be hanged, so that means that someone wants me dead."

"Aye, true enough. Nay just dead, either, but your good name weel blackened."

"Exactly. So I have sent word to Simon asking him to come here, stressing an urgent need to speak with him."

Tormand was pleased that he sounded far more confident of his decision than he felt. It had taken him several hours to actually write and send the request for a meeting to Simon. The voice in his head that told him to just turn his back on the whole matter, the same opinion that Walter offered, had grown almost too loud to ignore. Only the certainty that this had far more to do with him than with Clara had given him the strength to silence that cowardly voice.

He had the feeling that part of his stomach's unsteadiness was due to a growing fear that he was about to suffer as James had. It had taken his foster brother three long years to prove his innocence and wash away the stain to his honor. Three long, lonely years of running and hiding. Tormand dreaded the thought that he might be pulled into the same ugly quagmire. If nothing else, he was deeply concerned about how it would affect his mother, who had already suffered too much grief and worry over her children. First his sister Sorcha had been beaten and raped, then his sister Gillyanne had been kidnapped—twice—the second time leading to a forced marriage, and then there had been the trouble that had sent James running for the shelter of the hills. His mother did not need to suffer through yet another one of her children mired in danger.

"If ye could find something the killer touched, we could solve this puzzle right quick," said Walter.

Pulling free of his dark thoughts about the possibility that his family was cursed, Tormand frowned at his squire. "What are ye talking about?"

"Weel, if ye had something the killer touched we could take it to the Ross witch."

Tormand had heard of the Ross witch. The woman lived in a tiny cottage several miles outside town. Although the townspeople had driven the woman away ten years ago, many still journeyed to her cottage for help, mostly for the herbal concoctions she made. Some claimed the woman had visions that had aided them in solving some problem. Despite having grown up surrounded by people who had special gifts like that, he doubted the woman was the miracle worker some claimed her to be. Most of the time such *witches* were simply aging women skilled with herbs and an ability to convince people that they had some great mysterious power.

"And why do ye think she could help if I brought her something touched by the killer?" he asked.

"Because she gets a vision of the truth when she touches something." Walter absently crossed himself as if he feared he risked his soul by even speaking of the woman. "Old George, the steward for the Gillespie house, told me that Lady Gillespie had some of her jewelry stolen. He said Her Ladyship took the box the jewels had been taken from to the Ross witch and the moment the woman held the box she had a vision about what had happened."

When Walter said no more, Tormand asked, "What did the vision tell the woman?"

"That Lady Gillespie's eldest son had taken the jewels. Crept into Her Ladyship's bedchamber whilst she was at court and helped himself to all the best pieces."

"It doesnae take a witch to ken that. Lady Gillespie's eldest son is weel kenned to spend too much coin on fine clothes, women, and the toss of the dice. Near every mon, woman, and bairn in town kens that." Tormand took a drink of ale to help him resist the urge to grin at the look of annoyance on Walter's homely face. "Now I ken why the fool was banished to his grandfather's keep far from all the temptation here near the court."

"Weel, it wouldnae hurt to try. Seems a lad like ye ought to have more faith in such things."

"Oh, I have ample faith in such things, enough to wish that ye wouldnae call the woman a witch. That is a word that can give some woman blessed with a gift from God a lot of trouble, deadly trouble."

"Ah, aye, aye, true enough. A gift from God, is it?"

"Do ye really think the devil would give a woman the gift to heal or to see the truth or any other gift or skill that can be used to help people?"

"Nay, of course he wouldnae. So why do ye doubt the Ross woman?"

"Because there are too many women who are, at best, a wee bit skilled with herbs yet claim such things as visions or the healing touch in order to empty some fool's purse. They are frauds and ofttimes what they do makes life far more difficult for those women who have a true gift."

Walter frowned for a moment, obviously thinking that over, and then grunted his agreement. "So ye willnae be trying to get any help from Mistress Ross?"

"Nay, I am nay so desperate for such as that."

"Oh, I am nay sure I would refuse any help just now," came a cool, hard voice from the doorway of Tormand's hall.

Tormand looked toward the door and started to smile at Simon. The expression died a swift death. Sir Simon Innes looked every inch the king's man at the moment. His face was pale and cold fury tightened its predatory lines. Tormand got the sinking feeling that Simon already knew why he had sent for him. Worse, he feared his friend had some suspicions about his guilt. That stung, but Tormand decided to smother his sense of insult until he and Simon had at least talked. The man was his friend and a strong believer in justice. He would listen before he acted.

Nevertheless, Tormand froze with a growing alarm when Simon strode up to him. Every line of the man's tall, lean body was tense with fury. Out of the corner of his eye, Tormand saw Walter anxiously rise and place his hand on his sword, revealing that Tormand was not the only one who sensed danger. It was as he looked back at Simon that Tormand realized the man clutched something in his hand.

A heartbeat later, Simon tossed what he held onto the table in front of Tormand. Tormand stared down at a heavy gold ring embellished with bloodred garnets. Unable to believe what he was seeing, he looked at his hands, his unadorned hands, and then looked back at the ring. His first thought was to wonder how he could have left that room of death and not realized that he was no longer wearing his ring. His second thought was that the point of Simon's sword was dangerously sharp as it rested against his jugular.

"Nay! Dinnae kill him! He is innocent!"

Morainn Ross blinked in surprise as she looked around her. She was at home sitting up in her own bed, not in a great hall watching a man press a sword point against the throat of another man. Ignoring the grumbling of her cats that had been disturbed from their comfortable slumber by her outburst, she flopped back down and stared up at the ceiling. It had only been a dream.

"Nay, no dream," she said after a moment of thought. "A vision."

Thinking about that a little longer, she then nodded her head. It had definitely been a vision. The man who had sat there with a sword at his throat was no stranger to her. She had been seeing him in dreams and visions for months now. He had smelled of death, was surrounded by it, yet there had never been any blood upon his hands.

"Morainn? Are ye weel?"

Morainn looked toward the door to her small bedchamber

and smiled at the young boy standing there. Walin was only six but he was rapidly becoming very helpful. He also worried about her a lot, but she supposed that was to be expected. Since she had found him upon her threshold when he was the tender of age of two she was really the only parent he had ever known, had given him the only home he had ever known. She just wished it were a better one. He was also old enough now to understand that she was often called a witch as well as the danger that appellation brought with it. Unfortunately, with his black hair and blue eyes, he looked enough like her to have many believe he was her bastard child, and that caused its own problems for both of them.

"I am fine, Walin," she said, and began to ease her way out of bed around all the sleeping cats. "It must be verra late in the day."

"'Tis the middle of the day, but ye needed to sleep. Ye were verra late returning from helping at that birthing."

"Weel, set something out on the table for us to eat, then. I will join ye in a few minutes."

Dressed and just finishing the braiding of her hair, Morainn joined Walin at the small table set out in the main room of the cottage. Seeing the bread, cheese, and apples upon the table, she smiled at Walin, acknowledging a job well done. She poured them each a tankard of cider and then sat down on the little bench facing his across the scarred wooden table.

"Did ye have a bad dream?" Walin asked as he handed Morainn an apple to cut up for him.

"At first I thought it was a dream but now I am certain it was a vision, another one about that mon with the mismatched eyes." She carefully set the apple on a wooden plate and sliced it for Walin.

"Ye have a lot about him, dinnae ye?"

"It seems so. 'Tis verra odd. I dinnae ken who he is and have ne'er seen such a mon. And if this vision is true, I dinnae think I e'er will."

"Why?" Walin accepted the plate of sliced apple and immediately began to eat it.

"Because this time I saw a verra angry gray-eyed mon holding a sword to his throat."

"But didnae ye say that your visions are of things to come? Mayhap he isnae dead yet. Mayhap ye are supposed to find him and warn him."

Morainn considered that possibility for a moment and then shook her head. "Nay, I think not. Neither heart nor mind urges me to do that. If that were what I was meant to do, I would feel the urge to go out right now and hunt him down. And I would have been given some clue as to where he is."

"Oh. So we will soon see the mon whose eyes dinnae match?"

"Aye, I do believe we will."

"Weel, that will be interesting."

She smiled and turned her attention to the need to fill her very empty stomach. If the man with the mismatched eyes showed up at her door, it would indeed be interesting. It could also be dangerous. She could not allow herself to forget that death stalked him. Her visions told her he was innocent of those deaths, but there was some connection between him and them. It was as if each thing he touched died in bleeding agony. She certainly did not wish to become a part of that swirling mass of blood she always saw around his feet. Unfortunately, she did not believe that fate would give her any chance to avoid meeting the man. All she could do was pray that when he rapped upon her door he did not still have death seated upon his shoulder.

Secrecy and intrigue ignite dangerous passions in New York Times *bestselling author Hannah Howell's seductive new novel . . .*

It is whispered throughout London that the members of the Wherlocke family are possessed of certain unexplainable *gifts*. But Lord Ashton Radmoor is skeptical—until he finds an innocent beauty lying drugged and helpless in the bedroom of a brothel.

The mystery woman is Penelope Wherlocke, and her special gift of sight is leading her deep into a dangerous world of treachery and betrayal. Ashton knows he should forget her, yet he's drawn deeper into the vortex of her life, determined to keep her safe. But Penelope is no ordinary woman, and she's never met the man strong enough to contend with her unusual abilities.

Until now . . .

Please turn the page for an exciting sneak peek of Hannah Howell's IF HE'S SINFUL, coming in December 2009!

London, fall 1788

There was something about having a knife held to one's throat that tended to bring a certain clarity to one's opinion of one's life, Penelope decided. She stood very still as the burly, somewhat odiferous, man holding her clumsily adjusted his grip. Suddenly, all of her anger and resentment over being treated as no more than a lowly maid by her step-sister seemed petty, the problem insignificant.

Of course, this could be some form of cosmic retribution for all those times she had wished ill upon her step-sister, she thought as the man hefted her up enough so that her feet were off the ground. One of his two companions bound her ankles in a manner quite similar to the way her wrists had been bound. Her captor began to carry her down a dark ally that smelled about as bad as he did. It had been only a few hours ago that she had watched Clarissa leave for a carriage ride with her soon-to-be fiancé, Lord Radmoor. Peering out of the cracked window in her tiny attic room she had, indisputably, cherished the spiteful wish that Clarissa would stumble and fall into the foul muck near the carriage wheels.

Penelope did think that being dragged away by a knife-wielding ruffian and his two hulking companions was a rather harsh penalty for such a childish wish born of jealousy, however. She had, after all, never wished that Clarissa would die, which Penelope very much feared was going to be her fate.

Penelope sighed, ruefully admitting that she was partially at fault for her current predicament. She had stayed too long with her boys. Even little Paul had urged her not to walk home in the dark. It was embarrassing to think that a little boy of five had more common sense than she did.

A soft cry of pain escaped her, muted by the filthy gag in her mouth, when her captor stumbled and the cold, sharp edge of his knife scored her skin. For a brief moment, the fear she had been fighting to control swelled up inside her so strongly she feared she would be ill. The warmth of her own blood seeping into the neckline of her bodice only added to the fear. It took several moments before she could grasp any shred of calm or courage. The realization that her blood was flowing too slowly for her throat to have been cut helped her push aside her burgeoning panic.

"Ye sure we ain't allowed to have us a taste of this, Jud," asked the largest and most hirsute of her captor's assistants.

"Orders is orders," replied Jud as he steadied his knife against her skin. "A toss with this one will cost ye more'n she be worth."

"None of us'd be telling and the wench ain't going to be able to tell, neither."

"I ain't letting ye risk it. Wench like this'd be fighting ye and that leaves bruises. They'll tell the tale and that bitch Mrs. Cratchitt will tell. She would think it a right fine thing if we lost our pay for this night's work."

"Aye, that old bawd would be thinking she could gain something from it right enough. Still, it be a sad shame I can't be having me a taste afore it be sold off to anyone with a coin or two."

"Get your coin first and then go buy a little if'n ye want it so bad."

"Won't be so clean and new, will it?"

"This one won't be neither if'n that old besom uses her as she uses them others, not by the time ye could afford a toss with her."

She was being taken to a brothel, Penelope realized. Yet again she had to struggle fiercely against becoming blinded by her own fears. She was still alive, she told herself repeatedly, and it looked as if she would stay that way for a while. Penelope fought to find her strength in that knowledge. It did no good to think too much on the horrors she might be forced to endure before she could escape or be found. She needed to concentrate on one thing and one thing only—getting free.

It was not easy but Penelope forced herself to keep a close eye on the route they traveled. Darkness and all the twists and turns her captors took made it nearly impossible to make note of any and every possible sign to mark the way out of this dangerous warren she was being taken into. She had to force herself to hold fast to the hope that she could even truly escape, and the need to get back to her boys who had no one else to care for them.

She was carried into the kitchen of a house. Two women and a man were there, but they spared her only the briefest of glances before returning all of their attention to their work. It was not encouraging that they seemed so accustomed to such a sight, so unmoved and uninterested.

As her captor carried her up a dark, narrow stairway, Penelope became aware of the voices and music coming from below, from the front of the building which appeared to be as great a warren as the alleys leading to it. When they reached the hallway and started to walk down it, she could hear the murmur of voices coming from behind all the closed doors. Other sounds drifted out from behind those doors but she tried very hard not to think about what might be causing them.

"There it be, room twenty-two," muttered Jud. "Open the door, Tom."

The large, hirsute man opened the door and Jud carried Penelope into the room. She had just enough time to notice how small the room was before Jud tossed her down onto the bed in the middle of the room. It was a surprisingly clean and comfortable bed. Penelope suspected that, despite its seedy location, she had probably been brought to one of the better bordellos, one that catered to gentlemen of refinement and wealth. She knew, however, that that did not mean she could count on any help.

"Get that old bawd in here, Tom," said Jud. "I wants to be done with this night's work." The moment Tom left, Jud scowled down at Penelope. "Don't suspect you'd be aknowing why that high-and-mighty lady be wanting ye outta the way, would ye?"

Penelope slowly shook her head as a cold suspicion settled in her stomach.

"Don't make no sense to me. Can't be jealousy or the like. Can't be that she thinks you be taking her man or the like, can it. Ye ain't got her fine looks, ain't dressed so fine, neither, and ye ain't got her fine curves. Scrawny, brown mite like ye should be no threat at all to such a fulsome wench. So, why does she want ye gone so bad, eh?"

Scrawny brown mite?, Penelope thought, deeply insulted even as shrugged in reply.

"Why you frettin' o'er it, Jud?" asked the tall, extremely muscular man by his side.

Jud shrugged. "Curious, Mac. Just curious, is all. This don't make no sense to me."

"Don't need to. Money be good. All that matters."

"Aye, mayhap. As I said, just curious. Don't like puzzles."

"Didn't know that."

"Well, it be true. Don't want to be part of something I don't understand. Could mean trouble."

If she was not gagged, Penelope suspected she would be gaping at her captor. He had kidnapped the daughter of a marquis, brought her bound and gagged to a brothel, and was going to leave her to the untender care of a madam, a woman he plainly did not trust or like. Exactly what did the idiot think *trouble* was? If he was caught, he would be tried, convicted, and hanged in a heartbeat. And that would be merciful compared to what her relatives would do to the fool if they found out. How much more *trouble* could he be in?

A hoarse gasp escaped her when he removed her gag. "Water," she whispered, desperate to wash away the foul taste of the rag.

What the man gave her was a tankard of weak ale, but Penelope decided it was probably for the best. If there was any water in this place it was undoubtedly dangerous to drink. She tried not to breathe too deeply as he held her upright and helped her to take a drink. Penelope drank the ale as quickly as she could, however, for she wanted the man to move away from her. Anyone as foul smelling as he was surely had a vast horde of creatures sharing his filth that she would just as soon did not come to visit her.

When the tankard was empty he let her fall back down onto the bed and said, "Now, don't ye go thinking of making no noise, screaming for help or the like. No one here will be heeding it."

Penelope opened her mouth to give him a tart reply and then frowned. The bed might be clean and comfortable but it was not new. A familiar chill swept over her. Even as she thought it a very poor time for her *gift* to diplay itself, her mind was briefly filled with violent memories that were not her own.

"Someone died in this bed," she said, her voice a little unsteady from the effect of those chilling glimpses into the past.

"What the bleeding hell are ye babbling about?" snapped Jud.

"Someone died in this bed and she did not do so peacefully." Penelope got some small satisfaction from how uneasy her words made her burly captors.

"You be talking nonsense, woman."

"No. I have a gift, you see."

"You can see spirits?" asked Mac, glancing nervously around the room.

"Sometimes. When they wish to reveal themselves to me. This time it was just the memories of what happened here," she lied.

Both men were staring at her with a mixture of fear, curiosity, and suspicion. They thought she was trying to trick them in some way so that they would set her free. Penelope suspected that a part of them probably wondered if she would conjure up a few spirits to help her. Even if she could, she doubted they would be much help or that these men would even see them. They certainly had not noticed the rather gruesome one standing near the bed. It would have sent them fleeing from the room. Despite all she had seen and experienced over the years, the sight of the lovely young woman, her white gown soaked in blood, sent a chill down her spine. Penelope wondered why the more gruesome apparitions were almost always the clearest.

The door opened and, before Penelope turned to look, she saw an expression upon the ghost's face that nearly made *her* want to flee the room. Fury and utter loathing twisted the spirit's lovely face until it looked almost demonic. Penelope looked at the ones now entering the room. Tom had returned with a middle-aged woman and two young, scantily clad females. Penelope looked right at the ghost and noticed that all that rage and hate was aimed straight at the middle-aged woman.

Beware.

Penelope almost cursed as the word echoed in her mind. Why did the spirits always whisper such ominous words to her without adding any pertinent information, such as what she should *beware* of, or whom? It was also a very poor time for this sort of distraction. She was a prisoner trapped in a house of ill-repute and was facing either death or what many euphemistically called a fate worse than death. She had no time to deal with blood-soaked specters whispering dire but unspecified warnings. If nothing else, she needed all her wits and strength to keep the hysteria writhing deep inside her tightly caged.

"This is going to cause you a great deal of trouble," Penelope told the older woman, not really surprised when everyone ignored her.

"There she be," said Jud. "Now, give us our money."

"The lady has your money," said the older woman.

"It ain't wise to try and cheat me, Cratchitt. The lady told us you would have it. Now, if the lady ain't paid you that be your problem, not mine. I did as I was ordered and did it quick and right. Get the wench, bring her here, and then collect my pay from you. Done and done. So, hand it over."

Cratchitt did so with an ill grace. Penelope watched Jud carefully count his money. The man had obviously taught himself enough to make sure that he was not cheated. After one long, puzzled look at her, he pocketed his money and then frowned at the woman he called Cratchitt.

"She be all yours now," Jud said, "though I ain't sure what ye be wanting her for. T'ain't much to her."

Penelope was growing very weary of being disparaged by this lice-ridden ruffian. "So speaks the great beau of the walk," she muttered and met his glare with a faint smile.

"She is clean and fresh," said Cratchitt, ignoring that by-play and fixing her cold stare on Penelope. "I have many a gent willing to pay a gooldy fee for that alone. There be one man waiting especially for this one, but he will not arrive until the morrow. I have other plans for her tonight. Some very rich gentlemen have arrived and are looking for something special. Unique, they said. They have a friend about to step into the parson's mousetrap and wish to give him a final bachelor treat. She will do nicely for that."

"But don't that other feller want her untouched?"

"As far as he will ever know, she will be. Now, get out. Me and the girls need to wrap this little gift."

The moment Jud and his men were gone, Penelope said, "Do you have any idea of who I am?" She was very proud of the haughty tone she had achieved but it did not impress Mrs. Cratchitt at all.

"Someone who made a rich lady very angry," replied cratchitt.

"I am Lady Penelope—"

She never finished for Mrs. Cratchitt grasped her by the jaw in a painfully tight hold, forced her mouth open, and started to pour something from a remarkably fine silver flask down her throat. The two younger women held her head steady so that Penelope could not turn away or thrash her head. She knew she did not want this drink inside her but was unable to do anything but helplessly swallow as it was forced into her.

While she was still coughing and gagging from that abuse, the women untied her. Penelope struggled as best as she could but the women were strong and alarmingly skilled at undressing someone who did not wish to be undressed. As if she did not have trouble enough to deal with, the ghost was drowning her in feelings of fear, despair, and helpless fury. Penelope knew she was swiftly becoming hysterical but could not grasp one single thin thread of control. That only added to her terror.

Then, slowly, that suffocating panic began to ease. Despite the fact that the women continued their work, stripping her naked, giving her a quick wash with scented water, and dressing her in a lacey, diaphanous gown that should have shocked her right down to her toes, Penelope felt calmer with every breath she took. The potion they had forced her to drink had been some sort of drug. That was the only rational explanation for why she was now lying there actually smiling as these three harpies prepared her for the sacrifice of her virginity.

"There, all sweets and honey now, ain't you, dearie," muttered Cratchitt as she began to let down Penelope's hair.

"You are such an evil bitch," Penelope said pleasantly and smiled. One of the younger women giggled and Cratchitt slapped hard. "Bully. When my family discovers what you have done to me, you will pay more dearly than even your tiny, nasty mind could ever comprehend."

"Hah! It was your own family what sold you to me, you stupid girl."

"Not that family, you cow. My true parents' family. In fact, I would not be at all surprised if they are already suspicious, sensing my troubles upon the wind."

"You are talking utter nonsense."

Why does everyone say that? Penelope wondered. Enough wit and sense of self-preservation remained in her clouded mind to make her realize that it might not be wise to start talking about all the blood there was on the woman's hands. Even if the woman did not believe Penelope could know anything for a fact, she suspected Mrs. Cratchitt would permanently silence her simply to be on the safe side of the matter. With the drug holding her captive as well as any chain could, Penelope knew she was in no condition to even try to save herself.

When Cratchitt and her minions were finished, she stood back and looked Penelope over very carefully. "Well, well, well. I begin to understand."

"Understand what, you bride of Beelzebub?" asked Penelope and could tell by the way the woman clenched and unclenched her hands that Mrs. Cratchitt desperately wanted to beat her.

"Why the fine lady wants you gone. And, you will pay dearly for your insults, my girl. Very soon." Mrs. Cratchitt collected four bright silk scarves from the large carpetbag she had brought in with her and handed them to the younger women. "Tie her to the bed," she ordered them.

"Your customer may find that a little suspicious," said Penelope as she fruitlessly tried to stop the women from binding her limbs to the four posts of the bed.

"You *are* an innocent, aren't you." Mrs. Cratchitt shook her head and laughed. "No, my customer will only see this as a very special delight indeed. Come along, girls. You have work to do and we best get that man up here to enjoy his gift before that potion begins to wear off."

Penelope stared at the closed door for several moments after everyone had left. Everyone except the ghost, she mused, and finally turned her attention back to the spectre now shimmering at the foot of the bed. The young woman looked so sad, so utterly defeated, that Penelope decided the poor ghost had probably just realized the full limitations of being a spirit. Although the memories locked into the bed had told Penelope how the woman had died, it did not tell her when. However, she began to suspect it had been not all that long ago.

"I would like to help you," she said, "but I cannot, not right now. You must see that. If I can get free, I swear I will work hard to give you some peace. Who are you?" she asked, although she knew it was often impossible to get proper, sensible answers from a spirit. "I know how you died. The bed still holds those dark memories and I saw it."

I am Faith and my life was stolen.

The voice was clear and sweet, but weighted with an intense grief, and Penelope was not completely certain if she was hearing it in her head or if the ghost was actually speaking to her. "What is your full name, Faith?"

My name is Faith and I was taken, as you have been. My life was stolen. My love is lost. I was torn from heaven and plunged into hell. Now I lie below.

"Below? Below what? Where?"

Below. I am covered in sin. But, I am not alone.

Penelope cursed when Faith disappeared. She could not help the spirit now but dealing with Faith's spirit had provided her with a much needed diversion. It had helped her concentrate and fight the power of the drug she had been given. Now she was alone with her thoughts and they were becoming increasingly strange. Worse, all of her protections were slowly crumbling away. If she did not find something to fix her mind on soon she would be wide open to every thought, every feeling, and every spirit lurking within the house. Considering what went on in this house that could easily prove a torture beyond bearing.

She did not know whether to laugh or to cry. She was strapped to a bed awaiting some stranger who would use her helpless body to satisfy his manly needs. The potion Mrs. Cratchitt had forced down her throat was rapidly depleting her strength and all her ability to shut out the cacophony of the world, the world of the living as well as that of the dead. Even now she could feel the growing weight of unwelcome emotions, the increasing whispers so few others could hear. The spirits in the house were stirring, sensing the presence of one who could help them touch the world of the living. It was probably not worth worrying about, she decided. Penelope did not know if anything could be worse than what she was already suffering and what was yet to come.

Suddenly the door opened and one of Mrs. Cratchitt's earlier companions led a man into the room. He was blindfolded and dressed as an ancient Roman. Penelope stared at him in shock as he was led up to her bedside, and then she inwardly groaned. She had no trouble recognizing the man despite the blindfold and the costume. Penelope was not at all pleased to discover that things could quite definitely get worse—a great deal worse.

More by Bestselling Author
Hannah Howell

__Highland Sinner	978-0-8217-8001-5	$6.99US/$8.49CAN
__Highland Captive	978-0-8217-8003-9	$6.99US/$8.49CAN
__Wild Roses	978-0-8217-7976-7	$6.99US/$8.49CAN
__Highland Fire	978-0-8217-7429-8	$6.99US/$8.49CAN
__Silver Flame	978-1-4201-0107-2	$6.99US/$8.49CAN
__Highland Wolf	978-0-8217-8000-8	$6.99US/$9.99CAN
__Highland Wedding	978-0-8217-8002-2	$4.99US/$6.99CAN
__Highland Destiny	978-1-4201-0259-8	$4.99US/$6.99CAN
__Only for You	978-0-8217-8151-7	$6.99US/$9.99CAN
__Highland Promise	978-1-4201-0261-1	$4.99US/$6.99CAN
__Highland Vow	978-1-4201-0260-4	$4.99US/$6.99CAN
__Highland Savage	978-0-8217-7999-6	$6.99US/$9.99CAN
__Beauty and the Beast	978-0-8217-8004-6	$4.99US/$6.99CAN
__Unconquered	978-0-8217-8088-6	$4.99US/$6.99CAN
__Highland Barbarian	978-0-8217-7998-9	$6.99US/$9.99CAN
__Highland Conqueror	978-0-8217-8148-7	$6.99US/$9.99CAN
__Conqueror's Kiss	978-0-8217-8005-3	$4.99US/$6.99CAN
__A Stockingful of Joy	978-1-4201-0018-1	$4.99US/$6.99CAN
__Highland Bride	978-0-8217-7995-8	$4.99US/$6.99CAN
__Highland Lover	978-0-8217-7759-6	$6.99US/$9.99CAN
__Highland Warrior	978-0-8217-7985-9	$4.99US/$6.99CAN

Available Wherever Books Are Sold!

Check out our website at
http://www.kensingtonbooks.com